MURDER ABOARD THE *TITANIC*

An officer caught Henry by the elbow. "What are you doing on the bridge?"

"I must see the captain. There's a murderer on board."

"He can't deal with it now, man. He's got the whole ship to worry about. Can't you see what's going on?"

"But he's just killed a woman."

"Did you see it?"

"No, but—"

"We'll deal with it in good time. Now, make yourself useful below. Calm the passengers down. That's an order, sailor."

Henry swore at the man under his breath. As he climbed down the ladder, he noticed that the angle of the steps was more pronounced than before. There was a perceptible tilt of the deck towards the bow. The *Titanic*, he realized, was sinking.

As he walked along the deck listening to the merriment of the passengers around him, he realized that circumstances had forced him to become Tarr's judge, jury and executioner.

Would he have time for vengeance before the *Titanic* plunged to the ocean floor?

TITANIC

A Novel

by Tony Aspler

SEAL BOOKS
McClelland-Bantam, Inc.
Toronto

TITANIC

A Seal Book / July 1990

Doubleday Canada Limited edition published 1989

ISBN 0-7704-2372-8

Seal Books are published by McClelland-Bantam, Inc. Its trademark,
consisting of the words "Seal Books" and the portrayal of a seal, is
the property of McClelland-Bantam, Inc., 105 Bond Street, Toronto,
Ontario M5B 1Y3, Canada. This trademark has been duly registered
in the Trademark Office of Canada. The trademark, consisting of
the words "Bantam Books" and the portrayal of a rooster is the
property of and is used with the consent of Bantam Books, 666 Fifth
Avenue, New York, New York 10103. This trademark has been duly
registered in the Trademark Office of Canada and elsewhere.

PRINTED IN CANADA

COVER PRINTED IN U.S.A.

U   0 9 8 7 6 5 4 3 2

To my friend Gordon Pape,

for fictions past and those to come.

Monday, July 10, 1911

THE SUN BURNED like a wound in the West Virginia sky. A hot wind blew swirls of dust among the wooden shacks where the miners sat waiting in doorways, carbines across their knees. Dust, the color of dried blood, settled on their boots.

Behind the miners' shacks, rows of tents billowed out in the wind. Washing hung from tent guy lines in an attitude of surrender. The sign over the company store rasped as it swung on unoiled hinges, "Brandon Iron and Steel Company" spelled out in bleached blue and gold letters. On the hilltops surrounding the town the wheels of the bankheads rocked slowly as the wind agitated their cables.

Five days earlier, as a signal for the strike to begin, a Greek immigrant named Stavros Tikas had set off a dynamite charge at the entrance to the mine. The company guards who were smoking inside when the roof caved in were still buried under tons of rock.

Two men stepped over the railway tracks and walked up the street past the company school towards the company church. One carried a leather satchel. Their black suits and straw hats betrayed them as bosses.

A miner spat tobacco juice as they passed.

"A dollar sixty-eight a week," someone shouted. "You call that wages?"

A door opened, and a heavy-set, bearded man with a revolver in his belt strode onto the porch of a wooden building. He planted his legs apart and placed his fists on

1

his hips. On his shirt he wore a deputy's badge. There were half-moons of sweat under his armpits. His eyes were shaded by the wide brim of his hat.

"You guys from Mr. Tarr?" he shouted.

The two men nodded.

"Get in here."

The deputy looked up and down the street then at the encircling hills before disappearing inside. The windows were barred and shuttered.

The room was hot. From a kerosene lamp hung a coil of flypaper, a sticky graveyard for a battalion of flies. The room was sparsely furnished with a rolltop desk, a wooden filing cabinet and a combination safe. In the centre was a table with four chairs around it. Three men wearing ties and badges sat with their feet on the table. Tacked to the wall was a map of Virginia, next to it, a rifle rack.

"Which one of you is Hislop?" demanded the deputy.

"I am. I'm sorry we're late. The train had to take on water in Hagerstown."

Hislop, tall, sallow-faced, with the unctuous demeanor of an undertaker, handed the deputy the satchel.

"Who's he?"

"His name is Henry Blexill. Mr. Tarr's butler," said Hislop. "He's only been in Mr. Tarr's employ for a week."

The men smirked and exchanged glances.

"Mr. Tarr thought I should accompany Mr. Hislop," said Henry. "Purely for security reasons."

His voice immediately identified him as English. The deputy glared into his sun-reddened face, and was met with a look of tolerant inquiry.

"Did I say something wrong?"

The deputy poked the nearest of his colleagues in the back, then said, "Well, lookee here. Maybe his lordship can settle the strike for us. I hear them English can talk the birds down from the trees."

The men laughed, showing brown teeth. Hislop looked anxiously at Henry, who merely smiled.

"Prob'ly knows more about dealing with wops than we do. Whaddaya say, English?"

"If you'd be so good as to conclude our business, we'll be on our way," replied Henry. He held his straw boater as if he were about to have his photograph taken. His shoulders were broad, and the muscles of his upper arms swelled under the heavy material of his black jacket.

The men slapped their thighs and guffawed loudly.

"Ain't he somethin'," the deputy roared. "How about we keep him here? He's funnier than a fartin' mule."

"Perhaps you'd like to communicate that sentiment to Mr. Tarr," offered Henry.

At the mention of Tarr's name the men stopped laughing. The deputy scowled and opened the satchel. From it he withdrew a canvas bag. He loosened the drawstrings and emptied the contents onto the table. Bundles of bank notes tumbled out.

"Twenty thousand dollars, gentlemen," said Hislop. "If you'd be good enough to sign this receipt."

The men at the table licked their lips as the deputy scooped up a bundle and riffled through it.

"Got to count it first."

"Each of those is one thousand dollars," said Hislop, "You have my word as a man of the cloth."

"My, my. A butler and a preacher man. Mr. Tarr sure knows how to look after hisself," mused the deputy.

He threw the bundle on the pile. Then he crossed to the safe and bent down, working the combination lock between his thumb and forefinger. The other men gazed fixedly at the wads of bank notes on the table.

"May I ask how you intend using the money?" asked Henry.

"To fight the unions, son." The deputy looked at Henry. "And keep America clean."

"And how will you do that?"

"Henry," said Hislop, catching the younger man's sleeve. "It's time to go."

"No, I'm curious. It's a lot of money for a fight."

"Why don't you just sashay back to Noo York City like the preacher man says? You do your job, and let the Baldwin-Felts Detective Agency do ours."

Henry ignored the implied threat.

"Those miners have guns. They wouldn't have armed themselves unless they'd been threatened."

The deputy moved in front of Henry and stared into his face. His eyes were bloodshot from lack of sleep.

"Yesterday I shot a miner. He was trying to organize a meeting. Since then they've been buying up all the guns and ammunition they can lay their hands on from the neighboring towns."

"Why did you stop their meeting?"

"What is this? Are you some kind of son of a bitch radical?"

Before Henry could respond, the sound of a rifle shot echoed off the hills.

"Lock the money in safe," shouted the deputy as he ran to the door.

He stepped into the street and drew the revolver from his belt. Henry followed him out and saw him point the gun at the sky. The man fired three shots in quick succession.

The noise galvanized the camp into action. The miners spilled out onto the streets carrying pick handles and Colt revolvers. Several had Winchester rifles and flour sacks filled with ammunition slung over their shoulders. They looked around to see where the shots had come from.

Almost immediately the coughing sound of an automobile engine could be heard approaching from the direction of the railway tracks. A truck chassis with iron wheels and armor-plated sides rolled up the sun-baked street. It looked like a huge steel outhouse on wheels. It lumbered up the street towards the church, then turned in a large arc. From a slit in its flank a Hotchkiss machine gun spewed a hail of bullets into the miners' shacks.

The miners shouted in a language Henry had never heard before. They fired at the armored car but their bullets ricocheted off its metal walls.

The chattering of the machine gun drew more men from the wooden houses. Curious to witness the strange object, they were cut down by its fusillade.

Stunned momentarily by the suddenness of the attack, Henry watched, appalled, as the miners were mown down. The deputy pointed at a lane adjacent to the main thoroughfare and stabbed his finger in that direction. The armored car turned down the lane, heading towards the sea of tents. The gunner inside kept firing.

"Stop him! You must stop him!" yelled Henry, grabbing the deputy by his shoulders.

"Too late," he said, and shrugged.

His three colleagues had taken up defensive positions behind a horse trough, their rifles trained on the fleeing miners.

The miners who bolted for the safety of the rocks beyond the encampment were caught by a sudden volley of shots from snipers positioned in the underbrush on the high ground.

One of the wooden shacks suddenly exploded in flames. The wind bent the fire and carried it to the next tinder-dry dwelling. One by one the shacks ignited like the candles of a giant birthday cake.

Women clutching children burst screaming into the street. Panic-stricken, they ran in all directions, only to be driven back into their blazing homes by a volley of shots from the deputy's men.

"Oh, my God, you'll massacre them all!" yelled Henry.

The deputy whirled on him.

"If you don't start back the way you came, mister, one of these is for you."

He cocked his revolver and pressed it against Henry's temple, dislodging his straw hat. Behind Henry stood Hislop, white-faced and trembling in the heat.

"Henry. There's nothing we can do."

Henry could feel the warm barrel against his head. The acrid smell of spent cartridges filled his nostrils. With a sudden upward movement of his right forearm, he knocked the deputy's wrist away, forcing it against the timber wall. At the same time he drove his left fist into the man's solar plexus.

The deputy doubled over and dropped the revolver.

Henry threw an uppercut but the man pulled away, and the blow slid harmlessly off his shoulder. Henry stood back, fists raised, squaring to fight.

"You're going to die, mister," hissed the deputy, and with a roar he hurled himself at Henry.

Henry sidestepped and threw a short jab to the deputy's head, cutting him over the right eye. The deputy raised his fingertips to his face and felt the blood.

"Burke! Price! Peters!" he yelled. "Get over here!"

"The gun," Henry called to Hislop, but the preacher remained rooted to the ground.

The deputy advanced. Henry circled to put himself between the man and his revolver. His only chance was to drop his assailant before the others arrived, then pick up the weapon.

The deputy threw a barrelhouse left, which Henry easily blocked and countered with a right cross. The man grunted. Henry followed with a straight left, which sent the deputy staggering backwards.

"Just stay right where you are, English, with your hands in the air."

Three Winchester repeating rifles were trained on his back. Henry raised his arms.

"Hold him," growled the deputy.

Three pairs of hands grabbed him, pinning his arms behind his back. As Henry tried to break free, the deputy punched him in the face. He could hear a roaring in his ears as the pain travelled through his body. Then his head snapped back again as another blow landed. And another. The deputy was a blur. Henry raised his leg to fend off the advancing figure but an arm pulled sharply across his windpipe making him gag.

Blood ran from his nose. He wondered if it was broken. Another punch landed, and he could hear someone laugh.

Suddenly there was a shot, and the men released him in surprise. He sank to his knees.

The Reverend Clifford Hislop held a smoking revolver in both hands, swinging it uncertainly in a wide arc to cover the four men.

"No more," he shouted. "You'll kill him."

"That's the general idea," sneered the deputy.

In the distance, as if in another world, the sound of the Hotchkiss gun rattled off the surrounding hills.

"You're not going to use that again, preacher man, so why don't you just put it down and get your dumb friend out of here before you both get hurt."

Hislop edged towards Henry and helped him to his feet.

"You keep back now," said Hislop.

His voice had risen an octave and sounded close to hysteria.

Still groggy and smarting with pain, Henry allowed himself to be led towards the railway tracks.

Hislop took a handkerchief from his pocket and dabbed at Henry's lips.

"I didn't think I could do it," said Hislop. His voice was trembling with excitement. "I don't believe in violence."

"Well, thank God you believe in self-preservation," said Henry, gingerly feeling his nose.

"Mr. Tarr's not going to like this."

"I'm sure they'll be only too ready to apologize," replied Henry, indicating the bodies of the dead miners lying in the main street.

He counted seventeen. The corpses looked like piles of old clothes. Dust had already begun to settle on them. Halos of flies hovered over the blood. How many more of them were along the narrow lanes leading to the tents?

In the distance the machine gun clattered then stopped. A few more shots rang out from the hills, then there was silence.

"Welcome to America," said Henry. "Life, liberty and the pursuit of happiness."

As they approached the railway tracks he saw an engine drawing a single carriage shunt slowly by. The curtains over the windows were drawn. The carriage was painted blue and trimmed with gold, the colors of the Brandon sign. On the centre panel was a coat of arms. He had seen it before. The same device was carved on a stone escutcheon over the doorway to Thaddeus Nugent Tarr's New York mansion.

Henry watched the private train glide past until it crossed an iron bridge and disappeared into the heat haze that welded the purple mountains to the brown land.

Thursday, July 13, 1911

THADDEUS TARR SAT in his canopied bed, arms folded. In his gray silk pyjamas, with the initials TNT monogrammed over his heart, he looked like an angry, beached whale. The financial pages of the *New York Times* lay open across his knees. He reached over to the walnut humidor on his bedside table. It was embossed with the coat of arms of Napoleon III. From it he withdrew a long black cigar.

"How badly was he hurt? Could he walk?"

The Reverend Clifford Hislop, raw-boned, funereal in black, stood at the end of the bed blocking Tarr's view of his wife's portrait. Tarr had commissioned it from the fashionable Italian painter Giovanni Boldini on their honeymoon in Paris twenty years before.

"His face is marked up, sir. He told me to tell you he's been laid up with food poisoning."

Tarr laughed.

"It was unfortunate, sir. If things had gone according to plan there would have been no violence."

"Sometimes it takes the sight of blood to bring people to their senses," growled Tarr. "Did he put my men in danger?"

Hislop made a move to reach for the sulphur matches in a cut-glass container by the humidor. Tarr waved him away.

"I believe Henry was concerned for the well-being of the miners," said the preacher.

"It's my well-being he should be concerned with,"

9

snapped Tarr. "I'm bleeding, Hislop. Every day that strike goes on I lose three hundred thousand dollars."

"The shooting started before the leaders could be paid off, Mr. Tarr. We were lucky to escape with our lives."

The banker folded the newspaper neatly and placed it on the floor by his bed.

"What I want to know is can he be trusted? Loyalty, Hislop. That's what counts."

"He comes from a different culture, Mr. Tarr. He is unfamiliar with the way things are ordered here."

Henry Blexill had been awake since the first milk wagon had trundled up Fifth Avenue. He heard Lily, the upstairs maid, place a cup of tea on the bare floorboards outside his door. Tarr had not bothered to carpet the floors at the top of the house where the servants lived. Typical of the man, Henry thought. The polished herringbone parquet of the mansion's lower floors flamed with the finest Tabriz, Bokara and Kirman rugs.

"Tea, Mr. Blexill," he heard Lily call. "Hope you're feeling better."

Each night since his return from Brandon three days ago, Henry had awoken in the early hours soaking with sweat. The smell of cordite and dust lingered in his nostrils. His face and ribs still hurt from the beating. There was a bruise on his left cheek and a cut on his lip.

Images of the West Virginia massacre kept pulsing behind his closed eyelids. Bearded men dancing, tripping, bouncing like puppets to the yammering of the Hotchkiss gun. Yet there had been no accusations, no public outcry, no policemen pounding on Tarr's door. Only a mealymouthed editorial in the *New York Times* calling for the regulation of corporate combines.

The man responsible for the deaths of so many workers slept unconcerned between silk sheets two floors below Henry. And tonight Tarr would be holding a dinner party for J.P. Morgan and six other prominent New York bankers who had applauded his stand. No doubt a council of war, thought Henry, on how to fight President Taft's proposed anti-trust legislation. Regulation was bad for bankers. Nothing must threaten their community of interest.

Henry knew things were done differently in America, but there had to be justice for those immigrant miners shot down in the dust. He had only been in Tarr's employ for two weeks yet he realized his fate was now inextricably bound to Tarr's, and his nights would be haunted by dancing corpses in bloody shirts until the banker settled this account. He had thought of resigning but he had nowhere to go. It was not a butler's place to confront his master, but by remaining silent he would be condoning Tarr's action.

As he lay in bed staring at the stuccoed ceiling, he thought back to the day he had first crossed the banker's path.

Thaddeus Nugent Tarr, with a cigar in his mouth and his piercing black eyes, was the first American Henry had ever met. Tarr had visited Cumerworth Hall at Lord Rutherland's invitation in 1909. He had seemed out of place in England as he sat drinking port with the old man in front of the fire while sheep grazed on the downs beyond the window. Tarr had worn a black opal on his little finger and held a gold-headed cane across his knees.

For all his money, thought Henry, the banker still had the instincts of the Wyoming barbed-wire salesman he once was.

In March 1911, Lord Rutherland had gone bankrupt as a result of some disastrous stock speculation and was forced to sell Cumerworth by public auction. The staff who had served his family for generations was let go.

Two days before he left Cumerworth Hall, Henry received a letter from the American banker inviting him to come to New York as his butler. The proposed salary was three times what Lord Rutherland had paid him. With no other prospects in view Henry had accepted the offer. The era of Cumerworth and what it stood for was ending. Men like Thaddeus Nugent Tarr represented the new order. Reluctantly, Henry bought a steamer ticket and a map of the United States.

Henry rose painfully from his bed and dressed. There was no point delaying the inevitable. He would have to face Tarr.

Cook was already at the stove when Henry entered the kitchen carrying the morning's mail.

"The face looks better now, Mr. Blexill. You'll be more careful on those cellar steps now, won't you."

"Indeed I will, Mrs. Garvey. What's the menu for tonight? I'd like to fetch the wines."

"Steak. Well-done steak. That's all he ever eats. Breakfast, lunch and dinner, if I gave it to him."

"Well, I have some 1895 Clos Vougeot shipped by Champy Père et Fils, which should go nicely. What else?"

"Lobster in cream sauce to start. Mr. Morgan's favorite. And cheese to finish. Stilton."

"I suppose he'll want champagne as they arrive. He's got a lot of Krug in the cellar. I'll bring up three bottles of Schloss Johannisberg Riesling Spaetlese 1900 for the lobster and the Dow 1878 for the Stilton."

"Just names to me." Cook sniffed. "Dow 1878."

"Vintage port." Henry laughed. "The British Empire floats on port. Not surprising he likes it, really."

The staff always referred to Tarr as "he," never by his name except for Nichole, Mrs. Tarr's secretary and her daughter's chaperone.

"Did you know, Mrs. Garvey, after his breakfast every morning he drinks a glass of port mixed with olive oil. Barbaric. Thinks it's a tonic."

A motor car honked its horn as it passed a horse-drawn ice wagon on Fifth Avenue. Through the kitchen window, which was at sidewalk level, Henry could see its yellow-spoked wheels bumping over the cobblestones. Yellow wheels meant Mr. Vanderbilt. Mr. Gould, who lived on the other side of the street, owned a black Pope-Toledo, but he never drove it himself. The upstart Guggenheims had two cars, both white Pierce Arrows. Tarr kept a Detroit Electric, which he hardly used, but he ordered the chauffeur to leave the garage door open.

In the summer Tarr insisted that the front door of the

house stand open, too, so he could scandalize passersby
with a glimpse of the William Bouguereau nude that hung
in the hall. It was a portrait of a woman with long black
hair rising from her bath. Cook would instruct the new
maids to shut their eyes whenever they passed it. Nichole
had laughed when Lily reported this. Cook had been
Nichole's enemy ever since.

One morning, when the sunlight from the hall windows
set the model's flesh glowing, Henry caught Nichole standing in front of the painting. He was refilling the port
decanter in the library. Through the open door he could
see her profile as she looked up at the rosy nude. She ran
her hands slowly over her breasts, down her ribs, then
over her hips to her thighs. When he accidentally chinked
the glass top against the decanter she wheeled around and
grimaced angrily in his direction. Then she laughed deep
in her throat.

"Are you a watcher, too?" she said.

Those were the first words Nichole addressed to him.

"If you mean, do I admire the female form, Miss Linley,
then the answer is yes."

Henry gazed at the street thinking about Nichole. A
shadow passed the window. It stopped, and he caught
sight of a pair of man's heavy boots dulled with mud. The
toes were pointed towards the house, as if the man were
turning his back on the wind to light a cigarette. Henry
saw the dead match fall, and the man moved on.

It was odd to see boots like that in summer on Fifth
Avenue, he thought, but he forgot about it when Lily
came into the kitchen with a pile of change in her cupped
hands.

"I hope you did what I told you," said Cook to the
young woman.

"Yes, ma'am." Lily made a face at Cook's back. She put
the money on the kitchen table and took a glass bowl from
a shelf. She placed the coins in the bowl and poured
boiling water from the kettle over them. Henry watched
her, fascinated.

"What are you doing, Lily?" he asked.

"Washing his change."

"Are you serious?"

"He makes me iron his dollar bills, too. I guess he can't stand wrinkled money."

"You never get rid of the smell of blood," said Henry.

He watched Lily dry the coins on her apron and begin to apply polish to them. She made them gleam like the Georgian tea service that sat, unused, on a tray in the library.

"You see that silver?" Tarr had asked when he conducted Henry around the mansion on his first day in New York. "It once belonged to President Garfield. Bet you never heard of him."

Another trophy, Henry had thought. Like me.

Lily wiped her fingertips on her sleeves, arms crossed over her imperceptible chest.

"Is it true Miss Rhonda got kicked out of school for thieving?" she asked.

"And where did you hear such a terrible thing, child?" demanded Cook.

"Elsie, the florist's assistant, told me when she delivered the flowers this morning. Her sister's a nurse at Gorton. Fancy."

Cook said nothing and gave the stock pot several vigorous stirs. *Like father, like daughter, she's thinking,* said Henry to himself. He had only seen Rhonda once, the first night he had served at table. Rhonda had been home from school for the weekend.

The heavy silence in the kitchen was broken by a bell tinkling overhead. Three pairs of eyes swivelled up to the bell box, to see which bell was ringing. The letter *B* for *butler* agitated wildly in the box.

"He wants you," said Cook.

"Not me, the mail," said Henry.

He put the stack of envelopes on a silver tray and reached for his jacket.

"Can you find out if Mrs. Tarr's joining the men for dinner? She hasn't been out of her room for days," said Cook. "I'll need white fish."

A green baize door at the top of the kitchen stairs separated the servants' quarters from the main hall. Henry walked across the hall floor on the balls of his feet so the pink marble would not ring under his steel-tipped heels—an economy his father had taught him.

At the centre of the hall a huge staircase rose to a half landing. Guarding it on either side were twin suits of medieval armor with broadswords held by metal gauntlets between metal feet. Just as there had been at Cumerworth Hall.

There were other reminders of Cumerworth Hall around Tarr's mansion. The habitual decanter of port with two glasses on a tray in the library. The matched pair of Purdy shotguns that never left their glass case on the landing. And the portraits. Holbeins, Vermeers and Gainsboroughs hung without thought of period or style. Tarr's instant ancestors.

Henry had grown up at Cumerworth Hall. His father had been Lord Rutherland's valet until he collapsed and died of a burst appendix on St. Swithin's Day, 1901. Henry was eighteen when he succeeded his father. He had started in Lord Rutherland's service as a stableboy and had once held a horse for the Prince of Wales.

His caustic tongue got him into trouble with his peers, and he was constantly having to defend himself with his fists. Lord Rutherland witnessed one fight and saw some pugilistic talent in Henry, which he encouraged by building a ring behind the stables. He invited challenges from neighborhood boys in his protégé's fighting weight. Money would change hands among the grooms.

Henry went on to become county champion. His idol was John L. Sullivan, the Boston Strong Boy, whose career he followed avidly in the English press. He clipped every mention of the boxer and gummed it into a large scrapbook.

Henry mounted the stairs. He could see that the door on the landing directly above him was slightly ajar. As he turned on the half landing, it was shut without a sound. The Reverend Clifford Hislop watched and listened. Like the Pinkertons, his was the eye that never slept.

Henry knocked quietly on Tarr's bedroom door.

"Come," roared the voice from inside.

"You rang, sir?"

"Of course I rang, Blexill. Why in hell do you think you're here? Have you got the mail?"

Henry waited while Tarr went through the letters. On the pretext of screening the household from threatening mail, he would open envelopes addressed to his wife, Cornelia, his daughter, Rhonda, Nichole Linley, Clifford Hislop and every member of the staff who lived under his roof.

Henry could tell which letters were dangerous by the shabbiness of the paper and the badly penned block capitals. They were either begging notes or death threats. Since Brandon, the death threats had doubled. In response Tarr had hired private detectives to guard the house. Wherever he went he surrounded himself with a phalanx of Pinkerton men.

Tarr read all the offensive letters before tearing them up, muttering, "Cranks, lunatics, vermin," as he did so.

It's almost as if he enjoys being the target of so much envy and hatred, Henry thought.

"Now. Is everything in order for tonight?" demanded Tarr, when he had finished reading.

"Yes, sir."

Henry remained impassive. A good butler, his father used to say, shows no emotions.

"Everything's got to be a hundred per cent. There's a lot riding on this dinner."

According to the below-stairs gossip, this was the first time J.P. Morgan would set foot in Tarr's house. Yet they all knew that Morgan was an ever-present spectre in Tarr's life. The shadow he cast darkened Tarr's sky. Morgan was everything Tarr wanted to be, so rich and powerful he could not be touched.

Tarr was obsessed with the man. Every morning Henry watched his employer tracking the master of money's intricate network of voting trusts, stock ownerships and directorships. Morgan, Tarr once told him with unabashed admiration, controlled three national banks, three life-insurance companies and ten railroads. He also held the reins of such industrial giants as General Electric, AT&T, International Harvester, Western Union and the world's largest corpration, U.S. Steel.

Morgan and his partners, Tarr enumerated with reverence, held seventy-two interlocking directorships in forty-seven of the largest financial institutions and corporations of America. The combined worth of these directorships alone was ten billion dollars. Morgan's personal collection of art, rare manuscripts, ceramics and tapestries was valued at fifty million dollars. Tarr's face had flushed with an excitement that bordered on the sexual when he delivered the coup de grace.

"When you put it all together, Blexill, the House of Morgan and its affiliates directly control aggregate resources worth twenty-two point five billion dollars. D'you know how many zeroes that is?"

Henry did not, nor did he care. It was obscene to talk about money. He had never heard Lord Rutherland mention the price of anything. But in this brash new society everything was reduced to a price tag.

Yet behind Tarr's admiration for Morgan's achievements, Henry sensed a burning desire to get the better of the man. Nichole had confirmed this when she had told him about the Crash of 1901.

The day after the incident with the painting, Nichole had come into the kitchen while he was making himself a cup of tea.

"How about one for me?" she had asked.

They sat at the kitchen table, and he had let her talk. She seemed to be the kind of woman who needed to fill silence with indiscretions. He had not initiated the conversation about Tarr. He had merely observed that his employer seemed to spend an inordinate amount of time talking about J.P. Morgan.

"Well, you know why, don't you?" said Nichole, then she leaned towards him with her elbows on the table. She held her teacup in both hands as she recounted the story.

Steam from the cup curled around her dark eyelashes. He realized then how beautiful she was.

"Eight years ago, Mr. Tarr was the majority shareholder in the Tennessee Coal, Iron and Railroad Company. When the market took a dive, the railroad was threatened with bankruptcy. He was forced to go to Morgan cap in hand for a loan. Morgan doesn't lend money. He gives credit. You can imagine what it did to Mr. Tarr to go begging like that. Anyhow, Morgan bailed him out, but he also purchased all the company's saleable bonds, and he got control of the stock. It seems Morgan really wanted the railroad. That was when he was putting together U.S. Steel. You must have read about it in England. It was in all the newspapers. Well, Mr. Tarr never forgave Morgan for that."

Henry had watched the way her nostrils flared when she emphasized certain words. It was as if she felt her conversation could not hold his attention and she needed some physical movement to make him concentrate on her face. In a household where everything revolved around one man, small wonder the rest of us use harmless stratagems to hold the interest of the others, he thought.

Henry waited until Tarr had finished reading.

"If I may, sir, I would like to speak to you about Brandon."

"What about Brandon?"

"As you see, sir, I got into an altercation. Men were being shot indiscriminately. I felt it was my duty to try to stop it."

"Your duty is to me, Blexill."

"Yes, sir. I would not want circumstances to reflect badly on my employer."

"Don't speak in riddles, man. What are you trying to say?"

"I saw your private train. Naturally, I assumed that you were there and had witnessed what had happened."

"You can set your mind at rest on that score. I was in Cleveland at a directors' meeting."

"Well, sir, the armored car had flanged wheels for run-

ning on railway tracks. It would have had to be brought in
specially. The attack on the miners was planned. It wasn't
a spontaneous action. A signal was given to start shooting."

"If that's the case, Blexill, the men were going against
my orders. There was to be no bloodshed. State troopers
ordered the armored car. But if they overstepped the
mark I'll make sure they're punished. All right?"

"Yes, sir. Perhaps the company might see fit to make
some financial accommodation to the widows and orphans
of the dead miners."

Tarr shifted angrily in his bed.

"Now look, Blexill. I'm prepared to listen to you because you're new here but don't think you can—"

The banker stopped short when the door to the adjoining room opened and Cornelia Tarr entered. She wore an
embroidered Chinese robe that touched the floor. It covered her body without giving her any shape. Her wrists,
which protruded from the wide silk arms, were slender,
white and vulnerable. Her thinning hair was concealed
under a turban.

"Why, Henry, whatever have you done to your poor
face?"

Henry turned in the direction of the musical voice with
its gentle southern inflection. Cornelia had her own bedroom at the end of the landing. Frail and tremulous, she
lowered herself onto a leather chair as far from the window as she could get.

"A mishap with a belligerent door, madam. I assure you
it will not happen again."

He glanced at Tarr, who smiled.

Henry had spent his first afternoon off at the New York
Public Library reading the *Social Register*. It was no
Debrett's Peerage, but it gave him an idea of the pecking
order in this frenetic city. Cornelia, he had learned, was
the youngest daughter of an old Georgia banking family
named McKinley. The book gave no information on Tarr's
background.

The librarian had suggested he would find "the real
cream of New York" in William McAllister's "List of Four

Hundred." The names had been compiled by a society columnist at the request of Mrs. William Waldorf Astor, whose private ballroom could accommodate only four hundred people. There was no reference there to either Cornelia or Thaddeus Nugent Tarr. A cursory reading of the list of the city's elite suggested that Cornelia, with her background, deserved to be numbered among them. Obviously Tarr's antecedents had precluded him his inclusion in the list, and, by association, hers. Perhaps New Yorkers were not so naïve after all.

"And please tell Nichole—" Cornelia paused after uttering the name as if she had forgotten what she was about to say "—that Miss Rhonda will be arriving on the Boston train tonight. I'd like Nichole to meet her with the automobile." Then she added vaguely, "No, don't bother, Henry. I'll tell her myself."

Her flutelike voice rose at the end of her sentences, making every statement sound like a question.

"Very good, madam."

Henry liked Cornelia Tarr. There was something of the late Lady Rutherland about her. She knew instinctively how to deal with staff. Unlike Tarr, whose every word was a bullying command.

Tarr scowled at his wife. "There's something I want to say to Henry in private, Cornelia."

"Very well, dear," she said. She rose, birdlike, from her chair. When she moved she seemed even more insubstantial.

"You take care of that face now, you hear?"

"Yes, madam."

"How long have you been with me, Blexill?" asked Tarr, after Cornelia had shut the door behind her.

Tarr called him "Henry" when his wife was present, but "Blexill" in front of the other servants or when they were alone.

"Two weeks today, sir."

"Two weeks. You like working here, do you?"

"I've just started, sir," Henry equivocated.

"So you have. So you have. Fix my tonic, will you?"

Tarr waved towards the decanter of port that stood on

the Louis XIII table in front of the window. Beside it was a silver urn filled with olive oil. Henry poured a measure of oil into a glass, added a couple of ounces of port then stirred the mixture with a spoon until the two had mixed. He held his breath so he would not have to smell the concoction.

"I sent you to Brandon because I wanted to see how you would react," said Tarr. "It was a kind of test. I could have sent a Pinkerton with Hislop, but I wanted to get a bead on you."

"I was just trying to stop people getting killed, sir."

"People get hurt when they try to smash the system, Blexill. In this country anything's possible as long as you play by the rules. It's the duty of men like me to protect those rules for the good of everyone else."

"If I may be permitted, sir, a system that has to be protected with armored cars I hardly think is—"

"You are not paid to think, Blexill."

Henry could feel the muscles in his shoulders tensing. He placed the glass on a tray and held it out for Tarr to take.

The banker studied him for a moment without moving.

"Drink it," he said.

"I beg your pardon, sir."

"Drink it. It'll do you good. Full of iron."

"If you don't mind, it's a little early in the day for me."

"You weren't listening to me, Blexill," shouted Tarr. "I said drink it, and that is an order."

Henry pressed his teeth together. If he refused, he knew Tarr would fire him. He would be out on the street in a strange city with no references. Slowly he raised the glass to lips and took a sip. The sweet, oily mixture made him gag.

"All of it."

Henry shut his eyes and knocked back the glass. His whole body shuddered.

"There. That wasn't so hard, was it?" Tarr smiled.

Henry could feel the bile rising in this throat.

"I knew you'd drink it. You know why? Because you

had no choice. I can read men, Blexill. I know when they're bluffing. When they've been pushed to the wall. That's what makes me a good businessman. I got all this by knowing that. By being a wolf among foxes." Tarr laughed and made a circle with his hand to encompass everything in the room as proof of his statement. "But you, Henry, I'm not sure about you."

"May I go now, sir?"

"You've just shown me you can be obedient, Henry. But can you be loyal? Loyalty to an employer, that's the American way. That's what makes a well-oiled clock."

"Yes, sir."

"Yes, sir. No, sir. You don't mince words, do you, Henry?"

"Sir?"

"Lord Rutherland wasn't like you, so it's not just because you're British. Or maybe it is. Working-class British."

"Lower-middle-class, sir," corrected Henry, stung by the description.

"Lower-middle-class," repeated Tarr, mimicking Henry's accent.

Henry's efforts to control his heaving stomach were making him perspire. "At the risk of spoiling your carpet, sir, I really must ask you to excuse me."

Tarr began to laugh and dismissed him with a wave of the hand. As Henry moved hastily down the stairs, Tarr shouted after him: "Loyalty, Henry. That's the key."

Thursday, July 13, 1911

SHAKING WITH ANGER and indignation, Henry headed for the gymnasium Tarr had built in the basement. He stripped off his jacket and shirt and began to pummel the punching bag. Leaning his shoulders against the bag, he drove his bare fists deep into its canvas belly as if it were Tarr he was hitting.

It felt good. Like the early days at Cumerworth Hall. His father had rigged up a bag in the stables and had coached Henry in London rules—bare knuckles and wrestling throws. He had Henry lift bails of straw to strengthen his arms and shoulders. Boxers had to be strong. A fight lasted until one contestant conceded.

His anger spent, Henry stood back from the bag and began to jab at it, circling in the stance John L. Sullivan used. Feet spread wide, back straight, knees slightly bent, weight distributed evenly on both feet.

The iron ring that supported the bag on a chain squeaked each time Henry struck. He began to move faster, bobbing and weaving, flicking out straight lefts before closing with short hooks and crosses. He feinted with a left then shifted his weight to throw a right. The bag seemed to groan under his punches, swaying dizzily, complaining on its chain.

He had forgotten about Tarr and was completely absorbed in his defenseless opponent when Nichole entered the gym. Her dark hair was piled up on her head in the fashion of the day. She wore a lavender-colored silk dress with an open Dutch collar, which exposed her long neck.

"Is that anyone I know?" she asked, smiling as she approached behind him.

Henry stood upright and held the bag still.

"A little morning exercise, Miss Linley," he said, breathing heavily.

He looked around for his shirt, uncomfortable to be without it in the presence of a woman.

"Are you blushing, or is it just the exercise? Don't worry. I've seen men without their shirts before."

I'll wager you have, thought Henry. It was common knowledge that Tarr visited her room at night. Cook once told him that Nichole behaved as if she, and not Mrs. Tarr, were mistress of the house. "Gives herself airs, that one," Cook had said, "and we all know why. Small wonder Miss Rhonda is as wild as she is. Some chaperone."

Nichole reached out and touched a U-shaped scar on his chest, just visible above the neckline of his undershirt.

"Did that happen at Brandon?"

Henry drew back from the butterfly touch, which sent shivers through his body.

"I'm sorry," she said. "Is it painful?"

"How do you know about Brandon?"

"You don't think for a moment I believed your story. Men like you don't fall down stairs."

"It happened long ago, when I was in England," said Henry. "I was kicked by a mare in heat."

He reached for his shirt and pulled it on.

Nichole frowned and brushed some imaginary dust from her sleeve. "Apparently, I'm to pick up Rhonda from the Boston train at six o'clock. I thought you might drive the automobile since it's the chauffeur's day off."

"It would be my pleasure, but he needs me here for his dinner party, Miss Linley. There are the wines to decant."

"You make me sound like an old spinster, calling me Miss Linley. Couldn't you call me Nichole?"

Henry smiled. He could do better than that. He could take the pale, oval face in his hands and lift it to his. He could kiss the crimson-painted lips and press the slim body against his own.

He was moving towards her when the house was suddenly rocked by what felt like an earthquake. Plaster dust fell from the ceiling, and the punching bag broke away from its chain.

Henry's first thought was that a gas main had blown, and that the floor above mght cave in on them. He grabbed Nichole's hand and ran for the stairs. He could hear servants calling to each other in panic.

Henry raced into the hall where the suits of armor were still rattling from the vibrations of the explosion. The blast had blown the massive front door off its hinges. Out of the smoke and dust staggered an apparition of a man in tattered clothes, his flesh blackened and seared. The man was groaning and shaking. Blood ran down his legs and arms.

Henry caught the man as he fell. "Get a doctor," he yelled at Nichole, who stared in horror at the injured man.

"Bomb," whispered the ghostly figure, then his head rolled back.

Henry eased him gently onto the Bokara rug.

Tarr's voice thundered from the landing above: "Not on the carpet, you fool! Put him on the floor." Tarr, wearing a quilted dressing gown, bounded down the stairs. "Is he alive?" he demanded.

Henry felt the man's heart. It was still beating faintly.

"Yes, but he's badly hurt, sir."

Henry noticed that there were tiny pieces of white material sticking to the man's wounds. He touched one, which left a white powder on his fingertips.

It looked like flour. The bomb, he reasoned, must have been hidden in a flour sack when it was detonated. The image of the Brandon miners, their flour sacks filled with ammunition, flashed through his mind. The man whose feet he had seen that morning, the man with the muddy boots, must have planted it.

Lily's frightened face appeared from behind the green baize door.

"Get out," yelled Tarr. "Get back to work."

He bent until his lips almost touched the injured man's ear.

"Who did it, Collins?" Henry heard him whisper. "It was the Macklins, right? Was it the brother or the son?"

The man's eyes flickered but his mouth was too full of blood to speak.

Tarr turned away and cursed. "Was it Brandon?" he asked. He dug his fingers into the man's shoulder.

The only response was the gurgling sound of air bubbling up through the blood in the man's throat. The head fell to one side, and the blood flowed purple onto the pink marble. Tarr shook his head in disgust and rose to his feet.

"Check on the damage," he ordered Henry as he strode upstairs, muttering angrily to himself.

On the half landing he bumped into Hislop.

"Try your Divine Science on him," shouted Tarr, and he disappeared upstairs, slamming his bedroom door behind him.

Henry and Hislop exchanged glances. Hislop reddened.

"Spirit is immortal truth. Matter is mortal error," murmured the preacher. "There is nothing I can do for the dead but pray for them."

"And we have seen a lot of death, have we not, Mr. Hislop?" said Henry.

The Reverend Clifford Hislop took a leather-bound Bible from his pocket. He had wound the red ribbon, which marked the pages, so tightly around his index finger it had turned the flesh bluish-white. Outside, the sound of an approaching siren whined on Fifth Avenue. Two policemen in tight-fitting blue uniforms darkened the doorway.

"Who's in charge here?" demanded one, looking at the blast-burned body. "Has anybody called an ambulance?"

"A doctor has been called," said Henry. "This is Mr. Tarr's residence."

As if conjured by the uttering of his name, Tarr appeared at the head of the stairs.

"Radicals, gentlemen." His face was stern as he descended. "Bombing private property again. It's a disgrace.

We're not safe in our beds. The mayor will hear from me, you can bet on that."

"Did you know the deceased, sir?" asked the second policeman.

"Collins was his name. Raymond Collins. A Pinkerton man hired by me to protect my family and my property from exactly this kind of murderous outrage," shouted Tarr. "We'll talk about it in the library."

His manner softened as he approached the two policemen. They fidgeted and looked at each other, uncomfortable in such lavish surroundings.

"I have a great respect for the police, gentlemen. I should tell you that I am entertaining J. P. Morgan here tonight, as well as other influential men of our city. Now I don't want any publicity, you understand. These men don't take kindly to newspapermen with cameras snooping around."

As he passed Henry, he whispered, "Bring up a couple of bottles of bourbon."

He smiled at the policemen, took them by the arm, led them into the library and closed the door behind him.

Henry's first concern was the wine cellar. The bomb had exploded at the side of the house nearest to the cellar. The night before, he had taken four bottles of Dow 1878 from the racks and stood them on the tasting table. Once the sediment had settled, he could decant them for the Morgan dinner party.

He hurried down the basement stairs to check on the wines, but his way to the cellar was blocked by the strong-room door, which had been blown open. Henry had never been inside the strong room, where Tarr kept his private papers. Only Tarr had a key.

Henry switched on the light. Tarr's papers were everywhere, and the room looked as if burglars had ransacked the place. The force of the blast had thrown the file drawers from their wooden cabinets and deposited their contents in a heap. Files, account books and papers littered the floor. Tarr, who was fanatically tidy, would not be pleased to see the mess. It would be hard work to put his papers in order again.

Henry smiled and was about to leave when his eye was caught by the label on the nearest file: "Morgan—Northern Securities Case."

He knelt and fanned out several files like a hand of cards. "Morgan—International Harvester." "Morgan—Museum Bequests." "Morgan—36 Madison Avenue." Each file was dedicated to some facet of J.P. Morgan's affairs, an entire archive with financial reports, newspaper clippings, railroad balance sheets, copies of *Banker's Magazine*, stock-market analyses—all neatly indexed in Tarr's hand.

The man is insane, thought Henry. Tarr's obsession with the latter-day Medici reminded him of a cartoon he had once seen in *Punch*. A tiny fish is about to take a baited hook. So intent is the fish on swallowing the bait that he is unaware of a slightly larger fish behind him with its jaws open. And behind the larger fish is an even larger one, jaws agape. And so on until the sixth fish, which is huge and will devour the other five. Henry saw Tarr as the biggest fish. But Morgan was the man in the boat who would haul in the catch when the fish had swallowed each other in sequence.

He picked up a file marked "Morgan—Staff." Inside was a sheaf of single sheets of paper. The uppermost page had the name Alice Burbank printed in block capitals in the top left-hand corner. Under the name were the words, "Receptionist-Telephonist." The page below was labelled, "Bernard Coates, Actuary," the third, "Marsden J. Dewey, Accounts Payable."

Short paragraphs described each person's function at Morgan's Wall Street office, their interests, their salaries, their home addresses. It was the kind of information that only someone inside Morgan's operation would know, or that a private detective could accumulate.

He was about to reach for another file when he heard a footfall on the stairs. Guiltily, he began to shuffle the heap of files into some semblance of order.

"What are you doing in here?"

Hislop stood in the doorway staring at him as he busied himself with the scattered files. The next one he picked up was marked, "Brandon—Consolidation."

He stared at Hislop, unable to speak. He looked at the file again. All the information about Brandon was there, neatly filed.

"Well?"

"Mr. Tarr asked me to check on the damage," Henry improvised.

"You know this room is off limits. Only Mr. Tarr comes in here."

"Then Mr. Tarr can clean up the mess himself," Henry said as he dropped a pile of papers on the floor.

"He's waiting for the bottles of bourbon he asked for," added Hislop.

"You have remarkably good ears," replied Henry as he pushed past the preacher.

Hislop said nothing. He was inspecting the buckled lock and looking suspiciously at Henry. "Just get the bottles from the cellar and I'll take them up," said Hislop.

His tone, Henry noticed, had softened. Effeminate, deeply religious and obsessed with knowing exactly what was going on, the Reverend Clifford Hislop continued to be something of an enigma to Henry. His position in Tarr's household seemed to rest solely on his relationship with Cornelia. He was her touchstone of faith, her nurse, her confidant. The banker seemed to tolerate his presence with ill-concealed contempt. Yet Hislop had his uses for Tarr, as well. It was Hislop who had been entrusted with the delivery of twenty thousand dollars to the Brandon militia. What other dubious errands had he run on Tarr's behalf? Although he was a man of the cloth, he seemed to have a singular ability to override his Christian conscience when executing the banker's wishes.

In the corridor Henry could smell the sweet, raisiny bouquet of vintage port emanating from the wine cellar. The bottles must have smashed on the flagstones, he thought.

He could hear the sound of an ambulance bell coming from the street. Too late; the man was dead. Another victim in the war over Brandon. With a heavy heart he opened the cellar door.

"Oh, no."

The four bottles of vintage port lay in wreckage on the floor. The port spread like a pool of blood. Lord Rutherland used to say the 1878 port was the last of the great vintages. It was the port Henry had served to Tarr on his visit to Cumerworth Hall, the port Tarr insisted be laid down in his own cellar. These were the last four bottles.

"I'm sorry," said Hislop. He placed a hand on Henry's shoulder as if he had been bereaved. "Show me where you keep the bourbon, and I'll take it up to Mr. Tarr."

Alone amid the wreckage of those precious bottles, Henry wondered why they had more claim on his sympathy than the poor wretch who had died upstairs. He felt chastened by his indifference to the fate of a private detective who had been blown apart trying to protect Tarr's mansion. Tarr had told the police that the bombing was the work of radicals—Emma Goldmann, Russians, agitators according to the press, anarchists and people like that. Their names were in the newspapers all the time. Boils on the Statue of Liberty, Tarr called them. They held meetings in church halls in Queens and the Bronx. The police arrested them whenever they spoke.

But he had distinctly heard Tarr ask the dying man if it was the brother or the son. Tarr had also referred to Brandon. That suggested he knew the reason for the bombing, and who had planted the bomb. But why had he not informed the police?

The answers were in those files. Henry was sure of it.

He breathed in the scent of the port as he mopped the floor and grieved for the dead miners and the lost bottles. One bin of old claret had also been destroyed—Chateau Margaux 1871, Lafite 1875 and Haut Brion 1890, wines that had just become ready for drinking. Wines that could never be replaced.

By the time he had finished, a locksmith was already at work fixing a new lock on the door to the strong room. From upstairs came the sound of carpenters replacing the hinges of the front door. *Tarr hasn't wasted any time*, he thought. Everything had to be back to normal for the arrival of Midas.

Henry approached the locksmith. "That looks like a sturdy one," he said.

The man in blue overalls stood back and admired his handiwork. "Keep out Houdini, that will." He grinned.

"You've done a grand job. If you'll give me the keys I'll take them to Mr. Tarr."

The locksmith reached into his pocket and took out a ring with two keys on it.

"Saves me a journey. D'you mind signing this work order so I can get off home?"

When the locksmith had gathered up his tools and climbed the staircase to the tradesman's entrance on Thirty-sixth Street, Henry took out the keys, removed one from the ring and attached it to his own set of house keys.

Now he had access to Tarr's private papers. All he needed was the opportunity to study them at leisure without any prying eyes.

The sound of the brass knocker on the front door echoed through the hall and down the stairs into the kitchen where Henry was looking for the small silver tray. Every object brought to Tarr by the serving staff had to be presented to him on a silver tray. The tray, which had a slight dent in it from a pistol shot, had once graced the desk of Victor Emmanuel, King of Sardinia.

Henry climbed the stairs and went through the hall, checking the marble for signs of blood on the way. There were none. A faint odor of disinfectant hung in the air. Henry opened the door.

A man with a camera stood on the steps. He had a press card tucked into the band of his straw hat. A notebook protruded from his pocket. He wore a shapeless brown tweed suit, a spotted bow tie and a striped shirt. The collar was too large for his neck. His bony face suggested cynicism, boredom and fatigue all at the same time.

"May I help you?"

"My name's McGillivray. From the *New York Times*. I'd like to see Mr. Tarr."

"Mr. Tarr is—"

Before Henry could complete the sentence, Tarr called out angrily from the library. "Who is it?"

"A gentleman from the *New York Times*, sir," Henry replied over his shoulder.

"Throw him out."

Henry looked at McGillivray. The journalist had obviously heard Tarr's response but was making no effort to move.

"Mr. Tarr is inviting you to leave," said Henry.

"Maybe he'll send me an engraved invitation."

"Maybe I'll send you one."

McGillivray craned his neck to peer inside the door. Henry blocked his view. The reporter shrugged and took a business card from his breast pocket.

"Here," he whispered. "Call me if you know anything about Brandon. It could be worth your while."

Henry shut the door in his face. His action was motivated not by loyalty to Tarr but by his resentment of McGillivray's intrusive curiosity. He stood, listening, inside the door, tempted momentarily to supply the journalist with all the information he would need to expose Tarr. Let the newspapers put the banker on trial.

But there was something cowardly about informing on one's employer. The score could only be settled face to face. Marquis of Queensbury rules. The British way.

What was it about Brandon that had brought McGillivray to Tarr's doorstep? He must have made the connection between what happened at the mining camp and the explosion. Henry could understand why the Hearst newspapers would be swarming around: Tarr was fabulously wealthy, and scandals involving the rich were the theatre of the poor. What could be more dramatic than blood and money? But the *New York Times*? Surely they were above such gutter journalism. What did McGillivray know that could threaten Henry's employer?

"What did he want?" demanded Tarr, who had come to the library door.

"The bomb must have attracted him, sir."

"I'll have no reporters hanging round my front door! Do you hear?"

"Yes, sir."

At that moment the knocker sounded again.

"If it's another of them I'll send him packing with an ass full of buckshot," Tarr roared.

Henry waited until Tarr had retreated into the library before he opened the door.

A boyish messenger in a purple and blue button-studded uniform stood moving from one foot to the other on the top step. He wore a pillbox hat secured under his chin by a leather strap.

"For Mr. Tarr."

He handed Henry a creamy envelope, then held his hand out. The flap of the envelope was sealed with red wax, which bore the imprint of J.P. Morgan's signet ring.

Henry gave the boy some change and put the envelope on the silver tray. Next to it he placed the new strongroom key.

Tarr was seated at his desk when Henry entered the library.

"I have the key to the new lock on your store room downstairs, sir. And this envelope has just arrived."

Henry watched Tarr pick up the key and put it in his waistcoat pocket. Tarr was more interested in the envelope, especially when he saw the seal on the back. He ran his fingers over the paper as if the message inside would be unlocked at their touch. Slowly, he took a jade letter opener from the drawer and slit the envelope open. He unfolded the creamy paper inside and read the handwritten note.

Henry saw the blood drain from his face.

Tarr clenched his fists around the letter opener until it snapped in two. He began to tremble. With a look that could freeze stone he turned and said through clenched teeth: "There'll be one less for dinner tonight, Blexill. Mr. Morgan—it seems—has been called out of town."

Friday, July 14, 1911

EVERY YEAR IN mid-July, Thaddeus Nugent Tarr moved his household from the Fifth Avenue mansion to his eighty-acre estate in Westchester for the summer season.

To Henry, who was witnessing it for the first time, the event was like a military manoeuvre.

A private train transported family and servants, their combined luggage, Tarr's favorite armchair and a large electric humidor filled with a three-month supply of black cigars.

Two days before their arrival, Mrs. Grady, the Westchester housekeeper who was in permanent residence, opened up the house with the help of the three gardeners. Sheets were pulled from furniture; fires were lit in every fireplace to dispel the damp. Beds were made. Surfaces were dusted and mirrors polished. Cut flowers were placed in all the rooms, and a stock pot was started on the stove in the basement kitchen.

A fleet of hired cars delivered the Tarrs, their retinue and luggage to Grand Central Station one hour before the train's departure, at noon. A packed lunch was served on board, and the servants were instructed not to sing in case they disturbed their employer in his private car. At Mamaroneck they alighted, and were picked up again by the fleet of hire cars for the fifteen-minute drive to the estate. The cavalcade was a welcome sight for the merchants of the small fishing village on Long Island Sound.

This year an extra carriage was coupled to the train to

accommodate the five Pinkerton agents Tarr had hired to guard him and his family on the estate.

Henry's first sight of the blue and gold carriages sitting at the station brought back images of Brandon: the train, the dust, the heat haze and the flies circling above the miners' bodies. Why had he not told McGillivray what he had witnessed? The mere act of articulating what he had seen would have lessened his burden. He had tried to talk to Hislop about it, but the preacher had raised his eyes and intoned, "It is for God alone to make judgements."

"But didn't you see how they were forced to live? Don't you care about poverty?" Henry had protested.

"Why do you damn the rich?" was Hislop's response. "Have you never thought that poverty might be a sign of God's displeasure? The rich can do God's work, too, Henry. God is manifest in good works."

At that point, Henry realized Tarr had a housebroken preacher under his roof.

Henry sat alone in the servant's carriage fingering the key ring in his pocket. There had been no chance to sneak down to the basement and have a look at the files. Hislop, whose pathological curiosity led him to roam the house at all hours of the day or night, was liable to report Henry's movements to Tarr.

The protocol for the train journey dictated that Thaddeus and Cornelia Tarr occupied the carriage furthest from the engine. Rhonda, Nichole, Hislop and any of Rhonda's friends who might be accompanying her as house guests sat in the next carriage. The rest of the staff crowded into the carriage coupled to the coal bin. This year the Pinkertons travelled in the car nearest the coal. They used Tarr's electric humidor as a card table.

Another departure from the ritual this year was the absence of the wayward Rhonda. She had been sent to her Aunt Hortense in Atlanta. For the sake of a peaceful summer, Cornelia had asked her eldest sister to entertain Rhonda. "Thaddeus," she wrote, "has enough on his mind without having back talk at every meal from the young miss. They are really like two peas in a pod."

Ten minutes out of Grand Central Station the door of the servants' carriage opened and Nichole walked purposefully down the aisle to where Henry was sitting. There was silence for a moment, then a low buzz of conversation as hands raised to mouths.

"Do you mind if I join you?"

"If you don't mind wagging tongues," said Henry.

"Hislop's getting on my nerves," said Nichole, unconsciously mirroring Henry's thoughts. "The man's always watching me with his piggy little eyes. Have you noticed? They're the color of ground glass."

Henry breathed in her lavender scent as she sat beside him. He wondered why she had come to join him.

She inclined her head towards him as if she were about to share a confidence.

"I heard a funny story about Mr. J.P. Morgan. You'll appreciate this. Up until this season he was commodore of the NYYC."

"NYYC?" asked Henry, turning towards her.

"The New York Yacht Club. Where have you been? Anyway, he had a china service on board that black steam yacht of his, the *Corsair*. It was specially designed for him with two little flags: the commodore's pennant and the club ensign. Well, the day he resigned he had the crew bring the complete set up on deck. Then he told his guests to smash every piece. He even threw a soup tureen in the water so they could use it as a target. Isn't that amusing?"

She laughed and touched his sleeve.

"The dogs must have had a tough time," said Henry.

"Dogs?"

"The retrievers."

"What do you mean, retrievers?"

"Hunting dogs, to bring back the kill. But I imagine Mr. Morgan has only lap dogs."

He wondered if Tarr had heard the story. If he had, he'd try to outdo Morgan this summer with a clay-pigeon shoot from the deck of his yacht or something equally vulgar. Henry had come to recognize that Tarr felt impelled to compete with the Wizard of Wall Street on every level. When his employer had heard that Morgan's European agents outbid Kaiser Wilhelm for a copy of the Luther Bible, Tarr had tried to buy it from them.

The German emperor, it was reported, was furious at having lost the precious volume. At the first whisper of royal displeasure, Morgan had presented the Bible to Kaiser Wilhelm personally. Noblesse oblige. A gift from the American emperor to the German. In return the delighted Wilhelm bestowed upon Morgan one of the empire's highest honors—the Order of the Black Eagle.

Tarr had been consumed with envy when he learned of the decoration. He quizzed Henry about it for days, fretting over it, clutching at any opportunity to make the magnanimous gesture for royalty. When the *New York Times* reported that King Edward's horse, Minoru, won the Derby, Tarr instructed Henry to send Edward a Nebuchadnezzar of Krug.

"With the greatest respect, sir," Henry had replied, "one doesn't send champagne to the King of England."

Tarr rose from his chair and thundered: "If it's good enough for me, god damn it, it's good enough for him!"

Henry smiled at the thought of the enormous bottle being delivered to Buckingham Palace by Berry Brothers and Rudd. Number Three St. James Street was just around the corner from the Palace. He used to order Lord Rutherland's wines there. Five generations of His Lordship's family had been weighed on Berry Brothers' ancient coffee-mill scales. And they were in good company. Emperors, kings and heroes had sat on the ancient machines to have their weight recorded, like so many sides of beef.

"What are you thinking about?" asked Nichole.

"I was just wondering how much Mr. Tarr weighed."

"Well, I wouldn't ask him right now if I were you. He's in one of his moods."

Tarr's carriage was laid out like a drawing room. The furniture was pushed against the curtained windows, to allow him room to pace. Cornelia sat on an overstuffed chesterfield, sipping hot water flavored with cloves.

Tarr, hands locked behind his back, marched up and down in front of her.

"I don't understand it. The market's firm. Silver's off a quarter of a cent. U.S. Steel's up a point. Money's cheap in London, and yet every one of my goddammed stocks is falling."

"I'm so glad we're out of Manhattan," said Cornelia, trying to divert her husband. "All that unpleasantness."

"I'm talking about stocks, Cornelia. Millions of dollars!"

"Maybe it's because President Taft wants a corporation tax."

"Nonsense. The whole Exchange would be down. I tell you somebody's out to get me. They're trying to depress the value of my shares by dumping them on the market. There's no other reason for them to fall."

Tarr continued his pacing.

"It must be Morgan. Morgan and Hill and that fancy boy, Fisk. Or Jay Gould, the son of a bitch. They're probably sitting in the Union Club this minute conspiring against me. Well, they're not going to get the better of Thaddeus Nugent Tarr, god damn it!"

"We'll be safer in the country," said Cornelia. "They won't follow us here, will they? The radicals, I mean."

Tarr stopped and turned to face her.

"You have to understand, Cornelia, a man of destiny is always a target. Look at Lincoln. Garfield. McKinley. All you can do is protect yourself and what is yours."

"At least in Westchester the servants won't be pestered by newspapermen." She sighed.

"What?"

"Clifford told me they've been knocking on the servants' door again."

"Who?"

"A man from the *Times,* I believe. I suppose it might be worse. It could have been the *Daily News.*"

With all the force he could muster, Tarr threw his unlit cigar against the carriage door. It bounced off the frosted glass and rolled across the carpet to Cornelia's feet.

"Why didn't he tell me?"

"Perhaps he didn't think it important. Why are you so upset, dear? Surely we've got enough money. You don't have to carry on so," she said softly.

"It's not the money," roared Tarr. "It's power. Control. It's about being bested by timber wolves like Morgan!"

"Please don't shout. You know it gives me headaches."

Tarr let out a snort and took two deep breaths. "I'm sorry, my dear. It makes me so mad. I want to build something. A monument. Something for the world to see that's American. And they all try to claw me down."

Tears rose in Cornelia's eyes. She patted the chesterfield next to her. Tarr sat beside her, and she rested her head on his shoulder.

"But I'll win in the end," he said. "They were never in the barbed-wire business."

They sat rocking gently together to the motion of the train, watching the smoke blow past the windows.

"What do you think of the new man?" asked Tarr.

"Henry?"

"Yes."

"He's a real gentleman."

"I don't trust him."

"Thaddeus, whatever do you mean?"

"Your Clifford found him going through my files."

"Surely not."

"Caught him redhanded in the strong room. But there's nothing to worry about. I've turned the problem over to the agency. They will deal with it."

"Don't do anything rash, dear. A good butler is so hard to find these days."

"Nothing you need worry about, Cornelia. Loyalty above all. That's all I ask. By the way," he said, "I have a business meeting tonight."

"But Thaddeus," she protested, "our first night."

"I know, I know," he said, and kissed her lightly on the forehead.

Friday, July 14, 1911

AT MAMARONECK STATION, Henry helped Nichole down from the train. Her hand was cool. When her feet touched the platform she looked into his eyes and gave his hand a gentle squeeze.

"Thank you, kind sir," she said.

Cornelia Tarr stepped down from her carriage at that moment, and Henry could see that she had witnessed the exchange. He thought of choosing a different car from Nichole's for the drive to the estate but then he decided the damage had already been done. He opened the door of the black Pope-Toledo and slid in next to her. Taking the driving blanket, he spread it over her knees.

"In case it's windy," he said.

She smiled at him, and he slid his hand under the blanket, searching for hers.

He felt the roundness of her thigh under the silk of her dress, then the warmth of her fingers as they interlaced with his. Neither spoke. Both looked straight ahead. Secrecy had heightened the pleasure he felt. He desperately wanted to turn his face to hers and kiss her but he kept staring at the back of the chauffeur's neck while Lily, on his other side, chattered away about a fish her uncle had once caught in the Sound by stunning it with an oar.

The procession pulled through the open wrought-iron gates in the early afternoon. Henry looked at the house in amazement. It was a perfect replica of a fifteenth-century British castle, complete with moat, drawbridge and portcullis. Set on top of a hill, it dominated the countryside.

"He had it shipped over from England," said Nichole, "stone by stone."

Henry remembered the furore in the British press when an American oil magnate had tried to buy a Shakespeare folio from the British Museum. "The great art treasures of Europe," thundered the *Times*, "all seem to be destined for the private pleasure of Yankee bankers whose good taste is measured only in zeroes."

Tarr's acquisition of the old castle must have provoked the same response, Henry thought—another example of England's heritage being plundered at will by New World millionaires.

A wistful smile played on Nichole's lips as she gazed at the castle.

"How would you like to own something like that?" she said.

"All it takes is a surfeit of wealth," he replied.

She looked at him oddly. The irony of his remark escaped her. "Don't you ever wish you were rich?"

"The trouble is, Miss Linley, the wrong people have the money, and they never have enough of it." He called her Miss Linley for Lily's sake. No point in creating gossip.

He had, in fact, often wondered what it must feel like to be able to buy anything one wanted without having to think of the cost. But for the lottery of the cradle he might have been born into a wealthy family. But he knew he could never have started from scratch as Tarr had done. To become as rich as Tarr took a special kind of perverse genius, a grinding single-mindedness of purpose Henry did not possess. His sense of irony would have constantly deflected him from the blinkered, driving pursuit of money.

Nichole's voice broke into his thoughts.

"That's the gatehouse where he entertains his shooting buddies."

The house looked startlingly familiar to him. Then he realized it was a replica of the lodge at Cumerworth, a half-timbered, Tudor-style building on two floors where Lord Rutherland's head gamekeeper used to drink the midnight hours away with a notorious poacher.

Henry looked along the curve of the gravel driveway from the gatehouse to the castle. Wide enough to accommodate two automobiles abreast, the drive was delineated by tall rhododendron bushes on either side. Newly raked and watered, it twisted around ancient oak trees. The setting was as English as Constable or Turner could have wished.

The lawns, Henry noticed, formed part of a nine-hole golf course. Studded along its fairways were such unnatural hazards as ornamental iron sculptures of animals: deer, bear, moose, lions. The metal creatures were pitted with buckshot.

"When he's had more port than is good for him," Nichole explained, "he gives his guests guns and they go up on the battlements."

Mrs. Grady and the skeleton staff were lined up inside the courtyard as the procession of cars rumbled over the drawbridge. Reluctantly, Henry withdrew his hand from Nichole's as the chauffeur opened the car door.

After the initial greetings, the Manhattan staff helped the chauffeurs take down the luggage. Cornelia Tarr disappeared inside on Hislop's arm while her husband asked the head gardener how his strawberry beds were faring. It was the first question he asked each year. Tarr had heard that Morgan grew strawberries on his estate.

"Here, let me take that," said Henry as Nichole struggled under the weight of a suitcase.

"There are three others," she said. "The matching blue ones."

"Henry!"

Tarr, looking every bit the country gentleman in Harris tweed breeches and jacket, approached him as Henry set Nichole's luggage on the cobblestones.

"I'll be dining in the gatehouse tonight at nine. I want you to set for two. Champagne, Chambertin, Port. Nothing fancy. A cold supper will do. Get one of the chauffeurs to drive it down. Tell him to leave it in the ice-box. I don't want to be disturbed."

Henry knew Cornelia Tarr drank only cognac. Obviously her husband was entertaining someone else.

When Tarr turned away, Henry caught the look of fury on Nichole's face. Her neck went red, and she stared after Tarr's retreating figure, breathing heavily. He almost couldn't believe her features were capable of such venom. Her eyes blazed with hatred.

After unpacking Tarr's luggage and settling himself in his room, Henry walked around the castle on the pretext of familiarizing himself with its layout. He hoped he might run into Nichole.

The ground level was one large space with a massive fireplace at the northern end. The floor of square flagstones was smooth and shiny with the patina of centuries. Brightly colored Oriental carpets were scattered randomly to relieve the rigid symmetry of the room. Old battle standards hung from oak rafters, and crossed swords and shields decorated the walls. The arches above the squat, heavy pillars had been plastered and painted blue. The ceiling with its concealed lighting was sun yellow. A magnificent oak refectory table stood in the centre of the room, with sixteen high-backed leather carvers placed along its flanks. Pink and white roses in ornate silver bowls shone against the ancient black oak of the table.

Mrs. Grady had explained the routine. The family dined here when they had guests. When they were alone they took their meals in their rooms.

At the four corners of the great hall, stone stairs led to four square, crenellated towers, which were joined by arched walkways. The rooms in the towers were small. Each member of the Tarr family occupied a separate apartment. Nichole had a room in Rhonda's suite. Hislop, as Cornelia's spiritual adviser and confidant, was in her suite. Tarr had commandeered the tower with the best view of Long Island Sound. He could walk from his bedroom onto the battlements. Against the wall next to his four-poster bed he kept a rack of shotguns for the pleasure of downing anything that flew overhead.

The fourth tower was reserved for house guests. The staff lived in the basement rooms and in cottages out of sight of the castle, where the land sloped away towards the game forest.

"That bell's for you, Mr. Blexill," said Mrs. Grady. They were sitting in the kitchen, and Henry was enjoying a cup of tea with the cook. She looked like the twin sister of Mrs. Garvey, with her wide girth and putty-colored face. Her hair had been dyed carrot red. The two women hated each other and would never remain under the same roof together. Mrs. Tarr had worked out a diplomatic compromise. When the family moved to Westchester Mrs. Garvey took her annual holiday with her sister in Baltimore.

"The mistress always has sandwiches the first night. She won't eat them and she'll complain that the room's damp even though I aired it before she came. I always do."

"She's at the top of the stairs in the south turret, right?"

"That's it."

Henry had asked the housekeeper about the rooms so he could find out where Nichole slept. Nichole's sudden anger had bewildered him, and he had not seen her since.

Cornelia's rooms overlooked the driveway. From her bed next to the window she could see the gatehouse. The oak trees cast long, purple shadows across the lawn.

When she answered Henry's knock, her voice was frail and weak.

The oak door creaked on its hinges, and Henry made a mental note to oil it.

"Thank you, Henry." Cornelia was wearing a turban. She smiled at him as he placed the tray on her bedside table. A copy of *Vanity Fair* lay open beside her.

"I'm not really hungry," she continued. "It's the damp air. I feel chilled to the bone. I'd like a fire. And draw the curtains, if you would. I find twilight so sad."

She picked up the magazine and studied the portrait of a woman.

"Would you just look at this?" she asked. "You know Macy's, the store, don't you, Henry?"

"Yes, madam. At Thirty-fourth Street."

"Well, there's a picture here of Mrs. Walter Scheftel, the youngest daughter of Isadore Straus, who owns Macy's.

What is the world coming to when shopkeepers' daughters are celebrated in such a fashion? And the bodice of her dress is cut so low."

"Yes, madam."

Henry crossed to the window and unhooked the sash that held back the heavy damask curtains. As he was about to draw the curtains together he saw a light go on in the gatehouse. Tarr's Palmer-Singer Six-Sixty, with its canvas top down, was parked by the front door.

"Is that my husband's car outside the lodge?" asked Cornelia.

"I believe so, madam."

She nodded sadly and stared into the blackness of the fireplace. Henry checked his pocket watch. It was eight forty-five.

"Tell me, Henry," said Cornelia. "Do you like it here in America?"

He was startled by the question and paused before answering.

"I'm very content, madam," he replied. He knelt in front of the fire and piled logs onto the kindling wood.

"But don't you miss England?"

"I miss the sense of order. In America I never know what to expect."

Cornelia sighed. "Yes, I know what you mean. Did you know that when Queen Victoria died she had her coffin lined with Prince Albert's dressing gown? I can understand that. When it rains I have these premonitions . . ."

Her voice trailed away with the thought. Henry, on his knees, waited for her to continue, but she merely stared at the curtains. In the direction of her husband.

He applied a match to the wood shavings and watched with satisfaction as the flames caught.

"If ever you have anything on your mind, Henry, you will come and talk to me, won't you?" asked Cornelia.

Henry frowned into the fire. What could she possibly mean? "Certainly, madam, if there is anything bothering me."

"I just don't want anything to happen to you," she said. And she added, "To any of us."

Henry pulled himself up and drew the wire-mesh curtains across the fire.

"Will there be anything else, madam?"

"Yes, Henry. If you wouldn't mind. A little cognac. To help me sleep."

"Very good."

"Wherever I go," she said suddenly, "I have the feeling there's someone watching me. When will it end?"

The question was not addressed to Henry. Cornelia had turned her head away, and she dismissed him with a wave of her hand.

The castle's wine cellar was next to the kitchen. Its bins contained the same kinds of wines and spirits as those in the Fifth Avenue cellar. Henry picked out a bottle of cognac and took a balloon glass from the cabinet in the great hall. He placed them on a silver tray and covered them with a cloth.

On the stairway to Cornelia's room he sensed someone was following him. He paused and listened. Hearing nothing, he put it down to his imagination. Perhaps a ghost had been transported along with the stones. Or maybe Henry had become infected with the paranoia that distracted the mind of Cornelia Tarr.

She did not register his presence when he deposited the cognac tray next to her untouched sandwiches. At the door he wished her good night. An expression of irritation formed around her mouth as she waited for him to close the door.

He felt a deep sense of pity for her. A lonely woman seeking solace in a cognac bottle, old before her time. He could see from her gaunt, nervous face, that she had been beautiful once. He imagined Cornelia before she had met Tarr. Hair in ringlets, dressed in ribbons and crinolines, sitting outside her father's antebellum mansion, playing with a fan through endless afternoons of sunshine and magnolia blossoms. Rhonda had some of her looks, but the daughter's sharp nose she got from her father.

The steel-tipped heels of his shoes echoed down the stone steps. The purple glimmer of evening filtered through the glassed-over slits in the tower wall.

"Henry."

He heard his name whispered. He stopped and looked around. In a niche in the wall from which archers once rained arrows on their enemies stood Nichole. Cradled to her chest she held a bottle of burgundy in its straw sleeve.

"You walked right by me before," she said, playfully. "Am I that invisible?"

"I thought I smelled your perfume."

"I need your expertise." She was speaking in a confidential whisper. "You're the only one around here with a corkscrew. Did I choose well?"

Henry slid the bottle out of the straw and looked at the label in the half light.

"Chambertin Tête du Cuvé 1875, shipped by Chauvenet. You certainly did. Is this for Mr. Tarr?" He felt vaguely annoyed that Nichole should take a wine from the cellar without consulting him.

"No, it is not for Mr. Tarr," said Nichole, smiling.

"Then what's it for?"

"It's for us."

She looked at him, her face tilted to one side, and slid the straw sleeve slowly over the upright bottle.

"What was all that about, this afternoon?" he said.

"Nothing. Sometimes he makes me so mad. Well, are you going to join me or not?"

With the dim light behind her Henry could not see Nichole's face. He breathed in the smell of her. The smell of lavender in sunshine. Why, suddenly, was she making advances to him? She had been angry when Tarr said he would be entertaining at the gatehouse and did not want to be disturbed. It could only be another woman. And that must be the reason Cornelia had taken to her bed.

Nichole took a step towards him and placed her fingertips on his cheek. She moved them slowly across his lips.

"You have a beautiful mouth," she said.

He touched her fingertips with his tongue then pressed his lips into her palm. She drew his face towards her and kissed him softly. He returned her kiss fervently. She drew back and emitted a sound that was half a groan and half a sigh.

"Are you in love with me, Henry?" she whispered.

"I don't know."

"Please be."

Henry felt himself stirring. Tarr was occupied in the gatehouse. Cornelia had her cognac bottle. The rest of the night belonged to them. He would deal with the consequences in the morning. It had been such a long time since he had made love to a woman.

But a voice in his head kept warning him to resist. For a butler to act like this was utter madness. His life had always been governed by other people's rules. He had known the boundaries; he had known what was expected of him. But in America the old certainties no longer seemed to work. In England, butlers did not get beaten up in mining towns. Their masters' houses were not bombed. And here was a woman who was asking for love. A beautiful woman. The mistress of his employer.

"I'll get the glasses," he said.

"Give me five minutes then come to my room," said Nichole. "Make sure no one sees you. And don't forget the corkscrew."

Filled with a sensation of pleasurable excitement, Henry crossed the great hall. As he was about to open the glass cabinet, the Reverend Clifford Hislop materialized by his side. He wore a pair of woollen gloves with the fingertips cut off. His fingers, pale as worms, clutched a copy of *Mesmerism and Christian Science* by Frank Podmore.

"Do you think you could light the fire down here, Henry? The light in my room is barely adequate to read by."

Henry cursed him silently.

Hislop followed him as he moved quickly to the far end of the hall. "Let me help you," Hislop said as Henry took a taper from a pewter mug on the mantel and lit it. The fire was already set, and needed only to be touched with a flame.

"There is really nothing to be done," said Henry as he hunkered down. "It will either catch or it won't."

Hislop placed a hand on his shoulder.

"Why don't you like me? Is it because of Brandon?"

Henry looked up. The man's thin, ascetic face reminded him of a gloomy painting he had once seen in the National Gallery.

"You did nothing."

"I'm not a man of action. I just want to be your friend."

Henry rose to his feet and looked at Hislop. "The fire will catch," he said. He gave the logs some unnecessary thrusts with the poker. "Now, if you'll excuse me."

Henry moved away. He could feel Hislop's eyes watching him. Then he heard the creaking of leather as the preacher lowered himself onto the sofa in front of the fire. *His back is to me*, thought Henry. He reached inside the cabinet and took down a decanter and two glasses. Glancing at the end of the hall, he saw Hislop put his book down, slip to his knees and close his eyes over praying hands.

"Did anyone see you come in here?"

"No."

"What took you so long?" Nichole sat on the end of her bed watching Henry tap the sealing wax away from the top of the bottle with the handle of his corkscrew.

"I was waylaid by Hislop. He wanted to be my friend."

"I knew it! I knew he liked men!" She laughed and clapped her hands.

Carefully, Henry wiped the exposed neck of the bottle. From his vest pocket he took a candle stub and lit it.

"My. We do come prepared, don't we?"

She watched as he drove the point of the corkscrew down with powerful turns of his wrist. Holding the bottle on the table, he took the strain and eased the cork free.

He squeezed the end of the cork and sniffed it.

"Fine," he said, and lit the candle. The flame guttered in the draft and was reflected in Nichole's eyes. The only other source of light was the log fire, which cast a rosy glow. Nichole sat next to it, and her face bloomed a rose-petal pink.

Henry took the wine bottle in his right hand and the

empty decanter in his left and angled them together over the candle flame until the neck of the bottle was fully illuminated. With a sure, steady motion he began to pour the wine into the decanter. The fragrance of tar and violets rose and filled his nostrils.

Henry smiled with satisfaction. He stopped pouring when he saw the ruby rivulet in the neck become muddied with sediment. He held the decanter in front of the candle and admired its contents, as clear and velvety as a prince's robe. Deep in the eye of the wine, he saw a king's ransom in rubies.

"Magnificent," he said.

He poured a couple of ounces into one of the glasses. Holding the glass by the base, he swirled the wine around with a quick circular motion of his wrist. He sniffed and took a little into his mouth, sucking in air as he did so. He let the mature burgundy play over his tongue to warm and unlock its flavors. The wine was sweet and as silky as flesh, with a taste of ripe raspberries warmed by the summer sun. The taste lingered on his palate and filled his head.

"Do you always make love to your wine?" asked Nichole.

"Of course." Henry smiled. "Wine unlocks the secrets of the heart."

She took the glass from his hand and drained its contents without taking her eyes off him. When it was empty she slid it out of reach before he could pour more wine into it.

"Later," she said. "I don't want to lose all my secrets."

He took her by the hand and raised her to her feet. He drew her gently towards him and kissed her. He could taste the sweetness of the wine on her lips. She stood back from him, one hand on his chest, smiling.

"This is how I want to remember you," she said. "With the firelight in your eyes."

Slowly she began unbuttoning the sleeves of her dress.

They made love on the creaking bed. Passionately at first, eager for each other. They were swimmers coming up for air after a long dive. Drowning in each other's flesh, gasping for breath as they broke the surface.

When they had finished they lay back on the pillows and sipped the wine. Contented. A sickle-shaped moon shone through the window.

Nichole traced the U-shaped scar above Henry's heart with her finger.

"I didn't intend this to happen," she said.

"And yet you wanted me to be in love with you."

"All women want to be loved."

"And to love."

"Yes. But it's never that simple. You're a butler."

"And you're a chaperone."

"I'm not a chaperone," she replied. "Don't ever call me that."

"And what's wrong with being a butler?"

He could feel her slipping away from him. Nichole took another sip of wine. She had covered her breasts with the sheet. Their thighs were touching.

"When I was a little girl my mother told me that the only thing that saved a woman from service was money. It didn't matter how you got it as long as you had it. I was fourteen. My father had left her. And she said to me, 'If I had my life to lead over again, I'd forget what they taught me in Sunday school.' "

"There are other things, Nichole. Money is not a panacea."

"I'd rather be miserable with money than without it. Tell me something, Henry. Honestly. Do you always want to be a butler?"

Henry propped himself up on his elbow.

"I'm not ashamed of being a butler. That was what I was trained for."

"But you can be anything your heart desires! You just have to want it. You could be a boxer."

How could he explain to her? Society cast you in a role the moment you were born. You were fixed like a pinned butterfly, and all you could do was strive to be the best at your allotted task. He could work to become the finest butler who ever lived but that would not turn him into

Lord Rutherland or give him Cumerworth Hall. You were what your class dictated.

He had once believed this as firmly as he had once believed in God, yet what he had experienced in America had raised doubts in his mind. English society was stratified like layers in rock, fossilized, but in America thieves like Tarr were today's aristocracy. Tomorrow they might be bankrupt, which would throw them to the bottom of the heap again. Everything was mobile here; people were in motion, sliding up and down the social scale as though it were an elaborate game of Snakes and Ladders.

"How did you get this job with the Tarrs?" he asked to fill the silence between them.

She sighed and pulled her knees up, causing a draft under the sheet.

"I've got all sorts of hidden talents. How many women do you know who can drive a car? Can you?" She paused. "I used to be a dancer. Here, feel my thighs. Dancer's thighs. He saw me in an operetta at Booth's Theatre and sent me flowers. Gardenias. He took me to dinner a few times. Gave me presents. It's hard for a working girl to resist."

"But living here. Working for him. How did that happen?"

"Confession time?"

"Secrets of the heart."

"Okay. About four years ago, he brought me back to the Fifth Avenue house. Rhonda had been sent home with a note from her principal, and she surprised us. Mr. Tarr told her he had hired me as her chaperone. And that was it."

"And how did Mrs. Tarr take that?"

"I think she was secretly pleased. I also act as her companion. Answer her letters. Help her shop. That way there's no scandal."

"She knows, though, doesn't she?"

"We don't discuss it," said Nichole, suddenly cold. "She has Hislop. He has me."

"But you must want more than that."

She turned her back to him, and he felt an involuntary shiver pass through her body.

"One day," she said, giving each word equal weight, "I shall marry a very, very wealthy man."

He reached out to stroke the curve of her buttocks.

"Don't!" she said, and pushed his hand away.

Henry lay back and stared at the ceiling. The wine had lost its sweetness for him. Nichole's abrupt change of mood confused him.

"It must be half past one, at least," said Henry. "I'm up at six. I'd better go."

Nichole said nothing.

Reluctantly, he eased himself out of bed and padded across the cold stone floor to where his clothes lay over the back of a chair. Moonlight reflected off the nape of her neck, white as marble.

He was about to speak when he heard a scraping sound outside the door.

A rasping voice called, "Nichole."

She sat bolt upright in bed, eyes wide in alarm.

"Oh, my God!"

Before either of them could move, the door burst open and Tarr propelled himself into the room. His hair was awry, and Henry could see that the white shirt under his smoking jacket was stained with port. He was breathing heavily as if he'd been running.

Tarr took in the frightened face of Nichole and the naked figure of Henry silhouetted against the window.

"You!" he yelled and lunged towards Henry, who grabbed his clothes and moved behind the table to protect himself.

"Don't, sir. Don't make me hit you."

"Thaddeus!" screamed Nichole.

It was the first time Henry had heard her call Tarr by his Christian name, and it startled him. Tarr stopped dead and looked quizzically at Nichole. Diverted, he directed his anger at her.

He tore the covers from the bed and, with a roar, threw them at her. The jumble of blankets hit her and fell to the floor. A corner of the sheet dropped into the grate and caught fire.

"You'll burn the house down," screamed Nichole.

"Good! Then we'll all burn together," roared Tarr.

He pointed an accusing finger at Henry who had pulled the sheet from the fire and was stamping out the flames with his bare feet.

"I could have you killed for this! So help me, if it's the last thing I do, I'll see you never work again. Ever. Anywhere! Get out of my house this minute!"

The moon was veiled modestly in a wispy shawl of cloud when Henry, suitcase in hand, eased the front door shut behind him. The cobblestones in the courtyard were slick with dew. The lawns were silver in the moonlight, and the blooms on the rhododendron bushes had turned to gold. A barn owl hooted into the wind.

Henry had visions of Tarr driving him off the property with salvoes of buckshot from the battlements.

His feet were blistered from the fire, and he shivered in the unseasonal chill of the damp morning air. The gravel crunched loudly under his feet, and the animals of the night darted around the roots of the old oak trees. Halfway down the driveway he turned and looked at the castle. The curtains in Cornelia's room had been drawn back, and he thought he saw someone standing at the window but he couldn't be sure.

Henry felt angry and resentful. He imagined Nichole facing Tarr's wrath alone, and wondered if he should go back. But Tarr had fired him. He could not believe that he was out of a job. For the first time in his life, he had no place to sleep. He was deep in the Westchester countryside in the middle of the night, and he had nowhere to go. Tarr's words rang in his head. "I'll see you never work again. Ever. Anywhere." Henry knew the banker had the power to make good his threat.

I have to leave New York, he thought. *Get back to England. Lord Rutherland will give me references. I can expect nothing from Tarr.*

But first he had to retrieve his clothes from the Fifth Avenue house, and the little money he had saved. His immediate problem was getting back to the city.

"Just hold it right there."

The voice came from the shrubbery.

"Drop the valise and put your hands behind your head."

Henry did as he was told. Out of the corner of his eye he could see a shadow emerge from the rhododendrons. The moonlight glinted on the barrel of a Smith & Wesson .38 revolver.

"Now turn around real slow."

He was facing a bearded man in a broad-brimmed hat.

"Open the suitcase."

"I'm Mr. Tarr's butler, Henry. We were on the train together."

The Pinkerton man knelt down, pointing the revolver at Henry's stomach as he felt around in the suitcase. Satisfied, he stood.

"Where are you going this time of night?"

Henry thought quickly. "I was taking Mr. Tarr's hunting clothes to the gatehouse."

"Sorry to have troubled you. Go about your business."

Henry clamped the suitcase shut and walked down the driveway. He was conscious of the man's eyes on him as he walked slowly towards the gatehouse. He would have to go in and wait until the man had moved on. Perhaps there was something to eat in the ice-box. There would be no train until the morning. He would have to walk fifteen miles to the Mamaroneck station and sleep the rest of the night there.

The door to the gatehouse was open, and Tarr's Palmer-Singer was still parked outside. When he had first seen the car from Cornelia's window, it had been parked parallel to the wall. It was now backed up to the front door. Maybe Tarr had dropped his lady friend off somewhere. But the tire marks in the fresh dew showed Henry that the car had merely been turned around.

The gatehouse was in darkness now, except for the glow from the embers in the grate. In case the Pinkerton man was still watching him, Henry entered without looking back.

Through the gloom he could see that the ground floor was divided roughly in two: a kitchen and scullery on one side and a larger sitting room on the other. Old English hunting prints adorned the walls, and three sofas covered in a floral pattern were placed box-shape in front of the fireplace. A poker protruded from the dying coals.

At the centre of the box made by the sofas was a large, square coffee table. On it were two trays with wine glasses, empty bottles and the remains of dinner.

Henry put down his suitcase and crossed to the table. On one of the plates was an untouched chicken breast. He wrapped it in a napkin and slipped it into his jacket pocket. Perhaps there was more food in the kitchen. He moved around the table by the fire, and suddenly his foot slipped on the parquet flooring. He looked down and saw a little pool of wine on the polished boards. Tarr or his friend must have knocked over a glass. Tarr more likely. Henry had seen port stains on his shirt.

His butler's instincts told him to look for a fallen glass. He kneeled to check under the chesterfield furthest from the windows, and he saw more wine on the floor. There were spots on the Dutch tiles in the hearth where the ornamental andirons extended from the fireplace. It was almost as if someone had hurled a full wine glass. He dipped his finger in the pool and sniffed it.

It didn't smell like port. It smelled salty-sweet. Henry studied the tips of his fingers in the moonlight.

It was blood. The stains on Tarr's shirt must have been blood, too.

He thought he heard a floorboard creak overhead. Was it Tarr's guest? Or a Pinkerton man? Or had the Brandon miners finally caught up with Thaddeus Nugent Tarr?

Henry needed something with which to defend himself. He tiptoed to the grate and drew the poker slowly from the fire. Its handle was warm and wet. Sticky with blood.

Hastily, he thrust it back into the coals.

He could hear the sound of running footsteps outside,

coming towards him down the lawn. Rubber soles squeaking on wet grass.

He wiped his bloody hand on his trousers and moved quickly to the door. Using the car as cover, he bent and crept to the front of the gatehouse. He stood up in the shadows and pressed his back against its whitewashed wall.

He heard the crunch of gravel as someone approached the front door. The sound was tentative, as if the person was unsure of what or whom he was looking for.

Henry waited. He could feel his heart pounding in his chest. He tried to make sense of what he had seen. The finished meals, the empty wine bottles, the pools of blood, the poker stuck in the coals.

Someone had been struck with that poker. There was blood everywhere, but there was no body. Tarr had run directly to Nichole, his shirt all blood-stained. He had not raised the alarm for the Pinkerton men who guarded the property. If his life had been in danger, surely they would have been the first people he would have summoned.

Now there was someone snooping around the gatehouse. The steps on the gravel were too unsure to be those of a Pinkerton agent on guard duty.

Then Henry realized that his fingerprints were on the poker.

Henry knew there were ways to identify a person from fingerprints. He had read it in the newspapers. Ever since Sir Francis Galton had published his *Fingerprint Directory* fourteen years ago, police forces on both sides of the Atlantic were using this new science to trap criminals.

If the poker with his prints on it fell into the hands of the police, he could be charged with murder. He could just hear Tarr telling them, "Yes, it was the same night I fired him." Whoever it was who had been bludgeoned to death in the lodge, it would be Henry Blexill who would go to the gallows for it.

I must get that poker.

He strained to listen for the interloper at the door of the gatehouse. The sound of the crickets rang in his ears. He heard the footsteps turn on the gravel, then the muffled, wet sound of shoes on dewy grass once more. He waited until he could hear nothing. Then he darted to the car and peered into the darkness. Whoever it was had been swallowed up by the night.

A cloud had covered the moon, melting the lawns into the black of the trees.

Stealthily, he returned to the sitting room. He no longer cared if there was someone in the rooms above him. His only concern was to clean his fingerprints off the poker handle.

In the darkness he felt his way around the sofas, trying not to walk where he remembered the pools of blood to be. He ran his hands over the empty trays on the coffee table until he found a napkin, then knelt at the edge of the hearth. He wrapped the material around his right hand and reached forward for the poker.

It wasn't there.

Frantically, he swept his hand along the cast-iron firebox. The metal burned his fingers.

He took a box of matches from his pocket and struck one. He held the flame aloft and searched wildly for the poker.

Somebody had taken it. Somebody upstairs, or the person who had just visited the lodge then disappeared into the night.

Henry struck another match. By its tiny flag of light he manoeuvred himself towards the stairs. The pools of blood glistened blackly at his feet. Carefully, he worked his way up the staircase to the landing on the second floor.

His foot creaked on a floorboard, and he eased his weight gently off it. He looked around for something to use as a weapon, but the upstairs rooms had not been opened up. Everything was draped under heavy white sheets.

Henry stood in front of a closed door. He took out a handkerchief and gripped the brass handle. Slowly, he turned it and inched the door ajar. Standing back, he pushed it with his foot. The door swung open, whining on its hinges. The room was empty.

He felt sweat running from his armpits.

He tried the next door. He heard a scratching sound, and something ran over his foot. He jumped back. A mouse skittered across the floor and disappeared into the wainscotting.

Henry eased open the door and found himself in a study. There was a desk by the window. The middle drawer was open, as if someone had reached for something in a hurry and forgotten to close it. Fearful of leaving other prints behind, he touched nothing, merely glancing quickly around the room.

There was no one upstairs.

He was about to descend when the night outside was suddenly illuminated with a bright orange light. Then he heard the cough of an engine starting. He drew back from the landing window and looked down. First he saw the twin beams of the Palmer-Singer's headlights. Then the car itself came into view. The top was up, and he could not make out who was driving. He watched the sleek body slide out of the open gates onto the highway. It picked up speed as it travelled in the direction of the railroad station.

Henry waited until the sound of its engine was drowned by the incessant, metallic chirping of the crickets. They struck the ear like millions of tiny knives being sharpened on whetstones.

He felt cold and weary as he began to walk towards the station. The croaking of bullfrogs rose from the creeks on either side of the road. A heavy mist hung over the mud-packed highway, and in the distance he could hear the mournful foghorn of a tanker on the Sound. Like the mating call of a behemoth.

He wondered if he should go to the police. But what would he tell them? There was no body, and the murder weapon with his fingerprints on it had disappeared. They would say he was trying to revenge himself on his employer for having been dismissed.

And what had Tarr done? He was wearing his smoking jacket, which meant the occasion was informal. Otherwise he would have asked for his dinner jacket to be laid out.

He had ordered a cold meal, which he had served himself. Nine o'clock was later than he usually dined. Perhaps he had wanted to make sure Mrs. Tarr was in bed. If it had been an assignation he would naturally entertain in the gatehouse rather than the castle.

There was blood but no body. Why had Tarr come to Nichole? And where was the car going at two o'clock in the morning?

These thoughts exercised Henry's mind as he walked to the railway station. He realized he had left his suitcase in the gatehouse. Tarr would find it and know that Henry had seen the blood.

Tarr probably had the poker, and he was probably taking it to the police.

The idea alarmed Henry. He considered going back to retrieve the suitcase, but he realized it was too late. His best course of action was to get as far away from Tarr as he could.

Through the mist he saw a pair of headlights approaching. It could be Tarr returning with the police.

He threw himself into the long grass by the roadside, his heart bucking wildly against his rib cage. As the car roared past he recognized Tarr's Palmer-Singer. Tarr sat in the passenger seat, gripping the walnut dashboard with both hands.

Next to him in the driver's seat, her face bluish-white in the moonlight, was Nichole Linley.

At that moment Henry knew they had just disposed of a corpse.

Saturday, July 15, 1911

HENRY DOZED FITFULLY on a baggage trolley as he waited for the morning train. His shallow sleep was disturbed by dreams of blood. The menacing face of Tarr rose before him. He saw Nichole, driving the Palmer-Singer like a dead person, trying to run him down.

He awoke at first light. He was cramped and stiff, and his clothes were damp. He ran his fingers over his stubbly face, wishing the stationmaster would arrive so that he could wash, at least. He took the cold chicken from his pocket and ate it, then wiped his fingers on the napkin and threw it into the garbage can next to the station door.

He wondered if this was one of the railroad lines owned by Tarr. Would Tarr have alerted the train detectives to look for Henry?

He paced the platform, his eyes following the tracks into a white horizon to the north. Two silver needles in the morning mist. To the south, unseen, lay the skyscrapers of Manhattan. Grand Central Station, a short walk from Thirty-sixth and Fifth.

In his haste to fire Henry, Tarr had forgotten to ask for the return of the keys to the Fifth Avenue mansion. So Henry would have no trouble gaining access by the servants' entrance.

A train pulled into the station belching smoke into the white morning sky. Henry, rumpled and unshaven, was happy to be seated. The conductor eyed him suspiciously as he paid for his ticket. He closed his eyes and fell asleep the moment the train pulled out of the station. He awoke with a jolt at Grand Central, suddenly apprehensive again. He moved quickly through the deserted streets to Tarr's mansion.

As he opened the door, he noticed there was a man leaning against a lamppost on the west side of the avenue. Henry moved with deliberation. Once inside the kitchen he stood on a chair beside the side of the window and pulled back the curtain. He saw the man fold his newspaper and settle against the lamppost once more. Pinkerton, he thought.

He took the back stairs to his room at the top of the mansion. It seemed strange to be there, knowing he would never see the place again. Even though the house was empty, Tarr's malevolent presence seemed to hover in the rooms like a force of nature, and Henry could not break the habit of walking silently on the balls of his feet.

He decided he would pack his belongings and leave the mansion as quickly as he could, in case Tarr had informed the Pinkerton agency that Henry was no longer allowed inside. He took a suitcase from the closet and opened it on the bed.

Then he realized he had the house to himself. At last, he could spend as much time as he needed reading Tarr's files.

He finished packing and took the suitcase to the kitchen, then made his way along the corridor to the strong room. Once inside, he pulled open a drawer of the walnut cabinet to look for the Brandon files. He found three of them, "Acquisition," "Legal" and "Consolidation."

The legal file was full of press clippings in chronological order, most taken from the *New York Times*. The first, datelined Brandon, West Virginia, July 11, 1911, gave an eye-witness account of the massacre. The headline read: "45 Dead, 20 Hurt, Score Missing In Strike War."

The same information was repeated in the first paragraph of the story. The writer added, "The battle that raged with uninterrupted fury between mine guards and miners on the property of the Brandon Iron and Steel

Company lasted for fourteen hours until State Troopers were called in."

The second paragraph suggested that the writer had embroidered facts he had heard second hand. McGillivray? "The Brandon camp today is a mass of charred debris, and beneath it is a story of horror unparalleled in the history of industrial warfare. In the holes that had been dug for their protection against the rifles' fire the women and children died like trapped flies when the flames swept over them."

The image of the armored car returned. Henry saw it trundling up the dusty street, spitting fire. Sickened by the memory, he turned to the next clipping, an editorial.

"The Brandon miners have no justification for murdering men whose only offense is that they are seeking to earn a living without a permit from the United States Mine Workers of America. The trouble was started by the strikers killing a non-union man who was walking to work without their permission."

The piece ended with a call for an inquiry into the steel trust, which the Brandon Iron and Steel Company was seeking to join.

On the same page was a letter from a banker named Jim Gordon. Henry recognized the name—he would have been one of the guests at Tarr's dinner party for J.P. Morgan. "The Brandon Iron and Steel Company," Gordon wrote, "had been forced to employ guards to protect their men who desired work. As Mr. Tarr well said, this issue is not a local but a national one. He is doing his patriotic duty in endeavoring to protect his men in their right to earn an honest living without paying tribute to the labor leaders, and in standing for this right he should have the approval of all who love justice and true freedom."

Pencilled along the margin was a notation in Tarr's hand: "Get other directors to write!"

Next was a document tied with blue ribbon. It was titled, "Macklin versus Tarr, State of West Virginia, September 23, 1909."

Henry untied the ribbon and opened the document. It was couched in extravagant legal jargon. To Henry's untrained eye it appeared to be a statement of claim by George and Arnold Macklin accusing Thaddeus Tarr of swindling them out of three iron-ore mines. According to the Macklin brothers' sworn deposition, the banker had acquired their mines by false pretenses. Their association with Tarr began when they needed capital to construct a railroad from Brandon to Pittsburgh so they could ship their high-grade iron ore. They had approached Tarr, whose railroad ran closest to their property, through the foothills of the Allegheny Mountains. Initially, Tarr had purchased five hundred thousand dollars' worth of bonds in their company.

Soon, it appeared, the banker was lending the brothers large sums of money to help them exploit their ore deposits. The document supplied figures and listed the dates the money was deposited in the company's Charleston City Bank account. In return for financing the expansion, Tarr had demanded company stock as collateral. At his suggestion, to "improve operational efficiency," the Macklins merged the three mines into a single corporate entity called the Brandon Iron and Steel Company. This manoeuvre required additional injections of capital, which the banker willingly supplied.

"All the while Mr. Tarr protested that he had no interest in acquiring the company," George Macklin was quoted as saying. "But when the loan reached $2.3 million he called it in. And he gave us twenty-four hours to repay."

Unable to raise the money, the Macklins were forced to default on the loan, and Tarr acquired control of the mines. The Brandon Iron and Steel Company, said the deposition, had at the time an estimated value of $27.5 million.

Henry shuffled through the rest of the papers. There were no others relating to the court case. What had happened when George and Arnold Macklin had taken Tarr to court over the disputed mines?

The brother or the son. What had Tarr meant by that?

Were the Macklins the men Tarr suspected of bombing his house? And who was the son? By due process of law, it would appear Tarr had won the court case. He was, after all, still in control of Brandon. But something else must have happened. Henry riffled through the three files again, but found no answers to his questions.

Perhaps there were some papers filed under "Macklin." He pulled out the drawer labelled K to M. His fingers skipped over the tabs. There was nothing under "Macklin." As he was about to slide the drawer closed, his eye was caught by a file headed "Lord Rutherland—Argentine."

He pulled it out and stared at the buff-colored folder. Why would Tarr have a file on Lord Rutherland? Henry had no idea that there had been any dealings between the two men other than an invitation to visit Cumerworth. They had taken a glass of port together. They had talked for two hours at most. Lord Rutherland had seemed relieved when Tarr called for his top hat.

Henry opened the file. On top was an envelope addressed to Tarr in Lord Rutherland's spiky handwriting. There was no mistaking the color of ink the old man used for his correspondence—emerald green. Among Henry's daily chores had been the responsibility to insure that the inkwells in the study were full. There was a small green stain the size of a guinea on the carpet under the desk where he had overfilled the cut-glass inkwell on his first effort.

He was about to take the letter out of the envelope when he heard the sound of a door closing overhead.

Henry froze. Somebody else was in the house. Could it be the Pinkerton man checking on him? Was it a Brandon miner, crazed with grief over the loss of his family, looking for Tarr? Had Tarr told the police where to find Henry?

He stuffed the file down the back of his trousers and edged his way towards the open door. He could hear steps in the hall, and the muffled thump of the green baize door swinging into place. The intruder was coming down to the basement.

Henry switched off the electric light and waited in the darkness.

He debated whether to call out but decided against it.

He did not want to become embroiled any deeper in Tarr's affairs. He wanted nothing to hinder his escape. But what if the intruder had a bomb and was about to try once more to destroy Tarr's home? Henry could be blown up at any moment.

The footsteps stopped. Then he heard the irregular clang of metal striking metal. It sounded as if someone were trying to force a lock with a crowbar. The door to the cellar was secured with a padlock.

Every artery in his body pulsed with apprehension as Henry stood with his back to the wall. The cellar was down a short corridor. Overhead, he could hear the clicking of heels on the Fifth Avenue sidewalk. His neck prickled, and beads of sweat stood out on his forehead.

He eased himself around the corner. In the darkness he could make out a shadow bent over a lock and an arm trying to lever the lock away from its wooden surround.

The figure was hunched in concentration and did not hear him approach, although the sound of his heart seemed to bounce off the walls.

"Miss Rhonda!"

The girl jumped back, dropping the metal tool. It hit the stone floor with an echoing clang.

"Henry! You gave me such a fright."

"I thought you were a burglar. What are you doing here?"

"I got bored with Aunt Hortense. And Atlanta in July is impossibly hot, so I came back here."

"But your parents are in Westchester."

"I know. I'll call Mummy later. I just wanted some time to myself. They keep trying to force EYMs on me."

"I don't understand."

"Eliglble young men. They're all so wet."

"And may I ask why you were trying to get into the cellar?"

"I just wanted a bottle of champagne," she said, poised, unconcerned with what he thought. "I'm old enough, you know. We have it all the time at coming-out parties. My best friend Annabel, her beau drank it out of her shoe at

the May Ball. Isn't that romantic? Except she said it was
all squelchy when she danced."

Henry handed her the keys.

"Why don't you get it for me?" asked Rhonda, and she
smiled at him.

"Because I no longer work for your father."

"Why ever not?"

"He fired me last night."

"Fired you? What for?"

"I think you'd better let him explain."

"But what will we do for a butler?"

"I'm sure your father will find someone. Well, goodbye,
Miss Rhonda. It was a pleasure to have served you."

He gave her a slight bow and turned.

"Wait. What are you going to do?"

The less the Tarr family knew about his immediate
plans the better Henry liked it.

"I shall look for employment elsewhere."

"But you'll need money," said Rhonda. "Come with
me."

She lifted her skirt and raced up the stairs, through the
green baize door, across the hall and into her father's
study. Henry followed, and watched her from the study
doorway. She dragged the circular library steps to a section of the bookshelves on the far wall, then climbed to
the top. Reaching up, she slid out a heavy, leather-bound
volume and opened it with her back to him. When she
emerged from the study she had five freshly ironed ten-
dollar bills in her hand.

"Here," she said. "I'm sure my father owes you wages
anyway."

Henry hesitated. It was two months' salary.

"Go on, take it. I do it all the time." She giggled. "He
never knows."

"Thank you. I'll consider it a loan," he said. "May I ask
you a question?"

She moved closer and smiled at him. "Of course."

"Did you ever hear your father mention a man named
George or Arnold Macklin?"

"Are they single? If they are, Mummy probably did."

"No, I suppose you'd call them middle-aged. Your father had some business dealings with them."

"I never listen when Daddy talks business," said Rhonda. "Now I get to ask you a question."

"Fair's fair."

"On your first night here when you served at table, you never looked at me. Why?"

"I was trained that way, Miss Rhonda. Eye contact for a butler is bad form except with the master of the house."

"And if the master of the house isn't there?"

Henry looked at her in the half light. She was no more than a girl.

"Perhaps if you were ten years older and I was a banker like your father. . . ."

"Don't you find me attractive?"

"You have your mother's good looks."

Rhonda made a face. "It's Nichole, isn't it?"

"Miss Rhonda, you have a very active imagination."

"You men. Whenever we state the obvious you say it's imagination."

The mansion door closed behind him with a thud. Henry stood on the stone steps, suitcase in hand, wondering where he should go. Fifth Avenue, no longer deserted, appeared to him at that moment to be charged with movement and energy. Carriages flashed by; car horns honked, horses whinnied. Every sound seemed louder than usual.

The New York air smelled of cement and horse droppings. Shoppers filled the stores and restaurants. Ladies with parasols and hats as large as lamp shades strolled along Fifth Avenue, their dresses brushing the sidewalks.

Cut adrift from the security of an established household, Henry began to panic. Having to make decisions about his future made his stomach churn. All his life he had been in service. There had always been someone to tell him what to do. There was a routine, a rhythm. He merely reacted to orders or anticipated needs. He knew where he belonged and what was expected of him. He was not used to thinking about himself. He had known what he would be doing until the day his employer pensioned him off, the old family retainer, trusted and loyal, put out to pasture.

But now he was alone, faced with the implacable hostility of Thaddeus Nugent Tarr, and with no employment and no prospects. Without a roof over his head, in a country that was still foreign to him.

He had never felt so defenceless. The horse-drawn trolleys and the honking cars, the pedestrians moving purposefully along the sidewalks, the street vendors and the shoeshine boys all seemed hostile to him, as if they were part of some giant conspiracy against him orchestrated by Tarr.

He had to get back to England as quickly as possible. He had to secure passage on a liner before Tarr could make good on his threat. There were sailings every day on White Star and Cunard liners with romantic names like *Oceanic, Adriatic, Lusitania* and the newly launched *Mauretania.* Their comings and goings were chronicled in the *New York Times* with special mention of celebrity passengers. But he had no idea of how to get a job on board a ship.

He needed an ally. Perhaps that reporter from the *New York Times* could help him. McGillivray. He took the man's card from his pocket. Charles McGillivray. City Desk.

Suitcase in hand, he headed towards Times Square. The newspaper office was situated in the Times Tower, a twenty-five-storey pink-granite confection in Italian Renaissance style, which stood where Broadway, Seventh Avenue and Forty-second Street converged.

At the reception desk in the marbled hall he asked for McGillivray.

The woman checked her roster and spoke to Henry through a circular hole in the glass that surrounded her desk.

"Second floor." She pointed to the elevators.

The city desk, Henry discovered, was located at the far end of the newsroom. The noise of typewriters was deafening. Round-shouldered men in shirt-sleeves and braces hunched over desks, still wearing their hats. Cigar butts burned in saucers, and there was much shouting and movement up and down the narrow aisles.

Henry found McGillivray behind a mound of yellowing newspapers.

"Excuse me," he said. "My name is Blexill. You gave me your card."

"Yes?"

The journalist seemed annoyed at the interruption, although he did not appear to be doing anything but drinking coffee from a cup without a handle. His feet were up on the desk, crossed at the ankles. There was a hole in his right sole.

"You came to see Mr. Tarr a few days ago. I'm his butler."

"Oh, yes. Step into my office, Mr. Blexill."

McGillivray swung his legs from the desk and stood up, extending his hand.

"Can we talk somewhere?"

"Sure. Let's go to the water cooler."

McGillivray took a pad from his jacket pocket, which was hanging from the back of his chair, and led the way through the maze of desks. Outside the newsroom they sat on a leather sofa next to the water cooler.

"What have you got for me?" asked McGillivray, flipping open his pad.

"Actually, I was hoping you might help me."

The reporter laughed. "That's a switch."

"I want to get a job on a liner that will take me back to England."

"Why?"

"Because I no longer work for Mr. Tarr and I would like to go home."

"Fired you, did he? English butlers don't usually get fired. What happened? Hand in the till?"

"I was not on duty when I should have been."

"Boy, you guys really take your work seriously, don't you?"

"Will you help me?"

McGillivray got himself a paper cup of water from the fountain.

"Perhaps we can help each other, Mr. Blexill. I have a contact at White Star Lines. I could put you in touch. In return you can give me something on Tarr."

Henry felt tense. While he had no loyalty to Tarr, the idea of opening the family closets for a reporter was repugnant to him. McGillivray must have sensed his reticence because he began talking again.

"Fascinating man, your ex-boss. The new breed of American businessman. Owes nothing to what goes on on your side of the pond. Into everything, railroads, coal, steel, silver. You name it."

"The only thing I'm prepared to talk about is Brandon," said Henry.

"Good. Maybe we can do business, then."

"Do you know anything about two brothers named George and Arnold Macklin?"

"They used to own the Brandon mines," McGillivray replied. "They brought a lawsuit against Tarr a couple of years ago. It was a long legal battle, but Tarr came out with the whole shooting match. The Macklins had to settle out of court."

"Why did it take so long?" Henry asked.

"My guess is that Tarr dragged it out as long as possible. He had the money to keep it going. The Macklins were broke."

"What was the settlement?"

"The brothers got $750,000. Total."

"That's all? For a company worth nearly thirty million dollars?"

"Yep. When old George Macklin heard, he had a heart attack at his desk. I covered the funeral. Tarr sent a wreath. Arnold Macklin threw it into the church furnace."

"How old is Arnold Macklin?"

"Let's see. He was five years younger than George. He must be in his late fifties now, and still a bachelor," McGillivray said.

"What about George? Did he have any children?"

"One. A son called Schuyler."

The brother or the son.

"Is there any chance of a government inquiry into what happened at Brandon?" Henry asked.

"Naw, the Senate would have moved by now. It's a dead issue."

"What would it take to have the files reopened?"

"Some new evidence, maybe."

"What if I told you that twenty thousand in cash was paid to the deputy sheriff on duty in Brandon the day of the massacre."

McGillivray whistled. "How do you know?"

"I saw it. I helped to deliver it." Henry recounted in detail what had transpired that fateful day. McGillivray took notes.

"I'll need confirmation from this guy Hislop. Otherwise it's your word against Tarr's."

"What do you mean?"

"Well, why would you and a preacher carry that much money on public transportation when Tarr was at Brandon in his own private train?"

"He wasn't there. He was in Cleveland at a directors' meeting."

"He was there, my friend. I covered the story and I interviewed him the night of the massacre."

Saturday, July 15, 1911

SO TARR HAD lied to him about Brandon. Tarr had been there all the time, and Tarr had ordered the armored car. Henry had wanted to believe, as Tarr had said, that the murderous machine was only there as a show of force, a deterrent to violence.

Henry's heart raged as he headed for the White Star offices on Broadway. In his pocket was a note from McGillivray to a man called Rattigan. Henry felt like a coward for running away, but now that McGillivray knew the truth the story would come out.

It all rested on the Reverend Clifford Hislop. Henry had told the journalist that he could find the preacher at Tarr's Westchester estate. He would be there until the summer's end, when Tarr gave the order for the move back to Manhattan.

If McGillivray approached Hislop, how would Hislop react? There could be no exposé without the preacher's co-operation. Henry realized that a denial from Tarr backed up by Hislop would make his story sound like the fanciful tale of a disgruntled employee bent on revenge.

But if Hislop's conscience finally got the better of him and the story did break, it would be in Henry's interest to be as far from Tarr as he could get. The poker with his fingerprints on it was still in Tarr's possession.

He waited in line for the omnibus that would take him to the Battery. His suitcase became heavier by the minute. When the bus arrived he was grateful to be seated.

He watched the brown façades of the new cast-iron buildings along Broadway. They seemed so permanent in their classical style, with solid pillars and wrought-iron balconies. They reminded him of London and the clubs Lord Rutherland belonged to.

The conductor rang the bell and announced, "Beaver Street, State Street, Bowling Green." The stop before had been Wall Street, which sent a shiver down Henry's spine. Tarr's office building was number seven, within hailing distance of the Stock Exchange.

He stepped down from the bus in front of the White Star Lines building. The midday sunshine had given way to a light rain. Men were sheltering under the trees in Bowling Green Park opposite. Henry hurried inside the Palladian entrance with its heavy lintel and imposing oak doors.

"Excuse me," he said, as he approached the reception desk. "I'm looking for Mr. Rattigan."

"That's me," said a man in a shapeless suit and bow tie. He was bald, and there was a large purple stain above his right ear.

"Mr. McGillivray from the *New York Times* asked me to give you this." Henry handed the note across the counter to Rattigan.

The man's lips moved as he read the typed message. "You looking for a berth?"

"No. I mean, I was thinking of a wine steward's job."

"That's a berth. Let's see your book."

"Book?"

"Seaman's book. Certificate of Continuous Discharge."

"I'm afraid I don't have one. You see, I'm a butler and I have to return to England. I thought I might work my passage."

The man looked up and grinned. His teeth were stained with tobacco. He leaned back in his seat and tucked his thumbs into the braces under his jacket.

"Limey, are you? My Dad's from Southend. Sounds just like you. You've got to have a book before I can let you sign on."

"How do I get it?"

"Takes time. I could fix it for you. For a fee."

"How much?"

"Two bucks."

"I'll give you five," said Henry, "if you can get me a job on the next White Star liner that sails."

The man regarded him suspiciously. "Cops after you?"

"No," said Henry, looking him squarely in the eye. "My father needs an operation, and I have to get back home to help out."

"Sorry to hear it. Wine steward. Don't get many openings for wine stewards. Last one I placed was on the *Republic*." The man laughed and clearly expected Henry to do likewise. When he got no response his face became serious. "January twenty-second, round-trip luxury cruise to the Mediterranean by way of Gibraltar, Alexandria, Palermo and Genoa. Rammed by an Italian immigrant ship, the *Florida*, in a fog fifty miles south of Nantucket. Four dead."

"Thank you," said Henry, "that's all I needed."

"Gimme an hour, then come back, okay? Ask for me if I'm not here." The man winked at him. "Leave your case if you like."

With an hour to kill, Henry sauntered down State Street to the South Ferry. The wind blew off the bay and stirred the water into tiny whitecaps. The rain had abated. The water had turned the color of gun metal, and above it the Statue of Liberty held her torch aloft, eternally welcoming.

How different that symbol was from Britannia, he thought. How very English she was in her plumed helmet, gracefully seated on her sea-girt rock. Her right hand held the oval shield embossed with the crosses of St. George, St. David and St. Andrew; her left a trident. Every schoolboy carried her around in his pocket, on the back of the penny.

Lord Rutherland had given Henry his first penny after he had gone three rounds with the old aristocrat's nephew, Charles Sinclair, who was down from London for the weekend. Lord Rutherland had shown Henry the image on the back. "Britannia," he had said, "the spirit of Old England. She first appeared on a Roman coin, Henry. The model for this one on your penny was Frances Stewart, Duchess of Richmond, in the time of King Charles II."

When he was a child growing up at Cumerworth, Henry thought Lord Rutherland knew everything there was to know. But he had not known how to stave off bankruptcy.

Tugs were pulling a two-funnelled liner up the Narrows between Brooklyn and Staten Island, making for Ellis Island. Another boatload of immigrants from Europe with dreams of gold. They would end up in mining towns like Brandon, digging in the earth to enrich men like Thaddeus Tarr.

Soon Henry would be heading the other way with a leaden heart, leaving Nichole behind him. There was no Cumerworth Hall to return to, but at least its former owner would give him references. Unless the old man had died. The thought saddened Henry. When he was released from service, Lord Rutherland had given him his blessing, as he might have done to a son setting out on a great adventure. "Go to America," he had said. "That is the future for young men like you, Henry."

He dearly wanted to see the old aristocrat again. All life's certainties seemed to reside at Cumerworth, and its owner had dispensed the wisdom of ages as he sat by the fire with a blanket across his knees. Perhaps he could unravel the mystery of Brandon.

But he had his own secrets, it seemed: his dealings with Tarr. An English butler knew more about his master than the master's wife did. But Henry had had no idea the two men were involved in some business venture until he had discovered the file.

That file!

For hours he had been walking around with it pressed against the small of his back. He reached under his jacket and slid it free. He opened it carefully so the wind couldn't carry its contents into the slate-colored water of the East River.

He took the letter from the envelope. The heavy white

paper was embossed with Lord Rutherland's coat of arms, under which was printed "Cumerworth Hall."

"My dear Tarr," the letter began. "I would like to thank you for having dispatched the geologist's report with such alacrity. It arrived this very morning—" Henry checked the top right-hand corner of the letter for the date, January 17, 1909 "—and I can tell you it was balm in Gilead for this old man who is more than due some sunny tidings for a change. If what your scientific chappie says is correct then there should be a bit of money in it. I have asked my nephew, who handles my affairs these days, to make the necessary financial arrangements. I will keep in touch by wire and look forward to hearing from you in the near future. Yours most sincerely, Rutherland."

Henry checked the file, but there was no copy of a geologist's report. Only a letter addressed to Tarr in what appeared to be Spanish from a man who signed himself J.R. Ongania.

The file tab said "Lord Rutherland—Argentine." In all his years of delivering mail to the breakfast table at Cumerworth Hall, he could not recall a single letter from South America. What connection could the old aristocrat have with Tarr that involved the Argentine? If he could find someone who spoke Spanish perhaps the letter would tell him. He folded it and placed it with Lord Rutherland's letter into a single envelope, which he put in his inside jacket pocket. Then he took the file cover, tore it into small pieces and threw them into the water.

He pulled his jacket collar up against the wind and looked at his watch. The hour was almost up.

He turned away from the dockside. On the boardwalk above him he caught sight of a man in a straw hat leaning over the railings. Immediately their eyes met the man pulled out a newspaper and concealed himself behind it.

Henry was certain it was the man who had been watching Tarr's house that morning. A horse-drawn van passed between them, blocking his view. When it had moved on the man had vanished.

Why is Tarr having me followed? I have to get out of

New York as soon as I can. He hurried back to the White Star Line office.

There was a woman at the reception desk. She was trimming a pot of flowers, pulling off the brown leaves. She wore her hair like Nichole, swept up in the fashion of the day. There was lace around her collar, and her fingers were stained with ink. Henry asked for Mr. Rattigan.

"Eddie," she called in the direction of the frosted-glass door behind her.

Rattigan appeared, ducked behind the door and reappeared with Henry's suitcase. He held the handle with both hands as if reluctant to relinquish it before he had received his money. With a nod of his head, he beckoned Henry to one corner of the hall. In a conspiratorial whisper he said: "You're in luck, fella. An assistant steward on the *Oceanic*'s got a burst appendix. I signed you on. She sails tomorrow at noon. Here's your book."

"How difficult will it be for someone to find me?" asked Henry as he took out his wallet.

"They won't unless I tell them," replied Rattigan, his eyes fixed on the bills inside.

Henry's only sea-going experience had been his trip to New York as a passenger on a Cunard liner, *Carmania*. He found the *Oceanic* much more luxurious. Its marble bathrooms and staterooms were lavishly furnished in Louis XV and Queen Anne style. The first-class cabins and public rooms were panelled in mahogany, oak and satinwood. When she was launched in 1899, the chief steward told him, the seventeen-thousand-ton *Oceanic* was the biggest steamer of her day.

The sense of lateral movement disturbed him at first, but he soon got accustomed to decanting claret while the deck rolled under his feet. He kept himself apart from the other crew members, fearful lest Tarr had discovered his whereabuts. In his off-duty hours he would walk on deck to escape the tobacco-charged atmosphere of the cabin he shared with eleven other members of the dining-room staff.

There was a woman who dined alone with a book who reminded him of Nichole. Two days out she was joined by a man and no longer brought her book to the table. In the darkness of his berth, late at night, he would lie awake among his snoring shipmates thinking about her and the way she smiled. Very much like Nichole. He wondered what had happened to Nichole. She had been left alone to face Tarr's wrath. Had she ever thought of leaving the banker and running away to Henry? She must know he would return to England to Cumerworth Hall. If she thought about it, she would realize the only way he could get back to England was to work his passage on a liner. If their positions had been reversed he would have found her. Perhaps he should write to her—but he knew Tarr opened all the mail.

The thought reminded him of the letter from the Argentine. He asked around the crew if anyone spoke Spanish. The next day a waiter named Vergara from the second-class dining room cornered him menacingly in the kitchen.

"What you want with Spanish?" he demanded.

The man was short and fierce and seemed ready to fight at some perceived affront to his nation and its flag. But he smiled condescendingly when Henry explained he needed a letter translated.

"From a woman? You English with your one language."

Henry ignored the jibe at his unilingualism. "It's a business letter. I'll pay you a pound."

"Two," said Vergara.

"All right, but you have to write it out for me."

The next day the little Spanish waiter was back, scratching his head.

"There are many words I do not understand," he complained. "It is all about mining."

"If they're technical terms they'll probably be the same in English," said Henry. "Just write them down as they are."

Two days later, Vergara handed him the translation and demanded his two pounds. Henry paid him and retired to the steward's washroom. He locked himself in a cubicle and read the document.

It was headed "Assay report of the Los Cobres mine near Catua, by Jorge Raphael Ongania, Geologist and Surveyor, October 30, 1908."

Los Cobres. Henry remembered Lord Rutherland raising a glass of port and toasting the name as he stared into the dining-room fire.

He continued reading. "On instructions from Mr. T.N. Tarr, I, J.R. Ongania, attest that I conducted a week of field studies of the Los Cobres mine between September 3 and September 10 of this year. Preliminary investigation showed that it had not been worked for several years. Samples of rock taken from tabular (Vergara had written a question mark after the word) and lenticular (?) bodies at levels of fifteen, thirty, fifty and one hundred feet indicated Mesothermal (?) and Epithermal (?) deposits. Field inspection confirmed later by laboratory analysis showed a variety of gangue (?) minerals present, namely quartz, calcite, ankerite, siderite and rhodochrosite. Traces of silver and zinc were also found, as were some cinnabar and stibnite crystal formations.

"With respect and regret I must inform you, my dear sir, that the percentage and quality of silver recovered from these deposits does not warrant the expense of further exploration. The Los Cobres mine is not a commercial proposition."

So Tarr had been pedalling a worked-out silver mine.

He took Lord Rutherland's letter from his pocket. It was dated nearly three months after the letter from J.R. Ongania. "It arrived this very morning and was balm in Gilead for this old man who is more than due some sunny tidings for a change."

What had Tarr told him to elicit such a response? For some reason, Lord Rutherland had been anticipating a sudden windfall from the mine. Yet Ongania had stated that Los Cobres was virtually worthless.

Was that why Lord Rutherland had invited the American banker to Cumerworth—to set up a business deal?

The old aristocrat might provide Henry with more ammunition to fight Tarr, he thought.

But when the *Oceanic* docked at Southampton Henry had no time to search for Lord Rutherland. The ship had a two-day turn-around, and his shore duties included restocking the cellar. He had no home in England. There was only the sea.

He rented a room in the terraced house of the second-class pantryman, who lived at Portswood, just outside the town. When he was off duty, he walked down to the hall of the National Union of Stewards, hoping he might find a letter from Nichole waiting for him there. But there was nothing for him.

He sat on a bench, resigned that he had lost touch with her for good. He wrote a letter to Lord Rutherland, explaining his new circumstances and saying that he would visit him once he had the address. He sent it to Cumerworth Hall, with a note on the envelope saying "Kindly Forward to Addressee."

Henry felt trepidation about the return trip to New York on the *Oceanic*. As the liner eased against the dock in America, he scanned the faces below, looking for serious-faced men among the smiling, waving crowds. He took a tiny room behind the Seaman's Friend, where he scoured back copies of the *New York Times* to see if McGillivray had unearthed new evidence against Tarr. He found nothing. Surely the journalist would have been in touch with Hislop by now? And if McGillivray had contacted Hislop, he might also have met Nichole. He would know if she was safe.

"Oh, it's you, the busted butler." McGillivray smiled at him from his desk. "I wondered when you'd turn up."

"I've been looking for your story, Mr. McGillivray."

"What story?"

"About the money." Henry glanced furtively around and lowered his voice to a whisper. "The twenty thousand dollars Tarr sent to Brandon."

McGillivray shook his head as if he had forgotten the punch line of a joke.

"You still on about that? Your preacher buddy Hislop told me you'd probably keep rooting in the garbage heap. What's the point of carrying on a vendetta?"

"When did you speak to him?"

"A week ago."

"Did you ask him why he delivered the money?"

"Yes."

"Well, what did he say?"

"It was a used to build a school."

"A school!"

"Yeah, a school to teach miners' kids English."

"And you believed him?"

"I don't believe anybody, Blexill. Not even a man of the cloth. Especially a man of the cloth. I'm a newspaperman. A born cynic. I have to see things with my own two eyes. So I went to Brandon. I saw the goddamn school."

So that's how Tarr settled his conscience, thought Henry.

"But don't you see? It could have been a different twenty thousand. To make Tarr look good. There was a whole private army down there. He had to pay them somehow."

"Look, I don't know what you stand to gain by your vendetta. Thaddeus Tarr is not someone I want to tangle with unless I have a sworn affidavit that the guy pulled the trigger himself."

"I'll get it for you," said Henry.

"You really hate him, don't you?"

"Yes, I hate him. If you'd seen what I've seen you'd hate him, too."

McGillivray said nothing. He regarded Henry with a frown, his hands plunged deep in his pockets. Henry turned to leave in disgust.

"No, don't go for a moment. You could be right. Maybe we treat the Rockefellers and Morgans and Tarrs different from other mortals. But, damn it, they are different. I'm going to show you something. I shouldn't, but what the hell."

The journalist opened the top drawer of his desk with a key on a long chain attached to his belt. He took out a file and handed it to Henry. Inside was a single sheet of paper.

"Have you ever head of Agnes Milo?" McGillivray asked as he scanned the typewritten page.

Henry shook his head.

"She's an actress. A singer or something. Done a few Broadway shows. Now read that."

"Agnes Milo's Career in Jeopardy" ran the headline. "Actress Breaks Back in Elevator Fall."

According to McGillivray's story, Agnes Milo sustained serious injury when the private elevator of a Wall Street office plummeted twelve floors and crashed in the basement. Engineers investigating the accident reported that the braking system had mysteriously failed.

"She was in the wrong place at the wrong time," said McGillivray. "She was in Tarr's office."

"Seven Wall Street," said Henry. "Why don't you say so, then?"

"There's no point. You see, that story will never see the light of day. You know why? Because the publisher called me in and told me to forget I had ever written it. That's the kind of power your ex-employer has, my friend."

"I know that elevator," said Henry. "It's his private one, right up to his suite on the twelfth floor. It works on a key. She would have to have one to use it."

"So Tarr was fooling around with an actress. What's new?"

"That accident wasn't meant for her."

"What's your guess?"

"Somebody tampered with the lift. They thought Tarr was the only person using it."

"Brandon miners would know all about lifts and braking devices."

"There are a lot of people who would like to see Tarr dead, Mr. McGillivray. But I want to see him in a court of law, where he belongs. That's why we must get a government inquiry."

"We?"

"If I get you the evidence you need, would you publish a story?"

"In spite of what you might believe, Blexill, journalists do have a code of ethics. But martyrdom isn't part of it. Let's just say I'd make sure it got to the right people."

Henry smiled and extended his hand. "You can reach me through White Star Lines. By the way, did you get to talk to Nichole Linley, Mrs. Tarr's companion?"

"The good-looking one? No, it was tough enough to talk to Hislop."

"I'd appreciate it if you would. She could be in as much danger as I am."

Wednesday, September 13, 1911

AS A BUTLER, Henry understood service, and he adapted easily to the myraid demands of ocean-going passengers. His willingness to work had caught the attention of the *Oceanic*'s chief steward, who moved him from the cabins to the second-class dining room. Here Henry displayed such flair with the wine list that diners asked him to recommend wines for them. They enjoyed watching him decant old claret in a rolling sea when the glasses were sliding across the table. And Henry liked the informality of the vacation-like atmosphere. He found himself smiling. His father had always taught him to keep his smiles for below stairs. "A good butler," he used to say, "is invisible."

The sea, the incessant, ever-changing sea, began to break down Henry's inbred sense of how life was ordered. The unpredictability of waves made him question his own purpose. Experiencing the ocean's sudden storms and in-explicable calms, its sunsets and far horizons, he saw possibilities he had never recognized before. New patterns emerged. The movement of the deck under his feet and the flux and flow of passengers excited him. He began to doubt if he could ever work on land again, where everything was fixed in the aspic of social expectation.

In his work, as assistant steward third class on the *Oceanic*, Henry came into contact with immigrants like himself, disgruntled men returning home disenchanted with the New World. They reminded him of the Brandon miners. They fretted and sulked their way across the

Atlantic, singing maudlin songs in Gaelic, Italian or Greek, hanging on to the bar in the rough sea. In the saloon they drank frothy beer chased down with shots of whisky, then had to be helped to their cabins.

Henry quickly became a fixture on the transatlantic route. On his third trip he was promoted to the first-class dining room over the heads of other stewards with longer service. Before each voyage he would read the passenger list, looking for names he knew, always wary lest Thaddeus Tarr was sailing. Each time he arrived in Southampton he checked the National Union of Stewards' hall for mail. On one trip he decided that, if there was no reply from Lord Rutherland, he would visit Cumerworth. The villagers would know what had become of the lord of the manor.

He was standing in line waiting to pay his union dues when he saw a diminutive woman in a cloth coat and a shiny black straw hat festooned with cherries. She was fending off a tall uniformed man with her umbrella, much to the amusement of the predominantly male audience in the dusty hall. The man appeared embarrassed at being the centre of attention, yet he persisted in trying to catch the lunging woman.

Henry noticed her red cheeks. He saw some undisciplined wisps of hair fall from under her hat. She exuded such zest and animal high spirits that he felt immediately drawn to her.

"Just calm down, Kittie," hissed the man. "We'll go somewhere and discuss it."

"I'm not going anywhere wiv' you," shouted the woman. "You just take yer 'ands off of me." Her eyes were shining with tears.

The man made a sudden grab for her wrist, and the umbrella fell to the floor. "Now don't make a scene, Kittie."

The men laughed as her captor folded his arms around her and lifted her off the ground. The woman kicked, impotent as a child in his grasp.

"Put me down!"

Henry moved out of the line and approached the man.

"The lady said she wants to be put down."

The man turned his attention to Henry. He had one arm around the woman's waist, as though she were a doll.

"Butt out, sailor, if you know what's good for you," the man growled.

Henry could see from his uniform that he was a chief steward on the White Star Line. He was the same height as Henry, but heavier.

"Do as the lady asks."

The woman squirmed and struggled against the powerful arm that held her. Her breath came in short gasps.

"You're 'urting me, you great ox. Put me down!"

"And who's going to make me?"

"I am," said Henry.

"You and whose army?"

The spectators began to murmur, sensing a fight.

Henry raised his fists and adopted a John L. Sullivan stance. The crowd moved closer, instinctively forming a ring. The man bared his teeth and loosened his grip. The woman slid to the floor. The impact of her weight on the splintery boards caused motes of dust to dance in the sunlit air.

The man took off his peaked cap and held it for someone to take. He unbuttoned his jacket, still smiling. Henry maintained his position, bent legs two feet apart, fists extended away from his body at chin level.

The man took off the jacket and threw it behind him.

"You're going to regret this, fella."

He turned his back on Henry as he rolled up his shirt sleeves. Then suddenly, without warning, he whirled and threw a punch, which caught Henry on his right ear. Henry staggered. He covered up as the man pounded at his face with both fists. He could hear the crowd cheering, egging him on, not wanting the fight to end.

Henry slipped a couple of punches and measured his opponent with a straight left. The man came back swinging wildly. Henry countered with a combination left and right to the solar plexus. The air rushed from the chief steward's mouth like twin blasts on a ship's whistle.

He grabbed Henry, pinning his arms, and butted his forehead to Henry's face. Henry could feel the bone in his nose give. Then a rush of blood cascaded over his lips and chin.

The man stepped back, smiling in satisfaction. He cocked his fist and aimed for Henry's damaged nose. Henry waited for the punch, and at the last second pulled back his head. The man went off balance when the blow did not land. Henry drove his right fist into the man's heart. The steward groaned and lurched forward. As he toppled to the floor, Henry caught him on the point of the jaw with a left hook. The man went down in a heap, bounding on the floorboards. The crowd cheered.

Henry gingerly touched his nose. The woman came rushing forward, her expression a mixture of anger and concern. She brushed past him and dropped to her knees beside the recumbent figure of the chief steward.

"Mr. Kirkbride, Mr. Kirkbride, are you all right?"

Henry stared at her in amazement. She turned her face to him.

"Why did you go and ruin it for me? Why couldn't you just mind your own bees' wax?"

"You're welcome," said Henry, and walked out of the hall into the autumn sunlight holding a handkerchief to his bleeding nose. He moved aimlessly along a row of terraced houses with peeling doors and rain-stained windows, reflecting on the mysteries of the female mind.

All the way to Cumerworth Hall in the rocking railway carriage, Henry found his thoughts coming back to the woman named Kittie. He had come to her rescue like a knight of old, and she had sent him about his business as if he had been her attacker. He was intrigued by her and he wondered where she lived and which ship she sailed on. He was so preoccupied with her that he almost missed his stop. Then the conductor's call of Tinsley Green broke into his reverie.

Cumerworth Hall was perched above the village, which sat on the Surrey-Sussex border. Henry walked from the station along the winding lane, with a hedgerow on one side and the estate wall on the other. From the road he could see the roof of the stables where he had worked as a boy. The prancing-horse weather vane was still there.

When he arrived at the entrance to Cumerworth Hall, the iron gates were closed. Through the bars he could see women in white pushing elderly people in wheel chairs up and down the flagstone terrace that ran on either side of the entrance hall.

A sign on the gatepost read: "Tinsley Green Sanitorium—Visitors By Appointment Only."

All the windows had their blinds drawn, and the gravel driveway, which used to meander through the trees, had been replaced by an arrow-straight macadamized road right up to the Gothic façade. The new road had displaced several old oaks, elms and horse chestnuts.

A magpie fluttered out of a hawthorn tree behind him. Henry gazed at the gray façade of Cumerworth Hall. It saddened him to think that the old house had been reduced to this.

He walked slowly into the village. Agatha Gimblett, who ran the general store in Tinsley Green and who knew everything there was to know about the comings and goings of its three hundred inhabitants, did not, however, know where Lord Rutherland had gone.

"You might try London. His nephew lives there somewhere. The one who used to come down here for the point-to-point."

Henry thanked her and bought a quarter of a pound of acid drops.

On the train to Southampton, Henry puzzled over where Lord Rutherland might be. He remembered the old man used to stay at his club when he went up to London to see his solicitor. Henry thought it was near Berry Brothers in St. James, because Lord Rutherland always brought back a bottle of port with him. The next time he could get the days off he would travel to London.

It was dark as he made his way to Portswood from Southampton Station. He was depressed about Cumerworth. Even in England the old order was passing. The vitality had drained away, and everyone talked about America as the land of the future.

Wearily, he climbed the stairs to his room. He could hear the pantryman arguing with his wife in the kitchen. Then there was the sound of smashing crockery. She was throwing teacups at him again. Henry longed to be at sea, away from their constant bickering and the smell of boiled cabbage and laundry that assailed his nose each time he opened the front door.

As he approached his bedroom, he could see light in the crack under the door. There was no reason for the electric light to be on in his room. He cleaned his room himself, and the pantryman's wife never entered it except to lay fresh linen at the end of his bed.

He heard a creak from inside the room and saw a shadow slide across the floorboards. He moved quietly to the door and knelt down to the keyhole, but the key was in the lock and he could see nothing. He put his ear to the door. He could hear the sound of a drawer being pulled open. He felt his heart begin to quicken. Tarr had found him.

He wondered if he should make his way quietly down the stairs and alert the pantryman that there was a stranger in the house. The two of them could tackle the intruder. But the less his landlord knew of his private life the better.

He visualized the room. There was one window giving out on the back of the house. He had left it open. The bed was opposite the door. Next to it, set against the exterior wall, was a small chest of drawers, and beside that was a wardrobe. From the sounds within, the intruder was going through the drawers. His back would be to the door. If Henry burst in he could surprise him.

Slowly he turned the handle and inched the door open. The bedside lamp cast an orange glow, which illuminated a black form bent over an open drawer. Henry propelled himself into the room and wrapped his arms around the intruder's body, lifting him bodily into the air. He was surprisingly light.

"Bloody 'ell!" shrieked a high-pitched voice. "You love fighting, don't you?"

"You!"

An astonished Henry lowered the woman to the floor.

"How did you get in here?"

"I told your landlord you asked me to clean your room 'cause it's like a pigsty," she said, smoothing her coat.

"But why?"

"Why? I've got nowhere else to go, that's why. Thanks to you."

"I don't understand."

"I was thrown out of me digs. I 'ad lodgings with Mr. Kirkbride's sister."

"I'm sorry," said Henry. "What was that all about, anyway?"

" 'E's the chief steward on the *Celtic*. 'E told me 'e could get me a berth on the *Titanic* if I was nice to 'im."

Henry had heard all about the *Titanic*, the world's largest man-made object. She was to be the jewel of White Star's fleet, a new sister ship for the *Olympic*. J.P. Morgan had been at her launching in Belfast. Twenty-two tons of tallow and soap had been used to grease her passage down the slip and into the River Lagan. No champagne bottle was cracked across her bows as she slid into the water. She was scheduled to be fully fitted out and ready for service in March. And all the White Star crews—firemen, stokers, greasers, stewards, cooks and pantrymen—were vying to be on the maiden voyage of the most luxurious liner ever built.

"And I ruined your chances."

"Them and me reputation."

"Are you laundry?"

"Stewardess, if you don't mind," said the woman. "My name's Kittie Boyer."

"Henry Blexill."

"I know. I asked about you at the 'all."

The pantryman's voice could be heard shouting at his wife from the kitchen below. His angry words were punctuated by another salvo of crockery smashing against the wall.

"They was arguin' when I came in," said Kittie. "Why can't men and women get along?"

"Would you like a drink? There's a pub on the corner."

"I make you nervous, don't I? I can tell. You 'aven't looked me in the eyes once. It's the old butler routine, isn't it?"

Kittie Boyer discomfited Henry. She said what was in her mind, and what was in his. He had never met anyone quite like her before. She was like a child who knew too much for her own good. She took his arm and smiled at him as they walked down the street. He felt curiously excited by her.

They entered the saloon bar of the Rose and Compass and settled into a curved leather seat. Kittie ordered a port and lemon, Henry a pint of ale. She unbuttoned her coat, and he caught a glimpse of the curve of her breast as she slid the garment off her shoulders.

She placed her fingertips on the marble tabletop as if she were about to play the piano. Her profile was reflected in the engraved mirror behind her. She had the delicate face of a porcelain doll. Her upper lip was thin, and she had compensated for it by putting rouge on it in the shape of a bow.

"I'm a cockney sparrer," she said, aware that he was studying her. "A bird, a little bird." She flapped imaginary wings.

"I can hear," said Henry.

A woman in a grubby shawl came shuffling over to their table. Her eyes were rheumy, and there was spittle dried white at the corners of her mouth. She held her hand out.

"Hello, grandma," said Kittie. Then she poked Henry in the ribs. "Give 'er the price of a pint."

Henry gave the woman tuppence, and when she had shuffled out of earshot, he said, "Was she really your grandmother?"

"Lord love you, no." Kittie laughed. "You don't know much about the working classes, do you, 'Enry."

"I suppose I don't."

"Well, why should you, spending all your time with the toffs. I can teach you. First thing to remember is when a gentleman saves a lady from a fate worse than death, 'e 'as an obligation to 'er."

"What kind of obligation?" Henry smiled.

"Finding 'er a place to live since 'e got 'er kicked out of 'er digs."

"I could speak to my landlord."

"If you think I'm moving in with you, 'Enry Blexill, you've got another think coming."

"No, he has another room to let."

"I can't afford much."

"I'll help out if necessary. After all, a gentleman has an obligation."

Kittie took a sip of port, then pulled back with an exaggerated gesture to study Henry.

"You're not a bad-looking bloke when you smile. The *Titanic* could be good for you, too, y'know. Just think of all them nobs who'll want to be on its maiden voyage. And all them lovely tips. So what're you goin' to do to get us a couple of berths, then?"

"I'll work on it," said Henry. "I sail for New York in the morning."

He reached for her hand, but she drew it away quickly and buried it in her lap.

The prospect of having Kittie live under his roof pleased Henry. He had not realized how lonely he was. While Kittie did not arouse in him a passionate desire, as Nichole had, her teasing presence made him feel alive again. The idea of sailing with her on the *Titanic* intrigued him. When the *Oceanic* docked in New York, he headed straight for the White Star Line office and asked to see Eddie Rattigan.

Rattigan greeted him like a long-lost brother.

"Henry Blexill, as I live and breathe. How the heck are you?"

"Fine, just fine. I need a favor, Mr. Rattigan. I want to get a berth on the *Titanic*."

"You and everybody in the merchant marine. They'll be picking the best."

"And there's a young lady, a stewardess on the *Celtic*. Her name's Kittie Boyer."

Henry slid a five-dollar bill across the desk.

"What did you say her name was?"

"Kittie Boyer."

"I'll see what I can do."

"Thank you."

"Not at all. Anything for a friend. Oh, by the way, I had a guy in here last week asking about you. I said I never heard of you."

"Did he show you any identification?"

"No . . . but I always knew you were running from the cops, son."

The wind blowing off the East River was funnelled up Broadway by the tall buildings on either side of the avenue. Henry pulled his jacket up around his ears as he walked. Someone was asking questions about him. Obviously, Tarr had not given up. *He's trying to frighten me*, thought Henry. The incident with Agnes Milo must have unnerved the banker. Had he set detectives on all his enemies?

A black Detroit Electric cruised by him and slowed. No one got out, and Henry was aware of two men sitting in the front seat wearing soft black hats. The brims hid their eyes. He quickened his pace as he passed the car, trying hard not to look back. He heard the change of gears and a popping sound as the car began to move. He was standing on the corner of Fulton Street. At the intersection a policeman with a whistle in his mouth was directing traffic. He had stopped the cars and trolleys on Broadway and was waving the Fulton Street traffic across.

Henry stole a glance at the black sedan. It was stopped behind a cream-colored Pope-Toledo Runabout with its canvas top down. The policeman changed his hand signal, turned ninety degrees and began to wave the Broadway traffic forward. Henry stepped out into the road, and suddenly he heard an engine accelerating. With a screech of tires the black automobile careened around the corner and swerved towards him.

Henry threw himself onto the sidewalk, hitting his shoulder against the paving stones. He saw an arm protrude from the passenger window. There was a flash, then another. He saw the flames spit from a gun. Shards of cement stung his cheek. With a roar the car accelerated. He heard a woman scream as he picked himself up and began to run. He heard the policeman's whistle blow, but he kept running up Broadway.

He did not stop until he reached Times Square. His lungs ached from the sudden exertion, and he gasped for breath as he burst through the door of the *New York Times* building.

McGillivray. He had to see McGillivray.

A haze of cigar smoke hung over the newsroom like a curse. Under its blue pall, journalists hunched over their typewriters. The backs of their shirts were dark with perspiration. McGillivray was on the telephone when Henry approached his desk. He held the earpiece wedged against his shoulder as he took notes with his left hand. The position made him look deformed.

"Jumping Jesus!" exclaimed McGillivray when he saw Henry. Into the mouthpiece he said, "I'll call you back." He looked up. "What the hell happened to you?"

"Somebody tried to kill me," said Henry. "They tried to run me down, then they fired two shots."

"Here, sit down. You look terrible."

McGillivray rummaged in a drawer and took out a flask of bourbon. He splashed a measure into a coffee cup and handed it to Henry.

"And you're going to tell me it was Tarr."

"Who else would want me dead? He must have found out I've been talking to you."

Henry took a gulp of bourbon. McGillivray looked around the newsroom then bent closer to him.

"You were right," he said. "I found the engineers Tarr hired to repair his elevator. They say the cables on the braking system had been filed through."

"You're going to go with the story then?"

McGillivray shook his head.

"But why?" Henry asked. "I came to you because you're the only one who can help me. What happened to me just now means Tarr believes I'm getting close to something that could hurt him. You say you need proof. I don't have it yet. But I know how to get it. If anything should happen to me in the meantime you'll know it's because of him. There are two people who can give me the information I need. One is my old employer in England, Lord Rutherland. I'm still trying to find him. The other is Nichole Linley."

McGillivray tapped his teeth with a pencil as he listened.

"I'd forget about Nichole Linley, sport. I already talked to her."

"You talked to her?"

"Yes."

"Where?"

"At Tarr's estate. I posed as a florist. Some spread he's got."

"Is she all right?"

"She looked just fine."

"Did she ask about me?"

"She said you're wanted for murder."

Henry half rose from his chair. If McGillivray believed Nichole, he could pick up the phone and have Henry arrested on the spot.

"And what do you think?"

"Relax, Blexill, I've got connections with the police. I checked, and you're not on their files. But why would she say something like that?"

It became increasingly apparent to Henry that his only hope was to find Lord Rutherland. Only watertight evidence against the banker would be good enough for McGillivray. Nichole had closed ranks with Hislop. She must have taken her cue from Tarr. She was probably too frightened to do anything else. She had been driving the car the night Henry thought Tarr disposed of a body; Nichole might be an accessory to murder. McGillivray had asked Henry why Nichole had called him a murderer.

"She must have been referring to Brandon," he said. "I was there with Hislop, remember. I couldn't stop the massacre."

The *Oceanic* returned to Southampton, and Kittie met Henry at the dock.

She waved a gloved hand as he carried his duffle bag down the gangway.

"Good to see you, 'Enry. I missed you."

"And I missed you."

"Sure you did, running around with all them fancy women in New York City."

He went to kiss her, but she pulled her face away.

"I didn't expect to see you," said Henry, annoyed by the rebuff. "I thought the *Celtic* sailed on Tuesday."

"Coal miners' strike," said Kittie. "I don't mind. I'm solid with the miners."

"And how's the landlord?"

"'Is missus is down to 'er last teacup. By the way, there's a letter for you at the union 'all."

It was the one he had sent to Lord Rutherland, stamped "Return to Sender." The words "Gone Away" were scribbled in pencil across the front.

"I'm going to have to go to London, Kittie. Want to come with me?"

"No, thanks. Can't stand the place. Ran away from it when I was fifteen. But you can bring me a souvenir."

Henry had not been to London since he was a boy. The city seemed so sombre and reserved compared to New York. The carriages along Piccadilly seemed less grand than they used to. The concierge at Whites, Lord Rutherland's club, informed him that Lord Rutherland was no longer a member. He had resigned some months ago. When Henry pressed him to look at the records of members' addresses, the concierge said it was not possible. A proffered sovereign had the desired effect, and the man returned ten minutes later with an address written on a piece of paper. "Care of Massingdale, Trent, Calder and Attinger, 53 Staple Inn, High Holborn WC 1."

Lord Rutherland's solicitors.

"And why, pray, do you wish to contact Lord Rutherland?" asked Kenneth Attinger, recently returned to chambers following a roast beef lunch at Simpson's. He had the ruddy, self-satisfied glow of a man who not only knew where his next meal was coming from but could not wait to attack it.

"I used to be in his service, sir. I lived at Cumerworth Hall for twenty years, first as a stableboy and then as his Lordship's butler."

Attinger nodded. "Lord Rutherland is, ah, living in somewhat reduced circumstances. I don't know if he would care to see you."

"I'm aware that he had to dispose of Cumerworth."

"Yes."

"You must have acted for him in the matter. I realize you have professional considerations, but I'd appreciate it if you could tell me why he had to sell the estate."

"Why does anybody have to sell anything these days? He needed the money."

"But why so suddenly?"

"To pay debts, I presume."

"Did it have anything to do with a silver mine in the Argentine?"

Attinger's eyebrows rose perceptibly.

"I'm not at liberty to discuss Lord Rutherland's affairs with you, Mr. Blexill."

"Of course. I understand." Henry changed his strategy. "I was hoping you might be able to put me in touch with him, sir. You see, I came all the way from America to find him. I'm considering marriage and my father, before he died, made me promise I would seek his Lordship's approval of the lady in question before I did."

The idea jumped into his head, and with it the image of

Kittie's mocking smile. The solicitor studied him for a moment.

"An American lady?"

"No sir, British."

The man nodded. He withdrew a leather-bound book from the drawer of his desk.

"Lord Rutherland has a set of rooms behind Notting Hill Gate. Number 3-A Dawson Place. I would suggest you drop him a note before you call. He is, after all, well on in years. Well, good day, Mr. Blexill, and, ah, congratulations on your forthcoming nuptials."

"Thank you," said Henry, rising. "One last thing. Who owns Cumerworth now?"

"It's a sanitorium, I believe."

"Does it belong to an American?"

"Why, yes." He added, "Like so much of England these days."

"A banker named Tarr?"

"That is correct. He was the original purchaser. But he had the title deed changed several months ago. I effected the transfer myself," said Attinger, with obvious distaste.

"To his wife's name? Or his daughter's?"

Attinger said nothing.

He took one last shot.

"It wouldn't have been to a Miss Nichole Linley, would it?"

"You seem to be remarkably well informed, Mr. Blexill."

Friday, October 20, 1911

SO NICHOLE HAD finally bagged her golden goose. She was the mistress of Cumerworth Hall. But at what cost?

Had Tarr deeded it to her for the price of her silence? Or did she have some other secret knowledge she could hold over the banker? Small wonder she had told McGillivray Henry was a murderer. It wasn't fear that had motivated her to lie to McGillivray. She was just protecting her investment.

But how had Tarr been able to acquire Cumerworth Hall in the first place? It was typical of the man that he had destroyed Lord Rutherland's ancestral home by turning it into a money-making sanitorium.

These thoughts preoccupied him as he waited in line for the omnibus to Notting Hill Gate. He did not have the time to write to Lord Rutherland and wait for his reply before calling on him, as the lawyer had suggested.

"Coal strike! Coal strike! Read all about it!"

A scruffy urchin in a soft cap with a bundle of newspapers under his arm harangued passersby with the headlines. Henry bought a copy just as his bus arrived.

At Marble Arch traffic was held up for a protest march by the men whose actions had created the headlines. Welsh and Scottish miners had joined their colleagues from eight English counties. They had descended on London to press their claim for a minimum wage. As they marched ten-deep down Park Lane towards the Houses of Parliament, they shouted slogans and waved placards vilifying Prime Minister Asquith. Mounted police and constables on foot lined their route.

Henry watched their clamorous progress. The sight of them brought back images of the Brandon miners fleeing before the spitting Hotchkiss machine gun. West Virginia seemed far from the terraces and parks of London.

Kittie sympathized with the coal miners, but Henry knew the strike would have repercussions on both of their lives. The shortage of coal had made it difficult for the White Star Line to fuel its ships. Several sailings had been cancelled, and stocks were consolidated for use by the largest vessels.

The construction of the *Titanic* had been held up because of the strike. But these hoarse-voiced men with their faces seamed with coal dust had to eat, too.

As he waited for the traffic to move again, Henry opened the newspaper and scoured the pages for any reference to Tarr.

In the foreign news section, Henry's eye was arrested by a headline: "American Magnates Called To Steel Trust Inquiry." Thaddeus Nugent Tarr was mentioned, along with J.P. Morgan, Andrew Carnegie, John D. Rockefeller, the Moore brothers and John Gates. The prominent industrialists and bankers had been subpoenaed by the House of Representatives in an investigation into something called the Steel Trust.

The story detailed how Morgan had parlayed three companies he controlled—Federal Steel, National Tube and American Bridge—into the United States Steel Corporation, the largest steel conglomerate in the world. The idea had been brought to Morgan in December 1900. Four months later he put together a combine, which cost him $793 million.

More than half the cost was the price he had to pay to Andrew Carnegie, who owned the company that controlled America's largest deposits of iron ore.

To subsidize the enterprise, Morgan issued bonds, preferred shares and common stocks to a value of nearly one and a half billion dollars. A frenzied American public, hungry to ride on the financial coattails of the Wizard of Wall Street, had taken up his offer of U.S. Steel stock with feverish abandon.

The Steel Trust, which the government sought to dissolve, was made up of twelve corporations under the control of J.P. Morgan. The industrial giant owned sixty-five per cent of America's iron and steel, one thousand miles of railroad, and one hundred and twelve ore-carrying vessels; and he possessed vast reserves of iron ore, coal, limestone and natural gas. The very size of U.S. Steel threatened British interests overseas, the newspaper writer concluded. He also pointed out that Morgan's partners chaired the finance committee and the executive committee.

So, the Brandon Iron and Steel Company is part of U.S. Steel, Henry thought. No wonder the financial community backed Tarr in his fight against the striking miners. But Tarr's name was not among the board of directors of U.S. Steel listed in the story.

I'm in good company, thought Henry. *J.P. Morgan must really hate him, too.*

Smiling, he took out the envelope with the letter from Jorge Raphael Ongania and began to reread it.

Dawson Place was a quiet, rather shabby back street where once-elegant Regency homes had been converted into rooming houses. The front garden of number 3-A was overgrown with brambles, weeds and choking vines. The paint was peeling off the forlorn façade, and a milk crate full of empty bottles stood on the top step. The portico smelled of cats.

There were six different bells, each with its own name written on a piece of cardboard and slid into a brass window. The one at the top read simply, "Rutherland." Henry pressed it and waited.

Nothing happened. He pressed it again. Eventually he heard a shuffling sound behind the glazed panels in the sun-blistered door, then the sliding of a bolt. The door opened, and a gray-haired woman in a man's cardigan over a pink slip asked him what he wanted. She held a long-haired cat in the crook of her arm.

"I've come to see Lord Rutherland."

"Did you ring his bell?" demanded the woman.

"Yes."

"Well go and knock on his door, then. He's a bit deaf. Top of the house."

Henry climbed the dark stairwell. It reeked of cooking odors and dust. He paused on the landing outside Lord Rutherland's room and listened. A victrola was playing Elgar's "The Dream of Gerontius." He knocked on the door. The music stopped abruptly and a thin, faded voice called, "Come in."

He turned the handle and pressed the door open. A rush of suffocating heat almost pushed him backwards. He stepped inside and there was Lord Rutherland, seated by a gas fire with a blanket around his shoulders.

The room was cluttered with objects Henry recognized from Cumerworth Hall—a brass coal scuttle with a blue and white delft handle, a sculling oar with its blade painted maroon, a telescope, a huge globe, an Indian rug. Objects the old man probably had not been able to sell, or from which he refused to be parted.

The walls were lined with books. Next to Lord Rutherland's chair stood the victrola with its great bell pointing directly into his ear, its turntable still revolving slowly.

"Good afternoon, m'lord."

"Henry? Henry, my dear boy. Come in, come in."

Lord Rutherland made a move to rise, but the effort was too great. He fell back into the chair and closed his eyes. His skin was drawn tight over his cheekbones, but his neck was swollen. The little light that filtered through the grimy windowpanes illuminated his pallor. His hair was long and unkempt.

"Lord Rutherland, it's so good to see you."

"How kind of you to call. Sit down, sit down and tell me all about yourself. Are you still boxing?"

"I don't have much time these days, I'm afraid."

"You'll have to speak up, my boy. The old ears aren't what they used to be. Nothing is," he added, glancing around the room.

Henry sat in the chair opposite the old man. His heart wept to see him living in such circumstances. He always pictured Lord Rutherland in hunting scarlet sitting erectly on his favorite bay, accepting a stirrup cup on a chill autumn morning with the dogs yelping and his horse's breath shooting from its nostrils like steam.

"Tell me about America, Henry."

Lord Rutherland listened avidly as Henry talked about the skyscrapers of New York and the shops along Fifth Avenue, of the automobiles and the marching bands. "Everything in America is a parade," he said.

He talked about Westchester and how he had left Tarr's employment to join the White Star Line. But he did not mention the reasons for his abrupt departure. He said nothing to upset the old aristocrat who listened to him as if he were creating a tale of high adventure.

"And are you married yet, Henry?"

"No, m'lord, but there is a lady I am fond of."

"Splendid, splendid. There's a bottle of sherry on the sideboard, Henry. Cyprus, I'm afraid. But let's both have a snifter. If you'd be so kind."

Henry rose and poured two glasses.

"It's quite like old times, m'lord," he said. "Do you have someone to look after you?"

"My nephew drops in from time to time. You remember young Charles. You thrashed him once behind the stables. Remember that?"

"Yes," said Henry, smiling. "But how do you manage?"

The old man shrugged.

"My needs are modest these days. I learned to get along on very little when my wife died."

His hand shook as he took a sip of sherry, spilling it on the blanket.

"May I ask you, if it's not an impertinence, why you sold Cumerworth?"

"Debts, Henry. Made a fool of m'self in the market. My own damn silly fault. Overextended m'self. A great pity. Six generations. I was hoping to hand it down all of a piece to Charles."

Henry took a sip of his sherry.

"I remember hearing you once talk about a silver mine."

"That's it. Los something or other. South America. Looked like a good thing. That Tarr fellow who gave you a job when I had to let you go, he had it surveyed. Supposed to be full of silver."

Slowly, painfully, under Henry's patient questioning the story began to emerge.

In May 1909, Lord Rutherland had invited Thaddeus Tarr to Cumerworth to discuss a business venture. Rents from the family properties were no longer sufficient to maintain the estate. The idea of selling off a portion of the ancestral land was anathema to Lord Rutherland, so he looked around for other means of raising capital. Among his holdings was a dormant silver mine in the Argentine that his father, the major general, had acquired in the 1880s as a gambling debt. Against the advice of his friends in the City, Lord Rutherland decided to reactivate it. To do so he needed capital. Rather than mortgaging the estate to raise the financing, he looked to the New York money market. His wife was American. She still had connections there. The name of Thaddeus Nugent Tarr was mentioned.

Lord Rutherland wrote to Tarr, who was obviously flattered by the approach. He sailed across the Atlantic. He then bought fifty per cent of the silver company and agreed to fiance a geological survey of Los Cobres.

On the strength of what Lord Rutherland called "a highly encouraging report," Tarr had convinced him that they should take the company public on the New York exchange.

"Buy all you can, he told me. The price will go through the roof. Well, it did for a while, and I borrowed money to buy as much as I could. Tarr kept urging me to get more. Then the bubble burst. And I was left holding a lot of useless paper. I've no one to blame but m'self. Pure greed."

Henry was stunned. Thaddeus Tarr had pressed his partner to buy shares in a silver mine he knew to be worthless. Yet he had somehow convinced Lord Rutherland the mine would make him rich. He must have watered the stock, then secretly unloaded his own inflated shares on the market. But why? What could have motivated Tarr to destroy the old aristocrat?

"Do you still have that geologist's report on the mine?" asked Henry.

"Yes, I had it framed. I thought it would make my fortune. It's hanging up there."

"May I?"

"Of course, dear boy."

Henry crossed to the wall, took down the dusty frame and wiped the glass with the palm of his hand. The document was hand-written, in English. Its wording was more or less the same as the translation of Ongania's report Henry had received from the Spanish waiter. Except for one crucial detail—the final paragraph. "With respect, I am happy to inform you," it read, "that the percentage and quality of silver recovered from these deposits suggests a lode of spectacular size. The Los Cobres mine should be immediately activated and strictest security assured to avoid uncontrolled speculation."

Had Tarr bribed the translator to falsify the document? Or had he written it himself?

The graceful, flowing hand was not Tarr's.

Henry held the frame up to the light. He studied the slant of the looping letters and the thinness of the line.

"Ah, yes," he said, as he recognized the penmanship of the Reverend Clifford Hislop.

Wednesday, April 10, 1912

HENRY LEANED AGAINST the boat deck railing and looked down the cliff-like side of the *Titanic*. All was right with the world. He and Kittie were aboard, members of a crew of nine hundred and fifteen.

Sixty feet of riveted steel below him, Southampton dock swelled with passengers, friends and well-wishers. They spilled out of the long, narrow customs shed. They milled around the gangways and the crane derricks, filling the air with a communal sense of wonder at the monstrous black hull that dwarfed everything around it.

The corrugated iron walls of the customs shed were painted green, the same color as the boat-train engine that stood panting smoke after its run from London. The brown and cream carriages of the London and South West Railway had already disgorged a contingent of well-heeled travellers on the first leg of their journey to New York. They would cross the English Channel to Cherbourg, pick up more passengers and freight, then steam to Queenstown at Ireland's southern tip before heading out into the Atlantic.

The coal miners' strike had ended in March. Still, the *Oceanic* and the *Adriatic* had to sacrifice their coal bunkers so the *Titanic* could sail. Her twenty-nine boilers devoured six hundred and fifty tons of coal a day.

Of all the crossings Henry had made, none rivalled this one for the sense of excitement and anticipation it engendered among passengers and crew alike. Below him, first-class passengers brushed shoulders with second-class ticket-holders and bundle-carrying immigrants. Rich and poor mingled under the shadow of the *Titanic's* black belly. In their feathered hats and silken toppers, cloth caps and lacquered straw bonnets, the passengers called to each other in loud voices and snapped photographs, bending backwards to frame as much of the liner as possible in their viewfinders.

A brass band played marches to speed the passengers aboard. The ship's whistles on her two forward funnels split the warm spring air with a throat-clearing blast. Twin plumes of white steam shot into the overcast sky and vanished in the wind gusting off Southampton Water. The air smelled of seaweed, oil and wet coal.

Next to Henry, young Georgie Skinner cupped a cigarette in his palm and gazed down on the carnival scene. The wind blew his corn-silk hair behind him. A blue ensign snapped and ruffled at the *Titanic's* stern.

"You 'eard about the coal fire in Bunker Number 10? Been burning ever since they left Belfast."

Henry tugged at his waiter's jacket and watched a woman in a green coat stepping from a carriage. She held a Pekinese under one arm. With her free hand she lifted her dress, and he caught sight of the white silk of her stockinged calf.

"The old man would never sail if he thought it was dangerous," Henry replied without turning his head. "It's not coal you should worry about. It's ice. The *Lord Cromer* ran into an ice field off the Grand Banks last week. Dented her plates below the waterline."

"Where's the Grand Banks when they're at 'ome?" asked Georgie.

"Hundred and fifty miles off Newfoundland. I wouldn't let the chief steward catch you in uniform with a fag in your face, young fella me lad. He'll have your guts for garters."

Henry treated his assistant with avuncular affection. Georgie's knowledge of wine left something to be desired, but his smiling cheerfulness and the ease with which he dealt with his betters made him an invaluable backup.

"If you're clocking the birds, Mr. B., take a gander at that one down there. Not bad for a Wednesday afternoon, eh?"

Henry squinted in the direction of Georgie's pointing finger. The woman was suddenly obscured from his view by a large man in a black frock coat and top hat. The man's bulk seemed to fill the entrance to the gangway. He carried his stomach protectively in front of him as if it were a tray loaded with expensive crystal.

"Oh, my God!" exclaimed Henry.

Instinctively, he pulled back from the railing. His hands felt sticky, sticky with the blood of an unknown victim. He could never wash the blood off.

"The man in the black top hat. Is he boarding?"

Georgie leaned over the side.

" 'E's 'aving 'is picture taken. Big fella. Yank, is 'e?"

"His name's Tarr. One of the richest men in America. I was his butler once—until he fired me."

Georgie stared at Henry. "Blimey, you should see your face."

Henry had gone white. He clenched the railing as he stared down at the imposing figure of Thaddeus Nugent Tarr. His expression was cold with contempt and hatred. For a man who had received death threats almost daily, Tarr still looked very much alive, Henry thought. Other people died, but Tarr survived unscathed.

Henry watched Tarr pose with his entourage for the obligatory pre-boarding photograph that would appear in the social pages of the *Tatler* or *Vogue* magazine.

"A great black spider," said Henry, "surrounded by his prey."

Cornelia, eyes opened wide, stood to her husband's right, leaning slightly into him. She wore her habitual turban to cover her thinning hair. Behind Cornelia stood Hislop, twitching like a ferret, watching Tarr, forever anticipating his needs.

Rhonda, on her father's left, was the only one who smiled. At eighteen, life was still an adventure.

Next to Rhonda stood Nichole, perfidious Nichole, mistress of Cumerworth Hall. She had called Henry a murderer. Her face was partially veiled by the hat she wore. She must have sensed that someone was scrutinizing her, because she looked up, shielding her eyes against the sudden sunshine with a gloved hand.

The *Titanic*'s whistles roared again, a baleful sound like the death rattle of a wounded dinosaur. The Blue Peter pennant was run up the foremast, and from the first-class entrance on C Deck Henry could hear the voice of the purser, amplified by a megaphone, calling, "All ashore that's going ashore." Passengers on the Promenade Deck were waving to friends on the dock and throwing streamers. Five attendant tugs waited to take up the slack on their lines. They were named for Greek gods and heroes— *Vulcan, Neptune, Ajax, Hector* and *Nestor*.

Henry began to shiver uncontrollably. He recalled the last words Tarr had spoken to him: "You have my word, Blexill. I'll see you never work again. Ever. Anywhere!"

There would be no way to avoid Tarr now. And once Tarr had spotted Henry, he would make good his threat. That would be the end of Henry's career with the White Star Line—and with Cunard, Hamburg-Amerika or any other transatlantic shipping company, for that matter.

If it came to a showdown, what did Henry have in his arsenal? It was too soon to confront Tarr with what he knew. It would be his word against the banker's, and what proof did Henry have that Tarr was a murderer?

Henry thought about jumping ship. Then he remembered Kittie. By running, he would be abandoning her. Their relationship had blossomed since his return from London. He had bought her a silk shawl, and as he put it around her shoulders he had kissed her neck.

She did not back away. Nor did she return his kiss.

"I have news for you," he said. "I heard at the hall that I'm going to the *Titanic*. Wine steward in first class."

"I'm very 'appy for you," she said. There were tears in her eyes.

"The best news of all is that you've got a berth, too."

"You fixed it!" she screamed. "You marvellous bloody man." And she ran into his arms.

As these memories played through Henry's mind, the chief steward marched up behind him and tapped him on his epaulette with a sheaf of Marconigrams.

"You're on duty, Blexill. Smarten up."

Henry turned and looked straight into the face of Alan Kirkbride.

In his alarm at seeing Tarr, he had forgotten that Kirkbride had been transferred to the *Titanic* as chief steward. Henry would report directly to him. The two men stood facing each other in silence.

"I'll be watching you," said Kirkbride as he handed Henry the sheaf of papers.

"What are these?" asked Henry.

"Requests for champagne to be delivered to first-class cabins. Now hop to it." He turned to Georgie. "And what's your name, sailor?"

"Skinner, sir."

"Where's your cap, Skinner?"

Henry glanced at the Tarr family tableau below him.

"I see Mr. Tarr's coming aboard. I didn't notice his name on the passenger list," Henry said.

Kirkbride consulted the clipboard he held.

"His baggage is going to B53. Booked in the name of McKinley."

Henry nodded. Obviously, Tarr was anxious to keep his travel plans to himself. The passage had been booked in Cornelia's maiden name.

Tarr's accommodation was the best the liner had to offer. He occupied the suite that had been built specially for J.P. Morgan, whose International Merchant Marine Company owned the White Star Line. Henry knew that it must have cost more than four thousand dollars—a far cry from the weekly wages of a Brandon miner, he thought.

Wednesday, April 10, 1912

CORNELIA TARR GAZED up at the shining black hull of the *Titanic*.

"It's like a leviathan," she said to Hislop. "It makes me giddy just to look at it. How can something so big float?"

"They're telling us to get on board, Daddy," said Rhonda.

"They can wait a moment longer. They won't sail without me." Tarr smiled. "You've got to hand it to these Brits. They sure know how to build a navy."

Nichole put a gloved hand to her hat as a sudden breeze threatened to dislodge it.

"Something you'll be able to tell your grandchildren, Rhonny," said Tarr, putting his arm around his daughter's shoulder as if he were making a present of the liner to her. "You sailed on the maiden voyage of the world's most expensive ship. This baby cost seven point five million dollars."

Hislop stood behind Cornelia, protecting her from the jostling crowds. His eyes darted from face to face, never lingering long enough to establish contact.

From his vantage point high above the dock, Henry kept his eyes on Tarr as the banker moved towards the gangway. Henry studied the man with the same morbid fascination he had once felt for an adder he had seen at Cumerworth Hall. The snake used to slither out of its hole every morning to sleep in the sun. Henry was eleven then, and he knew adders were poisonous.

One day he saw a large swelling in the snake's belly. It

was obviously digesting a field mouse. Repulsed, he had thrown a rock at it and broken its back.

If Henry had a rock in his hand now, he would have felt a compulsion to hurl it at the advancing figure of Thaddeus Nugent Tarr.

Visitors streamed down the gangway in response to the urgency of the ship's whistles. There was a jam of bodies as Tarr pressed his way up the gangway. Just as he reached the step, Henry saw a man in a straw boater catch the banker's arm. He had a notebook in his hand and a press card tucked in the band of the straw hat.

Henry saw Tarr turn and speak angrily to the man. Then Tarr raised his cane. He appeared about to strike the man. Then Hislop stepped between the two of them and dragged Tarr away, as a tug might pull a liner to the safety of deeper water.

Henry watched as the journalist slunk away. Tarr made a path for himself through the milling crowd at the foot of the gangway.

Henry looked over the customs shed, across the railway tracks to the gray slate roofs of the workmen's cottages along Chapel Road. He wondered if Tarr could have him arrested on the high seas.

One long blast of the ship's whistles signalled the departure of the *Titanic*. On the bridge, Captain Edward J. Smith, wearing his medals on his blue uniform, gave the order for the mooring lines to be slipped. The tugs began to take up the slack.

"We're moving," said Rhonda, looking out the square window in Tarr's sitting room.

The majestic liner began to inch away from the dock amid cheers from onlookers and from passengers crowded against the railings.

Tarr had booked one of two suites of cabins that had their own private promenade decks. His was on the starboard side, cabins B51, B53 and B55. There were two bedrooms, which he and his wife would occupy, a sitting room, a private bath and a trunk room. Rhonda, Nichole and Hislop were in single cabins nearby.

"We should be celebrating," said Tarr. "Order my usual and tell Nichole to get me a passenger list, Hislop. Let's see who else is on this tub."

Henry sat in the wine room off the first-class restaurant and thumbed through the Marconigrams Kirkbride had handed him. The wine room was next to the cold room, where fruit and flowers were stored.

"'Ere's a weird one," said Georgie Skinner, replacing the telephone receiver on its hook. "They want a bottle of cognac, a bottle of vintage port and a decanter of olive oil."

"Tarr," said Henry. "The cognac's for his wife. Port and olive oil is a tonic he takes every morning."

"Blimey, must make 'im run like a fiend."

"Leave it to me," said Henry. "Here, take this champagne to the smoking room."

There was no point in delaying the inevitable, he thought. He selected a Hine Vieille Grande Champagne 1888 from stock and a bottle of Taylor's 1898. From the kitchen he took a small jug of olive oil. He placed them all in the centre of a silver tray. He added four balloon glasses, two port glasses and two teaspoons. Holding the tray above his shoulder, he backed through the door into the restaurant's reception room, then into the corridor where the first-class cabins on B Deck began. He threaded his way carefully through the excited passengers who were exploring the blue-carpeted corridors.

He wondered what Kittie was doing. She was in charge of the stewardesses who serviced the second-class cabins. It would be difficult for them to see much of each other on their first passage together, especially with Kirkbride watching Henry, waiting for him to make a mistake.

As he approached B51, Henry stopped and pulled down his jacket with his free hand. Outside the door stood a man, his fist raised as if he were about to knock. He was listening at the door. Henry recognized the silhouette of the Reverend Clifford Hislop.

"Good afternoon, Mr. Hislop," he said.

The thin, cadaverous face turned towards him and what little color it had seemed to drain away to an ashen pallor. Hislop's knuckles were still poised at the door. His mouth dropped open.

"Henry! I thought you were . . ."

"Dead? Is that what Mr. Tarr told you?"

"But you disappeared. There was no word. All this time, Henry. What was I to think?"

"There were good reasons."

Hislop smiled wanly and stretched out his hand as if to touch Henry. Then he brought the tips of his fingers to his lips and patted them, perplexed. "Do they know you're on board?" he asked, trying to recover his composure.

"Not yet."

"Give that to me. I'll take it in."

"I'm afraid not. Against company rules."

"I was only thinking of Mrs. Tarr. The shock might upset her."

Henry knew that Hislop was dying to break the news of his presence to Tarr.

"Tell me, Hislop. Do you ever think about Brandon?"

Hislop gazed at him. "There is an order in all things. We must respect that order, otherwise we all perish. That is God's will." He knocked softly on the door and put his ear close to the wood, listening until he heard Cornelia's voice call, "Who is it?"

Hislop turned to Henry. "I won't have her upset. Understand?"

"I'm doing my job, that's all," said Henry.

"I am pleased to see you, though," replied Hislop, placing a hand on Henry's shoulder.

The door opened. The first person Henry saw was Rhonda.

"Well! Would you look who the cat dragged in."

"Rhonda, shame!" cried her mother.

"Miss Rhonda," said Henry with a slight bow as he entered. "Mrs. Tarr. It's a pleasure to see you again."

Cornelia's hands flew to her mouth. Her eyes were wide with disbelief.

At the sound of Henry's voice, Nichole turned from the window. Henry could see the color rising in her neck. She blinked several times and touched her hair nervously. He noticed how thin she had become. There were lines around her mouth and eyes. Yet for all the strain that showed in her face she was still beautiful. He nodded to her, but she did not respond. She stared at him for a long moment, then turned away and put both hands on the window frame as if she needed to support herself.

Henry felt suddenly awkward in their presence, and he took refuge in his old, formal ways. He set the tray on the table and busied himself with removing the wax seal from the cork of the cognac bottle by tapping it with the butt of his corkscrew. He wondered where Tarr was. The door to the adjoining cabin was closed. He heard the sound of running water through the wall.

"I would have liked to prepare you," said Hislop to Cornelia, but she dismissed him with a wave of the hand, her eyes fixed on Henry.

"Well, would you believe it." Rhonda smiled. "All together again. Daddy," she called. "Look who's here."

Henry poured a measure of brandy for Cornelia. Four pairs of eyes watched him. Four people waited for Tarr to appear.

The door opened and the banker stepped into the sitting room in his shirt-sleeves. Henry straightened, glass in hand.

"Good afternoon, sir."

Tarr stopped short and studied Henry in silence, heavy lids almost closed over his eyes. "Why didn't somebody tell me?" he hissed through clenched teeth. He looked angrily at Nichole, then at Hislop and finally at his wife.

"If you will allow me, sir, it has been a surprise for all of us," said Henry.

"You know I don't like surprises."

Tarr moved closer to Henry and took the glass from his hand. He lifted it to his lips and drained it in one motion, his eyes never leaving Henry's. He thrust the empty glass into Henry's hand.

"This should be an interesting trip," said Tarr, turning on his heel and leaving the cabin. He banged the door shut behind him.

The tugs' shrill whistles saluted the *Titanic* as she cleared the dock. In the cabin, a leaden silence had descended. Everyone watched Henry. He poured another glass of cognac and handed it to Cornelia.

Her eyes shone with tears. Her hands shook as she accepted the glass. "You left without saying goodbye," she said.

On the bridge, bandmaster Wallace Hartley led his seven-piece orchestra through a medley of ragtime tunes. The jaunty music was carried by the wind to the small craft tied up along the River Test.

When the tugs had manoeuvred the great liner to her turning arc, the musicians switched to light operetta. They played Oskar Strauss's "The Chocolate Soldier."

As soon as the *Titanic*'s majestic bow was pointed downriver, Captain Smith gave the order to start the engines. There were three huge brass propellers. Two were twenty-three and a half feet in height, the third was sixteen and a half feet. They slowly began to turn. The low hum from the engine rooms was the only sound that identified the *Titanic* as an ocean-going liner and not the grandest hotel in the world.

Her wash, combined with a displacement of thirty-five feet, was so great that it caused the water level in the estuary to rise dramatically.

Two smaller White Star liners, the *Oceanic* and the *New York*, were tied up at the dock on the *Titanic*'s port side. She passed them, then the water level fell in her wake, setting the empty vessels bobbing like corks.

The strain on the *New York*'s hawsers became too great, and one by one they snapped with sounds like pistol shots.

Henry heard the reports as he was polishing wine glasses in the restaurant. He hurried out on deck to see the *New York* being drawn away from the dock into the *Titanic*'s wake. Her stern was swinging in a quarter circle, on a collision course with the *Titanic*.

Henry could feel a sudden shudder under his feet.

"What's happening, steward?" demanded a woman. "Are we in any danger?"

"No danger, ma'am," replied Henry. "The captain's going full astern to cut down our suction. The tugs will hold the other ship fast."

And, sure enough, the attendant tugs were securing ropes to the port quarter of the smaller vessel to allow the *Titanic* to pass. She glided by within four feet of the rogue liner.

Oblivious to the drama on deck, Tarr sat at the writing desk in his cabin reading a stack of bon-voyage messages from bank colleagues and business associates. Next door, in the Jacobean-style sitting room, Cornelia nursed her brandy balloon. On the table in front of her was a pack of Tarot cards set out in rows.

"Are you doing that mumbo jumbo stuff again?"

Cornelia started at the sound of her husband's voice. She turned to see him standing in the doorway with a Marconigram in his hand.

"I thought they might tell me why Henry reappeared like that," she replied. "I never did believe he stole my necklace. You see how they came up? The king, the queen, the chevalier and the valet. All together. Oh, dear, it frightens me."

"Oh, for God's sake. Where's Hislop?"

"Clifford is unpacking."

"I want him here."

"Very well, dear. If you like, I'll get him for you."

Tarr was waiting impatiently at his desk when Hislop entered his cabin and closed the door behind him.

"You called for me, Mr. Tarr?"

"Cornelia's been at those damn cards again."

"Something must be upsetting her."

"It's Blexill. I want you to find out what he's doing on this boat. I want him off, understand?"

"I don't think I can arrange it until we get to New York, sir."

"Well, make sure he doesn't work for this shipping line or any other. That's the first thing you do when we dock. Understand?"

"Yes, Mr. Tarr."

"Now read this." The banker handed Hislop a yellow Marconigram. The message was hand-written on a post-office telegraph form, and was datelined Southampton.

"Have an interesting crossing," read Hislop. "Signed your friends at Brandon."

"Interesting crossing," growled Tarr. "I'll give them interesting crossing."

"What do you think it means?"

"How the hell do I know? Interesting crossing. That sure isn't miner talk. It's got to be the Macklins. They're trying to scare me, Hislop. There'll be no peace till I'm rid of them."

He moved quickly to the bed and began to rummage in his suitcase. From a side pocket he withdrew a soft leather bag and slipped it into his jacket pocket.

"Perhaps it's genuine," Hislop suggested. "A cable of good luck from the management."

Tarr regarded him with a look of unalloyed contempt. "You don't say interesting if you're genuine, Hislop. Have a great trip. Have a wonderful trip. But not interesting. You're thinking like a fairy boy again."

Hislop winced and swallowed. "Shouldn't we inform the authorities?"

"Just listen to me and don't interrupt. I'm going to deal with this my way. If Macklin and his nephew are on board this ship, you're going to find them. Is that clear? Ask around. But be discreet."

He pulled a gold bill clip from his vest pocket and counted off five ten-dollar bills.

"This should grease your way. Try second or third class.

And from now on I want you to stick close to me. You'll be my eyes and ears. They're not going to get another chance, because you're going to be my shield. Understand?"

Hislop nodded. He held the bills between his thumb and forefinger as though they were soiled rags.

Both men heard the ship's bugler summoning the first-class passengers to lunch. The tune he played was "The Roast Beef of Old England." Hislop left.

"I think Nichole is coming down with something," Cornelia said to her husband when he returned to the sitting room. "She's looking awfully peaky."

"The ocean voyage will do her good," said Tarr.

He pressed the electric bell above his head to call the steward for a menu. As he waited, he perused the passenger list.

"I see John Jacob Astor's on board," he said with satisfaction.

"He owns half the best real estate in New York."

"Is that child with him?" Cornelia asked.

"What child?" demanded Tarr irritably.

"You know—that eighteen-year-old he married. And he's almost fifty."

"Forty-seven," corrected her husband, who was punctilious about all numbers.

"Lily Frick told me the girl's pregnant. He always was an impulsive man. His grandfather married one of the Gibbes girls from South Carolina, you know. Friends of my granddaddy, Cornelius, after whom I was named. He was left twenty million dollars. Not *my* granddaddy—Colonel Astor's granddaddy. And here he is, a divorced man, gallivanting around Europe with a teen-aged pregnant bride. Why, she's the same age as Rhonda."

"Pity it wasn't Rhonda," muttered Tarr, his eyes scanning the passenger list. "Archie Butt, President Taft's adviser. Good. He could be useful. Listen to this. Sir Cosmo Duff-Gordon and Lady Gordon. These Brits and their dumb names."

"Does he have a son?" inquired Cornelia, but Tarr ignored her.

"Ben Guggenheim. Well, whaddaya know. I wonder which of his ladies he's bringing with him, the old dog. Charles Hays. You remember Chuck Hays. President of the Grand Trunk Railway. Tried to buy it from him once. Son of a bitch wouldn't sell. Where's Morgan?"

Tarr ran his eye down the list again but could not find Morgan's name.

"I don't see Morgan. I know for a fact he booked. I had it checked out in New York and London. Chairman of the company, he's got to be on board for the maiden voyage. He's the only reason we're here."

There was a knock at the sitting-room door.

"You rang, Mr. Tarr."

Georgie Skinner smiled ingratiatingly at the banker.

"I can't find J.P. Morgan's name on the passenger list." Tarr held up the list and shook it as if the name might fall out.

"I believe Mr. Morgan was booked, sir, but 'e cancelled 'is trip due to ill 'ealth."

Tarr sat bolt upright in the reproduction Hepplewhite chair.

"You mean he's not on board?"

"No, sir."

"He's got to be on board!"

"Thaddeus," warned Cornelia.

"God damn it! You mean I've come all this way for nothing?"

He crumpled the passenger list into a tight ball and threw it with all his might at Georgie. It struck him on the shoulder and bounced onto the carpet.

"Oh, Thaddeus," moaned Cornelia. "I'm sorry," she said to Georgie, who knelt and picked up the ball of paper. He placed it with overstated delicacy on the table. Tarr lay back on the sofa, breathing heavily.

"Okay, okay," he said. "Give him something. What's your name, son?"

"Skinner, sir, Georgie Skinner."

Cornelia dithered, looking for her purse. Georgie stood waiting.

"In my pocket," said Tarr, his voice suddenly weary.

He closed his eyes. A thin film of perspiration dampened his forehead.

Cornelia took the clip of bills from her husband's vest pocket. In a lost voice that tailed off in confusion, she asked plaintively, "What should I . . .?"

His eyes still closed, Tarr vented his anger on the sofa, pounding it rhythmically with clenched fists.

Alarmed, Cornelia handed Georgie the whole thing, gold clip and all.

"Ma'am?" he inquired uncertainly.

"Just take it," snapped Cornelia, "and please leave us alone now."

Georgie closed the door quietly after him, his face wreathed in smiles.

Wednesday, April 10, 1912

HENRY WAS SEATED in the wine room trying to collect his thoughts when Georgie Skinner came in, beaming.

"You're right about your ex-boss. 'E's filthy rich. You should see the tip 'e gave me. And this."

Georgie held up the gold bill clip. Henry recognized it immediately.

"He gave you that? Why? What did he say?"

Georgie recounted the sequence of events that led to Cornelia dismissing him with the money clip.

"So he thought Morgan was on board," mused Henry. "The bill clip must have been a mistake. He'd never give it away. You see the silver-colored strands? Those are bits of barbed wire from his first sale."

"I think the missus was in a bit of state. Didn't know what she was doing. Maybe I should give it back," ventured Georgie.

"Let me do it," said Henry, and he placed the bill clip carefully in the pocket of his uniform.

Rhonda had lunched alone in the Café Parisien, a replica of a sidewalk café adjacent to the main restaurant on the *Titanic*'s starboard side. Trellises on the walls supported a luxuriant growth of mock ivy. The cane furniture creaked when she sat down.

Through the bay window she could see into the restaurant where Henry went about his work. A young blond waiter smiled at her when she caught his eye.

On the table in front of her was an unfinished letter to a friend in New York. Bored with writing, she folded the notepaper and put it in her purse.

The last of the diners had left the restaurant and the waiters were clearing the tables. Henry saw her as soon as she entered. He watched her approach and caught her flashing a smile at Georgie as she passed him.

"Hello, Henry."

"Miss Rhonda."

He felt the old mask slip onto his face. He stood stiffly at attention.

She wore a pink chiffon taffeta dress. The material was weighted at the hem so that it fell in light folds. Over her shoulder was draped a length of matching silk mousseline.

Her hair was swept up, and Henry realized how like her mother she looked. She reminded him of the portrait in oils by Giovanni Boldini that hung in Tarr's bedroom.

Over Rhonda's shoulder Henry could see Georgie making a circle of his thumb and forefinger. The young waiter opened his eyes wide, stuck out his lower lip and nodded approvingly at Henry.

"Aren't you pleased to see me again, Henry?" Rhonda placed her purse on the table and held out her hands to him.

"It's always a pleasure to see you, Miss Rhonda." Henry made no move to take her hands. To cover her embarrassment, she curled them into fists and held them up in a fighting posture.

"Do you still box?"

"I beg your pardon?"

"Boxing," she said, punching him playfully in the ribs. "I used to sneak down to the gymnasium in the basement and watch you hit that old punching bag. You never noticed me. Nichole caught me once and said I was shameful. Do you think I'm shameful?"

"It's not my place to pass judgement."

"I never know what you're saying, Henry. Daddy's in a foul mood. He thought J.P. Morgan was on board, but the old goat cancelled."

She ran her fingertips along the linen tablecloth, then raised her head to look into his eyes.

"Is it true you slept with Nichole?"

Startled, Henry looked beyond her to see if Georgie was still there. There was a sardonic smile on her face.

"How old are you?"

"Eighteen. Cook said that's why Daddy fired you."

"Cook shouldn't be discussing such things with you."

"So it's true then!"

"Why don't you go and read to your mother? You know how it soothes her nerves."

Rhonda pulled a face and turned away from him.

"You know something, Henry? Even though you're a servant, you're more attractive than any of the men I know."

She smiled again at Georgie as she left the empty dining room. Henry watched her leave and then returned to clearing glasses from the tables.

"She's a real looker, isn't she?" said Georgie as he went by with a tray.

Henry nodded. "And you know something? I still owe her fifty dollars."

Henry had that amount in his wallet. He had carried his valuables with him since his locker had been broken into on the *Olympic*. Even the newspaper photograph of John L. Sullivan tacked onto the door had not deterred the thief from stealing his father's watch.

As he was setting glasses for the evening meal, he noticed that Rhonda had left her purse behind. He could discharge his debt now; he could put the money in the purse with a note, then have the purse returned to her.

Henry opened the catch and a letter fell onto the table. His first instinct was to put the letter back into the purse unread. But his curiosity overcame his scruples, and he sat at the table and opened the folded notepaper. The stationery was pale blue and headed Claridge's Hotel. There was no date, but the different colored inks suggested that the letter had been written over several days.

Dear Annie; London is gray and boring, full of dusty old museums with stuffed animals and dinosaur bones. Nobody seems to be young in England, even the men at the coming out parties. And everyone is on strike here.

Daddy, of course, was tied up with his business, so my jailer, Nichole, chaperoned me all over. Mummy is usually in bed with her "headaches."

The women here who think they are fashionable are laced into impossibly tight dresses and use words like "deevie" when they mean divine and "diskie" for disgusting. Isn't that a riot? And you should hear them talk. They're forever talking. In fact, nobody seems to do anything but talk. They even talked through Divine Service at St. Martin-in-the-Fields.

Mummy embarrassed me terribly by suggesting to the American ambassador over dinner that he try to get us an invitation to meet the King at Windsor Castle. The ambassador explained to her that the King was in Scotland somewhere. He said it as though everyone should know that. Daddy made things worse by telling the story about how he sent King Edward champagne for his horse or something. He even took a moth-eaten old letter out of his wallet to show everyone. I could have died. Daddy said the King of England never answers letters himself, and the reply was written by an equerry. Well, Edward couldn't have thought much of Daddy's champagne if he got a stableboy to answer.

Wherever we went in London people were talking about Captain Scott and how he was such a big hero. He had been beaten to the South Pole by a Norwegian called Amundsen, then he froze to death in his tent. He sounds more like a loser than a hero, but I know just how he felt because I nearly froze to death in an English country house.

A business friend of Daddy's, an earl with a glass eye that looks like a marble, invited us all down for the weekend. He has a large estate in Dorset, but the house is coming apart. One of the wings has almost fallen off. He kept hinting that Daddy might like to buy it. When Daddy said no, the earl produced his son.

Oh, Annie, you would have died. His name was Nigel and he had no chin. He never completed a sentence, and when he spoke he moved his lips like the llama we saw in the Bronx Zoo—remember? Well, the earl and Mrs. Earl kept pushing the two of us together. I kept trying to make excuses, but Mummy said I had to be polite.

Nigel took me riding and said I had a very nice seat, whatever that means. When we stopped by a river to rest the horses I let him kiss me. He squeezed me through my riding jacket and tried to get under my skirt. Then I saw a man wearing a deerstalker watching us through binoculars from the other side of the river. I could have died of shame.

The English, I've come to the conclusion, like watching. There was a man outside our hotel who kept hiding behind a newspaper whenever I looked his way. And the day before we left London to take the boat train to Southampton, I slipped out to go for a walk by myself in Hyde Park. It was the first fine day we had since we arrived, and I wanted to see the young officers cantering around Rotten Row in their guardsmen's uniforms.

As I was strolling through the park (I was wearing my lavender dress, the one with the lace across the bodice), a covered carriage slowed down and stopped in front of me. A woman in a heavy veil leaned out and called me by my name. I thought she must be a friend of Daddy's. When I approached, the coachman climbed down and tried to grab me and push me inside. Well, you know me. I kicked and struggled and finally broke loose. I gave the horses a good whack with my parasol, and the team bolted. The coachman ran after them, shouting, "Stop the blighters, stop the blighters." He forgot about me so I got away. Phew! Do you think it was a white slaver from Arabia?

You should have seen the look on Nichole's face when I told her. She wanted to take me straight up to Daddy, but I told her I would blame her for not accompanying me. Do you think that's mean?

The letter was unfinished. Henry folded it carefully and slid it into the purse. The way Rhonda had described the incident, it sounded like a kidnapping attempt. A veiled woman who knew her name. A coachman who used an expression no American would use. Did the Macklins have the resources to reach to London for their revenge?

He took his wallet from his hip pocket and counted off fifty dollars. On the back of a waiter's order pad he scribbled a note: "A debt repaid with thanks." He signed it with his initials, then slipped the bills and the note into the purse. He felt curiously guilty about his action and glanced around the room to see if any of the waiters had observed him. As his eye moved to the bay window that gave out onto the Café Parisien, he caught sight of a man in a straw boater looking in. When he looked again the face had vanished.

The Reverend Clifford Hislop knocked discreetly on Tarr's sitting-room door and waited to be summoned.

"I have some information for you, Mr. Tarr," he said as he entered. Tarr was pacing in front of the fireplace, hands behind his back. Cornelia was seated on the sofa, shoes off, with her legs tucked under her.

Hislop handed Tarr a piece of *Titanic* notepaper folded in four, and two ten-dollar bills.

Tarr opened the note and read the message written in a large, childlike hand: "Dear Sir; No body named of Macklin are in second or third class."

"You paid thirty dollars for this?" Tarr struck the paper with the back of his hand.

"I had to get the co-operation of the stewardess, Mr. Tarr."

"If Macklin's on board, do you really think he's going to use his own name?"

"I'm sorry, but this is outside my normal realm of activity."

"Well, here's something that's within your realm of competence," barked Tarr. "I want you to tell Nichole to have Mrs. Tarr's jewellery box locked in the purser's safe. Make sure she gets a receipt. And one more thing, Hislop. Tell her she's not to communicate in any way with Henry Blexill. Do you think you can do that?"

"Yes, Mr. Tarr."

"Good. Now get out of my sight."

Hislop blinked and looked at Cornelia for support. She smiled dreamily at him and raised her shoulders in the faintest of shrugs. He turned on his heel and left.

Nichole was in her cabin moodily staring out to sea when she heard a knock on her door. She opened it to find Hislop holding Cornelia's blue velvet jewellery box.

"Mr. Tarr would like you to have this deposited in the purser's safe, Miss Linley. A receipt is required." He added maliciously, "He also informed me that you are to have no communication with Henry Blexill." He smiled with satisfaction and closed the door.

The purser required an itemized list of Cornelia's jewels before he would give Nichole a receipt. He suggested that she use his private office to make the list.

She sat at his desk and began taking the pieces of jewellery out of the box one by one.

Cornelia had a preference for colored stones, and there were many large rubies and emeralds in diamond settings. Nichole took out a pair of diamond earrings and held them up to her lobes. She studied herself in the mirror fixed to the inside of the jewellery box lid. The pear-shaped diamonds swung lazily on their mountings, flashing white and blue and red in the lamplight.

Ropes of pearls, a diamond tiara, diamond rings the size of dice, brooches of gold and platinum, necklaces and bracelets. Nichole tried them all on, but none could bring a sparkle to the eyes in the mirror. She finished her list, gave it to the purser with the jewels, and waited for a receipt.

When she returned to her cabin she found an envelope containing a printed invitation slipped under her door.

"Captain E.J. Smith, R.D. (Commr. R.N.R.) invites Miss Nichole Linley to join him for dinner at the Captain's Table in the first-class restaurant, Wednesday, April 10, 1912 at 7:30 PM."

In the bottom right-hand corner were the words, "Black Tie."

"Oh, God," she said out loud. "How much longer?"

On the pretext of restocking the pantry with bottles from the champagne cellar, which was on the Orlop Deck, Henry worked his way down to E Deck, where Kittie bunked.

"Is there somewhere we can talk in private?" he asked her.

She took him into a laundry room off the broad corridor known to the crew as Scotland Road. The officers called it Park Lane.

"You're looking a bit queer, love," she said, when they were alone among the piles of bed linen.

"Tarr's on board. I knew one day it would happen."

Henry had told her about his time as Tarr's butler. She knew he had been fired, but not the circumstances that had led up to his dismissal.

"He said he'd make sure I'd never work again. Now he's found me," said Henry glumly.

Kittie held his face in her hands. She could read the anxiety in his face.

"'As 'e seen you yet?"

"Yes. I had to take an order to his cabin."

"Oh, 'Enry. What can we do?"

"Stay out of his way, I suppose. They're all here, his wife, his daughter, Hislop."

" 'Islop? Did you say 'Islop?"

"Yes."

"A Mister 'Islop from first class came down 'ere asking questions."

"What questions?"

" 'E wanted to know if there was a bloke named Macklin on board. 'E kept pushing money on me."

So they've followed him from London, Henry thought.

Kittie took the bills from her pocket and showed them to him. They had been recently ironed. Tarr's money.

"Not bad for a bottom drawer, is it, love?" She winked at him, but in his preoccupied state the nuance was lost on him.

"Oh, come on, 'Enry. It's not the end of the world. 'E fired you, so what can 'e do to you now?"

She kissed him quickly on the cheek. Then she drew back, a frown puckering her forehead.

"Is that woman on board as well?"

"Who?"

"You know. The one you told me about. 'Is mistress."

Henry's past reticence about Nichole had prompted Kittie to press him for information. Was she pretty? How tall was she? How did she dress? Henry had diverted any suspicion of his own involvement with Nichole by telling Kittie she was a kept woman. But he sensed Kittie could tell that something had passed between Nichole and Henry. Women somehow knew these things instinctively. He could see the anguish in her eyes now that she realized Nichole was so close.

"Yes," he said.

" 'Ave you spoken to 'er?"

"No, but I'll have to. She's the only one who can help me."

"You still like me, don't you, 'Enry?" said Kittie. Tears began to glisten at the corner of her eyes.

He took her in his arms and kissed her.

"You're trembling, 'Enry."

"There are ghosts I have to exorcise," he said.

"Ghosts?"

"When I left Tarr's house I made a promise to myself. I swore he would answer for certain things he did."

"So it's revenge you want because 'e fired you."

"No. It's not for me. One day I'll tell you, I promise."

"You can't fight the rich, 'Enry. They've got all the weapons."

"Truth is a big weapon."

Kittie put her arms around him and pressed herself to his chest. "You'll be careful, won't you? You're the only chance I 'ave."

Wednesday, April 10, 1912

THE SUN WAS beginning to set when the *Titanic* stopped engines off the French coast. At the port of Cherbourg, twenty-two passengers would disembark and two hundred seventy-four would come aboard. Among them were Benjamin Guggenheim, who had been finishing the season at Le Touquet; the Duff-Gordons, Sir Cosmo and his wife Lucille, the well-known dress designer, who had been visiting a couturier in Paris; and Mrs. Margaret Brown, who would in future years become known as the unsinkable Mollie Brown.

A fine sunset blazoned across the sky above Cap de la Hogue as Captain Smith gave the order to drop anchor. He checked his watch. It was six-thirty. The mighty ship rested on the still water, every light illuminated in a peacock display of pride.

In cabin B51, Thaddeus Nugent Tarr took a spring coat from the wardrobe and reached for his black top hat and cane.

"You and I will go up on deck and get some fresh air," he announced to Cornelia.

Cornelia sighed wearily and looked furtively at the cognac bottle.

Tarr moved towards Hislop and said quietly so that Cornelia would not hear: "You come, too. I want you to see who's boarding. You ought to be able to recognize the Macklins. You saw enough of them in court."

On the open Promenade Deck, they leaned against the

139

railing to watch the approaching tenders. The White Star Line's *Nomadic* and *Traffic* steamed out of the harbor, past the lighthouse, and nudged up against the *Titanic's* starboard side. The *Nomadic* carried first- and second-class passengers while the *Traffic* delivered the third-class ticket holders and the mails.

Tarr scrutinized the faces of the passengers as they negotiated the gangway between the tenders and the liner, searching for the Macklins.

"There he is!" Cornelia exclaimed.

"Who? Where?" exclaimed Tarr.

"Don't be so obvious," she whispered. "It's Astor and his child bride."

"Oh, for God's sake, woman," snapped the exasperated Tarr.

John Jacob Astor held a disdainful Airedale on a leash. He carried himself erectly, like a guardsman, his military moustache adding to the illusion.

His young wife, the former Madeleine Force, held his arm. The scandalous couple were the focus of all eyes. They had spent the past six months in Egypt to avoid newspaper reporters.

Cornelia Tarr watched their progress along the deck. As the couple passed Henry Sleeper Harper, whose family owned *Harper's* magazine, Harper scooped up his prize Pekinese, Sun Yat-sen, and turned away.

"Thaddeus Tarr!" A hand descended on Tarr's shoulder, and he wheeled around. "What brings you on board?"

Jim Gordon, a New York merchant banker, stood in front of them, smiling. He raised his hat to Cornelia, who took in his foppish clothes and lacquered nails. His hair was parted in the middle and pomaded flat to his skull, and he gave off the unmistakable smell of toilet water. From his high collar to his dove-gray spats, he looked as if he had just stepped out of a fashion plate.

"Hello, Jim. You remember Jim Gordon, don't you, my dear? Used to be on my Brandon board, till he resigned."

"Mrs. Tarr. Yes, pressures of work, I'm afraid. You know how it is."

"And this is the Reverend Hislop," said Tarr, gesturing vaguely in the preacher's direction.

"Good evening," said Gordon, and the two men nodded to each other. "I had no idea you were on board, Thaddeus. I went to Europe specially to be here. And you? What brings you to Europe?"

"Banking business. Got to get home for the baseball season, though, Jim. Starts tomorrow. Giants against Brooklyn at Washington Park."

"I didn't know you followed baseball."

"I don't. I just bought a half interest in the Giants. Coming thing. Lots of money there."

They stopped talking as John Jacob Astor strolled by. He looked resolutely in front of him so that he would not have to acknowledge his fellow passengers. Coming towards him was Robert W. Daniel, a wealthy Philadelphia banker, whom Tarr had once met at a dinner for Teddy Roosevelt. At the end of a straining leash, Daniel held a champion French bulldog he had just bought in London.

When the bulldog got the scent of Astor's Airedale, it suddenly turned and sprang, breaking the banker's grip on its plaited leather leash. The two dogs went at each other while Madeleine Astor began screaming, "Kitty, Kitty! Stop them, someone!"

"A dog named Kitty deserves all it gets," murmured Gordon. "Six to four the bulldog tears it apart."

"Betting man, are you?" said Tarr, interested.

Two stewards materialized from nowhere at the sound of the growls and snarls. They tried to separate the fighting dogs, fencing at them with collapsed deck chairs. The two combatants bared their fangs at each other as they were led away to their respective kennels on F Deck. The *Titanic*'s canine quarters were located next to the third-class galley.

"Anything to liven up a dull crossing, Thaddeus. What do you say we have a little wager on the ship's daily mileage?"

"Sure, why not.'

"One hundred dollars too steep?"

"Jim," said Tarr in mock reproach. "Don't penny-ante me. Let's make it worthwhile. A thousand."

"If you insist. I'll even take your personal cheque."

Tarr laughed.

"Why, Thaddeus," said Cornelia. "That's the first time I've heard you laugh since we left New York. You were reading something in the *Times* about Mr. Morgan."

Tarr coughed and turned back to Gordon. "There's a proposition I'd like to put to you, Jim. Why don't we talk after dinner?"

"Fine," said Gordon. "So long as it's not Japanese bonds."

They watched the *Nomadic* draw away from the *Titanic*'s side and disappear into the dusk.

When Gordon had taken his leave, Tarr turned to Hislop and whispered, "Did you see anyone we know?"

Hislop shook his head.

"Make sure you check at Queenstown. Understood?"

From his station by the buffet Henry watched Tarr's party thread their way through the restaurant to the captain's table. He could tell from Nichole's expression that she would rather have been elsewhere. But she had made the effort to look her best. He had forgotten how long and white her neck was, accentuated by the upward sweep of her hair and the smooth, creamy slope of her shoulders.

Captain Smith rose from his chair to greet Thaddeus and Cornelia Tarr as they arrived. Henry noted that the captain wore his dress whites. Pinned above his heart were his transport medal and Royal Naval Reserve decoration. With his pointed white beard and weathered complexion, Captain Smith looked the very incarnation of Britannia's regime of the sea.

Henry and the other members of the dining-room staff knew Captain Smith did not enjoy these particular duties of his command, and invariably he cut them short. But this was his last trip before he retired at the age of fifty-nine, and he was determined to show the company flag.

Henry could hear Smith's ringing voice above the hum of conversations around him.

"Good evening, Mrs. Tarr, Mr. Tarr. Do sit down. And this must be your charming daughter. I don't believe I've had the pleasure."

Tarr introduced Rhonda, then Nichole and Hislop. Cornelia was shown to the captain's right. There were two vacant chairs at the table. Captain Smith looked inquiringly at the maître d'hôtel, who said in a lowered voice: "Colonel Astor sends his regrets, captain. Mrs. Astor was somewhat disquieted by the canine incident on deck."

"Ah," said Smith. "In that case, perhaps Miss Tarr would do me the honor of sitting on my left."

He held the chair for Rhonda, then lowered his bulk into the one next to her.

"A fine boat, captain," said Tarr.

"Yes, indeed. May I suggest a bottle of champagne? After all, this is a celebration."

Before anyone could refuse, Captain Smith had raised his finger and nodded to the maître d'.

"Have the wine waiter send over a bottle of the Boy, if you please, William."

On a Royal Crown Derby plate before each diner was a postcard-sized menu. It was dated and decorated across the top with an engraving of the *Titanic* flanked by the Union Jack and the Stars and Stripes rising into a starburst sky. Simple English fare was on the menu: roast beef and fowl and boiled vegetables. The only exotica was curried chicken included by a service cook to evoke memories of the Raj for ex-colonial administrators and army officers.

"Tell me, captain, how fast can this boat go?" Tarr inquired casually as he perused the menu.

"She could make twenty-three knots under full steam, Mr. Tarr. But I don't think we'll be taking her that high. Mr. Ismay, our president, would relish having the riband on our maiden voyage, but why rush?"

"The riband?" inquired Rhonda. "What's that?"

"The blue riband is given to the liner that makes the fastest crossing of the Atlantic, my dear. Currently, the *Mauretania* holds it. She was up to twenty-six knots when she broke the record on her last crossing four days ago. Cunarders are built for speed. We're built for pleasure."

"I like that," said Tarr.

"I'm told that the French are putting their newest liner, the *France,* through speed trials on Friday," continued the captain. "By all accounts she can steam more than twenty-seven knots. Personally, I'd rather get there without looking wind-swept." He gave the company a beaming smile.

"So, how many miles do you reckon you do in a day?" pressed Tarr.

"Odd," replied Smith. "Mr. James Gordon asked me the very same question on my way down from the bridge."

"You mean he went up to the bridge? You didn't tell him, did you?"

"I suspected that his interest was out of all proportion to the triviality of the information, Mr. Tarr. I suggested that he wait until tomorrow noon when we post the day's run in the smoking room."

"Quite right." Tarr nodded. "A mighty fine ship, yes, sir. Mighty fine. And it's given me an idea."

"What's that?" asked the captain politely.

"With the opening up of the Panama Canal there'll be new opportunities for trade with Japan and South America. Why, I could charter a ship like your *Titanic* here and use it as an exhibition of American industrial know-how. Take the best products we have to offer and sail them right around the world. One great floating trade ambassador for Uncle Sam. What d'you think of that?"

"Ah, here comes the champagne," said Captain Smith, glad of a diversion. "Thank you, Henry."

At the mention of the name, all eyes swivelled to watch the White Star Line's most accomplished sommelier approach the table with a silver bucket on a stand. Protruding from its icy water was a bottle of Bollinger.

Henry felt their communal gaze as he placed a tall, flute-shaped glass to the right of each setting.

"It must be twenty past. A sudden hush has fallen on the conversation," observed Smith.

Cornelia looked at her husband, but his eyes were fixed on Henry. He looked like a cat stalking a bird.

"Why, didn't you know," said Cornelia, brightly, "Henry used to be our butler in New York."

"Really, Mrs. Tarr!" Captain Smith looked at Henry with renewed interest. "What an extraordinary coincidence. Your loss is our gain."

"Thank you, captain," said Henry.

"I had to fire him," said Tarr. "For disloyalty."

Everyone at the table stiffened. Tarr and Henry stared furiously at each other. Captain Smith dabbed his lips with his napkin and cleared his throat.

"Well, he's a first-rate wine steward," said Smith. "I suppose the White Star Line owes you a debt of gratitude, Mr. Tarr."

Henry smiled. He avoided looking at Tarr by concentrating on the bottle of champagne he had to open. He peeled away the lead foil and worked the wire muzzle free. Taking the bottle from the bucket, he dried it on a cloth. Then, holding the cork firmly in his left hand, he began to twist the bottle away from it with his right. The cork came away with a lover's sigh.

"I thought he'd make it pop," said Rhonda, disappointed. "At our parties we always do."

Captain Smith sensed the change of mood at the table.

"Lethal weapon, champagne," he said to Rhonda. "When I was a young lieutenant, more years ago than I care to remember, I once saw two first officers settle a wardroom dispute with champagne bottles at twenty paces."

"What happened?" asked Rhonda, intrigued.

"One lost a front tooth and the other broke a finger slipping on the deck."

Nichole and Tarr were the only ones who did not laugh. The banker continued to glower at Henry as he moved around the table pouring glasses. As he leaned over to pour Nichole's glass, he felt the pressure of her knee against his leg. He glanced down, and he could see that she was holding a note in her fingers, out of sight below the level of the tablecloth.

Henry glanced furtively at Tarr. Their eyes met, and Henry saw that the volcanic anger of old threatened to erupt at any moment.

"Have you discovered our swimming pool yet?" inquired Captain Smith, turning to Rhonda. "You'll find it on F Deck, starboard. I do hope you brought your costume. It's worth a dip. The *Olympic* and the *Titanic* are the first liners ever to have pools, you know. Six feet deep, thirty-two feet long, thirteen feet wide. Wonders never cease."

Henry looked at the square of paper in Nichole's hand. She was staring fixedly at Captain Smith. He bent to receive it but suddenly the hand whisked away and disappeared inside an evening purse. Hislop was watching them.

The orchestra's music was barely audible above the hum of conversation and the clatter of knives on plates. Outside the moon shone onto an oily black sea.

"How come J.P. Morgan's not on board for the maiden voyage, captain?" asked Tarr. "Seeing as he owns the line."

"Yes," replied Smith. "A great pity. He would have added lustre to such a landmark occasion. If you'll pardon the pun."

Henry carried the bottle around the table a second time, but Nichole made no move to take her hand out of her purse. He slid the champagne back into the ice bucket and returned to his station.

As soon as he was out of earshot, Tarr leaned across the table to Captain Smith.

"I don't want to tell you how to run your ship, but I'm surprised you'd hire a man like Blexill. Did you not ask for references?"

"The White Star Line has a special department for the hiring of sea-going personnel, Mr. Tarr. I'm sure everything was very thorough."

"Well, that may be, captain, but I have information that Blexill bribed his way into the company."

Smith registered his surprise.

"May I ask, sir, how you came by this information?"

"As I told you, Blexill used to work for me. I hired him without references. A man in my position can't be too careful about disaffected employees. So I had my people keep an eye on him."

"If you have proof, Mr. Tarr, I will pass it on to the proper authorities."

Tarr nodded. "I'll have Hislop cable New York and have the documentation sent to the White Star office there."

Cornelia quaffed her champagne to cover her embarrassment.

Nichole rose to her feet.

"If you'll excuse me," she said.

Captain Smith stood.

"I'll join you," said Rhonda.

"Stop fidgeting, young lady," said Tarr.

Rhonda pulled a face and sank back into her chair.

"Allow me to escort you, Miss Linley. I must be getting back to the bridge. A captain's life is not all fine dining, you know."

"If you'll excuse me, Mrs. Tarr."

"Of course, captain." Cornelia smiled, fanning herself with her menu card.

"Do enjoy your dinner, and please feel free to order what you like."

Captain Smith offered his arm to Nichole, and they walked towards the door. Both Tarr and Hislop watched their progress.

They were not the only men in the dining room watching Nichole. Through the window in the pantry door Henry followed Nichole's movement through the dining room, willing her to look his way. At the door Captain Smith gave her a slight bow and stepped outside. Nichole hesitated, seemingly not knowing where she should go. Henry saw her walk up to Georgie Skinner, who stood by the buffet table. They exchanged a few words, and Georgie pointed in the direction of the ladies' room. Nichole appeared to drop her purse, and Georgie knelt with her to pick it up. When they came into view again Nichole turned and walked in the direction Georgie had pointed.

Henry picked up a tray and headed towards Georgie. The young steward was facing the wall. When Henry approached he started guiltily. In his hands was an opened note. Henry could see the neat block capitals.

"That's for me, isn't it?"

"Right you are, Mr. B."

"Don't give it to me here. I want you to put it in your pocket and go into the kitchen. I'll be there in a minute."

Henry shuffled the dishes on the buffet table. Fresh lobsters, potted shrimps, soused herrings, galantine of chicken, corned ox tongue, cold roast beef and Cumberland ham—hardly any of it eaten. The crew would be served the leftovers for lunch, and what they could not eat would be thrown to the fish and the sea gulls.

He glanced over at the captain's table. Nichole had not yet returned to her seat. Kirkbride, the chief steward, was topping up the champagne glasses.

Henry made his way into the kitchen. Georgie winked at him as he handed over the note.

"You really are an old dog, aren't you?"

"You had to read it, didn't you?"

"Course. It might 'ave been for me."

Henry opened the paper.

"Henry," it read, "we must talk. Meet me on the Promenade Deck at eleven tonight, by the first lifeboat on the port side. Please be there."

Wednesday, April 10, 1912

AFTER DINNER, TARR instructed Hislop to escort the ladies to their cabins, then join him in the smoking room, where he had arranged to meet Jim Gordon for brandy and cigars.

Rhonda protested, saying that she wanted to go dancing, but her father was adamant. "Not tonight."

The smoking room was situated directly above the first-class restaurant. A magnificent staircase surmounted by a large glass dome led up to it. Heavy oak panels carved with flowers suggested the style of William and Mary, but the solid balustrades were given a sense of lightness and space by the wrought-iron scroll work that supported them.

In the centre of the wall at the top of the stairs was a clock, which read ten o'clock.

Tarr opted to walk rather than to take one of the three elevators just forward of the staircase. He walked behind a group of men in black tie, so he would not present himself as a target.

The smoking room was panelled in mahogany lavishly inlaid with mother-of-pearl. Above the woodwork were stained-glass windows. Deep leather chairs were set around iron-legged tables. At one end of the room was an open fireplace. Above the marble mantelpiece hung a painting by Norman Wilkinson, entitled "The Approach to the New World."

The large room, blue with cigar smoke and loud with the laughter of men drinking brandy, looked like a London club. Jim Gordon waved to him as he entered, then picked up his cigar from the ashtray and signalled the steward to bring his drink to a corner table. Tarr ordered a brandy for himself and refused Gordon's proffered cigar case.

"These are the only kind I smoke," he said, taking one of his black monsters from his vest pocket.

He bit the end off and spat it out on the floor.

Gordon winced and drew his crossed ankles nearer to his chair. "Any news of the market today?" he asked.

"Should be coming over the wires soon."

"Amazing, this new telegraph business. You'd think we never left Wall Street. Might be worth investing in."

The two men puffed on their cigars. Gordon waited for Tarr to broach the subject.

"About that proposition, Jim. But first I need your word that what I tell you is strictly confidential."

Jim Gordon's eyes glistened with greed.

"My lips are sealed, Thaddeus."

Tarr looked around before continuing. He pulled his chair closer to Gordon.

"It's railroads, Jim."

"Railroads? Now come on, Thaddeus. You know Morgan's got them all sewn up."

"That's what everybody thinks. That's what he wants you to believe," said Tarr. "I happen to know that the government is interested in buying the Copper River and Northwestern lines from Morgan and Dan Guggenheim."

"The Alaska road into the Bering coalfield?"

"That's the one. So you see, things are shaking loose. You probably know that James Hill controls the Northern Pacific and the Great Northern. Well, he needs a terminus in Chicago to link them. So he wants to buy the Chicago-Burlington and Quincy lines. That's eight thousand miles of track."

"Where would that leave Ned Harriman and his Union Pacific?" asked Gordon.

"Exactly! Harriman needs the Chicago-Burlington or he can't expand. He approached the board, but they won't sell to him. That made him hopping mad. With the Chicago-Burlington, Hill can open up in the west and screw Harriman to the wall."

"Where do you come in on this?"

"I'll tell you. Harriman heard that the Chicago-Burlington directors had agreed to sell to Hill at two hundred dollars a share. Way over market value. He came to me three days before I sailed for England. He was spitting nails. I got the two of them to sit down. We don't need railroad wars, Jim. Community of interest. Harriman asked for a third share of the Chicago-Burlington, but Hill turned him down flat."

"What did Ned say? He's a hot-tempered cuss."

"You know Ned. He puffed out like a bullfrog. 'This is a hostile act, and you must take the consequences.' Then he slammed out."

"So where does he stand?"

Tarr beckoned Gordon closer. "Harriman's going to buy up Northern Pacific without Hill knowing. Take all the marbles."

"But he can't," whispered Gordon. "The shares aren't available."

"They damn well are. I reckon it'll cost him seventy-eight million. He's picking them off a bit at a time, like a mouse at the cheese. The funny thing is, as the stock rises, Hill sells more."

"And you're helping Ned?"

"Damn right. The shares are going to go through the roof."

"Where do I fit in?"

"There's still a large block of Chicago-Burlington shares outstanding."

"Who has them?"

Tarr looked around the room, then took a swig of brandy. "Morgan."

"How much has he got?"

"At current market value, about seventeen million dollars' worth. I need them, Jim. But I don't want to alert the old fox. You're on his U.S. Steel board. Talk to him. Get him to sell to you."

"Why don't you go to Morgan yourself?"

"Morgan and I—" Tarr began, but he stopped when he saw Hislop standing in the doorway of the smoking room, peering through the haze.

"Let's just say there's a commission if you get them for me."

"Commission?"

"One million dollars cash. Deal?"

Gordon sat for a moment, tapping his fingertips together. "Deal."

"Oh, and Jim, no end runs. If Ned Harriman fails, I'll know who to finger. I always get my way. Remember Brandon."

"How can I forget," said Gordon, and he blew hoops of smoke into the blue air.

Henry stood in the shadow of a lifeboat and consulted his watch. It was five past eleven. The air was chilly, and wisps of cloud floated across the moon like chiffon in the wind. The only sounds he could hear were the hum of the engines and the steady splash of the *Titanic*'s wake.

A barrier separated the first-class promenade, on the port side, from the officers' promenade, which ended at the bridge. There were lifeboats on davits beyond the barrier, and Henry wondered if Nichole had been confused about their meeting place.

Twenty feet away a couple leaned against the railing and looked at the stars.

"That's Cassiopeia," he heard the man say. "Mother of Andromeda. She boasted she was more beautiful than the sea nymphs. For that, Neptune punished her by turning her into a constellation. So you'd better watch out."

His companion uttered a laugh like a little silver bell. It sounded like Kittie's laugh.

The couple moved away at the sound of a door sliding open. Henry saw Nichole step onto the deck and look tentatively around. She held her arms across her chest against a sudden chill.

"Henry?" she called softly at the shadow beneath the lifeboat.

"Over here."

He watched her move quickly towards him. Before he could speak she had put her arms around his neck. He pushed her away, and she stood in front of him with her head lowered.

"I know. I deserve it."

"You called me a murderer. How could you do that?"

She looked up at him, her eyes full of shame.

"I didn't mean to. He made me. You know how he can be. He kept telling me it was you."

"But you know it couldn't be. I was with you that night."

"When that reporter came asking questions about you I just wanted to be rid of him."

"But you told him I was a murderer!"

"That's what Thaddeus told me to say."

"Where is he now?"

"He's in the smoking room with Hislop. He's forbidden me to talk to you. But I have to. Someone is trying to kill him."

"Who?"

"I don't know. We're surrounded by detectives all the time. Before we left New York, there was an accident in his private elevator at the office. I'm sure it was sabotage. He's blaming everybody. Even you."

Nichole raised her tear-stained face and looked into Henry's eyes.

"He never forgives. You'll never be safe from him, you know that, don't you?"

The thought came to him quite suddenly. Tarr had sent her to him to find out how much he knew. Perhaps his presence on board had been unsettling for Tarr. Maybe Tarr was as upset as Henry.

"I've made such a mess of my life," Nichole said. "What am I going to do?"

"You can start by telling me the truth."

She began to sob. "He'll kill me if he finds I've spoken to you."

"Why would he kill you? He gave you Cumerworth Hall," Henry said coldly.

Nichole pulled away from him. "How did you know that?"

"I made it my business to find out."

"He gave me the sanitorium, the building, but not the land it stands on. That still belongs to him. He can tear the building down whenever he wants, and I don't get a thing. All the proceeds are ploughed back into the business. It's like a trust fund I can't touch. Don't you see? That's how he binds you to him."

"Why did he give it to you?"

"So I'd be loyal to him."

"I don't believe you, Nichole."

"It's true. You know how he feels about loyalty."

"A man doesn't just give away a thirty-seven-room mansion. It's because of that night, isn't it? The night he found me in your bed."

Nichole said nothing. She stood in front of him, shoulders drooping, her hands by her sides.

"I saw you driving back that night. I saw Tarr in the passenger seat."

Nichole turned her head and looked out to sea. Tears were coursing down her cheeks.

"If I'm going to help you, you're going to have to tell me what happened, Nichole. You owe me that, at least."

She nodded, still gazing at the silver line of the horizon. "Yes," she murmured. "I'm sorry. I'm so sorry."

She began to sob again, and Henry put his arms around her. He could feel the soft flesh of her shoulders and smell the lavender fragrance of her hair. He waited until she was still again.

"That night," she began, "Thaddeus was entertaining in the gatehouse." A sudden shadow passed over them as the moon slid behind a cloud. Nichole shivered again.

"Go on," prompted Henry.

"I never saw who it was. I thought it was a woman, but it wasn't. It was a man."

"How do you know?"

"I saw the body. He made me help him dispose of it."

"What did he look like?"

"He was short, with ginger sideburns, in his late thirties, perhaps. Thaddeus wouldn't say who he was. But when we lifted him out of the car—" she shuddered at the memory, and Henry held her "—a leather notebook fell out of his pocket, a sort of diary. I saw the initials M.J.D. engraved in gold across the bottom corner. I also saw the corporate symbol of the House of Morgan."

The House of Morgan. M.J.D. The initials struck a chord in Henry's memory. The man must have been one of Morgan's employees. Where had Henry seen those initials before? He remembered the day the New York house was bombed. He had found Tarr's files strewn over the basement floor. One of them, he recalled, was about Morgan's staff. Inside had been information on Morgan's staff. Who was M.J.D.? Henry remembered one name— Dewey, Marsden J. Dewey. He had been one of Morgan's bookkeepers.

Why would Thaddeus Tarr have entertained Marsden J. Dewey? Why bring him all the way out to Westchester? Tarr easily could have contacted the bookkeeper in Manhattan, unless it was a meeting neither man wanted known. Tarr had entertained Dewey in the gatehouse, not in his country home, so no one would know, not even his wife.

But why would a bookkeeper accept an invitation from the business rival of his employer? Obviously, Marsden J. Dewey was not an unwilling accomplice. What would have lured him to Westchester? Tarr must have made it worth his while.

With a sudden flash of revelation, Henry understood what had transpired in the gatehouse that Friday night. He knew Tarr so well in all his bullying, cajoling moods that he had only to close his eyes to recreate the scene.

Tarr had ordered dinner for two at the gatehouse. A cold dinner. That suggested the banker did not know

when he and his guest would be dining. He would have
had to pick Dewey up at the station. They would have
driven in silence—Tarr never spoke when he drove. Dewey
would have felt uncomfortable and stared out the window
pretending to admire the scenery in the dark.

Tarr would pull the car up to the gatehouse and park so
Dewey could alight without being seen from the house.
The two men would have sat opposite each other, a blazing fire illuminating their profiles. Tarr would have talked
about inconsequential matters until he had opened the
champagne. Dewey would have felt awkward, ill at ease, a
perfect victim for the hectoring Thaddeus Nugent Tarr.

Henry closed his eyes and imagined the conversation
between the two men.

"I appreciate your coming out here at such short notice,
Mr. Dewey," said Tarr.

Both men held glasses of champagne.

"Thank you," said Marsden Dewey. "You've really got a
beautiful place here, sir."

"All it takes is hard work and the courage of your
convictions, Mr. Dewey." Tarr beamed. "How long have
you been with J.P. Morgan and Company?"

"Fifteen years, Mr. Tarr," replied Dewey with pride.

"Fifteen years. Now that's what I like. Someone who's
dependable. Happy there, are you?"

Dewey shrugged. "I guess so. I wouldn't mind a raise."
He squirmed and coughed and pulled at his sideburns,
which were thick and luxuriant.

"We can never have too much money, can we, Mr.
Dewey?"

"I guess not."

The bottle of champagne was empty. Tarr lifted the
Burgundy decanter and poured two glasses.

He held up his glass to his guest, who did likewise.
They both drank.

"Enjoying the wine, Mr. Dewey? Chambertin. Napoleon's favorite, my butler tells me."

"I once went to a fancy dress ball as Napoleon," ventured Dewey, in an attempt to hold up his end of the conversation.

"Did you now? Well, you got the build for it. But what was I saying? Oh, yes. Knowledge. Knowledge is power, Mr. Dewey. It allows you to act from a position of strength. Take Wall Street. The little investor from Hoboken, New Jersey, is never going to make a killing. Why? Because he doesn't understand what's going on. He doesn't have knowledge. He buys shares like he plays the ponies, from a position of ignorance. He doesn't know about interlocking directorships or voting trusts. The way the banks work. The men who run the great companies of this country have money because they understand what makes things tick. In other words, they have the knowledge."

Dewey nodded.

"Did you know that one hundred and eighty men representing eighteen financial institutions in New York, Boston and Chicago hold between us seven hundred and forty-six directorships in one hundred and thirty-four corporations with aggregate resources of more than twenty-five billion dollars? You're a figures man. You can see what that means."

Tarr picked up a leg of cold chicken and took a bite. He fixed Dewey with a mesmerising stare.

"You know, Mr. Dewey, I believe that you sincerely want to be rich. I can see that in a man. You'd like to have all this."

With a wave of his chicken leg he took in the gatehouse, the grounds and the castle.

"I guess you're right, Mr. Tarr." Dewey took a gulp of wine, uncertain of what was coming.

"How much do they pay you?"

"Eighteen hundred dollars a year, sir."

"What if I were to tell you that I could give you some information that could make that much for you in twenty-four hours? That much and more."

Marsden Dewey blinked. A vein in his forehead began to throb. Tarr leaned over and refilled his glass.

"Well, what do you say, fella?"

"Why would you do that, Mr. Tarr?"

"Because Marsden Dewey would like to be rich."

"But what would I have to do?"

"Just invest in a certain stock I tell you about. A com
pany I'm about to buy will be issuing its second-quarter
report next week. When it's released the shares are going
to go like a rocket—because I'm going to make sure they
do. You could be in and out the same day."

"I appreciate what you're saying, Mr. Tarr. But why
me?"

"Ah," said Tarr. "Because of your knowledge, Dewey,
your knowledge. I'm prepared to trade knowledge with
you. I can make you a rich man♦ My information for your
information."

"What information?"

"As J.P. Morgan's bookkeeper you see how the capital
flows. Where it goes. It would help me a great deal if I
knew how and when it was spent."

"You're asking me to tell you how the Morgan finances
are conducted."

"Don't get me wrong, Marsden. I know a lot about
Morgan and his operation. I have a file cabinet full of
information on his companies. We sit on the same boards.
We have mutual friends. But there are some things I'd
like to find out sooner rather than later."

"But I took an oath of confidentiality, Mr. Tarr."

"Let me give you a hypothetical case. On April 11,
Morgan bought ten million dollars' worth of three-year
five-per-cent notes on the Erie Railroad. Erie needed to
go double track. They needed funding. The directors secured a loan with sixteen million par value as collateral.
Ten million of this was in convertible bonds."

Dewey stared at him in disbelief. "How did you know?
That's still classified."

"The point is, I know. But if I knew in April rather than
May I could have acted accordingly. You see, you wouldn't
be giving away anything I couldn't find out by myself.
What d'you say?"

Dewey took a sip of port. He stood and walked to the fire, resting his elbow on the stone mantel.

"If Mr. Morgan found out he'd fire me."

"He doesn't have to find out. It'll be our secret."

"But my neck would be on the line, Mr. Tarr. I don't want the promise of money. Look what happened in 1907. I want greenbacks I can hold in my hand."

"You want cash."

"Yes. Fifty thousand dollars."

"You have an inflated idea of your worth, Dewey."

"You could make millions. I'm only asking for fifty thousand."

"What if I threw you out the door?"

"You wouldn't do that, Mr. Tarr. I'm sure J.P. Morgan would be more than willing to reward me."

At the mention of Morgan's name, Henry thought, something would snap in Tarr's mind. In Henry's imagination, Tarr propelled himself from the sofa, knocking over his glass of port. So sudden was the attack that the little accountant did not see the blow coming. He took Tarr's fist full in the face. The force of it knocked him sideways. He cowered, holding his broken nose.

"Mr. Morgan will hear about this. You can count on that." He made a move for the door.

"You snivelling son of a bitch," yelled Tarr. Henry envisioned the scene as he picked up the poker from the grate and struck Dewey across the forehead. The accountant fell heavily and hit the back of his head on an andiron.

Tarr stood over him.

"Get up, man. Get up, I tell you!"

But Dewey did not move. A pool of blood began to spread over the stones.

Tarr knelt and put his ear to Dewey's chest. Hearing nothing, he rose. Angrily, he plunged the poker into the fire. The iron hissed as the blood turned to steam.

Henry saw Tarr shut off all the lights, open the door and look outside. There was no one in sight. He went to the car, turned it around and backed it up to the door. Then he opened the trunk and deposited the lifeless body of

Marsden Dewey inside. Then he went to Nichole Linley's bedroom.

Henry looked up at the night sky. Stars like champagne bubbles dotted the black velvet canopy high above him. Yes, he thought, that was how it could have been.

He turned to Nichole. "What happened after he threw me out?"

Nichole leaned against the railings and rubbed her arms for warmth. She stood in silence, staring at the deck.

"Nichole, you must tell me."

With the toe of her silk shoe she toyed with a flattened cigarette butt, pushing it back and forth in a half circle.

"I asked him what was wrong. He said we were going for a drive, that's all he would tell me."

"What happened then?"

"He led me to the gatehouse. We didn't talk. He opened the door to the car and handed me the keys."

"You didn't go inside the gatehouse?"

"No. I asked him where we were going. He said Echo Bay. I used to take Rhonda there when she was a young girl. Why are we going there in the middle of the night, I said. There's been an accident, he said. A man is dead."

"Did he say how it happened?"

"No. He said the man kept badgering him for money. You should have heard his voice, Henry. It sounded as if it came from the other side of the grave."

"Go on."

"He told me the man had gone berserk, and he pushed him away. The man must have fallen and struck his head."

"Did he think of calling the police?"

"I don't remember."

"Try. You must try."

"I don't think so. 'I'm going to get rid of him,' he said. I remember that clearly. 'I'm going to get rid of him.' "

"But wasn't he worried about the man being reported missing?"

"Why are you asking me all these questions?"

"He could have said he had surprised a burglar. A rich man like him—the police would have believed him."

"He said the Hearst newspapers were just waiting for something like that. He kept repeating it. 'I'm going to get rid of him. And you're going to help me.' "

"Did you say no?"

"How could I say no to him? He grabbed my arm and pressed his fingers into my flesh until I almost fainted. His eyes were so full of hate."

"Where was the body while all this was going on?"

"In the trunk."

"Did you pass anyone on the road? Any other cars?"

"No. No one. He started talking very quickly in the car. He held onto the dashboard, and the words just came tumbling out."

"Is that when he gave you Cumerworth?"

"No, that was later. When we got past the village of New Rochelle he pointed to a break in the trees. There was a track at right angles to the road. He told me to turn down it. The car bumped over the ruts, sending the headlights bouncing through the forest. After what seemed to be a five-mile drive the track broadened into a clearing, and I could hear the sound of water lapping against a dock. He told me to stop the car and turn off the headlights."

"Would you be able to find the place again?"

"I think so. There was a wooden dock and at the end of it there was a rowboat. He took the keys from the ignition and walked to the back of the car, unlocked the trunk and called me. I saw the body of a man cramped into the trunk space. His knees were pulled up to his chest. There was blood around his nostrils and a gash on his forehead. His hair was matted with dried blood. His head was resting on the andirons from the fireplace."

"Was there a poker in the trunk?"

"Poker? No, I don't think so. I'd never seen a dead person before. His lips were blue in the moonlight. It was horrible. I started to cry, and Thaddeus slapped me."

"Then what?"

"We lifted him out of the trunk, and Thaddeus tied his legs together with rope. He knotted the andirons around his waist. Then we carried him to the rowboat. He was heavy."

"You said a book fell out of his pocket."

"I didn't see it at first. Not until Thaddeus had put the man's body in the boat. He told me to keep watch while he rowed into the sound. There was a heavy mist coming off the water about forty feet from the shore. Soon the rowboat disappeared and all I could hear was the noise of the oars. I waited for them to stop. Then I heard a splash, like a fish jumping. I couldn't take it anymore. I went to the car and sat on the running board. That was when I saw the notebook on the ground."

"You picked it up?"

"Yes. Then I heard the creak of the oars again and I saw the rowboat coming back through the mist. I slipped the notebook between the buttons of my dress."

"Did Tarr see you?"

"No. When he came back, he was as calm as if he'd just returned from a croquet match on the lawn. 'Now, my dear,' he said, 'we're going back to the gatehouse, to clean up.'"

"Did you see anyone on the way back?"

"No."

"What about the poker? Do you know what he did with the poker?"

"What poker?"

"The poker he hit the man with."

"He didn't hit him with a poker. He just punched him. It was an accident."

"Are you sure you didn't see a poker?"

"No. I told you."

So Tarr had convinced Nichole it was an accident. But if she was telling the truth, somebody still had the murder weapon. If it had been Tarr, he would have disposed of it in Echo Bay along with the body. Henry debated whether to tell Nichole what he knew, that he had been in the gatehouse that night and that he had not been alone. He decided against it. Why give her information she could pass on to Tarr?

Yet in spite of his caution, Henry experienced a rush of excitement. If Nichole's story was true, she had given him the weapons he needed to fight Tarr. The banker's threats would be meaningless if Henry could prove Tarr was a murderer. For all his money and power, he would be vulnerable at last.

To the blood of the Brandon miners Tarr had added that of an unknown man from the House of Morgan. But this time he had done the deed himself.

"I've been living with the memory of it ever since," Nichole continued. "For months after, every night I dreamed of the blood. I was afraid to fall asleep. I tried to push it out of my mind. I was so tired I couldn't think anymore. But when I saw you come into the cabin it all came rushing back."

She started to sob again.

"Why didn't you go to the police? Tell them he forced you to do it?"

"He gave me Cumerworth Hall. I'd never owned anything before. I thought it would help me forget. Then time went by, and it was too late."

"What about Morgan? You could have gone to Morgan. He would have done something."

Nichole turned away and stared at the ocean.

"If Thaddeus found out I'd gone to Morgan he would have killed me," she said. Her face was set. "You know his temper. I had no one to turn to."

Henry put his hands on her shoulders and looked into her face.

"In the morning I'll take you to the captain. You tell him what you've told me. He can telegraph Queenstown and have the police waiting at the dock."

"No! I beg you. You mustn't tell anyone. Not until New York. You must promise me. On your word of honor."

"But why, Nichole? He won't be able to hurt you."

"Promise me."

"Why are you trying to protect him?"

"I'm trying to protect myself."

"All right. We'll wait until New York. But on one condition. You give me the proof that he did it. The notebook."

The notebook would be the one piece of hard evidence that would convince McGillivray to publish the story. With Nichole's testimony and his own the police would have to arrest Tarr.

As these thoughts passed through Henry's mind he suddenly realized that he had overlooked a whole aspect of the situation. A man like Marsden Dewey, with obligations and business responsibilities, does not just disappear off the face of the earth. His family, his colleagues and his friends would make inquiries when he did not turn up for work. It would have come to Morgan's attention that a member of his staff was missing. Surely a man like Morgan would want to know what had happened to one of his bookkeepers. The police would have been informed. Or perhaps Morgan had Dewey's disappearance investigated by his own people.

Suppose Morgan had hired private detectives to find out what had happened to Dewey. If Dewey had confided in anyone that he was going to see Tarr that night, the detectives would make inquiries in Westchester. They would find out that Henry had left the estate in the middle of the night, that Tarr had fired him and he had fled the country. His fingerprints were on the murder weapon, and Nichole had blurted out under McGillivray's questioning that he was a murderer.

What if Morgan's investigators had begun to put the pieces together? Rattigan had said that someone was asking questions about him at the White Star Line offices. Morgan owned White Star. And Henry was positive he had been followed when he was in New York.

He had thought it was Tarr's Pinkertons keeping him under surveillance. But what if it was J.P. Morgan?

Only Nichole knew the truth. Who would believe her now?

Was Morgan above the law, too? If he had evidence, he would have had Henry arrested. Unless . . . unless he was trying to avoid a scandal. A man like Morgan would hire people to deal with the matter. *He would have me killed while he's a continent away,* Henry thought. And what better place for an assassination than aboard an ocean liner! A knife through the heart in the dead of night, then over the side with the body. It could be anyone—a crew member, a passenger. Henry had met men at sea who would filet their grandmothers for a fiver.

Henry could hear the blood rushing through his veins. The terror he had felt that night in Westchester returned. The only way he could protect himself was to expose Tarr as Marsden Dewey's murderer. He would have to get the evidence to McGillivray before he was killed.

"Nichole, you've got to give me the notebook. I'm in more danger than you—"

The door to the Promenade deck slid open, and a shaft of light emerged. Henry pulled Nichole deeper into the shadows.

"Where is the notebook?" he whispered.

"In my cabin, in the side pocket of my suitcase."

"Good. I want you to go down to your cabin and—"

Standing in front of them, hands on hips, smiling archly, was Rhonda.

Nichole turned on her in anger.

"What are you doing up here? You're meant to be in your cabin."

"The cabin's stuffy, so I went for a walk. You know, second class is much more fun than first, Henry. They're all such fuddy-duddies in their wing collars."

"How long have you been here?" he asked, concerned that Rhonda might have overheard their conversation.

"Am I eavesdropping on a lovers' rendezvous?" Rhonda asked, grinning.

Nichole, pale with anger, approached Rhonda as if she were about to strike her.

"If you hit me I'll tell Daddy." Rhonda stood her ground.

"What will you tell him?" Nichole asked.

"That you and Henry are having an affair."

"That's not true," said Henry.

"Who cares?" Rhonda shrugged.

"If you say one word to your father, I'll tell him about your abortion," Nichole threatened.

Henry looked at Nichole in amazement. Rhonda glowered at her, and with as much dignity as she could muster she tossed her head, turned on her heel and walked to the door.

"An abortion?" asked Henry.

"Why do you think Cornelia sent her away to private school?" Nichole replied. "Just another of the Tarr family's dirty little secrets."

Thursday, April 11, 1912

A TWO-MASTED FISHING trawler dipped its flag in salute as the *Titanic* steamed its stately way up St. George's Channel towards Queenstown harbor. Viewed from the liner's A Deck, the vessel looked like a tiny metronome in the rolling sea.

"Up here you'd never know there are waves, would you?" said Tarr to Cornelia.

Hislop sat next to them. Their deck chairs were placed out of the wind, in the shelter of a wall near the Verandah Café and the Palm Court, behind the smoking room.

Tarr took a deep breath of sea air. "I slept like a baby. How about you?"

"You know I never sleep well in a strange bed, Thaddeus. I don't know why you always ask me that," said Cornelia.

For ten seconds an alarm bell rang several decks below them.

Cornelia looked nervously around her, clutching the arms of her deck chair. "What was that?"

"Crew's emergency rehearsal. The captain told you about it at dinner. Don't worry. The *Titanic*'s unsinkable. Why do you think there are none of those damn lifeboat drills?"

Cornelia sighed and picked a book out of her voluminous handbag. She watched a young boy in an Eton collar spin a top on the deck. The motion of the toy made her giddy.

"What're you reading?"

She studied the cover.

"A novel by H.G. Wells. *Tono-Bungay*."

"*Tono-Bungay*. Sounds weird."

"*Vogue* wrote very highly of it," said Cornelia. "An Englishman. He's very clever."

"What's it about?"

"A man who makes a fortune from a quack remedy. In North Carolina we call them snake-oil salesmen. Daddy used to run them off the property with a shotgun. Only this one's British."

"He'd like to have run me off the property with a shotgun." Tarr laughed.

Cornelia smiled and said nothing.

"Good morning, Thaddeus. Mrs. Tarr." Jim Gordon raised his hat with a velvet-gloved hand.

"Morning, Jim."

Gordon consulted his pocket watch and said: "Almost noon, Thaddeus. They'll be posting the ship's run. I've written down my guess and sealed it in this envelope. Are we still on?"

Tarr squinted up at him.

"Sure. I'll write mine on the outside. Hislop here can be my witness."

Above them, on the second-class promenade, some passengers leaned against the railing searching for celebrities. To one side stood a man in a straw boater. He watched Tarr tap his teeth with a fountain pen.

A diminutive bellboy in a pillbox cap secured with a leather strap under his chin marched self-importantly along the deck calling, "Mr. Tarr, Mr. Thaddeus Tarr," in a high-pitched voice.

The man in the straw boater pulled back from the railing.

"Over here," called Tarr.

The boy came over and handed him a yellow envelope. "Marconigram, sir," he said and waited expectantly as Tarr ripped it open.

"Give him something, Hislop," said Tarr as his eyes scanned the message. He scowled as he read.

"Not bad news, I trust," said Gordon.

Georgie Skinner came rushing into the wine room where Henry sat waiting. "They're all up on A Deck, tucked into deck chairs like toad in the 'ole. 'Im and 'is missus and the skinny-lookin' geezer."

Georgie, to whom the pursuit of women, especially those out of his class, was the only game, had readily agreed to act as look-out for his friend. Henry could nip into the lady's cabin now for a "quickie."

Henry knocked quietly on Nichole's door.

"Who is it?"

"It's me. Henry."

He heard the key turn in the lock. He looked up and down the corridor, then entered the cabin quickly and closed the door behind him.

Nichole was perplexed.

"I can't find the notebook. I've searched everywhere."

"You said you put it in the side pocket of your case."

"It's not there."

"Are you sure you brought it with you?"

"Of course, I'm sure."

"Could it have fallen out of the suitcase?"

"Impossible."

She showed him the suitcase. The pocket had a strong elasticized top. She threw the empty case on the bed.

"It could only be Rhonda."

"Do you realize what that means?" asked Henry. "If she gives it to her father, he'll see you kept it to use against him."

Georgie Skinner had positioned himself at the pantry door opposite cabin B69. From his vantage point he had a clear view of both staircases, fore and aft. If Tarr or Hislop came, he would have time to alert Henry. The door to Nichole's cabin was about six feet from the main corridor.

First-class passenger Mrs. Nellie Snyder swished by him in an extravagant hat plumed with ostrich feathers. He smiled at her and sniffed the air for her perfume. She stopped ten feet away and turned.

"I say, steward. When do we arrive in Ireland?"

"Very soon, ma'am," replied Georgie.

She nodded and continued on her way. By eleven-thirty, the *Titanic* would be dropping anchor off Queenstown to take on more passengers and to receive mail.

"Steward, do you mind helping me with this door?"

The voice startled Georgie.

Rhonda Tarr stood outside cabin B57, jiggling the key in the lock. He looked apprehensively down the corridor towards Nichole's cabin, then approached Rhonda.

"It doesn't seem to want to open."

"Let me try, miss."

The lock clicked back the first time he turned the key. He opened the door and held it for her to enter.

"How clever of you! No, don't go. I need you to open my window."

She closed the cabin door behind her and watched as Georgie unhooked the catch and pushed back the square pane. He could see the green coast of Ireland.

"What's your name?"

"Georgie Skinner, miss."

"Georgie Skinner. I'm Rhonda Tarr. Now that we've been introduced, there's something I'd like to tell you. I think you have the sweetest eyes I've ever seen."

Georgie went as pink as the dress Rhonda was wearing.

"Do you think I'm attractive?" Rhonda asked.

"Yes, miss," stammered Georgie, not used to such aggressive young women. In his limited experience it was the older, married ones who came into heat when they smelled the salt sea air.

"Do you know how to do the turkey trot?"

"Beg your pardon, miss?"

"The turkey trot. It's a new dance. It's all the rage in New York. I'll teach it to you."

"But there's no music."

"That's all right, I'll hum. Give me your hand. Now, put your other hand on my shoulder. Like that. Good."

Georgie Skinner liked the feel of her silk dress. Rhonda began to hum, and to bounce up and down to her own rhythm.

"Come on. Listen to the beat."

He tried to match her movements but he felt clumsy and ill at ease.

"You're not a very good dancer, are you, Georgie Skinner? What are you good at?"

She gazed at him provocatively, still holding his hand.

"That depends on what you mean, miss."

"And don't call me miss if you're going to kiss me. You were going to kiss me, weren't you? Without your cap."

Georgie took off his cap and moved closer to her. Rhonda closed her eyes demurely and waited. He placed his arms around her shoulders and leaned forward at the waist. His lips touched hers, and at their contact she moved closer to him. She pressed her tongue into his mouth and rotated it around his.

"Blimey!" said Georgie, breaking for air. "You're a right little firework, aren't you?"

Rhonda giggled and kissed him again.

"I hear bells. Do you hear bells, Georgie Skinner?"

"Bells. Yeah. That's our call. All hands. I've got to go, miss. Maybe we can, sort of . . ."

"You bet. Maybe the trip won't be so boring after all," said Rhonda.

When Henry left Nichole's cabin he looked up and down the corridor for Georgie, to give him the all-clear. But the young steward was nowhere to be seen. Henry frowned, irritated.

He made his way quickly to the restaurant and sat in the wine room to think. His immediate concern was to find the missing notebook. Without it he had nothing to give McGillivray. If Nichole was right and Rhonda had taken it, she must have it hidden somewhere in her cabin. The only person who could look for it without arousing suspicion was Kittie.

He raced down to E Deck to find her. She was preparing a room for the arrival of some new passengers. With all the movement on board, she would not be missed.

"Can't keep away from me, can you?" She laughed.

But the smile faded when she saw the concern in hi
eyes. She led him into the linen closet and they kisse
quickly.

"I need your help, Kittie. Please don't ask me what it'
about. I promise I'll tell you everything when we reac
New York."

Kittie began to fiddle nervously with the key chain tha
hung from the belt of her uniform.

"It's about Nichole, isn't it?"

Henry nodded. Her intuition never ceased to amaz
him.

Kittie backed away from him and busied herself with
brushing imaginary wrinkles out of a pile of sheets.

"You've been seeing 'er, then. Quite like old times, i
it?"

Henry frowned. He had not experienced jealousy from
Kittie before.

"It isn't what you're thinking."

"Why can't you tell me, then?"

"I don't want to put you in any danger."

"Danger! I'll give you danger. So, what did you talk
about?"

"Things in the past."

"Where? In 'er cabin?"

"Yes, in her cabin. Will you lower your voice?"

"Did you kiss 'er?"

"For God's sake, Kittie, no! Last night on deck she told
me about something that happened when I was working
for Tarr. This morning I went to her cabin."

"So, you've seen 'er twice. You don't waste any time, do
you?"

Exasperated, Henry grabbed her shoulders.

"Now listen to me. You can think what you want, but
there's nothing going on between Nichole and me. That's
finished. She told me something about Tarr last night but
I have to have proof. Her life and my life may depend
upon it."

"And what about our lives, 'Enry? Why are you gettin
involved with the likes of 'er again?"

"Because if I can find what I'm looking for I won't ever have to hide from Tarr again. He won't be able to touch me."

Kittie looked at him. There were tears in her eyes. Whenever he spoke of Tarr, his face hardened and the bones in his jaw stood out.

"But why does it 'ave to be you? Why can't she go to the captain?"

"Because I was there, and the captain wasn't. Please, Kittie, you have to trust me. If you love me, you must do this for me."

"What do you want me to do?"

"Search a cabin in first class. Pretend you're making the bed or changing sheets and towels, anything. I have to find a leather notebook with the initials M.J.D. in one corner. It's been stolen."

"And if I find it, what then?"

"Bring it to me."

"So you'd make a thief of me, too, would you, 'Enry Blexill?" She placed her hands on her hips and looked scornfully at him.

"Please, Kittie."

"Ever since you told me she was on board I knew she'd make trouble between us."

Tarr excused himself from Cornelia and took Jim Gordon by the arm. He lead him towards a sliding door, the entrance to the Verandah Café. As he passed Hislop, Tarr moved away from Gordon momentarily.

"Keep an eye out for the boarding passengers. Macklin is an Irish name," he whispered.

"Yes, sir."

"And by the way, Hislop, have you been in touch with New York about Blexill?"

"Not yet, but it's on my list, sir."

"Well, get to it," said Tarr sharply, and he turned to Gordon.

The two men sat at a table set for lunch.

"Jim. How long have we known each other?"

The banker pulled at the knees of his trousers and dusted his spats with his gloves.

"Nine, ten years?"

"You've done pretty well by me in the past, I'd say."

"Yes. And I'm grateful."

"I've put you on a couple of my boards. I've always been square with you, right?"

"Yes."

"Well, now I got a problem," said Tarr. "And I need your advice."

"I'm listening, Thaddeus."

"That cable I just got. It was from Washington. It says I'm directed to appear before the Stanley Committee of the Commission of Labor as soon as I can. It was signed by Stanley himself and by Champ Clark, Speaker of the House. What the hell do you make of that?"

"Stanley's committee is looking into conditions among steel workers. It's Vice President Sherman's pet project," Gordon replied.

"God damn Sherman and his anti-trust laws. Hasn't he caused us enough trouble? What do you figure they want?"

"Your guess is as good as mine, Thaddeus. But given the political climate I'd say they want to reopen the files on Brandon."

"Brandon is a dead issue. It's settled. We haven't had any more trouble there."

"But you know, from going to the Steel Trust inquiry last year, that the boys on the Hill are trying to make political capital out of it. There's a new mood in Washington. The social sap is stirring. Labor is flexing its muscles."

"It's that son of a bitch Taft trying to out-Roosevelt Roosevelt."

"He's just taking up where the colonel left off," said Gordon. "Forty-five anti-trust suits since he's been in office. Nearly twice as many as T.R."

"But why now? He's in the middle of a presidential race, Jim."

"He needs headlines, Thaddeus. He wants his name in front of the people. I hear he's running behind Roosevelt in Pennsylvania. The miners are all for Teddy. Taft needs something to swing them before Sunday's primary. You know Andrew's already declared for him."

"Carnegie's just doing it to spite Roosevelt. He'd climb into bed with Woodrow Wilson before he'd give Roosevelt the time of day."

"Yes, T.R. really took us all," said Gordon, laughing. "Coming cap in hand to Wall Street to finance his 1904 campaign, then treating us like lepers."

"You don't have to remind me."

"Andrew never forgave him for taking our money then denouncing us. Nor did Morgan. You remember at the end of his second term, when T.R. went off to Africa to hunt big game? Morgan said to me, 'I hope the first lion he meets does his duty.' "

Tarr was in no mood for anecdotes. "But who's behind this steel workers' investigation, Jim? Who's snooping around?"

"Some sociologist out of Pittsburgh, I understand. His name is John Fitch."

"Can he be bought?"

"I doubt it. He seems to be very well funded."

"Where's the money coming from?"

"The Russell Sage Foundation. Did you know Russell? His wife is very involved in philanthropies. Even gives to Jewish charities, I'm told."

"Who's the treasurer?"

"You mean who dispenses the money?"

"Yes."

"Didn't you know? J.P. Morgan."

Tarr breathed heavily through his moustache. "I might have guessed," he said, almost to himself.

"It's just a thought, Thaddeus, but there is a way you could head them off," Gordon offered.

"How?"

"Pull the rug from under the committee's feet. Before they ask you to testify, tell them you're going to make a gift of the Brandon mines to the American people. A foundation to be set up under federal auspices. The proceeds to go to the education of indigent miners' children, or some such. You'd be a hero, Thaddeus. And think of the tax implications. How much is Brandon worth? Seventy-five? A hundred?"

Tarr listened to the banker in horror.

"Are you crazy? Give away Brandon?"

"The grand gesture, Thaddeus. That's what the people expect from us. Look at Rockefeller. The old miser's everyone's favorite grandfather now. You don't really want them looking under the rocks at Brandon, do you?"

Tarr brought his fist down heavily on the table, causing the vase of tiny pink carnations to topple over. It rolled onto the floor, leaving a pool of water to seep into the tablecloth.

"I will not give up Brandon just to cosy up to a bunch of lily-livered socialists."

"You asked my advice." Gordon shrugged.

"I'm sorry, Jim. I didn't mean to get mad at you. It's just that things are going sour for me at the moment. You've probably seen the tapes. There's been a run on Tarr Investments stock. That's my holding company for the Jersey Central railroad."

"Is Brandon in there, too?"

"Of course it's in there, too. What the hell's that got to do with it?"

"How bad are you bleeding?"

"Plenty. Stock's down fifty-five points overnight. Something's going on. The rest of the market's like a mill pond. Somebody's put the word out to dump."

"Any idea who?"

"I've got my suspicions. It's no coincidence about this committee and the run on my stock. I'm not going to roll over and play dead, Jim. I'm going to fight. But first I have to protect myself. I need capital. I gotta buy up everything. If my stocks don't hold their value now, everything I own is just paper."

"What are you saying, Thaddeus?"

"This investigation could ruin me, Jim. Thirty years of sweat and blood down the drain."

"Maybe it's just a correction."

"Fifty-five points is not a correction!"

"All right. I'm listening."

"There are sixty million dollars' worth of Tarr Investments shares out there, Jim. Twenty are institutional, large blocks. They're the ones that were dumped. That tells me someone big is poisoning my well. It could be Hill, or it could be Morgan and his cronies. The point is I need a line of credit so I can buy up anything that hits the market."

"In round figures, Thaddeus."

"Forty-five, Jim."

Gordon whistled.

"You could organize a syndicate. I could secure the loan, god damn it. Hell, Brandon alone is worth twice that."

"Since the strike, no insurance company will touch Brandon stock."

"For Christ's sake, Jim, my name should be good enough. You know what I'm worth."

"I'll see what I can do when we get to New York."

"Today, Jim! By the time we get to New York, it may be too late. Cable your people. Look, if First City and you guys and maybe Chase split it three ways, with that kind of backing it would show confidence. I could turn it around."

"Sounds like someone found out what you're doing with Harriman and the Northern Pacific," said Gordon laconically. He noticed beads of perspiration forming on Tarr's forehead. "You have to ask yourself why there are no takers."

"Because some son of a bitch is sniffing through garbage cans and bad mouthing me on the Street."

Gordon gave a little laugh.

"What the hell's so funny?"

"I was just thinking. Community of interest doesn't account for a hill of beans when it comes down to railway ties."

"Are you going to help me or not, Jim?"

The wicker chair creaked as Gordon shifted his weight uneasily.

"If Morgan and Hill are behind this little adventure, you're not going to get Stillman at First City to come in. And if First City stands pat, Chase will do the same. I can't guarantee forty-five million, Thaddeus. I'd be too exposed. You find me two other banks, and I'll consider it. Okay?" He rose from the chair.

Tarr stood up, too, and held Jim by the lapel of his frock coat.

"You can telegraph them. Do it for me, Jim. You know I'm good for it."

"It would be easier to do over lunch at the Union Club," Gordon said, knowing that Tarr's application for membership had not been approved. Gordon heard the desperation in Tarr's voice. He enjoyed watching the banker squirm and wondered how far he would go.

"It'll be too late," pleaded Tarr. "Please, Jim. I've never asked you for anything before."

"All right. I'll cable my bank and ask the directors to see what they can do."

Tarr heaved a sigh of relief. "Thank you, Jim. I take that as an act of friendship. I won't forget it. By the way, don't mention any of this in front of Cornelia, okay? I don't want her to worry."

"My lips are sealed. But a word to the wise on this steel commission. I'd distance yourself from Brandon. If you don't want to get rid of it, my advice is to resign as chairman."

Tarr glowered at him.

"Just a thought, Thaddeus, just a thought."

Cornelia Tarr stood at the railing and watched the tenders nudging towards the hull of the *Titanic*. They looked like herrings rubbing up against a whale. A cool breeze gusted from the land, and she pulled her shawl more tightly around her shoulders. Hislop stood next to her, his eyes tearing in the wind as he studied the faces of the men boarding the liner.

Cornelia's eyes were fixed on the shore and the green hills that rose behind it.

"Did I ever tell you that my great-great-grandfather came from Ireland?" she said. "His people settled there with William of Orange. I have his diary at home. He married a Cabot girl in Washington. Louise Amanda, named for her aunt, who set fire to the governor's mansion during the Civil War. They had seven children. Five of them died."

She could see the faces of the Irish immigrants, who wore rough tweeds and soft hats. They were waving, excited, apprehensive, expecting a smile of welcome in return. Cornelia backed away from the railing. The ship's strident whistle made her jump.

"Must they do that? It's so hard on the ears."

Wafting up from the third-class stern deck, Cornelia and Hislop could hear the sound of the Uilleann pipes. Someone was playing "Erin's Lament." The keening melody expressed the pain and sadness of a man leaving his homeland, perhaps forever. Passengers on the first-class deck stopped to listen to the haunting, nasal whine of the pipes, moved by the sweet torment of the notes.

The sound agitated Cornelia, reverberating within her like harp strings plucked by the wind. In the core of the sound she heard intimations of disaster. She covered her ears with her hands.

People around her began pointing up at the fourth funnel, which towered above them. She looked up. At the top, gazing down, was the blackened face of a man. A stoker from the boiler room had climbed the inside of the ventilation shaft for a breath of fresh air. Cornelia, enervated by the music and the gull-like scream of the ship's whistle, read an unmistakable message of death in the man's black face. Uttering a rattling moan, she fainted.

Thursday, April 11, 1912

AS THE PASSENGERS streamed on board Henry stood at the end of the corridor that led to Rhonda's cabin. The confusion would make Kittie's job easier, he thought, but it would be prudent to keep watch in case Rhonda should return. He pressed himself against the wall when he saw Thaddeus Tarr coming down the main staircase towards the inquiry office. In his hand Tarr held a sheaf of telegraph forms.

Henry watched as Tarr instructed the clerk on duty. He lost sight of the banker as the crowd grew, thronging in happy groups around the vestibule of the first-class entrance. A man with a large camera passed him, craning his neck, obviously in search of someone. Protruding from his jacket pocket Henry recognized a folded copy of the *New York Times*.

"How do they expect us to find him in this crush?" Henry heard the man say to a colleague.

The accent was American.

Henry stepped forward. "Excuse me. Are you gentlemen from the *New York Times?*"

"That's right. We're looking for Thaddeus Tarr. Do you know where we can find him?"

Henry thought quickly. If they worked for the *Times* they could pass the word to McGillivray that he would soon have the evidence he needed. McGillivray could start making inquiries about Dewey. He could have the

Sound dragged for the body. Henry wondered where he could find a quiet corner to talk to them away from Tarr.

"I believe he's in the bar. If you two gentlemen would like to follow me."

As Henry began to move towards the staircase, Tarr turned from the counter and pressed his way through the crowd straight towards the two reporters.

"Say, isn't that him?" said the photographer. "Mr. Tarr!"

The banker stopped at the sound of his name. He looked into the faces of the two men, then at Henry.

"*New York Times,* sir," said the second man.

Tarr looked suspiciously at Henry.

"Did you speak to this man about me?" he demanded of the reporters.

"No, sir," they answered.

"All right then. What do you want?"

"The financial pages want an interview. I wonder if we could have a few minutes of your time?"

A smile began to spread across Tarr's sullen features.

"Of course, gentlemen. Would you like a drink?"

Henry watched Tarr steer the two reporters away from him. He swore softly.

"Blexill!"

He turned to find Chief Steward Kirkbride standing behind him.

"Get back in the restaurant where you belong."

Kittie searched through Rhonda's cabin, but it was Nichole she was thinking about. She had never seen the woman, and Henry had only described her as Rhonda's chaperone. She had vivid mental pictures of Tarr, Cornelia, Rhonda and Hislop. She could have picked them out of a crowd anywhere the way Henry had described them. But he hardly ever mentioned Nichole, and when he did he gave few details. This very reticence confirmed her suspicion that Henry had been in love with the woman. And, for all his denials, she sensed he was still in love with her.

Whenever she had questioned Henry about Nichole he had been evasive. Kittie knew Nichole must be beautiful.

Rich men's mistresses were never ugly, even if their wives were.

If it were Nichole's belongings she had been searching through, rather than Rhonda's, Kittie might learn more about her. Better still, she would like to talk to the woman. She had to know whom she was competing against for Henry's love.

For Kittie had realized that she was in love with Henry. Ever since she had run off to sea at the age of fifteen to escape a brutal, drunken father, there had been men in her life. She had no defences against them when they grabbed her—she could only deny them her lips. She vowed she would never allow anyone to kiss her save the man she would marry. And she had kissed Henry when he had given her the shawl he had bought for her in London.

He was different from the other men she had known. He was caring and gentle. He listened to her as she rattled on about everything under the sun. But he gave little away. She had to squeeze information out of him. She had teased him into telling her what he had discovered in London, that Nichole now owned the great house where he used to be in service. She must be a wealthy, beautiful woman who could get any man she wanted.

Kittie's eyes smarted with tears as she ran her fingers through the drawers of Rhonda's wardrobe trunk.

The notebook wasn't there.

She lifted the mattress from the bunk and felt underneath. She rummaged through the pockets of Rhonda's clothes; she looked in the night robe hanging behind the bathroom door.

Nothing.

She searched everywhere for the notebook. She desperately wanted to find it for him. She had never given Henry anything, other than her heart. And she was fearful of telling him that he possessed that, in case she lost him.

The notebook was nowhere in Rhonda's cabin. Henry had said that if it wasn't there, Rhonda might have hidden it in Tarr's suite.

Kittie closed Rhonda's door behind her and made her way up the corridor to Tarr's stateroom. She knocked softly. When she got no reply she opened the door with her passkey and slipped inside. It was the first time she had seen the suite, and she let out an involuntary sigh of wonder at the sheer opulence of the decor.

She moved around the sitting room, running her fingers over the perfect satin finish of the settee and the heavy velvet of the curtains. How fine everything was. If only she and Henry could have a room like this. She wanted a white marble fireplace just like the one in the suite, with a bevelled mirror above it and wall sconces with pretty shell-shaped lampshades.

"The notebook," she said to remind herself why she was there. She could feel her heart beating under the starched white apron of her uniform.

She looked around and spotted a small writing desk in the corner. She crossed over to it and was rummaging through the centre drawer when she heard a key slide into the lock. She froze, turning her head towards the sound. The door flew open and she saw a man she recognized as Mr. Hislop carrying a woman across the threshold. It must be Mrs. Tarr. Henry said she always wore a hat that looked like a turban.

"Oh, my Lord," she said.

Hislop stopped short when he caught sight of her. He looked more perplexed than suspicious.

"Wait," he said as he carried the woman to the settee and laid her down gently. The woman's eyes were glazed, and the faintest smile played about her lips.

"What are you doing here?"

"I was just checking to see if you 'ad enough stationery, sir," mumbled Kittie.

"I know you," said Hislop, pointing a finger at her. "You were downstairs. What's your name."

"Kittie, sir."

"Kittie what?"

"Kittie Boyer."

A moan emitted from the settee as Cornelia tried to raise herself to an upright position.

"Can I be of assistance, ma'am?" asked Kittie, taking advantage of Hislop's shift of attention.

"A little cognac," whispered Cornelia in a strangled voice.

Kittie looked at Hislop, who nodded towards the fresh bottle on the table.

She poured a measure and handed it to Cornelia, then watched as the woman took the glass as if she had been offered the nectar of the gods. She raised it to her lips and tilted it back until there was no more amber liquid left.

"That will be all," said Hislop.

Thankful to be dismissed, Kittie curtsied and made a hasty exit.

Outside the cabin she inflated her cheeks and opened her eyes wide, a comical expression of relief she had used since she was a girl. She placed her right hand on her heart to feel its pounding.

"So don't believe rumors, gentlemen. I'm as solid as the Rock of Gibraltar, as you can see." Tarr patted his stomach and smiled benignly. The two *New York Times* reporters sipped their bourbon.

"Tarr Investments shares are down significantly," said one, flicking through his note pad. The other set his camera on its tripod and lined Tarr up in his viewfinder. "Why do you think that is?" he asked Tarr.

"A technical adjustment. A question of liquidity at the moment, son. A lot of my resources are concentrated elsewhere."

"The word on Wall Street is that your directors want you removed from the board."

"That's a lot of hogwash. You should stick to reading your own newspaper and forget the lies Hearst prints."

"They say it dates back to the Brandon mines incident," pressed the journalist, undeterred by Tarr's blustering irritation. "Would you care to enlarge on that?"

"Look here. I'm sailing on the biggest ship in the world,

a marvel of British engineering and American money. Let me enjoy the trip. Come and see me in New York. You can meet the board. Then tell me who's in control."

"Is that all you have to say?"

"I know you guys have a living to make, so I'll tell you one thing. Jim Gordon at First City is organizing a forty-five-million-dollar line of standby credit. So you can see, gentlemen, I've got no worries. Rock of Gibraltar." He held up his bourbon.

"If you really want something to print, you can tell your readers I'm making a campaign contribution of a hundred thousand dollars to the next president of the United States, Theodore Roosevelt. You watch him walk away with Illinois."

Ever since his conversation with Jim Gordon, the idea that President Taft was working hand in glove with Morgan to destroy him had begun to fester in Tarr's mind. If Roosevelt were to defeat Taft—the colonel had turned on his former friend and secretary of war with alarming venom—then a grateful T.R. would repay the favor by calling off Sherman's watchdogs. There would be no inquiry into the Brandon incident.

None of the other Wall Street bankers would give Roosevelt a penny of financial backing because of his record. Tarr would be the only one.

"Now drink up, boys. Since I'm in such a good mood, I'll put a little something your way. Buy Northern Pacific. The shares are going to zoom. But keep it to yourselves, okay?"

From the corner of his eye he saw Nichole enter the bar and move purposefully towards him. He finished his bourbon in one gulp.

"That's all the time I have, gentlemen."

Nichole approached and spoke to him discreetly.

"I'm sorry to disturb you, Mr. Tarr. But it's Mrs. Tarr." She lowered her voice to whisper. "She fainted on the deck, and Mr. Hislop had to carry her to her cabin. She's asking for you."

"Northern Pacific," he said to the two reporters, shaking their hands as he left, "and it was Thaddeus Nugent Tarr who told you."

When he was out of earshot, he turned to Nichole.

"It's the cursed booze," he said. "Have you been feeding her brandy again?"

Before she could reply he strode towards the staircase.

When he entered the cabin with Nichole a few steps behind him, Cornelia was weeping convulsively. Tears had gouged deep tracks through the powder on her cheeks. A solicitous Hislop sat next to her stroking her hand. At the sight of her husband, Cornelia gasped for breath.

"Oh, Thaddeus, I want to get off this dreadful ship. We must all get off."

Tarr looked balefully at her, then at Nichole, then at Hislop. With an inclination of his head he told them both to leave.

At the door Hislop whispered to him, "There was a stewardess in here going through—"

"Not now," said Tarr.

When he was alone with his wife, Tarr sat on the settee with her and put his arms around her.

"In four days we'll be home, Cornelia. Everything's going to be all right."

He could feel her trembling. She seemed so frail and vulnerable, a frightened bird fallen from the nest.

"There's death on this ship, Thaddeus. I saw it. Please, let's get off while there's still time. We can take another ship, any one, but not this one."

"What are you talking about?"

"I heard it in the music. And I saw it. A face. A horrible black face coming out of the funnel."

"How much of that stuff have you been drinking? Look at me, Cornelia." Tarr held her at arms' length. She pressed her chin into her right shoulder, and her eyelids fluttered.

"Don't shout at me. Please don't shout at me. I don't want you to die. Rhonda? Where's Rhonda?"

"Nobody's going to die. This is the safest ship that ever floated. You heard what Captain Smith said at dinner. You know who else is on board. You don't think they'd be here if there was any danger. Men like Astor, Guggenheim, Vanderbilt, Sir Cosmo What's-his-name. Even Ismay, chairman of the line."

But Cornelia would not be pacified. She began to sob uncontrollably again.

"Listen to me." Tarr rubbed her back gently as he spoke. "I gotta get back to New York as fast as I can. I can't hole up in Ireland and wait for the next boat. There are too many things happening. I have to be back in the city. Everything I've ever worked for is tied up in this."

Cornelia turned away from him.

"I've never burdened you with my business problems before, sweetheart, but this is something I have to do."

Cornelia continued to weep. Her chest heaved, and she appeared to be having difficulty breathing.

"For God's sake, don't work yourself into one of your states," said Tarr. Exasperated, he crossed to the telephone and asked the operator to put him through to Captain Smith.

"I'm sorry, sir. Passengers cannot be connected to the bridge."

"If Captain Smith is not in my cabin in five minutes, none of my employees will ever take a White Star liner again. Do I make myself clear?" roared Tarr.

By the time the captain arrived, Tarr had succeeded in pacifying Cornelia.

"I'm sorry to get you down here, captain. But my wife . . . you have to talk to her. She wants to get off the boat."

"May I?" asked Smith, indicating the seat next to Cornelia.

Tarr nodded. The captain settled himself beside her and took her hand in his.

"Dear lady, I've been to sea for nearly forty-seven years. When anyone has asked how I can best describe my experiences, I say, uneventful. Of course, there have been winter gales and storms and fogs and the like, but in all my experience, I have never been in an accident of any sort worth speaking about. There was one minor contretemps with the *Olympic*, but we had hardly left port. I have seen but one vessel in distress in all my years at sea. The crew was taken off in a small boat. I never saw a wreck and never have been wrecked, nor was I ever in any predicament that threatened to end in disaster of any sort."

"Your hear that, Cornelia?" asked Tarr.

Cornelia made no reply. Captain Smith looked at Tarr, who nodded, encouraging him to continue.

"I wish I had a guinea for every time I've sailed the Atlantic," he said. "But you know, my dear lady, this is to be my last voyage. I'm retiring when I return to Southampton. The old salt home from the sea to tend his hollyhocks and roses. The old sea dog putting down land legs at last. I have a wife and a twelve-year-old daughter waiting for me. When a man has a child late in his life the time he has to spend with her is all the more precious. So you see, it's important to me to bring this great ship home in one piece. It would never do to blot my copybook on my last crossing, now, would it? After the *Titanic*, the sea holds no more challenges for me."

But Cornelia was not listening to him. She was staring at the clock on the mantel, crooning softly to herself. She did not even notice when Captain Smith rose to leave.

"Maybe the doctor can give her something," said Tarr at the door.

Cornelia began to cry when Captain Smith left. "Where is my daughter?" she asked plaintively.

"Easy now," said Tarr. "I'll find her. You just lie back and relax."

He kissed her on the forehead. Her skin was the color of the moon, and cold as marble.

"It wasn't there," said Kittie. "I looked all through her cabin."

Henry lowered a bottle of Clos de Charlemagne 1900

into an ice bucket. They were standing in the wine room, adjacent to the first-class restaurant.

What if she had given it to her father already? The consequences didn't bear thinking about. Kittie seemed to read his mind.

"So I thought maybe it was in 'er dad's cabin."

"You went in there?"

"Yes, but I didn't get much of a chance to look, because your Mr. 'Islop comes in carrying Mrs. Tarr."

"Carrying her?"

"Like a bride over the threshold, only she was all glassy eyed."

"He caught you looking?"

"Was I frightened. What're you doing 'ere? he said. Checking to see you've got enough stationery, says I!"

"Do you think he believed you?"

" 'E asked my name. He recognized me from yesterday when 'e came down to second class. You don't think 'e's going to report me, do you?"

Henry took both her hands in his.

"Kittie, I want you to promise me something. If anything should happen to me, I want you to contact a man called McGillivray who works for the New York Times. He's a reporter. Have you got that?"

"What do you mean, if anything 'appens to you?"

"Remember the name, McGillivray. Promise me. Tell him everything you know, everything you saw."

"I would if I knew what was going on. Why won't you tell me?"

"I will. I promise. When I have to. In the meantime, be careful. Watch out for Kirkbride."

As soon as her husband had left the room, Cornelia reached for the cognac bottle. Unable to find a glass, she removed the cork and put the bottle to her lips. The warming spirit calmed her nerves, and she steadied herself by holding on to the back of the settee. The *Titanic*'s engines had started again. She could feel the vibration through the soles of her feet. Outside the window the Irish coast began to move slowly away.

There was no escape now.

The pearls at her throat were choking her. She pulled at the catch, but it would not open. Feverishly, she tugged again and the string broke, sending a cascade of pearls bouncing like hail on the polished tabletop. Cornelia fell to her knees and buried her face in her hands.

It was in this position that Rhonda found her mother when she entered the sitting room.

"I'll pick them up, Mommy."

Gently, she raised her mother to a standing position.

"Oh, Rhonda, Rhonda," moaned Cornelia as she allowed herself to be led into the adjoining room.

"It's all right. You just get into bed."

"I have such hopes for you, my darling. A glittering match that all New York will talk about."

Rhonda unbuttoned her mother's dress and slid it off her shoulders. She pulled back the bedclothes and patted the sheet with the palm of her hand.

"Slip in, Mommy."

Cornelia, obedient as a child, did as she was told. Rhonda pulled the covers over her and looked down at the frail form. Cornelia Tarr made hardly any impression under the bedclothes. There were livid spots of red on her cheeks, intensified by the parchment-like pallor of her skin. The corridor outside echoed with the muted sound of the ship's bugler calling passengers to lunch.

"I'm very tired, my dear," said Cornelia. "I think I'll sleep now."

Rhonda kissed her mother's forehead.

"I'll be in the sitting room if you need me," she said.

Rhonda left the door ajar and sat on the sofa. She picked up a magazine and riffled through the pages. She thought about the young steward named Georgie. She would be careful this time.

She started at a knock on the door. She opened it and Nichole stood in the threshold.

"I've been looking all over for you."

"Well, now you've found me."

"Do you mind if we talk?"

"This isn't another lecture, is it?"

"No," replied Nichole coldly.

"Good. From the look on your face I thought I was going to get a finger wagged in my face."

"I believe you have something of mine, and I'd like it back, please."

"What are you talking about?"

"Something of mine is missing from my suitcase."

"What's that got to do with me?"

"I think you took it. I don't know how you got into my cabin, but you're the only one who knew where it was. You heard me talking about it last night."

"Maybe I did and maybe I didn't."

"Rhonda, don't play games with me."

"What am I supposed to have taken?"

"A notebook. It's of no use whatsoever to you."

"Then why are you so anxious to get it back?"

"It has . . . sentimental value."

"I was right, then—it is your lover's! I was hoping it would be interesting, but it's all in code, just figures and names. Very boring, really."

"Give it to me, please."

"Pretty please?"

"Pretty please."

Rhonda took the leather notebook from a pocket in the fold of her skirt. Nichole extended her hand, but the girl did not give it to her. Instead she turned the pages.

"Tell me who M.J.D. is, then I'll give it back."

"That's none of your business."

Nichole stamped her foot in anger.

"You are a dark horse. First Henry the butler, then the mysterious M.J.D."

"Give me that!"

Nichole lunged forward to grab the notebook, but Rhonda pulled it back at the last moment.

"Keep your voice down. You'll wake my mother."

"If you don't give it to me this instant—" Nichole began.

"What? What will you do?"

"Don't push me, Rhonda. I'm in no mood."

Suddenly, the cabin door flew open and Tarr's black form filled the doorway. His face was apoplectic with rage. Behind him stood Hislop, a lugubrious shadow.

"What the hell do you think you two are doing? Screaming at each other like a pair of fishwives. I could hear you down the corridor."

Defiant, Rhonda waved the notebook at her father.

"I only wanted to know whose this is. Nichole says it's hers. What do you think, Daddy?"

"Give it to me," demanded Tarr.

With a smile of triumph, Rhonda stepped forward to hand the notebook to her father. But before she could, Nichole, with the speed born of desperation, snatched the book from the girl, dashed to the open window and hurled it with all her might into the ocean. It fluttered momentarily in the wind. The covers opened and the pages flashed in the sunshine, black and white like a magpie. Then the notebook disappeared.

"What the hell do you think you're doing?"

"It was personal," said Nichole.

"It was her lover's," Rhonda chortled.

The *Titanic*'s first-class stewards and waiters were quartered amidships in large communal cabins on E Deck's port side along Scotland Road. Henry shared the space with twenty-seven other dining saloon waiters. His bunk was off to one corner, under Georgie Skinner's.

After dinner, when the passengers had left the dining room and he and Georgie had cleared away all the glasses and decanters, Henry smuggled out the heel of a bottle of 1846 Terrantez, a glorious Madeira. In the darkness of the cabin, lying back on their bunks listening to their shipmates snoring, he and Georgie sipped the rich, raisiny wine from delicate liqueur glasses.

"Great stuff, Madeira," whispered Georgie, leaning down.

"Mmm," Henry replied, but his mind was elsewhere.

Nichole had not been at the table for dinner. Nor had

Cornelia, which suggested that Nichole was dining in the Tarr suite to keep her company. When the request for a bottle of cognac had been transmitted to the bar before the bugle sounded, Henry was delivering champagne to the squash court on G Deck. Georgie had filled the order for him. He had reported to Henry.

"She just sat there staring out the window. And the old biddy in the turban sucking on the glass like there's no tomorrow. Just as I was going out, up she jumps, your lady, hands me a quid and whispers, 'Tell 'Enry the notebook's at the bottom of the Atlantic.' "

So Nichole had thrown it away. She had destroyed the only solid evidence to link Tarr to the murdered man. Angrily, Henry threw his blanket back and put his feet on the linoleum floor.

"Give me your glass. I'm going to take them back to the galley," he said.

"Don't bother. I'll do it in the morning."

"No. I can't sleep. I need some air."

He walked up to the Boat Deck. Perhaps it was best if he let the snake sleep in the sun. Why stir up ancient history? What did he have to gain by involving himself in Nichole's bizarre story? Maybe she had made the whole thing up for some crazy reason. It could be some elaborate, cruel plot cooked up between her and Tarr. If he went to Captain Smith now, he would be accusing one of America's leading financiers of murder on the say-so of a woman whose word could not be trusted. He had his own future to think about. His future with Kittie.

The moon cast a golden sheen on the water. The night air was cold, and he decided to go below. A late reveller was studying the clock in the first-class entrance, polishing his monocle on a silk handkerchief as he gazed at the twin female figures representing Hope and Glory.

Henry wished the man a good evening, pausing to listen to the faint buzz and click of a Morse code button. The operator in the wireless room behind the first-class stairway must be working late, he thought. Still wakeful, he decided to drop in. Wireless telegraphy was a novelty that fascinated him. He wondered how a sound could be transmitted over hundreds of miles without wire.

A light shone through the open door of the Marconi room. From its flat roof, four wires angled up to join those strung between the ship's masts, forming a gigantic antenna.

By contrast, the Marconi room was narrow and stuffy and packed with equipment. On the walls were three pneumatic tubes, which disappeared into the floor. Seated on a wooden bench, a pair of earphones lying on the table beside him, was a young man. His right hand rested on the table. In front of him was a pile of hand-written messages. Blue sparks arced across the Morse buzzer as if conjured by the slightest movement of his wrist. Henry waited until the operator had finished sending.

"Mind if I come in? The name's Blexill, first-class wine steward."

"That's a cushy job. I'm Harold Bride," said the boyish young man with prominent ears.

He couldn't be more than twenty-two, thought Henry.

"But keep it down. My chief operator, Phillips, is sleeping next door."

Henry nodded. "Tell me, how far can you send?"

"Depends, really. Guaranteed about two hundred and fifty miles. On a night like this when there's not much traffic and the atmospherics are right, maybe four hundred miles. In freak conditions it could go two thousand."

"Busy, are you?"

"Non-stop, mate. You'd think at twelve and six for ten words and nine pence for every one after that they'd be cautious. But not a bit of it. See this pile? That'd be a month's wages for me. Four quid a week, that's what the Marconi Company pays me."

"So you're not White Star."

"No, we're hired by Marconi. We're the British company. The Yanks get paid twice as much as we do. Bone of contention, that."

Bride was sending as he talked. It was second nature to him. His fingers beat out a rhythm on the buzzer. The dots and dashes emanating like angry wasps from the key would be translated into words by another ship's operator, who would then relay them on to a land station.

"It's a beautiful thing, this, and we've got the best there is. See this disk discharger? The most powerful one afloat. And this multiple tuner. I can pick up signals on more frequencies than any other ship at sea."

"What sort of messages do you get?"

"Other ships give us their position. Sea conditions, ice warnings. Lots of congratulations for our maiden voyage, greetings for passengers, stock market quotations, that sort of rubbish."

"What are you sending now?"

"A recipe."

"A recipe?"

"Yes. Lady Duff-Gordon went ga-ga over the chocolate mousse." He imitated the way he thought an upper-class English woman would say it. "She asked the chef to send the recipe to her cook in Paris." Bride laughed. "That'll cost her a couple of quid." He stopped sending for a moment and shifted his weight in the chair. "Listen, if you want to make yourself useful, you can sort out the pile I've already sent into classes. They're mainly first, but there are some seconds and a couple of thirds."

Henry took the pile of forms on his lap and began to sift through them.

"I reckon I've chosen a real coming business here," said Bride. "Telegraphy's the future. I'm counting on it."

Henry listened to the young man talk until his eye was caught by the address on one of the forms: J.P. Morgan, Grand Hotel, Aix-Les-Bains, Provence, France. The message was written in pencil in block capitals. "TNT TRYING TO RAISE 45 FROM CITY & FINANCIAL. BELIEVE SEEKING ALTERNATE FINANCING BANK OF MANHATTAN, WINSLOW LANIER AND ROTHSCHILD HAMBURG. WILL ADVISE." There was no signature, no indication who had sent it. In the top right-hand corner was a circled number. Someone was letting Morgan know Tarr's financial dealings. Morgan must have planted someone on board to watch the banker. Or to kill him.

"The purser must keep a record of who sends these messages, right? So they can be billed?" asked Henry.

"I s'pose so. Passengers pay up front when they hand them in," replied Bride.

Unseen by the operator, Henry slipped the cable into his pocket. He finished sorting the cables by class.

"Well, I guess I'll go below and get a little shut-eye. Might join you again when I can't sleep, Harold. Thanks for your company."

"Anytime," said Bride.

Saturday, April 13, 1912

CAPTAIN SMITH, AS was his morning practice, spent two hours inspecting the ship, from the engine room to the Boat Deck. Dressed in his white uniform, he led his entourage of officers and engineers through the galleys, the laundry, the bakery, the smoking rooms, the hospital, the dining rooms and lounges, the barbers' shops and the ballroom, the cargo holds, the pantries and the mail room. Wherever he went he saluted passengers, even in third class.

"How are matters in Boiler Room 6?" he asked the chief engineer.

"We finally got it out, cap'n."

A fire in the coal bunker of Boiler Room 6 had been burning ever since the *Titanic* had completed its sea trials two weeks earlier. Smith had ordered the mountain of coal to be hosed down continuously until the fire had been extinguished.

The only room the captain did not visit on his morning round was the Turkish bath, adjacent to the swimming pool on F Deck. Steam, he found, made his beard unkempt. Besides, the pre-luncheon hours, from ten to one, were reserved for lady passengers. The men had access to the baths between two and six.

Had he ventured into the Turkish bath that afternoon, Captain Smith would have found Thaddeus Nugent Tarr swathed in a white towel and in earnest conversation with Jim Gordon. The two men lay on ornately carved chaises longues, having emerged by stages from the steam room first to the temperate room and finally to the rococo splendor of the relaxation room. Its walls were tiled in green and blue, and the floor was a tile mosaic. Teak columns supported a beamed roof lit by crystal chandeliers. White bathrobes hung from hooks along the wall by the entrance.

Hislop sat in a chair just out of earshot of the two bankers, his legs reddened from the heat. Other men, draped in towels, slumbered like Roman courtiers after the feast.

"Cheer up, Thaddeus. I'll give you a chance to get your revenge," said Gordon, "double or nothing."

Tarr had lost one of the bets over the *Titanic*'s daily mileage. Gordon's guess was only five miles shy of the true distance, 386 miles. Tarr's cheque for one thousand dollars was folded in Gordon's wallet, which had been locked in a security box by the bath steward, along with his pocket watch and the diamond ring he wore on his little finger.

"Fine by me," said Tarr. He wiped the towel over his perspiring face.

Gordon looked at the mirrored ceiling. It was divided into great rectangles by gilded wood beams. The mirrors were hazy from the heat rising from steamed bodies. The portholes were hidden behind an elaborately carved harem screen, which diffused the daylight. The cooling room where the two men lay was larger than the entire galley for the third-class passengers.

"Reminds me of a brothel I once visited in Paris," said Gordon. "The women were all dressed like harem girls. Didn't shave at all. Armpits like camels, Thaddeus. The owner wore a black eyepatch like a pirate. When anyone paid with a gold coin she used to press it against her bad eye."

Tarr coughed impatiently. "Did you hear back from your people in New York?" He was propped up on one elbow, his stomach resting wetly on the polished wood of the seat.

"They had steam baths there, too. I like steam. Opens the pores. Gets rid of all the food and booze we pour down ourselves."

"I'm talking about New York, Jim. Did you hear about the loan?"

"Relax Thaddeus. It's Saturday. The weekend. They'll deal with it on Monday."

"You mean you didn't get them to call a special meeting? Hell, Jim. The market's open today, for Chrissake. I could be down another ten million."

"Let's see," said Gordon, inspecting his cuticles. "It's about eight in the morning on the east coast. The market's not open yet."

"Don't get smart with me, Gordon. It's my ass that's on the line here. I need that backing."

"I told you, Thaddeus. I'm doing what I can," Jim Gordon replied coldly. "If you're not satisfied, there are other bankers on board. But I'd be careful whom you speak to. If too many people know you're looking for that kind of money, they'll start reaching for a life raft, too."

Tarr glowered at him in silence.

Gordon stretched and sighed contentedly. He looked around the room at the recumbent figures dozing after their spell in the hot rooms.

"Tell you what. I'm going to make it easy for you. My bet is 520 miles. I've declared, so now the odds are in your favor. If you think it's more, all you have to say is one higher. Now, if you'll excuse me, I'm off to lunch with the Wideners."

Tarr watched him rise. "I'm skipping lunch," said Tarr. "Doctor says I should take off some weight. I think I'll steam for a bit. You'll tell me the minute you hear, won't you, Jim?"

"First thing," said Gordon over his shoulder.

Tarr looked at Hislop, who was staring at the retreating figure of Gordon. Tarr pulled the towel more tightly around his corpulent frame and beckoned the preacher over.

"A journalist from the *New York Times* interviewed me

earlier. He tried to suggest that the Brandon board was out to dump me."

"But you picked them yourself. They're your people."

"All except Morgan. Somehow he manages to slip through my fingers like water."

"Surely Mr. Gordon would know. He helped you finance the original stock issue."

"I wouldn't trust Mr. Fancy Pants Gordon further than I can spit. He had the nerve to tell me I should resign as chairman of Tarr Investments. Just because of the steel workers' commission."

"If your other directors have the same idea, Mr. Tarr, maybe you could turn it to your advantage."

"How do you mean?"

"Well, if it came to it, your price for stepping aside could be the loan you need."

Tarr cocked his head to one side and regarded the preacher through narrowed eyes.

"You know, Hislop, sometimes you surprise me. Underneath that pious exterior you have the mind of a medieval pope."

Hislop's face ignited in a rare smile.

"It is easier to balance a budget than minister to the needs of the soul," he said.

Tarr placed his feet on the tiled floor.

"There's one thing I'm curious about. You look right at home here. Do you spend a lot of time at the Forty-second Street baths?"

"I'm not sure I entirely understand you," replied Hislop.

"I'd lay odds you do," said Tarr. "I'm going for a steam now. You stay out here and keep an eye skinned. You'll enjoy that, I'm sure."

Tarr closed the door of the steam room behind him and sat on the pine bench. Alone, he unwrapped the towel, feeling the sweat erupt from his skin and roll down his body in rivulets. It felt good. The jungle heat made him drowsy, and he closed his eyes. He could hear himself breathing. The dank atmosphere was hot in his nostrils. His skin began to prickle.

Soon he became aware that the level of steam in the room had risen dramatically, and he could no longer see the door.

"What the hell's going on?" he cried out.

Vapor billowed from a grille above his head and tumbled down on him like scalding rags. With a roar of pain he leaped from the bench and staggered blindly towards the door, clutching at his towel.

The steam burned his eyes, and he shut them. Frantically, he groped for the door handle, cursing the attendant. He pushed, but the door would not open. He could hear the roar of steam, like a locomotive emptying its valves. The pipe on the ceiling began to vibrate and rattle against the pine planks. Tarr's flesh felt as if it had been stabbed by millions of red-hot needles. With all his weight, he pushed on the door. The steam scalded his nostrils and throat. He pulled the towel over his head and began to beat his fists on the door.

"Hislop!" he cried. "Somebody! Help me!"

He felt suffocated, and he began to choke. But when he opened his mouth to cry out, he could not breathe. He slipped to his knees, fighting for air, still pounding on the steam-room door.

"Help me, help me."

Suddenly the door flew open and he fell out onto the tiles, trembling with shock. When he opened his eyes, the first thing he saw was a row of paper slippers.

"Are you all right, Mr. Tarr?"

Hislop was bending over him. Next to him stood the anxious bath attendant.

"You really shouldn't take it that hot, sir," said the attendant. "It's bad for the heart."

Tarr lay panting on the tiles, unable to speak. He held up his arm, and the two men lifted him and helped him to a chaise longue. His body was the color of boiled lobster.

"Water," he said, his voice hoarse.

While the attendant fetched the water, Tarr drew Hislop closer.

"Did you see who did it?"

"I saw no one. I was the only one here, apart from a man in a white bathrobe who left a couple of minutes ago."

"What did he look like?"

"I'm afraid with all the steam I didn't get a good look at him."

"Typical," sneered Tarr. "I could have been boiled alive in there."

The attendant returned and handed Tarr a glass of water.

"Would you like me to call for the doctor, sir?"

Tarr shook his head. "How do you fix the heat inside?" he asked.

"There's a dial on the outside, sir."

"Well, go and check it, man."

The attendant crossed to the steam room and opened a cabinet on the wall. The dial had been turned up to its maximum.

"Good Lord!" he exclaimed, and hastily turned it down to its normal position.

Hislop, in his paper slippers, shuffled to Tarr's side and knelt.

"Find whoever did this, Hislop. Find him, and I'll make him wish that he'd never been born."

Henry Blexill made his way to the inquiry office near the first-class entrance. The purser's clerk, Ernest King, sat at the counter. Henry had sailed with him on the *Olympic*.

"Hello, Henry. So they let you out of the restaurant, did they?"

"On my break. Ernie, I've got a cablegram here and the passenger isn't sure if it's been sent or not. Can you check for me, please?"

The young man took the form and glanced at the number circled in the corner.

"It's paid for, anyway," he said. "See that number?"

"What's it mean?"

"Each cable coming through here is numbered like that so they get sent in order, unless there's a priority message."

"Can you tell who sent it?"

"They're logged by cabin number, in case there's a reply."

"What cabin sent this one, then?"

King reached for a leather-bound book on a shelf to his left. He licked his finger and began leafing through the pages. Finally, he stopped and ran his index finger down a line of figures.

"Here we are. It was handed in yesterday evening."

"Who was it charged to?"

"Suite B51—the American gentleman, Mr. Tarr."

"But that's not—" Henry checked himself. "Do you remember who handed it in?"

"Sorry, mate."

"Was it a woman?"

"Couldn't tell you. We were snowed under with cables yesterday."

Whoever sent the cable knew details of Tarr's financial manoeuvring, so it was someone with access to Tarr's papers, or someone he approached to discuss a deal. What if Nichole was spying on Tarr and sending information to Morgan? Tarr was obviously in financial trouble. If Morgan blocked off his avenues of credit, Tarr would be ruined. Was Nichole seeking revenge? If she was frightened of Tarr, she might give Morgan the ammunition to destroy him. Or perhaps the cable was sent by the banker Henry had seen Tarr whispering to in the smoking room the previous night.

One thing was certain: Nichole had not told Henry the whole story. Perhaps she had told him lies to entrap him. He would find out.

"They're in the Turkish bath," said Georgie, enjoying the conspiracy. "I followed them there. As far as I can tell, it's just 'is missus and your lady in B51. You really must 'ave it bad for 'er, old son."

"A lot of water under a lot of bridges," replied Henry.

He found Cornelia reclining on the settee, her knees covered with a rug, reading *Vogue* magazine. Untouched on the floor by her handbag was a copy of *South Sea Tales* by Jack London.

"Why, Henry! How nice to see you," she said, waving her hand abstractedly at him. "I asked Rhonda to have you call by yesterday, but I suppose she forgot. Young girls these days. Their minds are like cotton candy."

Henry looked around for some sign of Nichole.

"You know, it's a great comfort for me to see a familiar face." Cornelia's words were slurring and her hand movements exaggerated. "This ship makes me feel so sad. All these beautiful people. Such gaiety. They can't see what's going to happen. It's just like the time the lightning struck our palmetto tree. I had the same feeling then. A terrible chill that seems to come from inside my body."

"Would you like me to light the fire for you?"

"Yes, do that."

Henry knelt at the fireplace. It had already been set with paper, kindling wood and coal. Standing to one side was a set of bronze fire irons. He picked up the poker and levered up the coal to light the paper under it.

"You were lighting a fire the last night I saw you, I seem to remember," said Cornelia dreamily.

The night Tarr had killed a man. But that was just one of Tarr's crimes. What he had done to Cornelia was just as bad, Henry thought. He had squeezed all the life out of her. Even those Tarr professed to love he destroyed, only more slowly.

"What are you doing?"

"I'm lifting the coal with the poker to allow the air in, madam. It catches quicker that way."

"How very clever. I've always wondered what they were for."

What did she mean? Was she trying to tell him something? Henry heard her sigh.

"Do you ever miss your time with us?" asked Cornelia.

"I think of New York often, madam."

"Manhattan really is quite grand now, you know. More than London, in spite of the palace. Everything is so dowdy and gray in England. It was so much better in

Bertie's time, much more jolly. Thaddeus loves to tell the story of how Lillie Langtry popped a piece of ice down the prince's trousers at a shooting party, or the time Bertie had a donkey dressed up in a nightgown and hoisted into one of the guests' bedrooms. This George is really too sober altogether. Mind you, Thaddeus never did forgive him for not inviting us to his coronation. Had it been Edward, that would have been another matter. But you didn't answer my question."

"I suppose I miss my roots more," said Henry. "I grew up at Cumerworth Hall."

Where was Nichole? Georgie had said she was with Mrs. Tarr.

"Cumerworth Hall," repeated Cornelia, as if the name struck a chord in her memory.

"Lord Rutherland's estate. I was his butler before he went bankrupt."

"Ah, yes. That's where Thaddeus found you. Working for that deceitful man. You know, he tried to trick us out of a silver mine. You were much better off away from him."

So Tarr had painted Lord Rutherland as the villain. Henry said nothing.

Cornelia picked up her magazine. "I was reading as you arrived, Henry. Quite a coincidence, really. Where is it? Oh, yes. 'Mrs. Elise Hoffman Chapin of 35 West Forty-ninth Street will introduce her daughter, Katherine, at a tea.' You remember her elder sister, Veronica? She came to Rhonda's coming-out ball."

"I'm afraid I was no longer in your husband's employ when Miss Rhonda came out."

"No? That's right. It was the new man. What a pity. It was such a lovely affair. A costume party. Three hundred people crowded into our ballroom. Well, you can imagine. Rhonda went as Pierrette, and the room was hung with vines and masses of yellow roses. Mrs. Robert Hinkley wore green velvet and a coronet of shamrocks. She was a sensation, quite outshone poor Rhonda. She came dressed as the Emerald Isle and you should have seen her emeralds! Inherited them from her mother, you know. Mrs. O'Donnell Lee of Baltimore. What a splash she made."

"It sounds like a splendid affair, madam."

Henry wondered how he was going to extricate himself from having to listen to Cornelia's tipsy memories.

"Oh, it was . . . You never said goodbye, you know, Henry. One day you were there and the next you were gone."

She looked at him, blinking, a quizzical expression in her teary eyes.

"I'm sorry, madam. It was inexcusable of me."

She smiled and reached for the empty brandy glass. She held it out to him with a gesture that was half coquettish, half imploring.

"Never mind. We're all together now. One big happy family again. On this . . . this ship. The world's finest, most luxurious, unsinkable . . . prison. Who was it who said that going to sea is like going to prison with the possibility of being drowned?"

Her hand shook as Henry poured cognac into the outstretched glass. She looked at him reproachfully when he stopped and set the bottle down.

Through the window Henry caught a glimpse of Nichole. She was standing at the railing of the suite's private promenade, gazing fixedly out to sea. Her back was to him.

"Perhaps Miss Linley would like a touch of cognac against the damp," he suggested.

"Yes, do take one to her. She looks so pale."

Henry poured a glass and crossed the sitting room to the sliding door that gave access to the promenade.

Nichole did not move at the sound of his approach, and only when Henry touched her lightly on the shoulder did she turn towards him.

"I have to talk to you," he said.

"Please leave me alone. I can't stand much more of this."

"Here, take the glass, and listen. I want you to go swimming this afternoon when I've finished my restaurant duty. At a quarter to four I'll deliver a half bottle of champagne to the pool for you. We can talk there."

"No, Henry. I'm tired of it all."

"Just be there. I want to hear about you and J.P. Morgan."

Nichole's mouth opened, but no words came out. For a moment she stared into his eyes, frowning, then turned to look out to sea again.

Saturday, April 13, 1912

TARR SAT IN the smoking room across the table from Hislop. He was waiting for the steward to post the latest stock-exchange quotes telegraphed from London. In front of him was a glass of T.W. Samuels' bourbon. Hislop nursed a glass of seltzer.

"Another minute and I'd have been cooked alive," said Tarr. His skin still tingled from the scalding steam.

"Try to let your mind rise above the pain."

"Save that mystical claptrap for my wife, Hislop. It doesn't wash with me."

Hislop shifted his feet under the table and made a little coughing sound.

"And don't give me any of that bull about Brandon. A wop miner wouldn't have the imagination to boil me alive in a steam room. It must be the Macklins or someone they hired."

"If we don't know whom we're looking for," said Hislop, "everyone falls under suspicion—your fellow passengers, the crew, everyone on board."

"Blexill," said Tarr. "Don't forget Blexill. What the hell d'you think he's doing on board?"

"I would be very surprised—" Hislop began.

"Revenge, man. I fired him, didn't I? I'll tell you one thing. He could be trouble if they subpoena him for the Stanley Committee hearings."

"You were only doing your duty, Mr. Tarr. The newspapers said so."

Tarr rewarded Hislop with a contemptuous smile. "Well, I'm not taking any chances. Bad publicity now and Tarr Investments stock could really tumble."

"What do you suggest?"

"I'm going to make sure that Blexill won't be around to testify."

"Perhaps I can convince him that it would be in everyone's best interests for him to be unavailable, sir."

But Tarr was not listening.

"Did you hear anything from New York on Blexill?"

"They sent an abstract of the surveillance report. According to Rattigan, his girl friend is on board. He helped to get her the job."

"A passenger?"

"No, she's a stewardess. Her name is Kittie Boyer. She was the one I caught going through the desk in your suite."

"Blexill's girl friend was in my suite? Was anything missing?"

"Not that I could see."

"Pity."

"But she was the one I spoke to about the Macklins."

"How much did you pay her?"

"Thirty pounds, sir."

"In what denominations?"

"Three ten-pound notes."

Tarr pulled at his earlobe, a gesture Hislop knew from experience meant that his employer was carefully digesting the information.

"How much do you think a stewardess earns, Hislop?"

"I'm not altogether sure, but I would imagine about five or six pounds a month," replied the preacher.

"Good," said Tarr, and he took another swig of his bourbon.

The door to the smoking room opened and a tall, elegant man entered.

"Isn't that Butt?" said Tarr.

Major Archibald Butt, President Taft's adviser and confidant, walked purposefully towards the notice board.

"Major Butt," called Tarr. "Glad to see you."

The man turned at the sound of his name. "Mr. Tarr, isn't it?" The voice was deep, with a soft, southern inflection.

"Yes. I thought you'd be in Washington, what with Roosevelt and Taft squaring off."

"I convinced the president to let me have a brief holiday. I went to visit my brother in Chester." Butt smiled affably.

Hislop could see he was looking for a way to excuse himself politely, but Tarr was not to be denied.

"This Frelinghuysen measure, do you really think it's going to do any good?"

Four days before the *Titanic* sailed, the Senate had decreed that corporations registered in the state of New Jersey with capital of more than five million dollars would be taxed one hundred dollars instead of fifty for every million dollars of capital. Tarr had calculated it would cost him nearly twenty-five thousand dollars more in taxes that year. Morgan, he estimated, would have to pay a hundred thousand on the U.S. Steel Corporation alone. Wall Street was not happy with Senator Frelinghuysen.

"It could have been worse." Butt smiled. "You could be living in England. Ah, here comes the market news now."

A steward greeted them, then attached several sheets of paper to clips on the notice board.

"Wheat prices are rocketing," said Butt. "Must be the fear of winter damage pushing the prices up. And steel is rising, now that the British miners are back at work. Buoyant if not bullish, I'd say. If you gentlemen will excuse me."

Tarr was too engrossed in the list of figures to acknowledge Butt's departure. According to the latest numbers, his holding company, Tarr Investments, had suffered another setback. Its shares were down fourteen points.

"Look at that, Hislop," growled Tarr, hitting the paper with his knuckles, "and tell me it isn't a conspiracy to ruin me. If I were at home I could fight them. But I'm trapped on this ship like a flea on a dog. And I'm forced to rely on the charity of fops like Jim Gordon."

"Has there been no response to your cables?"

"I've contacted every major banking house in Europe—the Rothschilds, the Warburgs, the Deutsche Bank, Credit Mobilier—and not one of them has even had the courtesy to reply. Men I've been doing business with for years."

"Not even Mr. Harriman?"

"All Ned's assets are tied up in Burlington."

"Surely if you explained to Mr. Rockefeller that it was an opportunity to put one over on Mr. Morgan?"

"Rockefeller would love to have a go at Morgan, but not to save me. He was sniffing around Brandon, too, remember."

"Yes. Brandon."

"The vultures are circling, Hislop. They smell blood. Well, if it's blood they want, it's blood they'll get, but it won't be mine."

"I know I don't have to tell you, sir, but it's all a question of confidence."

"Confidence, yes. A show of confidence. Right. Everything's peachy. You've given me an idea, Hislop. I'm going to throw a party! The biggest, most extravagant party they've ever seen. For anyone who's anyone on this sardine can. The Astors, Guggenheim, that guy from Philadelphia, Thomas Cardeza who got on at Cherbourg, Archie Butt, George Widener, Jack Thayer, Charles Hay, Gordon, Ismay, Sir Cosmo What's-his-name. The whole bloody lot. Even Issy Straus. I'll show them who's got money." He slapped the table, and the steward looked inquiringly his way.

"It could work." Hislop nodded.

"Damn right," said Tarr, and he sat back, holding the lapels of his frock coat. "I remember what Seligman the banker once told me when I was raising money for the Brandon consolidation. Something his grandfather had told him. Old man Seligman came from Europe with a hundred dollars sewn into the seat of his pants. Ended up one of the richest men in America. On his deathbed he called all his grandsons to him. "I have one piece of advice for you," he told them. "To sell something you have to someone who wants it is not business. To sell something you don't have to someone who doesn't want it—that's business."

Hislop cradled his glass of seltzer in his long, bony fingers.

"And talking of business," said Tarr, "I want to talk to whoever's in charge of the stewardesses."

Henry held the tray at shoulder level as he negotiated the corridors from the wine room off the restaurant on B Deck to the pool on F Deck. Crew and stewards were not allowed to use the elevators. Henry used the forward staircase. As he descended to D Deck he passed a man who was coming up. The man was in his early thirties, and he sported a large moustache. His hair was wavy and parted in the middle. Their eyes met and locked for a moment. There was something about him that Henry found familiar.

But the features belonged to another place and an earlier time. As they moved away from each other, Henry tried to recall where he had seen the man before. The cut of his clothes was British. A passenger from another crossing, perhaps. But it troubled Henry that he could not place him. There was a furtive look about the man's eyes, as if their meeting had been unwanted.

The salty tang of sea water assailed Henry's nostrils as he pulled the door open to the swimming bath. The lifeguard, wearing a red-and-white bathing suit, was leaning on the railing that ran the length of the pool. He had a towel around his neck. Behind him, set against the wall, was a row of changing cubicles. The floor was fitted with non-slip porcelain tiles. There was a clock on the wall at the deep end. It was three forty-five.

Two children and a balding man were frolicking in the

shallow end. A stout woman was floating on her back and kicking her feet. She wore a rubber cap and a black costume with a ruffle at the waist, which only served to accentuate her girth.

Nichole was nowhere to be seen.

"You can't come in here with glass," said the lifeguard peremptorily as he spotted Henry's tray with the champagne bucket. "Captain's orders."

"I'm sorry," said Henry. "A passenger ordered champagne. But I don't see her here."

He ran his eye along the row of cubicles, thinking Nichole might still be changing. But all the doors were ajar. The two shower stalls at the end of the cubicles were also empty.

"False alarm," he said, shrugging at the lifeguard.

Henry went into the corridor. Perhaps Nichole would not come. He waited, undecided, as the door to the Turkish bath opened. A man emerged, his skin pink and glowing. An attendant held open the door. As Henry passed, the attendant stepped into the corridor.

"Boy, I could really use that right now," he said, eyeing the champagne. "What a day. A passenger nearly cooked himself in the steam room. Talk about a ruckus. Had to be an American, didn't it?"

Henry smiled sympathetically. "What happened?"

"Somehow the dial got turned full up and the door jammed. You should have seen him. He looked like a pink porpoise."

"Is he all right?"

"Yes," replied the attendant. "But it could have been really nasty. You know what these American millionaires are like."

Henry lowered the tray from shoulder height.

"His name wasn't Tarr, by any chance?"

"Yes, that's him. It's not round the ship already, is it?"

Henry did not reply. He was thinking about Thaddeus Tarr being trapped in a steam room. Tarr was too careful to let accidents like that happen to him.

"Would you show me the steam room?"

The attendant held the door open and pointed towards the dressing rooms.

"Go right through. There's no one in there. It's the door on the left."

Henry set the tray on a table next to a vacant chaise longue. The air was humid. He walked the length of the cooling room. In front of him was a pine wall with two doors. One was marked "Steam Room," the other "Hot Room." To the left of the steam-room door was a box; the heat-control unit was visible behind a glass panel. The small square window that gave access to the mechanism was unlocked; anyone could have opened it.

Henry moved to the steam-room door. He bent down until his eyes were level with the porcelain handle. The door had no lock. He opened it, trying to understand how it might have jammed. Perhaps the steam had swelled the frame, causing the door to stick momentarily, but it opened freely enough and swung easily on its hinges.

Henry ran his fingers along the edge of the door. Half-way down he felt a slight hollow in the wood.

At the matching point on the frame, he noticed two almost parallel indentations about an inch and half apart. It looked to Henry as if something had been wedged between the door and the frame.

He knelt and began to feel around on the floor. In a corner by the wall his fingers touched something hard. He picked it up. It was a piece of bone about two inches long, curved and polished, with a jagged end.

"A shoe horn," he said.

Someone must have followed Tarr into the Turkish bath. When Tarr was in the steam room alone, the other person had wedged a shoe horn into the door, snapped the end off and turned up the heat.

A person—it could only be a man, reasoned Henry—would have had to improvise the plan on the spur of the moment. Whoever it was must have known Tarr's movements.

He slipped the broken shoe horn into his pocket and stepped into the cooling room to retrieve his champagne tray.

In the corridor outside the Turkish bath he found Nichole wandering aimlessly.

"I almost didn't come," she said. Her eyes, he noticed, were red and swollen from crying.

"We can't talk here." Henry steered her with his free hand in the direction of the main staircase.

"What happened to the notebook?" he demanded in a low voice.

"I had to throw it overboard."

"Why? That's the only concrete piece of evidence we have."

"It's a long story," she replied wearily.

"I'm listening."

Nichole sighed. "It was Rhonda who took it," she said, and she told him the sequence of events that ended in her flinging the notebook into the ocean.

"Did Tarr recognize it?"

"I don't think so. Rhonda said it was my lover's diary. I had to do it, Henry. If he found out I'd kept it   " She did not finish the sentence. "I've got to go. He warned me not to talk to you." She began to move away.

"Wait a minute. Something's going on, and I'm going to find out what it is."

The tray was heavy in his hand, and he set it at the foot of the stairs.

"I must go. He told me to stay with Cornelia. He'll get suspicious if I'm not there."

"Listen. You've been lying to me ever since you got on board. Now I want the truth. There's a tea dance in the second-class smoking room on B Deck. I'm off duty in fifteen minutes. I'm going to my quarters now to get a civilian jacket. I'll meet you in there. The Tarrs wouldn't be caught dead in second class. We can talk in peace there."

"I can't come, Henry. Don't make me."

"You be there," he said, "at four sharp. Otherwise, I'm going to tell Tarr about you and Morgan."

"He'd kill you if you did, you know that."

"A party, sure, a party, why not?" Tarr paced the sitting room in front of the dumbfounded Cornelia. "Liven things up a bit. This place is like a morgue."

Rhonda clapped her hands. "Can I invite who I want?"

Tarr turned on her. "It's not your party. This is money rubbing up against money."

Cornelia exchanged glances with Hislop and lowered her eyes when her husband looked at her.

"There's a lot to do, and not much time. We'll need invitations printed. I'll talk to the chef. I'm going to empty this bark of caviar. There'll be champagne. We'll get our old pal Blexill to serve it. It'll be a party they'll never forget. Where's Nichole? She can get it started. Where is she, anyway?"

"I looked for her," said Hislop, "but I couldn't find her."

"Probably flirting with Henry," said Rhonda under her breath.

"We'll hold it tomorrow night," said Tarr. "A buffet dinner for eighty people or so. Just the cream. Hot and cold food. We'll get the band in. We'll get flowers. Like it was for Rhonny's ball."

His old energy had returned. Cornelia wanted desperately to reach for the cognac bottle, but she restrained herself.

"I don't know if I'll be feeling up to it, Thaddeus," she said, timidly.

"Of course you will. You'll have gotten your sea legs by then. I need you by my side, Cornelia. I'm not asking you to do anything. Just be there."

The walls of the second-class smoking room were oak-panelled, and the cream-colored ceilings, supported by oak pillars, were crossed with artificial beams. The small tables and leather tub chairs had been pushed back to the walls to allow space for dancing on the patterned linoleum floor. At the far end of the room the members of the orchestra, dressed in blue dinner jackets, were playing Victor Herbert's "It Happened in Norland." The floor was crowded with couples.

Drawn to the sound of the music, Kittie Boyer stopped outside the smoking room and eased open the door. Couples were waltzing. Through the crack in the door she watched them glide across the floor.

Then she saw Henry. He was out of uniform, and he offered his hand to a woman who was seated by a pillar. He escorted the woman to the dance floor. The company encouraged the crew to insure that passengers were involved. If a lady had no invitations to dance, pursers and stewards were instructed to step into the breach.

But the woman Henry was dancing with didn't look as if she needed any help in attracting a whole trolley car full of admirers, even if her face showed she'd rather be somewhere else. The way they acted together Kittie could tell they were not strangers. Though they weren't speaking, they seemed to communicate with each other.

It had to be Nichole. Kittie felt the blood rising in her cheeks. She closed the door with a bang.

Nichole's hand was cool in his. Through the satin of her dress he could feel her spine. He remembered how he had run his fingers down her back when they made love that night in Westchester. The lavender smell of her perfume wafted up from the exposed skin of her neck—the same perfume he had smelled on the castle stairs.

Nichole barely moved her feet, responding to the music with a gentle swaying of her head and shoulders.

Feelings Henry had denied then forgotten welled up inside him, drawn from him by the sentimental melody. Pleasurable and painful at the same time. He wanted to lift her face to his and kiss her. This contradictory woman, scheming, selfish, avaricious, yet vulnerable and unsure of herself—she could still make him want her.

Nichole did not speak, nor did she try to move away from him. They stood on the edge of the dance floor like lovers. For that moment Henry postponed the reason for their meeting. Enjoying the sight and smell of her, and the unspoken memory of the intimacy they once shared.

It was Nichole who broke the mood. She pulled back from him and looked him full in the face.

"So you found out about me and Morgan," she said defiantly. "And you'd tell Thaddeus."

"I just want the truth, Nichole."

"I don't think you really want to hear it. You know too much already."

"For God's sake. I'm an accessory. Like you. But I'm not going to let him win." Henry steered her to a quiet corner of the dance floor. "I want you to tell me where Morgan fits into all this."

Nichole started to tremble. "I have to sit down."

She moved to a vacant chair.

"Well? I'm listening."

Nichole sighed. "How did you find out?"

"It doesn't matter. Just tell me."

She looked at her feet and, in a voice he could hardly hear, she said: "If you must know, I used to be Morgan's mistress."

Morgan's mistress. The words beat into his mind like hammer blows. He knew he had no claims on Nichole, no right to feel jealous, but he did. Somehow the knowledge that she had been Morgan's lover was even more devastating to him than her relationship with Tarr.

"Or let's say, I was one of his mistresses," Nichole continued. "He has women all over the world, you know. He got tired of me eventually, like all the rest. The gifts and the money stopped, so I had to go to work. I went back to the theatre. That's where I met Thaddeus. And that's all there is. Are you satisfied?"

"Have you seen him since then?"

"No. When you're a J.P. Morgan reject, you don't get Christmas cards."

"Have you been in contact with him at all?"

"I told you. When Thaddeus took me in it was finished, over, done."

"Then why did you send him this?" He reached into his jacket pocket and pulled out the cablegram.

Nichole took it from him, unfolded it and read the message. He waited for her to answer.

"I don't understand. I didn't send this. I swear to you, Henry."

"If you're lying you're a very good actress, and you're being very stupid."

"Believe what you want. I don't care anymore." She turned away from him, flushing angrily.

"Whoever sent this knows Morgan."

"Everyone in first class knows Morgan."

"But they don't all know Tarr, and certainly they don't know he's looking for a huge loan."

If Nichole had not sent the cable, who had? Hislop, Cornelia or Rhonda? Or the banker Jim Gordon? Gordon would know the facts and figures, and he might have been discussing Tarr's affairs with his banking cronies on board. Any of them could have alerted Morgan.

The wording of the cablegram suggested that the sender understood finance. Yet the message had been charged to Tarr's suite. Was Tarr himself playing some Machiavellian game, tipping his hand to Morgan to set up a larger financial coup down the road?

"Somebody aboard this ship is trying to kill Tarr," said Henry.

"Do you think it's the person who sent this message?"

"No." Henry shook his head. "If they're trying to kill Tarr, why would they leave a trail like that? I don't believe the two are connected."

They sat in silence for a moment, watching the dancers.

"Someone tried to kidnap Rhonda in London," said Nichole finally.

"What happened?" asked Henry.

"All I know is what Rhonda told me, and you know how she loves to dramatize."

"What did she say?"

"She went for a walk alone in the park. There was woman in a coach. The coachman tried to snatch her."

"Did she describe the coachman?"

"Not really. She said he was young and his hair was parted in the middle. Oh, and he wore a wedding ring. Rhonda would notice that."

"Did Tarr go to the police?"

"He doesn't know about it."

"Why not?"

"Rhonda made me promise not to tell. I should have been chaperoning her. Against my express instructions, she snuck out of the hotel."

Henry thought hard. Could the man he had passed on the stairs be the coachman who had tried to abduct Rhonda? He knew he had seen that face before somewhere, but try as he might he could not find a setting for the face.

"I don't know exactly who it is yet or why they want to get Tarr, but I'm not going to let them. Tarr has to answer in a court of law for all the people he's destroyed. I want everything on record."

"That's very noble."

"I don't feel particularly noble. I could willingly strangle him myself."

"But what good is a court of law? You have no evidence."

"Thanks to you."

"I was only trying to protect myself. And you."

"Without the notebook, we can hardly expect Tarr to march into a police station and confess. If we bring a case against him he'll just hire a battalion of lawyers, and they'll get him off."

Nichole shook her head. Drawing closer to him, she kissed him on the ear and whispered: "Let Morgan do it."

"What do you mean?"

"The only way to destroy Thaddeus is to ruin him financially. That cable shows he's in trouble. He needs money, but Morgan will make sure nobody lends him any. All it takes is a word from him and every door closes. He saved Thaddeus once, but he won't do it again. There's too much at stake. Morgan will bankrupt him. That's the best revenge of all."

"How can you be so sure?"

"I know Morgan. He hates Thaddeus, and he can bankrupt anybody he wants to."

"And that's enough for you, that Tarr loses his money? What about justice? The law?"

"There are no laws where Thaddeus is concerned."

"That's up to the police."

"If you go to the police, I'll end up in jail."

"You think I should do nothing?"

Nichole shrugged. "It won't matter. I've been following the market. By the time we dock, Tarr Investments stock will be at rock bottom. He'll be finished."

"If someone on board doesn't get to him first," said Henry.

"Well, maybe he'll do us all a favor," said Nichole, callously. "It's much cleaner that way, Henry. Can't you see?"

"We're talking about a man's life, Nichole. You can't just forget there's a body at the bottom of Long Island Sound."

"It happens all the time. People disappear. You can't be responsible for the whole world."

Henry could hear the rattling of the Hotchkiss gun. In his mind's eye he saw men in bloodied shirts pressing the toes of their boots into the West Virginia dust.

"There are some things you don't forget," he said.

"The trouble with you is that you think like a servant."

"Yes, I probably do. That's why I want you to write down everything that happened that night. Just as you told me. Don't leave anything out."

"You really want to see me behind bars, don't you?" asked Nichole.

"It's all going to come out anyway. You can't just forget about it."

"But nobody will know unless you tell them."

"A man is dead, Nichole. And Tarr killed him."

"Why don't we wait and see what happens when we get to New York?"

"No. There is too much blood. He has to be stopped. But I can't stop him without your help."

The orchestra was playing "Miss Dolly Dollars." Nichole stared sadly at him. Her eyes were shining with tears.

"I'm sorry, Henry. It's too late for me."

Saturday, April 13, 1912

TARR HAD REQUISITIONED the Palm Court for his party, which would be held on Sunday after church services. Stewards would be stationed at the doors to keep out gate crashers.

"This bash will be talked about for as long as people remember the *Titanic*," said Tarr, swelling in anticipation.

Hislop listened, a notebook in his lap, while Rhonda wriggled in her seat, impatient to be gone. Cornelia sat apart from them on the settee, measuring the level in the cognac bottle with a practised eye.

"There'll be favors for the ladies and enough caviar to choke the entire stock exchange."

"But no one visits on Sunday afternoon," said Cornelia.

"We're in the middle of the Atlantic Ocean," growled Tarr. "Not on Fifth Avenue. What else is there to do, woman? Take a carriage around Central Park? Drive out to the Hamptons?"

Through a stupefaction of cognac, Cornelia watched the procession of stewards, pursers and waiters parade at intervals through the sitting room. Tarr had moved the desk into the centre of the room, and he sat behind it barking out orders as if he were in his Wall Street office.

"Looks as if you've hired the entire ship to cater your party, Thaddeus," she said.

"Why don't you go into the other room and do your jigsaw or whatever it is you're doing," he replied.

"I'll escort you back, Mrs. Tarr," said Hislop.

"Never mind, Clifford. I'm quite capable." Cornelia picked up the bottle and weaved her way to the door. "I'm going to lie down," she announced. When she got no response from her husband, she left, closing the door behind her.

"Hislop, I'm putting you in charge of the invitations," Tarr said. "You'll draw them up and have them printed. I'll give you the guest list."

"Yes, sir."

"Where's Nichole? I want her to take care of the decorations. Damn it, that woman's never here when I need her. Flowers," he said. "Make a note. Flowers everywhere. I want the room to look like the Botanical Gardens, do you hear? And candelabra. Lots of candles. Ladies always look better by candlelight."

Rhonda groaned.

"Don't think you're going to sit around, young madam. I want you to speak to someone about that bandleader, Hartley, or whatever his name is. There'll be ten guineas each for the musicians, and twenty for him. Tell him I don't want anything loud, no ragtime and no Broadway show-tune rubbish. And there'll be no dancing."

"Sounds like a swell party." Rhonda grimaced. She picked up a stack of Marconigrams from the table. "Your stock's fallen again, I see."

"Put those down," thundered Tarr. "They're not addressed to you. Now go about your business, missy."

"Who do I talk to?"

"Do I have to do everything myself around here? Find a steward."

"A steward. Thank you, Daddy. I know exactly who I'll talk to." She gave the two men a beaming smile and flounced out of the stateroom.

Tarr turned to Hislop. "Why are you leaving those cables around?"

"I'm sorry, Mr. Tarr."

"Get them out of my sight. Too many people know my affairs already. Now, what news on the steam-bath business?"

"I went to check with the attendant. As far as we can tell, it seems to have been a genuine accident, sir. According to the engineer the control is very sensitive. The wood is new. Sudden heat could have swollen the door."

"Maybe I should sue them. I don't believe a word of it. Do you?"

"I must give them the benefit of the doubt, sir."

Tarr glared at him. "Where's the chief purser?"

"I informed him you wished to see him, Mr. Tarr. I'm sure he'll be along."

Before Hislop had finished speaking there was a knock at the door.

"Ah, the chef," said Tarr. "Come in, come in."

The incident in the steam bath and the absence of the chief purser were temporarily forgotten as Tarr concentrated on the food he wanted served at his party. There would be whole barons of beef carved from the trolley, "just like Simpson's in the Strand." The chef recommended game birds for his British guests, pheasant, snipe, partridge, plover and teal, species Tarr had never heard of before. To make sure no guests would go hungry, there would also be rounds of spiced beef, Virginia and Cumberland hams, galantine of chicken and sides of smoked salmon. Pastries of all kinds and fresh fruit and a wide selection of French and English cheeses would be placed on a dessert table.

"I want Stilton, whole rounds of Stilton," said Tarr, "and decanters of your best port. Do you have any Taylor 1878?"

The head pastry chef was called in and instructed to concoct a replica of the New York Stock Exchange, executed in meringue, ice cream and chocolate. The banker made sketches of its facade from memory as a guide. The flagpole on the roof was to fly the Tarr family coat of arms, an heraldic device of medieval complexity recently purchased from a London genealogist.

"Now send your wine steward to me," commanded Tarr. "I want an inventory of all the champagne you have on board."

In her cabin, Cornelia could hear her husband's voice. She picked up a copy of the guest list, written in Tarr's spiky hand. Her eyes were misty as she looked down the page.

"Such beautiful people. The sadness of it all."

When Henry emerged from the tea dance he saw Kittie furiously polishing the staircase balustrade outside the smoking-room door. Her lips were pursed in anger.

"I saw you with 'er," she said when they were alone in the linen room. "I saw you dancin'."

"Kittie, I've told you. There is nothing between us. I had to talk to her. Some people are trying to kill Tarr, and I have to stop them."

"That's not your job. You're not a policeman. Tell the master-at-arms."

"If it's Nichole you're upset about, believe me, you've got nothing to worry about."

"All that business about a notebook. There was no notebook, was there? It was just something you made up so you and she could be together."

"Kittie, please."

"I don't understand you. Honest, I don't. All this talk about killing. What 'appens if you get killed?"

"Nothing's going to happen to me, I promise."

"But what's going on, 'Enry?"

"I can't tell you. For your own protection."

" 'Ow can we 'ave a life together if we can't be honest with each other? If you don't tell me, I'm only going to think the worst. If you have any feeling for me you'll tell me."

She had boxed him into a corner. If he told her she would be party to some dangerous information. If he didn't, she would be suspicious of his motives and of his feelings for her.

"What I'm about to tell you must never be repeated to anyone. For your own safety. Do you promise?"

"I promise."

He recounted for her the events that led to his firing by Tarr. Kittie listened without interruption.

"So," she said when he had finished, "the lady's got blood on 'er 'ands."

There was something in the way she said it that startled Henry. There was a tone of grim satisfaction in her voice, a cynicism, which suggested a toughness of mind he had not recognized in her before. He had anticipated expressions of shock and horror following his monologue, primary emotions that Kittie let loose at the kinescope or while reading love stories in ladies' magazines. But there were none.

"I was with Nichole today to try to convince her to write a confession," he said. "That's the only thing that I can pass on to McGillivray now. But she wouldn't do it."

"If 'e gave 'er Cumerworth 'all, why would she? She's in it with 'im right up to 'er eyeballs. Can't you see that? Oh, 'Enry, you're such an innocent. What 'appens if she runs to 'im now and tells 'im what you're after? 'E could be looking for you right now. And all because of 'er."

When Henry entered the restaurant, Georgie Skinner beckoned him over.

"Did you 'ear, your tubby friend, Old Moneybags, is 'olding a private party tomorrow in the Palm Court? 'E wants you be'ind the bar."

"Wonderful. You've just made my trip."

"And Kirkbride's been looking for you. Sounds like 'e wants to break you in 'alf."

Henry reached for his jacket.

"Break me in half, eh? Of course! Why didn't I think of that? Thanks, Georgie! Cover for me, will you? Tell them I'm down in stores. I won't be long."

If he had half the shoe horn, the other half must be somewhere. Maybe the man had thrown it in a waste bin or left it in the pocket of a bathrobe.

Henry descended quickly to F Deck and headed for the Turkish bath.

"One of my passengers says he left a watch in the robe he used earlier this afternoon," he told the attendant.

"Nothing's been handed in while I've been on."

"Mind if I check?"

"What time was he here?"

The attendant consulted his register. Henry looked over his shoulder and read the list of names. He saw Tarr's, Hislop's and Gordon's. There were several other names, all first-class passengers listed by their cabin numbers.

"Everyone has to register, right?"

"That's the regulations. Time in, time out."

"Mind if I look around?"

"Be my guest."

Henry felt the pockets of the robes hanging on the hooks. There was nothing in them. He crossed to the waste bin and rooted around inside. He found a few damp newspapers, several pairs of used paper slippers and a broken squash racket.

"What happens to the towels?" he asked the attendant.

"Passengers are asked to put them in that canvas basket on their way out."

Henry pulled the soggy towels from the basket. His search was rewarded. Near the bottom was the handle of the shoe horn.

He picked it up and fitted it against the broken piece. It matched exactly.

Printed on the handle was the name Weatherby and Sons, Jermyn Street, Piccadilly, W.1.

Lord Rutherland's boot maker.

Nichole responded slowly to the knock on her cabin door. She tucked a fallen strand of hair behind her ear and checked that the tears had not smudged her make-up.

"Who is it?"

"Stewardess, ma'am."

"I didn't ring for anyone."

"Miss Linley?" The voice was insistent.

Nichole frowned and unlocked the door. Standing on the threshold was a small, dark-haired woman in a crisply starched uniform. She was young and fresh-faced, with high cheekbones and deep brown eyes.

"Yes? What is it?"

"I'll close the door, if you don't mind."

"I'm very tired," said Nichole. "Can you come back some other time?"

"Me name's Kittie."

"All right, Kittie, do what you have to do and leave."

"Didn't 'Enry tell you about me?"

"What?"

"I'm a friend of 'Enry's. The wine steward. The one you was dancing with."

Nichole sat on the bed. "What do you want?"

"I know I'm taking a liberty coming to talk to you like this, but I 'ad to."

"Did Henry send you?"

"No, ma'am. 'E doesn't know I'm 'ere."

"Well, what do you want?"

" 'E told me the 'ole story."

"What story?" Blood rose in Nichole's cheeks.

"About 'im and you and Mr. Tarr and what 'appened that night."

"He told you!"

"Yes."

"Oh, my God!" Nichole's hands flew to her mouth, and her eyes opened wide in alarm. "You could be in great danger, you know."

"I'm not worried for meself, ma'am. It's 'Enry I care about. All this 'as been eating away at 'im. It's all bottled up inside. I 'ad to drag it out of 'im."

"You love him, don't you?"

"I want to marry him."

Nichole turned away and glanced quickly at herself in the dressing-table mirror.

"He never said anything," she said, quietly.

" 'E never told me much about you, neither," said Kittie. "That's the kind of man 'e is, I s'pose."

"Tell him he mustn't interfere anymore. Please, Kittie. You did say your name was Kittie, didn't you?"

"Yes, ma'am."

"He mustn't do anything. Or say anything. Then no one will get hurt. You must tell him that. Promise me."

"I think 'e's past listenin', ma'am. Too much blood under the bridge, you might say."

Nichole winced at the metaphor. "Why did you come here?"

"I wanted to tell you things maybe 'Enry wouldn't say. 'E wants to see justice done, ma'am."

"Justice," repeated Nichole, scornfully.

Kittie ignored the interruption. "Knowing 'im, I don't think 'e'll rest till 'e does. I feel 'im slipping away, ma'am. I don't want to lose 'im."

"Why should I help you?"

"Not me, ma'am. 'Enry. If you ever 'ad any feelings for 'im.

"It's not that simple."

"Yes, it is."

"Hah!"

"All 'e's asking is for you to write down on paper what you told 'im already."

"If I do that, I'm as good as dead," said Nichole.

"And 'ow much of a life can you enjoy livin' with it on your conscience?" asked Kittie.

The two women regarded each other in silence for a moment.

"What would you do in my place, Kittie?" asked Nichole.

"I'd look into my 'eart, ma'am."

Nichole dropped her shoulders, and the sigh she emitted was almost a sob.

"The heart is a clown, Kittie, dressed up in judges' robes."

*   *   *

The ocean was calm that night, but ships in the North Atlantic lanes had spotted ice, and were warning other vessels in the vicinity. The position they telegraphed was between forty-one and forty-two degrees north, forty-nine and fifty degrees west, in the Gulf Stream south of Greenland. Both eastbound and westbound ships reported encounters with ice fields and with individual bergs large and small.

Fifty feet above the *Titanic*'s forecastle deck, lookouts George Hogg and Frank Evans stamped their feet in the crow's nest as they scanned the horizon, wishing away the time when their watch would end at ten o'clock. The wind blew directly into their faces and made their eyes water.

On the bridge the officers of the watch found the air temperature noticeably colder than it had been the previous night. They called down to the galley for hot cocoa as the first-class passengers filed into the dining saloon for dinner.

Cornelia Tarr had retired to bed, urging her husband, Rhonda and Hislop to leave her behind. But Tarr insisted, over her protestations, that Nichole remain with her.

In the dining saloon Henry went about his business with professional detachment. He handed out wine lists and served bottles without his customary involvement. He could not concentrate. His mind was on Tarr. If he wanted to insure that the banker survived the voyage, surely the best thing he could do was to warn him that someone on board was out to kill him. But Tarr was used to death threats. He must know. Yet there was nothing Henry had seen while observing Tarr to suggest that his former employer had taken any measures to protect himself.

True, Hislop was continually by his side, but the preacher was a shadow not a shield.

Henry found himself in the ironic position of having to protect Thaddeus Nugent Tarr from the very fate he had wished upon him.

Tarr, he could see as he watched the man tuck his

serviette into his collar, was in better humor now, acknowledging the attentions of diners who had already received invitations to his party. Henry saw Jim Gordon approach the table, and he moved along the wall to be within earshot.

"Evening, Thaddeus," he heard Gordon say. "Looks like you got your revenge." The foppish banker pulled out a cheque and handed it to Tarr. "Two thousand dollars. Luck of the Irish."

"Just a good guess, Jim. Things are turning my way. I can feel it." Tarr beamed. "Any word from your people in New York?"

"Not yet. The captain tells me there's a backlog of cables. Some malfunction of the wireless equipment overnight, apparently. Good thing they didn't need it."

"Why don't you pull up a chair and join us?"

"Thanks but I'm dining with the Wideners tonight. George's wife's birthday, you know."

"You don't say," said Tarr, looking around to see if the couple was in the room. "I ought to send over a bottle of champagne."

"Eleanor doesn't drink," said Gordon, smiling as he moved away.

"See you tomorrow then, Jim. You got your invitation?"

"Oh, yes. The party. Enjoy your dinner."

"Damned snob," muttered Tarr under his breath. He patted the cheque in his breast pocket.

"Shall we double up for tomorrow?" he called after Gordon.

But the banker did not hear him, or pretended not to, as he threaded his way through the tables.

Cornelia Tarr's cabin was stifling hot. She had turned the electric heater up to its full power. She took off her turban, allowing her thinning hair to fall like cobwebs around her face. She wore an apricot-colored silk nightdress. She lay on the eiderdown, knees bent, working her thumbnail into the loose stitching along the seam.

"You look tired, Mrs. Tarr," said Nichole. "Why don't you rest?"

"My rings are hurting me," Cornelia said, pulling them from her fingers and handing them to Nichole. "I'm beyond tiredness, my dear Every time I close my eyes I see such horrors."

"My mother used to say that nightmares never come back if you tell them to somebody when the sun shines."

Cornelia smiled. "How I wish I were a child again."

"I know." Nichole sighed. "If only we didn't have to grow up."

Cornelia placed her fingertips on her eyelids. "What do you see when you close your eyes?"

"Nothing," said Nichole. "Just blackness."

"You know what I see? I see the family portraits in my daddy's house in Atlanta. All the way up the staircase. Six generations of McKinleys. You wouldn't think that would frighten me, would you? Family should be a comfort. At the top was a creaking step. At night it held a special terror for me when I was a girl. Next to it hangs great-grandfather Emerson Whitby McKinley. He served as Robert E. Lee's aide-de-camp in Virginia until he was killed. The night before the surrender he was accidentally shot in the eye by one of his own infantrymen. When I close my eyes I see the blood spurting from his torn socket, flooding down his thin, angular face and spreading in a great purple stain over his powder-blue uniform."

"Oh, Mrs. Tarr."

"And that's not all, child. In my mind I hear the crack of thunder and lightning. The same sound I heard when the palmetto tree was split in two and consumed by flames. I was watching that night from my bedroom window. It burned like a giant sulphur match. Lit up the sky for miles around, and turned the leaves of the magnolia trees to gold."

In the silence between them they listened to the low hum of the ship's engines. A steward passed along the corridor outside, calling late-comers to dinner.

Cornelia held up a feather she had pulled from the hole she had made in the eiderdown and blew on it. She let it go, watching it rise in the heavy air then float down.

"Poor little bird," she said.

"Are you sure you don't want anything to eat?" asked Nichole.

"Eat? No, thank you."

"Are you all right? Would you like me to turn down the heat?"

"No. It reminds me of Atlanta in August. Remember how sore our wrists got from all that fanning? No, you wouldn't remember. You were a baby, Rhonda. Just a baby."

Nichole looked at the cognac bottle on the night table.

"How like your father you've grown. Not like my side of the family at all. You seem to be so wrapped up in your thoughts all the time."

"I'm sorry. Do you mind if I get a fan from my cabin?" asked Nichole. "I'll only be a moment."

"Go ahead, child. I'll wait for Daddy. Daddy's gone for a drive. He'll be back soon."

Nichole closed the cabin door quietly behind her and stood listening for a moment.

She heard the clink of glass against glass. Cornelia Tarr would not miss her; she would be thankful for her absence. Instead of heading for her cabin, Nichole turned into the vestibule of the first-class entrance and descended the staircase.

One deck below, she approached the inquiry office.

"May I help you?" asked the clerk.

"I would like to send a telegraph to New York," she said. "How soon will it arrive?"

"It should be delivered first thing in the morning, ma'am."

"Good."

Nichole took the form and pencil he slid across the counter. In block capitals she wrote: "Dear Mother.

Legal assistance vital. Please contact your lawyer immediately. Have him meet *Titanic* on arrival. Urgent. Love, Nichole."

She looked around nervously as the clerk logged the cable.

"Name and cabin number, please."

"Linley. B71. How much is that in dollars?"

The man counted the words and did a quick calculation on the back of the form.

"Twelve dollars and fifty cents, ma'am."

Nichole opened her purse and paid. She waited until she had seen him stuff the form into a brass cylinder tipped with rubber and place it in the pneumatic tube above his head. With the push of a button and a rush of air, her message was on its way up to the wireless room on the Boat Deck.

Nichole walked slowly back to Cornelia's cabin and knocked on the door.

"It's Nichole, Mrs. Tarr."

There was no reply. She knocked again, then opened the door. The sweet smell of cognac assailed her nostrils.

"Mrs. Tarr?"

The room was in darkness. She felt her way to the bed and fumbled for the lamp. The heat was oppressive.

Cornelia was not in bed. The balloon glass was on the night table, but the cognac bottle was missing.

Nichole went to the bathroom. The light was on, but Cornelia was not there.

She felt her heartbeat beginning to quicken. She raced into the sitting room, then Tarr's bedroom. There was no sign of Cornelia, and no evidence to suggest that Cornelia had decided to join her husband for dinner.

Nichole dashed into the corridor, searching frantically, but there was no one there. She returned to the suite and broke a fingernail as she tugged at the sliding door to Tarr's private promenade.

The moon created a pattern of squares along the covered expanse of deck. She moved to the railing and looked down. Sixty feet below her, the *Titanic*'s wash rolled into creamy phosphorescence.

The cold wind slapped at her face. She felt giddy and sick.

"Oh, my God. Please no."

The vastness of the ocean spread out to a black horizon. Nichole backed into the sitting room. In desperation she began to pull open the closets and run her hands through the clothes hanging inside.

Breathing heavily, she sat on the edge of the chaise longue, pressing her palms against her temples.

Tarr had asked her to look after his wife, and now she had disappeared.

Nichole rose, checked her face in the mirror above the mantelpiece and headed out towards the dining saloon.

Her eyes were blurred with tears as she walked down the corridor. What was she going to say to Tarr?

Ahead of her she could see dimly the figure of a man blocking her passage.

"Excuse me," she mumbled as she approached him.

The man stepped to one side, removed his hat and allowed her to pass. She noticed that his hair was parted in the middle.

She could hear the clatter of cutlery and the buzz of animated conversation as she neared the entrance to the dining saloon.

At the door, the maître d'hôtel bowed to her and inquired if she wanted a table.

She ignored him and walked quickly to Tarr's table.

Henry watched her as she bent to whisper in Tarr's ear. He saw Tarr's eyes swing from left to right as he listened. The agitation in Nichole's face suggested that her message was serious.

He watched Tarr rise and pull the serviette from his collar. Hislop stood, followed by Rhonda. The party moved towards the entrance. At the door, Henry saw Tarr stop and say something to Hislop. Both men glanced towards Henry. Then Tarr stormed out of the restaurant.

Hislop made his way through the tables to where Henry stood by the buffet, wine bottle in hand.

"Mr. Tarr needs you in his suite, Henry. Right away."

"I'm on duty, Hislop. I don't work for Mr. Tarr."

"Please. I beg you." He moved closer. "It's Mrs. Tarr," he whispered. "She's disappeared."

Henry's first thought as he rushed along the corridor was that Cornelia Tarr had met the fate the Macklins had designed for her husband. Then his mind began to formulate other possibilities. Did they intend to revenge themselves on the whole family one by one? Someone had already tried to kidnap Rhonda.

Tarr was pacing the sitting room when Henry entered the suite.

"God damned brandy," he was shouting. "It's rotting her mind. Rhonda, get your coat on and look for your mother on the Boat Deck. Nichole, you search the public rooms. Hislop, you take the bars."

The preacher's face was deathly pale.

"She didn't change or anything," said Nichole. "She must have gone off in her night dress."

"Are you telling me she's traipsing around with nothing on?"

Before Nichole could answer, Tarr turned his attention to Henry.

"Ah, Blexill. Now listen to me. Mrs. Tarr has wandered off somewhere. I don't want any scandal. You know the ship, so you're going to help us find her."

Tarr saw Henry glance at the open door leading to the promenade.

"Don't even think it!" Tarr shouted. "She wouldn't do that to me."

Henry crossed and slid the heavy door shut. If Cornelia Tarr had fallen or been pushed over the side, there would be no finding her now. By the time Captain Smith had turned the ship and lowered a lifeboat, Cornelia would have died of exposure, if she had not drowned as a result of the fall.

Henry looked at Nichole, who lowered her eyes.

"Why in God's name did you leave her alone?" shouted Tarr.

"There's no use shouting, Daddy," said Rhonda. "We're wasting time. Let's start looking."

"Where was Mrs. Tarr last seen?" asked Henry.

"She was lying on the bed in there," said Nichole. "I was only gone for a couple of minutes."

Henry went in and studied the bed. He saw the hole Cornelia had made in the eiderdown. There were feathers on the carpet. He had seen feathers in the corridor that led in the direction of the dining saloon.

"If Mrs. Tarr is wandering around the ship the captain should be informed," he said to Tarr.

"I'll talk to the captain when it's time," said the banker. "You just get looking."

Henry followed the trail of feathers as far as it led. He heard Nichole behind him. From the doorway of his suite Tarr was watching them.

"Go with them," Tarr said to Hislop.

Henry checked the reading room and the lounge through the windows as he passed. He was running. The promenade was deserted. He checked the first-class foyer by the aft staircase, and the smoking room behind it. A steward was putting out clean spittoons in preparation for the after-dinner crowd.

Nichole and Hislop were waiting anxiously for him when he entered the Palm Court Room.

"Any sign of her?" asked Nichole.

Henry shook his head.

"We'd better try the Boat Deck."

The night air was raw as they climbed the iron stairs to the Boat Deck. Their feet rang on the metal steps. The handrail was slippery with dew. Above them the stars shone as white as ice.

"She has an inner fortitude," said Hislop. "She has faith."

If Cornelia Tarr was still on the ship, thought Henry,

she would need all the warmth her faith and the cognac could give her.

"We'd better split up. Hislop, you take the port side. I'll take starboard. Nichole, you search the area where the deck chairs are stowed."

The air was like cold steel against his skin. Above him the telegraph wires were humming. He imagined Bride bent over his Morse buzzer, tapping away in his tiny room.

Shafts of light from the officers' quarters painted yellow squares on the deck.

Henry felt his way along the first lifeboat. The wind made its canvas cover flap against the gunwales with the thudding sound of a badly tuned drum.

He saw something on the steel plate at the base of a stanchion. He worked his way between the boats and knelt down.

It was an empty cognac bottle.

He picked it up and held the label to the light. Hine Vieille Grande Champagne, the brand he had delivered to Tarr's suite. The cork was missing.

"Over here," he yelled.

He could see two white faces come bobbing out of the darkness.

"Did you find her?" called Nichole.

"I found this," he replied, "by the railing here."

"Oh, merciful God," cried Hislop, grasping the railing with both hands as if to tear it from its mounting.

Nichole placed a hand on his sleeve.

"Who's going to tell Mr. Tarr?"

None of them moved. They just stared down into the blackness of an indifferent ocean.

Rhonda came running towards them.

"I've found her!" She stood in front of them, arms across her chest, rubbing her shoulders for warmth. "She's in the gymnasium.

The four of them headed inside. The long hall was dark, except where bars of silver light angled in through the windows. In the shadows at one end of the gym, Cornelia sat on the leather saddle of an electric camel. Rhonda's coat was draped around her shoulders. She held a metal bar rising from the pummel and rocked slowly back and forth, singing.

"Ride a cock horse to Banbury Cross to see a fine lady on a white horse. With rings on her fingers and bells on her toes, she shall have music wherever she goes . . ."

Henry watched as Hislop, Rhonda and Nichole helped Cornelia out of the gymnasium. They said nothing to him as they passed. He might as well have been invisible. He shook his head sadly.

He returned to the restaurant, which was almost empty. Georgie Skinner sidled over to him, smirking. "There's someone waiting for you in the wine room. You had better be quick. Kirkbride's been sniffin' around."

The walls of the wine room were honeycombed with racks. The lights were low, and the air was cooled by a small refrigeration unit.

Henry opened the door. In the dim light he saw Kittie, her back pressed against a wall of bottles.

"Kittie!"

"I thought you'd never get 'ere, luv. It's freezing."

"Did you find Macklin?"

"No," said Kittie, "better still. I got something for you."

From the folds of her uniform she produced an envelope. "A present."

He took the envelope. There was nothing written on the outside, and the flap had not been glued down. He slid out three sheets of notepaper and spread them flat. He recognized Nichole's handwriting, tiny and precise. He began to read.

Saturday, April 13, 1912. Dear Henry, I am writing this for you on the understanding that you will show it to no one until after we have landed in New York. That was our agreement, and I know you as a man of your word. What follows is a true and accurate account of events that occurred at the Westchester estate on July 14, 1911, as I recall them . . .

Henry looked at Kittie. She was smiling broadly.

"How on earth did you get this?"

"I introduced myself to Nichole. She's very pretty."

"But what did you say to her?"

"Women's talk, luv. I think she wanted to get it off 'er chest. 'Course she didn't want to do it at first. Took a bit of coaxin'. Then she stood up and kissed me on the cheek and told me to come back in an hour."

"Kittie, you're wonderful."

She blew on her nails and polished them on her chest in the time-honored gesture of self-congratulation.

"Got any mountains you want movin'?"

"It's all here," he said, scanning the letter. "Just what McGillivray asked for."

" 'Ide it away somewhere safe for all our sakes."

"Don't worry," said Henry, slipping the envelope into an inside pocket. The door to the wine room opened suddenly.

"Blexill!"

Henry turned slowly around. Standing in the corridor with his hands on his hips was Kirkbride.

"Get back in the restaurant. And you, young lady, you've just saved me a trip below deck. Purser wants to see you right away."

"It's my fault," improvised Henry. "One of my passengers left a watch in the swimming bath. I asked Miss Boyer to locate it."

"I said right away, girl."

Kittie smiled wanly at Henry and moved past him. Kirkbride followed her down the corridor.

Henry's first instinct was to make sure that Nichole's confession was stowed securely. Then he could intercede with the purser on Kittie's behalf. Experience had proved to him that his ship's locker was not safe. He needed a strong box.

Henry licked the flap of the envelope and sealed it. He

waited until Kirkbride and Kittie were out of sight, then descended to the inquiry office.

Ernest King was no longer on duty, and Henry did not know the new clerk.

"I have an envelope for the safe," said Henry.

"It's for first-class passengers only," replied the man.

His eyes were set close together, and Henry recognized in his pinched features the confined logic of the born bureaucrat.

"This belongs to a first-class passenger," said Henry. "The lady asked me to deposit it for her."

The clerk inspected the envelope, turning it over in his hands and squeezing it.

"Needs a name and a cabin number before I can accept it."

"Linley, Miss Nichole Linley. B71."

The man consulted the passenger list to confirm. "Cabin B71 is listed under the name of McKinley." His eyes registered the simultaneous emotions of triumph and suspicion.

"Three cabins and a suite were booked in the name of McKinley. That's Mr. Tarr's wife's maiden name. Mr. Tarr, as your list will tell you, is booked into B51," explained Henry, controlling his temper. "Please be good enough to hurry. I'm on duty in the dining room."

"I'm well aware which cabin is occupied by Mr. Tarr, but I can only accept articles registered in the same name as listed here."

"Look. The lady is in her cabin. She is seasick. She would have brought this herself, but she can hardly stand. Now be a good fellow and do her a favor. Just put her name on it, and cabin B71."

Henry waited impatiently as the clerk went through the process of printing the name and cabin number on the front of the envelope, then into the ledger. He turned the book around for Henry to sign.

Henry wathed the clerk cross to the gray-green Milner safe, turn the dial and pull open the heavy door by its great brass handle. He saw the man place the envelope on top of a blue velvet jewellery box, then shut the door, pull the handle downwards and spin the combination.

Satisfied, he turned away. Never in his life had he felt more like John L. Sullivan. Invincible.

Sunday, April 14, 1912

BY MORNING THE news that Stewardess Kittie Boyer had been caught stealing money from a first-class cabin had circulated among the crew. It was Georgie Skinner who brought the gossip to Henry as they were pouring orange juice for the passengers' breakfast. Immediately, Henry put down the jug and headed for Tarr's suite.

He took out the gold money clip and held it in his hand while he knocked. Hislop opened the door.

"I want to see Mr. Tarr," he said, controlling his anger.

Hislop opened the door to reveal Thaddeus Tarr standing by the window in his shirt-sleeves smoking a cigar.

"What is it, Blexill?"

"I believe this was given in error to one of my colleagues," he said, holding out the clip.

"So that's where it went!"

Tarr seemed delighted to have it back. He stroked his thumb over the strip of barbed wire embedded in the gold.

The door to Cornelia's cabin was ajar. Henry could see her propped up on the pillows with a glazed expression in her eyes. Rhonda was reading to her.

"And how is Mrs. Tarr this morning?"

"She's fine. You're not waiting for a tip, are you?"

"No, Mr. Tarr. There's a matter I'd like to bring to your attention. A stewardess has been accused of taking money from your suite. I know that's not what happened."

"The woman is a thief, Blexill. The money was in that drawer. Mr. Hislop caught her in the act."

"That's not true, and you know it."

"Then how did my money come to be in her possession?"

"Hislop gave it to her."

They both looked at the preacher, whose face turned crimson.

"I understand why you're taking an interest in such a sordid little affair, Blexill. Since the woman in question is your lover."

The look of surprise on Henry's face made Tarr laugh.

"You see, I know all about you. Perhaps you even put her up to it."

"Hislop, tell him. You gave her the money."

"Now why would Mr. Hislop give your lady friend money?" Tarr leered suggestively.

"Because he needed information."

"You can go now, Blexill," said Tarr.

"Tell him the truth, Hislop!"

The preacher cracked his knuckles and looked appealingly at Tarr.

"I said you can go now," growled Tarr.

"Remember Brandon, Hislop," said Henry, as he moved to the door. "How much more can you take?"

"Get out!" roared the banker. "Before I have you locked up for insubordination. You've seen what I can do. Let that be a warning to you to keep your mouth shut."

When Henry had left he picked up his jacket and patted the pocket that held his revolver.

"Has that material been sent to White Star yet?"

"It's Sunday, Mr. Tarr. The offices would be closed."

Tarr grunted. "I'm going to the barber for a shave before church," he said. "I want you to come along."

"But shouldn't I remain with Mrs. Tarr?" suggested Hislop. "In case she comes out of sedation?"

"Rhonda's perfectly capable of looking after her mother. The last thing I want to deal with now is a wife with DTs. Everything is collapsing around my ears."

"Once we get back to New York you'll be able to pull things round," said the preacher.

"You're a regular little Mary Sunshine, you know that,

Hislop? I've had seven replies. Seven. And all negative. The vultures are calling in their loans."

"There's still Mr. Gordon."

"Jim Gordon is one of them, for crying out loud. It's a god damn conspiracy, I tell you."

Barber August Weikman offered to take Tarr's jacket, to make him more comfortable while he was shaved. But the banker insisted on wearing it. He sat in the chair, glowering at the mirror.

Hislop stationed himself at the end of a padded bench by the door so he could watch the corridor.

The ceiling above him was hung with pennants and shoulder bags emblazoned with reproductions of the *Titanic*. Tacked to the wall were souvenir medallions, woven crests and tinted postcards depicting the great ship under full steam.

Tarr shut his eyes as Weikman tilted back the chair and wrapped his face in a hot towel.

"Someone is pulling their strings."

"I beg your pardon, sir?"

"I'm not talking to you. And take this damn towel off my face. Hislop, are you there?"

"Yes, Mr. Tarr."

"There's only one person who can do that—our old friend John Pierpont. He's the only one who could blackmail men I've done business with for years."

"You could be right, Mr. Tarr," agreed Hislop.

The banker squeezed the leather arms of the chair as his anger mounted. "Remember how they used to drink at my trough? Now they're turning on me like a pack of rabid dogs. And Morgan is the master of the hounds."

"Maybe you should set up a meeting with him when you get home."

"There are three more market days before we dock. Use your brain, man. It'll be too late. But Thaddeus Nugent Tarr isn't finished yet. I'll show them all. If they won't back me, I'll drag them all down with me, every last son of a bitch. I swear, Hislop, if Tarr Investments goes under,

I'll see to it that Wall Street comes with me. The Depression of 1904 will look like a cakewalk by comparison."

As August Weikman was stropping his straight razor, First Wireless Officer John Phillips received a message from the captain of the Cunard liner *Caronia*, en route from New York to Liverpool. It was addressed to the "Captain of the *Titanic*." Phillips logged it in at nine o'clock. It read: "Westbound steamers report bergs, growlers and field ice in 42° north from 49° to 51° west. April 12. Compliments, Barr."

Phillips shook Harold Bride awake and told him to take the message immediately to the bridge.

The *Titanic* was steaming on a course of south sixty-two west in a calm sea as Captain Smith read the cable. He nodded to his chief officer, Henry Wilde, and asked him to post the message on the bridge notice board.

"Insure that this is drawn to the attention of every officer as they come on watch," Smith said. On his way out he added, "I want all hands who aren't on duty at divine service. They are to distribute the company prayer books and collect them at the end."

Smith walked the short distance to his private sitting room, which was behind the wheelhouse. He sat at his desk to prepare himself for the forty-five-minute service he would conduct.

It was the custom of the White Star Line to hold Sunday services in first class and to invite worshippers from the other classes to attend. God warred with Mammon as passengers from steerage filed into the dining saloon, awed by the magnificence of their surroundings. They stared open-mouthed with wonder, touching the wallpaper and curtains, running inquisitive fingers over the bow-shaped backs of oak chairs and fluted columns. They whispered and pointed out prominent members of society, arguing noisily over which was John Jacob Astor and which hat concealed the face of Lady Lucille Gordon. They craned their necks and jostled with each other for aisle seats.

All the while, the orchestra played solemn music as

members of the congregation settled themselves in their seats.

Positioned near the restaurant entrance, Henry Blexill handed out prayer books from a trolley. The books were new, and their covers smelled of cowhide. He wondered how many of them would be returned at the end of the service.

He thought about Kittie, alone in her room. He was certain that Kirkbride had engineered her confinement. Once the service was over he would be off duty. He had to get Hislop alone. Only the preacher's word could set the record straight.

The doors at the far end of the room swung open, and Henry caught sight of Tarr with Hislop by his side. They pressed their way to their seats, leaving a vacant place between them.

Henry's gaze travelled across the faces in the saloon, looking for the man with the moustache and the wavy hair parted down the centre. The church service was the only occasion when other classes could legitimately walk the corridors of first class. But would the man show himself in such a public place? Henry watched Tarr swivel in his chair, visibly fuming that passengers from the lower decks had swarmed into his domain.

The orchestra stopped playing. The murmur of voices fell as Captain Smith strode into the saloon and placed his prayer book on the lectern. He consulted his pocket watch. It was ten-thirty. He nodded to William Hartley, who raised his baton. The musicians took up their instruments. The congregation rose as one.

During the opening hymn, Henry fixed his eyes on Tarr, who kept glancing around. The banker was trying to establish eye contact with various men in the room, but the men steadfastly refused to acknowledge him. Henry saw Tarr lean across to Hislop and whisper behind his prayer book. Hislop looked at the empty seat between them and shook his head as if he had no answer to Tarr's question.

Henry thought about the empty chair. The three women

must be in Mrs. Tarr's cabin. She was in no condition to be left unattended. The spare seat would be for Nichole or Rhonda—more likely for Rhonda, since Nichole was paid to look after Mrs. Tarr.

He wondered why Tarr would expose himself if he knew his life was in danger. He must realize there was a man somewhere on board waiting for another chance to kill him. An Englishman—for only an Englishman would use the term "blighter"—who had already tried to kidnap Rhonda in a London park. Rhonda and Cornelia were unprotected now. Would the man revenge himself on Tarr by murdering his family? No, it had to be Tarr. But whose orders was the would-be assassin following?

The banker knew Schuyler Macklin and his uncle by sight, and they would not be able to get near him. Tarr would be an easier target for an unknown assassin in London than he would be in New York, without his army of Pinkertons around him.

And how did Lord Rutherland fit into the scheme? Was it merely a coincidence that the shoe horn came from his boot maker's store? Heaven knows, the old aristocrat had reasons enough to wish Tarr dead. But he had no resources to hire a killer.

The congregation sat, and Captain Smith began to read the lesson.

Henry's mind kept working over the details of the mystery. Maybe he was following the wrong scent. Maybe the person who wanted Thaddeus Nugent Tarr dead had nothing to do with the Macklins or Lord Rutherland. Perhaps it had to do with railroads and a beautiful woman who had once been the mistress of J.P. Morgan, and who might well still be, in spite of her protestations to the contrary.

Morgan, as president of the White Star Line, should have been on board the *Titanic* for her maiden voyage. But he had cancelled his passage at the last minute. Why? Thaddeus Tarr was occupying the suite that had been specially designed for Morgan. If Morgan had wanted Tarr disposed of, he would have had the deed done in Europe

ather than on his boat. Or could he be sunning himself on
the Côte d'Azur while his financial rival was being killed?

The kidnap attempt may have been arranged to frighten
Tarr, to show him how vulnerable he was. But Tarr did
not frighten easily, and he would not be deterred from
attacking Morgan's railroad interests. And what if the Wizard of Wall Street had found out that Tarr had killed
Marsden Dewey, a trusted accountant Tarr was bribing to
spy on Morgan's intricate empire of companies and trusts?
In the mind of a robber baron like J.P. Morgan, such a
matter might be settled outside the law.

Morgan might not be on the *Titanic*, but he knew what
was happening. Someone on board was keeping him up to
date on Tarr's financial dealings.

Was that what Nichole meant when she warned Henry
to let Morgan take care of it? "He hates Thaddeus," she
had said. Did Morgan hate Tarr enough to have him
killed?

But Nichole had told McGillivray that Henry was a
murderer. What if the same information had been passed
on to Morgan? Tarr could have done it. Or Nichole.
Maybe the man with the moustache was waiting for Henry.

The congregation rose for the final hymn, "Oh, God,
Our Help in Ages Past." Henry saw the entrance door ease
open. A figure slipped into the room and moved behind
him. He could feel the hairs on his neck begin to prickle.
If he turned quickly he could catch the man off balance.
He stood still, holding his breath, trying to hear movement
over the chorus of voices. A hand touched his elbow.

He turned his head and looked down. Next to him stood
Kittie. She smiled at him and winked.

"They let me out."

She was beaming with pleasure.

"What happened?" whispered Henry.

"The purser said it was all a mistake, apologized and
gave me a raise. 'Ow d'you like them apples?'"

Shielded by the pile of prayer books on the trolley,
Henry took her hand and squeezed it. He looked at Hislop.
The preacher was singing, his eyes closed.

"By the way," said Kittie, holding a prayer book to her face, "I thought you ought to know. One of the stewards, Willie Burke, 'ad this bloke come up to 'im just now and offer 'im a fiver for a loan of 'is steward's jacket."

"Did he give it to him?"

"Yes. 'E said 'e needed it for a fancy-dress parade in first class, and 'e'd give it back right after."

Henry was aware of the schedule of entertainment for first-class passengers. There were no plans for a fancy-dress parade, certainly not on a Sunday.

At the stroke of noon, the *Titanic* sounded its whistles to signal the change of watch. The sombre grace notes reverberated through the ship. The sound awakened Cornelia, who had dozed fitfully all morning. She sat up unsteadily, still groggy from the sedative, not knowing where she was. Nichole placed a reassuring hand on her arm.

"It's all right," she said. "Everything's fine."

But when Cornelia turned her face towards her, Nichole saw the terror in the woman's eyes. The retinas were large and fathomless, and in their blackness they expressed such torment that she had to look away.

"Where is Rhonda?"

"At church with her father."

Cornelia lay back on the pillows.

"Get me some cognac, will you, dear?"

"Mr. Tarr instructed me not to," said Nichole. "Why don't I get you a nice cup of tea instead?"

Cornelia's fingers tightened around Nichole's hand. Her grip was surprisingly powerful. Her voice was measured and deliberate.

"If you want me ever to speak to you again you'll do as I ask."

"I can't take any responsibility, Mrs. Tarr."

"You never have, my dear, just do as I ask."

"Promise me you won't leave the room."

Tarr occupied himself by supervising the final preparations for his party. The Palm Court Room had been placed off limits to passengers while the staff decorated it according to the banker's lavish instructions. Long tables were set in the centre for the food. Flowers were placed in ornate Greek vases on each of the small tables. Great armfuls of roses had been woven into vines and strung from a central point in the ceiling.

Nichole found Tarr marshalling the stewards, directing the entire operation like a battlefield general. The dutiful Hislop sat near the revolving door that gave access to the smoking room. In front of him was a plate of sandwiches.

"What are you doing here?" Tarr demanded. "Why aren't you with my wife?"

"She's asking for cognac," said Nichole.

"Well, she can't have any. Hang that thing higher," he called to a waiter perched on a ladder. "I don't want my guests knocking into it."

"You'll have to talk to her, Thaddeus. She frightens me."

Tarr stopped and turned his attention to her.

"Frightens you? Cornelia frightens you? What the hell are you talking about?"

"Please, you must come to the cabin."

"Is Rhonda with her?"

"I thought Rhonda was with you."

"Damn that girl. She wasn't at church, either. Come on. You men get on with it. I want this finished by the time I get back."

During the afternoon, while the Palm Court was being decorated, the bridge received an ice warning from another White Star liner, the *Baltic*, relayed to her by the Greek steamer *Athinai*. Three minutes later, at one forty-five, the German vessel *Amerika* reported that she had passed two large icebergs. Marconi operator Harold Bride, having relieved John Phillips, relayed the sightings to Washington for the United States Hydrographic Office records.

Henry had been ordered by Kirkbride to tend the bar for

Tarr's party. The request for his services had been expressly made by the host. It was up to Henry to insure that there would be enough champagne and glasses.

"And be sure the glasses are clean," Kirkbride reminded him.

"There's nothing that makes champagne go flatter than a dirty glass."

"Are you trying to teach your grandmother to suck eggs?" asked Henry.

Kirkbride pushed his face close to Henry's. "You'll get yours before this trip's over. I promise you that."

Henry wondered if Kirkbride could be the one Morgan's people had hired. Since their fight over Kittie, he was looking for revenge. But some passenger had bribed a steward for his jacket. Henry had to smoke him out before the man could accomplish his mission.

On the pretext of checking the champagne supplies, Henry went in search of Willie Burke.

He found Burke playing cards with three other men. They sat on the edge of their bunks. Their table was a battered sea chest. Each had a pile of pennies in front of him.

Henry called Burke away from the game and asked him to describe the man to whom he had lent his steward's jacket.

"He was an ordinary sort of bloke. Brown hair, about your height. Young, with a moustache."

"What's his name?"

"He didn't give a name."

"You lent your jacket to someone and you don't know his name?"

"It was a spare I keep in the pantry in case something gets spilled."

"What cabin's he in?"

"Couldn't tell you. Not in second class, anyway. I know them all now."

So the man who attempted to kidnap Rhonda and who had tried to boil Tarr alive in the steam room was travelling third class. Ideal for anonymity. It would be simple for him to work his way up to first class on the stairs.

An Englishman who was determined to see Tarr dead. A stranger who could stalk him and choose the moment, just as he had seized the opportunity in the steam bath.

Trying to locate the man without knowing the name he travelled under would be difficult. Third-class passengers occupied four decks, D down to G, and were quartered at the ship's bow and stern. In the interests of delicacy and decorum, White Star regulations dictated that single men be berthed at the forward end of the *Titanic* and single women aft.

Third-class cabins accommodated from two to ten passengers. In addition, there were open berths forward on G Deck. The decor in the *Titanic*'s third class was in keeping with the ship's overall philosophy of comfort and luxury. The steel-plated walls might not have been hidden behind elegant wood panelling and woven tapestries, as they were in first class, but the furnishings and floor coverings of the third-class public rooms were the equal to many other liners' second-class facilities.

Henry was aware that seventy per cent of the *Titanic*'s third-class berth capacity had been booked. Seven hundred and twelve men, women and children. Apart from the English, Irish, Scots and Welsh immigrants seeking a new life in America, Henry noted as he read through the passenger list, there were French people, Dutch people, Poles, Scandinavians, Italians, Germans and Turks, as well as Arabs and Chinese people—a whole atlas of nationalities.

Henry recognized the names of two Welsh boxers, Leslie Williams, a bantam-weight, and David Bowen, the Welsh national light-weight champion, who were heading to New York for a series of bouts with American prize fighters. They shared cabin space with Eugene Daly, who wore a kilt and played the Uilleann pipes, whose plangent cry still haunted Cornelia Tarr's mind. Also in third class were Katherine Gilnaugh, not yet sixteen, who caught Daly's eye when they boarded in Queenstown. Anna Sjoblom, an eighteen-year-old from Finland who was seasick most of the time. Olaus Abelseth, a twenty-six-year-old Norwegian, on his way to farm in South Dakota; in his charge was the sixteen-year-old daughter of a family friend, bound for Minneapolis. . . .

Among this global microcosm Henry had to find an Englishman who wished to remain anonymous, but whose heart was bent on murder.

He questioned a few of the stewards and waiters on E Deck, but they were too busy to give him much time. He went back to the passenger list. The names were broken down by their point of embarkation, and the list specified citizenship.

If the man was a hired killer, he would probably be travelling with forged documents. He could have boarded at Southampton, Cherbourg or Queenston, but Henry reasoned that, if he had tried to kidnap Rhonda, he must have boarded at Southampton—he wouldn't have had time to cross to France or Ireland.

According to the list, one hundred and eighty-three British passengers had boarded at Southampton; thirty-seven were women or children. Which left nearly one hundred and fifty men.

Rhonda was the first person Tarr saw when he entered his suite, and she bore the brunt of his anger.

"You weren't in church, young lady."

"We're on a ship, Daddy."

"Don't you get smart with me, miss. I told you to be there. And when I tell you something, you do it."

"It was so crowded, I couldn't find a seat."

"I kept one for you."

"Please, don't shout, Thaddeus," Cornelia called from her cabin. "You know how it plays on my nerves."

Tarr shook a warning finger at Rhonda as he moved in the direction of his wife's voice. He closed the door behind him.

"That girl's running wild," he said. "No discipline. Why isn't Nichole doing her job?"

Cornelia shut her eyes. "Thaddeus, please. I can't stand much more. I feel so cold."

"How can you be cold? It's like a steam bath in here. I'll get the doctor."

"No. He'll only give me more pills."

"What about a massage? The barber tells me there's a masseur on board. That'll warm you up."

"I need a little cognac, Thaddeus. I can't seem to move. Cognac's good for my circulation."

"It's rotting your brain, Cornelia."

"You don't understand."

"I understand, all right. I'm trying to hold a lifetime's work together. Keep the dogs at bay. I have a daughter who's running around and a wife crazy on liquor. Why can't you help me? Why can't you be strong for once?"

"Oh, Thaddeus." Cornelia began to cry.

"Spare me the waterworks. You be dressed and ready by seven o'clock. I want you and Rhonda up there by my side. They've got to see that there's nothing wrong with the Tarrs. Understood?"

Passengers on the Boat Deck taking afternoon tea and scones noticed a sudden drop in the temperature. The thermometer on the bridge showed forty-three degrees Fahrenheit. The smell of ice was in the air. Stewards brought blankets for those who insisted on finishing their tea al fresco. The more pragmatic passengers retreated into the warmth of the lounge, leaving the stewards to bring their trays to them.

"No backbone, Americans," said Sir Duff-Gordon to his steward, as he watched the exodus from his deck chair. "Must be nearing ice. Ever seen a berg, Kirkbride?"

The chief steward, who enjoyed parading his knowledge, looked out to sea.

"Yes, indeed, m'lord," he replied. "A common sight at this time of year in these latitudes. April is particularly hazardous for icebergs in the Atlantic."

"But they don't just appear, do they?" inquired Lady Gordon.

"Actually, ma'am, they're broken-off bits of glaciers. In winter they get frozen in, but in the spring, when the temperature rises, they break loose from the pack ice. Then they float blindly around, driven by winds and currents south from Greenland into the transatlantic shipping lanes. Very dangerous, even the small ones, which are known as growlers. The large ones can be as big as buildings and older than civilization itself. Some date back one hundred thousand years."

"Really," said Lady Duff-Gordon, whose eyes were beginning to glaze over.

"But there's no need for concern, ma'am. Captain Smith has sailed these waters scores of times. And the *Titanic* has a double hull. We're virtually unsinkable."

Georgie Skinner was setting champagne bottles in silver buckets when Henry appeared in the Palm Court carrying two bottles.

"There's enough champagne to launch the entire British Merchant Marine, and you 'ave to get more." Georgie laughed. "Where you been?"

"There's a third-class passenger who may try to get in dressed as a steward. Keep your eyes peeled. If you spot him, let me know."

" 'E's got 'is priorities all wrong, mate. Looks like they'll want to bust out of this wake. I never saw such a dreary bunch."

The air was redolent with the perfume of roses. The food had been set out on great silver trays. In the centre, nestling in a bed of crushed ice, was a vast crystal bowl heaped high with caviar. The black eggs glistened like foxes' eyes under the chandeliers.

Waiters stood idly around, straightening cutlery and brushing non-existent creases from the tablecloths. The ship's orchestra tuned up in the corner, awaiting the arrival of the first guests. They were dressed in blue dinner jackets for the occasion.

A steward stood at the revolving door leading from the smoking room, and another was stationed by the sliding doors to the covered deck. They wore white gloves. They were ready to check the guests' invitations.

For his own security, Tarr had insisted that only those who had invitations would be allowed in. No free-loaders would be permitted to crash his party.

The orchestra began to play selections from "Cavalleria Rusticana" as Thaddeus Tarr, accompanied by Clifford Hislop, entered the Palm Court. He cast a critical eye over the room and nodded his approval. He spotted Henry and beckoned to him.

"This had better go off well," he said under his breath. "Tell them there's a hundred dollars in it for them. And make sure the champagne glasses are full at all times. Understand?"

"Yes, sir."

Tarr took his watch from his waistcoat pocket.

"Where is everybody? I said seven on the invitation, and it's already seven."

"People are less punctual on board," suggested Hislop in an effort to propitiate Tarr, who was already showing signs of detonation.

A man in a tight-fitting frock coat accompanied by an extravagantly dressed woman handed their invitations to a steward and made straight for the bowl of caviar. Henry began pouring glasses of champagne. Tarr took one before Georgie could lift the tray.

An elderly man appeared in the doorway and looked around, bemused. He had mistaken the room for the library, and was directed forward.

"Where's my wife?" Tarr demanded of Hislop. "Seven o'clock, I told her."

"Miss Rhonda is probably escorting her up now."

"Good evening, Mr. Tarr."

Tarr whirled around to face an overdressed woman in a large hat who was juggling a glass of champagne, a stick of celery and an evening bag.

"How very kind of you to invite us. Our card. We're from Baltimore. That's my husband over there by the roast beef trolley. Don't you love an ocean voyage?"

"Who are these people?" Tarr asked Hislop as he disengaged himself and crumpled the unwanted visiting card in his fist. "I thought 1 invited the quality. Where are Guggenheim and Astor? Widener? The bankers?"

"I imagine they'll be along," said Hislop. "It's still early."

The waiters glanced around impassively, trying to look busy even though there was nothing for them to do.

As Tarr waited impatiently for his guests to arrive, First Officer William Murdoch gave an order to Samuel Hemming, the lamp trimmer. "When you go forward, see the fore scuttle is closed as we're in the vicinity of ice. There's a glow coming from there, and I want everything dark before the bridge."

"Aye, aye, sir," said Hemming, and immediately went to batten down the hatch.

"Looks more like a wake than a party," Georgie whispered to Henry. "I take it all back," he said with a grin when he saw Rhonda come through the revolving door. She was holding her mother by the arm, and they walked slowly across the room.

Henry could tell that Cornelia had made a valiant effort to be there. As she passed him, he saw that her face was thickly rouged and powdered. She wore a chiffon gown, intricately embroidered across the chest with gold thread. Wisps of hair protruded from under her turban. The lighting on the ceiling accentuated the hollows of her cheeks and shadowed her eyes. She leaned heavily on Rhonda.

As they passed, Henry noticed an exchange between Georgie and Rhonda. The young steward winked at her, and she winked back.

Henry stepped forward and took Cornelia's other arm.

"Ah, Henry. Thank you," she said.

Between them, he and Rhonda led her to her husband, who was seated in a wicker chair. Cornelia smiled wearily at him as she sat.

"You see, Thaddeus," she said, spreading her palms in a gesture that took in her whole body. "Here I am. For what it's worth."

"Where's your jewellery? All that jewellery I've bought for you, and you're not wearing a thing."

"You had it locked up, dear, for safekeeping."

"For God's sake, woman, you've got to dazzle these people. Get 'em out of the safe."

"Oh, Thaddeus, must I look like a Christmas tree into the bargain?"

"You've got to look rich!"

"I haven't the energy."

"Can't you see she's worn out, Daddy?" asked Rhonda. "Anyway, everyone knows you're rich."

Ignoring Henry's presence, Tarr looked from his wife to his daughter. His neck was red with anger.

"They only know when they see it. Do I have to do everything around here myself?"

"Why don't I get Mrs. Tarr's jewellery box," offered Henry.

"No, I'll do it. Then I know it's done."

Tarr stormed out of the Palm Court, narrowly avoiding a collision with Georgie, who hovered behind Henry, holding a tray full of champagne glasses.

Henry was not the only witness to the scene. A man in a steward's short white jacket stood shivering in the cold outside the Palm Court. When Tarr left, the man moved into the shadows and worked his way quickly along the covered promenade.

The hatch was closed at the inquiry office counter. Instead of pressing the electric bell, Tarr hammered on the oak panel with his fist. Eventually, the hatch slid up and Ernest King's face appeared.

"Can I help you, sir? Mr. Tarr, isn't it?"

"Yes. I want my wife's jewellery out of the safe."

King took down the ledger. "Is it in your name?"

"I don't know. The box was deposited by my wife's secretary, Miss Linley."

King disappeared into the purser's office, and Tarr could hear the click of a combination lock. The clerk returned and slid the blue velvet jewellery box across the counter.

"If you'd like to check it, sir."

Tarr pulled the catch down, but it was locked.

"If it's not all there, you can be sure I'll be back," said Tarr.

"Do you mind signing for it? Here, next to the entry."

Tarr raised his pen over the page. His eyes fell on Henry Blexill's signature. It was in the column marked "Deposited By." Next to it was printed Nichole Linley's name and cabin number.

"What's this for?" Tarr pointed to the signature.

King turned the ledger around and studied the entry. "I'll check, sir."

"Well, hurry up, man. I don't have all day."

King retreated once more and returned with an envelope.

"I'll take that, too," said Tarr, signing for both items. He stuffed the envelope into his pocket before King could say anything. The clerk grimaced at Tarr's back as the banker moved across the vestibule towards the main staircase, the blue velvet box under his arm.

Tarr unlocked the door to his suite and went straight to Cornelia's cabin. He placed the jewellery box on his wife's dressing table and made a peremptory search for the key. Not finding it, he picked up a pair of nail scissors and forced the lock, snapping off a blade in the process. The sharp end of the blade was driven into his thumb, and he cursed aloud as blood began to flow.

He reached in his pocket for a handkerchief and instead brought out Nichole's envelope. Curious, he tore it open and began to read, unmindful of the bloodstain that began to spread where his thumb touched the paper.

Sunday, April 14, 1912

ON THE BRIDGE, the officer of the watch, Charles Lightoller, scanned the horizon. He had never seen the Atlantic so calm. There was no moon, but the cloudless sky was sequined with stars. Perfect for navigation. Below him on the forecastle deck a seaman lowered a canvas bucket over the side. He was drawing water to test its temperature, a practice performed at two-hour intervals throughout the voyage from the time the *Titanic* left Southampton until she docked in the Hudson River.

Lightoller adjusted his sextant, lined up on the pole star and took a bearing. The brass instrument felt cold against his cheek, and his fingers were numb. While Fourth Officer Joseph Boxhall plotted the ship's position on the navigation chart, Lightoller picked up the phone and rang the crow's nest.

"Is that you, Hogg? You and Evans keep a sharp eye out for ice," Lightoller said. "We've had several reports from other ships. Pass on the word to Symons and Jewell when they relieve you."

The lookouts would be finished their two-hour watch at eight o'clock. They were stiff with cold and looked forward to a hot chocolate below, illegally laced with rum.

In the wireless room, Harold Bride intercepted a message flashed from the Leyland Line steamer *Californian* to its sister freighter *Antillian:* "Latitude 42° 5 minutes north, longitude 49° 9 minutes west, three bergs five miles southwards of us. Regards, Lord."

He took it immediately to the bridge.

Two decks below, a man wearing a tweed sports coat over Willie Burke's steward's jacket made his way along the corridor, checking the cabin numbers. He found the one he was looking for, but he kept walking. He moved quickly to the gentlemen's lavatory amidships and slipped inside.

Locking himself in a cubicle, he removed a revolver from his tweed jacket, checked the chamber and slid it into his trouser pocket.

He took off the sports jacket and hung it on the hook on the back of the cubicle door. Emerging as a steward, he retraced his steps up the corridor.

A maid came out of a service pantry. She smiled at him as they crossed paths.

He stopped outside the door to B51 and looked up and down the corridor to assure himself there were no witnesses.

He knocked.

There was no reply.

He knocked again.

An elderly couple dressed as if for a motoring trip came out of cabin B63, forcing the man to press himself against the wall to let them pass. If he had arrived two minutes earlier, he would have seen Tarr emerge from his suite, walk a few paces down the corridor and knock on the door of B71.

"Oh, it's you, Thaddeus," said Nichole.

Tarr stepped inside and closed the door behind him. The only light came from the reading lamp above the bed. Their faces were in shadow. The single cabin was narrow, and there was little room for the two of them to stand. Nichole perched on the edge of the bed, offering the horsehair couch to Tarr.

"I guess you're wondering why I'm not at the party," she said.

Tarr picked up a bottle of perfume from the dressing table that stood between the bed and the couch. He sniffed it. "Got that for you in Paris, didn't I?"

"Yes. It's my favorite."

"Yes. Smells good on you. Why don't we have our own party down here, Nichole? Just you and me."

"I really don't feel like making love, Thaddeus. If you don't mind."

"Oh? Well, I do. Why don't you just take off your dress?"

"Please, Thaddeus." She placed a supplicatory hand on his knee. She could feel him trembling.

"Don't disappoint me, Nichole," he said.

His voice was husky and threatening. In the darkness his eyes seemed to burn with a feverish brightness. She stood up and began to unbutton the silk cuffs of her dress. He watched as she reached behind her neck and unfastened the buttons there. Slowly, she slid the dress off her shoulders and let it fall to the floor. She unlaced her bodice and stepped out of her underclothes. The chill in the air made her shiver, and the satin of the eiderdown felt cold against her back as she lay on the bed.

"Aren't you going to undress?"

"Not yet," said Tarr.

He stood and gazed down at her, letting his eyes wander over her shoulders, breasts and stomach. She could hear him exhale loudly through his moustache as he slipped to his knees beside her. Her flesh was stippled with goose bumps. He ran his hands over her like a dealer feeling the patina of a long-sought treasure. He stopped at her breasts and began to massage them, rubbing the nipples between his thumb and forefinger. Nichole trembled.

"Why don't you come in with me," she whispered.

Tarr said nothing. He just kept kneading her breasts, listening to her quick breathing.

"Not so hard," she said.

He slid his right hand down her stomach, between her legs, and inserted a finger into her moist flesh. His head lay on the pillow next to hers, his lips touching her ear.

"How much are you worth, Nichole?"

Nichole concentrated on the incessant motion of the finger working rhythmically inside her.

"Ten million? A hundred million? Two hundred million? That's right, sweetheart. Just close your eyes."

"Mm."

"Maybe more? Maybe three hundred million? Is that what you're worth, Nichole?"

She began to move her hips in a rocking motion, responding to the play of Tarr's finger. She arched her back and moved against him. Her lips were parted, and the light from the bedside lamp glistened off her teeth.

"Because that, my beauty, is what you and your friend Morgan could cost me in the end."

Her body went rigid and she fell back on the bed. She turned her head towards him. He was kneeling at her side, in an attitude of prayer, nodding his head.

"It was a long time ago, Thaddeus."

"How can I believe you, Nichole? And then there's this."

He withdrew her confession from his pocket only enough to let her see her handwriting, then tucked it away again. Nichole turned her face to the wall.

"How did you get that? Have you hurt him?"

"Not yet. But I will."

"Please don't, Thaddeus."

"I don't understand you, Nichole. I looked after you. I gave you Cumerworth Hall. And this is how you repay me. All I ever asked was loyalty."

Nichole stared at the fan on the ceiling. "I'm so tired of it all. I don't have your strength, Thaddeus."

"And what did you expect to gain from this? They'll never convict me of murder, you know."

"Don't you see what it's been doing to me all this time? I can't stand it anymore."

"You need a rest, my dear," said Tarr. "You and your friend Blexill."

"Henry knows nothing, I swear."

"Liar! You wrote this letter for him, lady. And it had better be the only copy."

He grabbed her by the shoulders and shook her. She

went as limp as the pillow under her head, offering no resistance. He threw her back on the bed.

"You used to make me feel so good," he said.

She lay there and concentrated on the fan. She was strangely at peace. She heard the sound of clothes being removed. She felt the suddenness of Tarr's weight on top of her pressing her hips down.

"Guide me in," he said.

She saw his face above her. His pupils were unnaturally large. She could hear the swishing sound of the ocean ringing in her ears.

"Oh, hear us when we cry to Thee for those in peril on the sea . . ." Two decks below, in the second-class dining saloon, a hundred voices were raised in the refrain of "Eternal Father, Strong to Save." The Reverend Ernest C. Carter was conducting a spontaneous hymn-singing evening. Accompanying the worshippers on the piano was Carter's wife, Lillian.

From the bridge, Second Officer Lightoller called down to the ship's carpenter, John Maxwell, who was in his workshop on G Deck, to ask him to watch the fresh-water supplies in case the tanks froze. He was giving the same instructions to the chief engineer, Joseph Bell, in the engine room when Captain Smith strode onto the bridge.

Captain Smith had dined in the à la carte restaurant as a guest of tramway magnate George Widener and his wife, Eleanor. Widener's other guests were Major Archie Butt, John Borland Thayer—the fifth John Borland Thayer—his wife, Maria, and William and Lucille Carter. The Wideners' twenty-seven-year-old son, Harry, a Harvard graduate, was also in the party. Over dinner Harry, a bibliophile, entertained his father's guests with the story of how he had acquired a Shakespeare first folio. He had paid a record ninety-six thousand dollars for it at a London auction house. "And just before I left New York for Europe, I narrowly missed a Gutenberg Bible," he added with a wave of his cigarette in its holder. "It eventually sold for forty-nine thousand. The theatre obviously commands more than the church."

George Widener had set up the dinner party the previous day, after he received Thaddeus Tarr's printed invitation. All the financiers and bankers on board had spontaneously discovered similar social engagements.

During dinner with the Wideners, Captain Smith made no mention of the ice. Nor did he or anyone else at the table refer to Tarr's party. Smith excused himself from the table before coffee was served, apologizing for the fact that he had to return to the bridge.

Lightoller greeted him when he arrived. "Evening, captain. Quiet night."

"There isn't much wind," said Smith, staring out at the water.

"No, sir, it's a flat calm. Pity we don't have the wind going through the ice region, though. It should be coming up soon."

"Exactly. No wind means no ripples round the base of an iceberg for the lookouts."

"Still, the night's clear enough," said Lightoller. "There'll be a certain amount of reflected light from the bergs."

"Yes, I suppose even if the blue side is up we'll see a white outline," Smith concurred.

The two officers gazed out into the star-spangled night. They could see the tiny points of light reaching across the sky to the horizon. Captain Smith pulled a pocket watch from his white dress uniform.

"Twenty past nine. I'm going to my quarters to bring the log up to date, Lightoller," he said. "If it becomes at all doubtful, let me know at once."

After the watch changed, Charles Lightoller phoned the crow's nest and repeated his message of vigilance to the new lookouts, Symons and Jewell.

In the wireless room, Jack Phillips was busy sending commercial messages to the Cape Race shore station. An exhausted Harold Bride was catching some sleep in the room next door. A message came in from the liner *Mesaba*: "In latitude 42° north to 41° 25 minutes, longitude 49° west to 50° 30 minutes west, saw much heavy pack ice and great number large icebergs also field ice weather good clear." There was no one to deliver the message to the bridge, so it sat under a paperweight on Phillips's desk.

Henry counted the bottles of champagne in the ice trays. Following Tarr's injunction, he had asked the waiters to circulate among the guests with open bottles, filling up glasses all the time. But there were almost as many waiters as there were guests. There were too few party-goers to consume the amount of wine that had been ordered.

A forced sense of gaiety permeated the room, sustained by the free-flowing champagne and the shrill conversation among people whose only common interest seemed to be the copious amounts of food and alcohol at their disposal.

Henry consulted his pocket watch. Tarr had been absent for twenty minutes or so, and the party was drifting aimlessly along without its host. He glanced at Cornelia, who sat apart from the concentration of guests at the food tables. She kept turning her head towards the door, an untouched glass of champagne on the table in front of her.

"I don't care for champagne," Henry heard her say to Hislop. "It's too fizzy, and it's always in motion. Enough to set one's nerves on edge."

"Would you like me to take you to your cabin?" inquired Hislop.

"Thank you, Clifford, but Mr. Tarr needs me here," said Cornelia. She turned to Rhonda. "What's keeping your father? He should be among his guests."

Rhonda, bored, shrugged her shoulders. "He said he was going to get your jewellery."

"My jewellery," repeated Cornelia, and a hand went to her neck.

"Would you like me to go look for him?" asked Hislop.

Cornelia smiled at him. "Considerate as ever, Clifford, but you relax. He'll be along. After all, it's his big moment."

"I don't know why Daddy did all this," said Rhonda, surveying the room. "They're like pigs at the swill."

"Rhonda!"

"Well, it's true. Look at them. I'm going to get a glass of champagne."

"Do you think you should?" asked Cornelia.

"Why not? I'm eighteen," she replied and walked across the room to where Georgie Skinner was counting used corks. She leaned over the table and said quietly to him: "If you can slip out with a bottle and a couple of glasses, we'll have our own party. You know where. Give me ten minutes."

On her way out, Rhonda winked at Henry.

"How did you like my wedding gift for you and Kittie?" she asked, smiling at him.

"Wedding gift, Miss Rhonda?"

"You're adorable when you look puzzled, Henry. I heard you and Daddy arguing. So I fixed it with the purser."

"What do you mean?"

"I told him it was me who took the money from Daddy's desk. But then I'm known for that, aren't I?

"And he believed you?"

"Of course. I cried a bit and said how sorry I was to create such a scandal. I'm really quite a good actress."

As she left the Palm Court, she narrowly avoided running into her father, who came into the room holding Cornelia's jewellery box.

Even though Henry had his back to the door he was aware of Tarr's return. There was something about the man's proximity that had always signalled itself to him. The muscles in his neck and shoulders would become tense. His every sinew and nerve end seemed to respond to the banker's presence.

Henry turned in time to see Tarr place a velvet box on the table in front of Cornelia. For some reason he could not understand, the sight of the box troubled him. He experienced a vague, unsettling sensation.

"You'd better have the key on you because I couldn't find it," he heard Tarr say. "Drew blood trying to open the damn thing."

"I'm sorry. You look flushed, dear. You shouldn't have hurried."

"Just give me the key."

"I have it in my purse," Cornelia said.

"Well, open it up and get on with it. I didn't go to all this trouble for nothing."

Cornelia sighed. She unlocked the box and lifted the lid. "Do you mind standing in front of me? I feel as if I'm dressing in public with all these people."

She took out the ruby and diamond necklace Tarr had bought her when Rhonda was born. She held the jewels against the sleeve of her dress. The blood-red rubies did not go well with the lime-colored silk.

"Don't fuss, woman. Just put the stuff on, for crying out loud."

Cornelia fastened the necklace.

"Now earrings, a brooch and a bracelet."

"But it's too much," protested Cornelia.

"You'll look beautiful in it," said Tarr through clenched teeth.

"But I can't mix rubies with emeralds. It's unlucky."

"Just put the damned things on!" he hissed.

Cornelia glanced at Hislop, appealing for him to intercede. But the preacher studied his fingertips in embarrassment. Tears rose in Cornelia's eyes.

"If it makes you happy, Thaddeus."

She put on the pieces he requested, then locked the box again.

"Here, you look after it," said Tarr, sliding the box across the table towards Hislop. "Now, I have some business to attend to. Mingle among the guests, Cornelia. Talk to people. You're meant to be the hostess."

Tarr picked up Cornelia's champagne glass, downed it in a gulp and marched through the revolving door into the smoking room.

The guests Tarr had so desperately wanted at his party were seated over coffee and brandy at a table in the smoking room as far from the Palm Court as possible. George Widener sat with his son, Harry, Jack Thayer, Jim Gordon, Ben Guggenheim and two other Philadelphia millionaires, Thomas Cardeza and William Carter. An aromatic haze of blue cigar smoke hung over them. They were laughing at a story Jim Gordon had just told as Tarr approached.

"Evening, gentlemen."

The laughter subsided as the men turned towards him.

"Hello Jim. Missed you at my party."

"Ah, Thaddeus. Sorry about that. Not very big on parties. A prior commitment."

"Seems like all you gentlemen had prior commitments."

There was an embarrassed silence during which the men sipped their brandies and knocked ash from their cigars. Nobody invited Tarr to sit down.

"Don't think I don't know what's going on," said Tarr, in a low, menacing voice. "I'm not a fool, you know." He held the back of Harry Widener's chair and rocked back and forth as he spoke. "I know what you guys are up to. But you're not going to bring down Thaddeus Nugent Tarr. Believe you me. I can tell when someone's putting the squeeze on me. All of you, you're in cahoots with Morgan. But I'm telling you now, it won't work. Because he won't be getting any more information."

He looked from one man to the next, but they avoided his eyes, shifting uncomfortably in their leather chairs. Angered by their silence, Tarr's voice rose. Other passengers in the smoking room turned to see who was shouting.

"You make me sick. You with your inherited money. Sure it's easy to have money when it's handed to you on a plate. But I started with nothing. Zero. And, by God, I made more than any of you. I didn't start with a family crest embroidered on my crib blanket. I didn't even have a blanket. You know what I had? An old flour sack. My mother lined it with newspaper to keep out the cold. That's what I started with. Now I'm worth millions.

"Have you seen the latest quotations?" asked Guggenheim, winking at Jim Gordon.

"Yes. And I know who's manipulating the market. But you guys are going to help me. Jim, and you, Thayer, and Carter here. Because if you don't I'm going to burst the bubble and we all go down the drain together. You can snub me, but you're not going to ignore me."

The men around the table avoided Tarr's eyes.

"That's why you're going to guarantee me sixty million dollars."

"And why would we lend you that kind of money?" asked Widener.

"You weren't listening very good, George. If you and your pals force Tarr Investments into bankruptcy, I'm going to drag you all down with me."

"And how do you propose to do that?" said Thayer.

"Easy. Just close the doors of my bank. Depositors don't like banks closing on them. It's un-American. It makes them nervous. And nervousness is contagious. They'll start taking their money out of your banks, too. Cause a run. Specially if I dump all my mining and railroad shares on the market at the same time. That'll really screw up the market."

"We could block you very easily," said Gordon.

"You could try, Jim boy, but this game's about confidence. And when investors lose confidence . . ." He made a diving gesture with his hand. "So, gentlemen. I'm going to my suite now. B51. I'll be waiting for your letters of credit. Sixty million dollars. I don't care how you slice up the pie between you. But you'd better do it. Because if you don't, the first thing I do when I get off this barge is put a lock on the front door of my bank."

Henry's apprehension that something was terribly wrong grew as he watched Cornelia sitting slump-shouldered under the weight of her jewellery. Hislop regarded her with an expression of pained sympathy.

Henry moved from behind the champagne table and crossed the floor to Cornelia.

"Good evening, Mrs. Tarr. May I get you anything?"

"Ah, Henry, how kind. A cognac, if you would."

He looked inquiringly at Hislop.

"I think it would be wiser if you had it in your cabin, Mrs. Tarr," said Hislop. "Why don't I escort you down? I can explain to Mr. Tarr."

Cornelia glanced in the direction of the smoking room.

"Well, maybe just for a few minutes."

"If you could take the box, Henry, I'll help Mrs. Tarr."

When Cornelia was resting on her bed with a glass of cognac in her hand, Hislop closed the door and turned to Henry.

"She'll be all right," he said. "You can get back to work now."

Henry made no move to leave.

"Somebody's trying to kill Tarr, you know," he said.

Hislop shook his head. "There are always crazy, envious people around. Mr. Tarr's money attracts them like flies."

"But this time it's different. It's not some immigrant miner who can't speak English or a crackpot Bolshevik radical. They've tried already, haven't they? Someone almost cooked Tarr in the steam bath. They just wedged the door shut and turned up the heat."

"The engineers said it was an accident. The door could have jammed."

"It didn't jam. Somebody used a shoe horn as a wedge. I found it. You were with him all the time down there, weren't you?"

"What are you trying to say?"

"It could have been you."

Hislop's face drained of blood.

"How dare you!"

"It's all right, Hislop. I know you wouldn't do that. But you'd like to see him dead."

"I don't have to listen to this."

"I wondered how long you could breathe Tarr's air. First there was Brandon. Remember the machine gun and those defenceless women and children? It plays on your mind, doesn't it? And there were probably things before that, things I don't even know about. A man with a conscience, a Christian conscience, a man of God like you, you couldn't live with memories like that for long."

"Of course the killing sickened me, but it wasn't his finger on the trigger."

"Does it matter whose finger it is? What about Westchester, the night he fired me?"

"Please leave me alone."

"It's too late, Hislop. Because it's not over yet. Tarr

killed a man that night. And that's on your conscience, too. A man who worked for J.P. Morgan. My guess is that Tarr was trying to get him to spy on Morgan. But something went wrong, and he killed the man. You were in the gatehouse that night, weren't you?"

"No."

"You might as well tell me, because it's all going to come out. The moment we dock in New York, I'm going to the police."

Hislop sat down heavily. His skeletal hands hung over his knees.

"What I did, I did to protect you," he said.

"Me?"

"Yes, you, Henry. I was reading by the fire when Mr. Tarr came running in that night. He didn't see me, but I saw him run up the stairs. I heard him shouting in Nichole's bedroom. I was concerned for Mrs. Tarr, so I went up to her. But she wasn't in her room. I looked outside and saw her running down the garden in her nightgown towards the gatehouse.

"I decided to go after her. When I got down there I looked in the window and saw you crouched by the fire. You had a poker in your hand. Mrs. Tarr was upstairs. I could see her looking down from the study window. When you left, I tried to get her to go back to the house, but she kept talking about the poker. She wouldn't leave until she had it. She found it, took some paper from the desk drawer and wrapped it up. Then she asked me to bury it."

"Why?"

"Because she loves her husband."

"She knew then?"

"Keep your voice down. She mustn't hear. Of course, she knew. But you were the last person to handle the poker. It had your fingerprints on it."

"Why didn't you go to the police?"

"She begged me not to. The shame of a trial would have killed her."

"So you decided to exact your own brand of justice."

"What are you talking about, Henry?"

"You sent a cable to Morgan telling him about Tarr's financial situation."

Hislop did not answer.

"In fact, you've been in contact with Morgan before. It was you who alerted Morgan that Tarr had booked passage on the *Titanic*. You knew Tarr's been dying to sit down with Morgan ever since Brandon. You've been feeding him inside information all these years, haven't you, Hislop?"

The preacher laced his fingers together. His knuckles were red. The backs of his hands were covered with ginger hairs.

"Yes," he admitted.

"Why? It's not the money."

"I don't accept money," said Hislop, standing.

"Then why?"

"Because he doesn't deserve what he has. Everything he made was by cheating and lying. And through it all he made fun of me. Snide little jokes all the time. He doesn't understand that I'm . . . different."

"Why did you suffer him all these years, then?"

"Cornelia needs me. If he were ruined financially, maybe he would leave her. Without his money he can do nothing for her."

"And what happens if he's murdered?"

"God moves in mysterious ways," said Hislop.

"God has nothing to do with this. I'm going to make sure the esteemed Mr. Tarr is delivered safe and sound in New York to stand trial for murder."

Hislop's sallow face contorted with anger.

"I will not let you do anything that will hurt Mrs. Tarr."

"Your solicitude is very touching."

"I suggest that you do nothing, Henry. I'm giving you fair warning. Just let matters take their own course."

"And if I decide to do otherwise?"

"Then I will feel compelled to present the proper authorities with some evidence. Evidence that will link you with the murder you're trying to pin on Mr. Tarr."

Henry nodded grimly. "You've been around him too long, Hislop."

"We do what we have to do, Henry. You see, I still have the poker with your fingerprints on it. I never did get around to burying it."

First Officer Murdoch trained his binoculars on an eastbound freighter's bridge. The Morse lamp was flashing.

"It's the *Rappahannock,* sir. She's had a bit of rudder trouble," said Sixth Officer James Moody.

"What's she saying, Mr. Moody?"

Moody deciphered the intermittent flashes of light that sped across the glass-like ocean.

"Have just passed through heavy field ice and seen several icebergs."

"Send an acknowledgement—message received, thank you, good night."

"Shall I inform the captain, sir?"

"No, it won't be necessary."

Nineteen miles north of the *Titanic,* in the ice field where the *Rappahannock* had damaged her rudder, another freighter was struggling with the growlers. The *Californian,* heading for Boston out of Liverpool, had shut off her engines. Her master, Captain Stanley Lord, asked his wireless operator, twenty-year-old Cyril Evans, if there were any other boats in his sending range.

"Only the *Titanic,*" Evans replied.

"Better advise her we are surrounded by ice, and that we're stopped."

"Aye, aye, captain." The operator went immediately to his cabin and beamed the message to his counterpart on the *Titanic.* Evans, at the end of his watch, was in a chatty mood and was hoping to have a conversation with a professional colleague. The message he sent began: "Say, old man, we are stopped and surrounded by ice."

In the *Titanic*'s wireless room, Jack Phillips had a pile of personal messages that had accumulated during the day. He was tired and testy and he cut Evans short: "Keep out. Shut up. I am busy. I am working Cape Race and you are jamming me."

Evans shrugged. "Charming," he said, and tuned in to eavesdrop on Phillips's outgoing messages.

As Henry walked to the Palm Court, his mind turned over the information he had gleaned from Hislop. The preacher would go to any lengths to protect Cornelia Tarr, and that kind of devotion made everyone around him vulnerable— Nichole most of all, since Henry's case against Tarr rested on her testimony.

Could Hislop be moved to violence against Nichole if he discovered the confession she had written? The feeling of unease he had experienced when Tarr appeared with Cornelia's jewellery box returned.

Then he understood why.

He had seen the envelope deposited in the safe. His friend Ernest King had placed it on top of the jewellery box, which was now in Hislop's possession.

Henry turned in mid-step and raced down to C Deck. At the inquiry office he rang the bell and waited impatiently for the hatch to slide up.

"You again." King smiled.

"Listen, Ernie. This is very important. I deposited an envelope in the safe for a passenger yesterday evening. Can you check to make sure it's still there?"

"What name?"

"Nichole Linley."

"She's with the Tarr party, right?"

"Yes."

"Well, Tarr himself just signed for it, not half an hour ago."

With a beating heart, Henry knocked on Nichole's cabin door. He had to warn her that Tarr had taken her confession from the safe. She would be in danger—from both Tarr and Hislop. Matters had gone beyond his control. He would have to tell the captain. He cursed himself for having put the envelope in the safe.

"Nichole," he called softly. "Are you in there? It's me, Henry."

He looked left and right, then knocked again, louder this time. He waited, but there was no response.

He took his passkey from his pocket and slid it quietly into the lock. He opened the door a fraction and peered in. The cabin was in darkness. An eerie gray light glowed from the window. Nichole was in bed, lying on her back. Only her head was visible above the covers.

He ducked inside and closed the door. The click of the lock startled him, and he looked at Nichole hoping the noise did not awaken her. The presence of a man in her room might cause her to panic.

He moved to her bedside and knelt down. Her head was turned to the wall. He could see the line of her cheek and that long, white neck he had kissed.

"Nichole," he said, gently touching her temple to waken her. Her skin felt warm, but she did not respond. He pressed his fingers into her shoulder, and her head lolled on the pillow towards him.

Her eyes were wide open and she wore a faint smile.

Henry backed away in horror. The couch caught him behind the knees, and he fell onto it.

"Oh, my God," he gasped.

He covered his hands with his face and began to sob.

The sound of seven bells drifted up to Fred Fleet and Reginald Lee, huddled together for warmth in the crow's nest.

"Half an hour more, Reg, and then it's kip time," said Fleet.

The temperature had fallen to below freezing. There was no wind, but the speed of the *Titanic*, which was travelling at more than twenty-two knots, made the air rush by them. They had no binoculars to stop their eyes from watering. None had been issued by the White Star Line for crow's nest duty, in spite of Fleet's repeated requests in Southampton to Second Officer Lightoller.

In front of them a slight mist hung like a shroud above the water.

"If we can see through that we'll be lucky," said Fleet.

The two men squinted into the distance. Suddenly, Fleet thought he saw a small, dark mass dead ahead.

He reached for the warning bell and rang it three times. Then he picked up the bridge phone.

"Are you there?"

"Yes," said Sixth Officer Moody. "What do you see?"

"Iceberg right ahead."

"Thank you." Moody put down the phone. "Iceberg right ahead, sir."

"Hard a starboard," ordered Murdoch.

In the wheelhouse, Quartermaster Robert Hitchens responded immediately.

Moody, at his side, confirmed the order. "Hard a starboard. The helm is hard over, sir."

The manoeuvre would swing the *Titanic*'s head to port. Murdoch telegraphed the engine room: "Stop. Full speed astern."

Murdoch pushed the ten-second-warning bell that signalled the closing of the watertight doors on the tank top, then activated the electronically controlled doors. Red lights flashed above the doors, and warning bells sounded.

Fleet and Lee, in the crow's nest, watched in agonized silence as the iceberg loomed up at them out of the mist. The *Titanic* was heading straight for it. The black, menacing shape grew larger and larger, and still the liner seemed to be riveted on a collision course.

The *Titanic* was steaming at twenty-two knots, just below her top speed. The lookouts were too unnerved to move. They held on to the railing in front of them and braced themselves for the impact.

Slowly, slowly the great bow veered to port. From Fleet's perspective, it looked as if the liner might slip by the iceberg without touching it. Thirty-seven seconds after he had first spotted the dark shape in front of him, the forecastle nudged against the black, shining iceberg.

It was as large and stately as a cathedral and it towered one hunded feet above the silent ocean.

The impact sent a cascade of ice on to the forewell deck. Deep in the bowels of D Deck, the shock dislodged a tray of freshly made breakfast rolls from the top of the bake oven. The rolls fell to the floor, bounced, then rolled like marbles.

In a forward coal bunker on the Orlop Deck, Trimmer George Cavell was caught in an avalanche of falling coal and had to dig himself out, gasping for air.

The dogs in their kennels on F Deck, next to the third-class galley, began to bark and jump in frenzy in their wire cages. The seamen in their bunks at the front of D Deck experienced the full force of the collision. Newly awakened for the twelve o'clock watch, Fireman John Thompson and his mates were thrown sprawling from their bunks.

"That was a narrow shave," said Fleet, as the iceberg glided past the crow's nest like the great black sail of a phantom ship.

The *Titanic*'s stern began to swing around in response to Murdoch's new order, hard a port. Then, suddenly, the officers on the bridge heard a loud grinding, groaning sound, like the death rattle of a leviathan.

To Tarr, smoking a cigar in his sitting room and playing a game of solitaire as he waited for the arrival of the bankers, it came as a slight jolt followed by a high-pitched scraping.

To Cornelia, sleepless in her bed next door, the sound was like someone tearing calico, or the ship's whistle screaming under water. She reached for the cognac.

Three cabins away, Rhonda and Georgie, lying still in each other's arms, could feel vibrations coming through the mattress.

"What was that?" asked Rhonda, propping herself on one elbow.

"Must 'ave dropped a propeller blade. Nothing serious," said Georgie. "Means a trip back to Belfast, probably."

The coat hangers jangled in the closet as they returned to their lovemaking.

Jim Gordon and his cronies in the smoking room debated what to do about Thaddeus Tarr's threat. The sound reminded them of a giant screwdriver being scraped across the metal hull.

Kittie was awakened in her bunk on E Deck. It was as if the whole side of the ship was being lashed with iron chains. She glanced out the porthole and saw a gray, luminous wall of ice slide by. The sound haunted her.

What they had all heard was a spur of ice, underwater, ripping a three-hundred-foot gash along the *Titanic*'s steel-plated hull, twelve feet above the keel on the starboard side, from just forward of the crow's nest to Boiler Room 5.

In the fifth watertight compartment from the bow, Leading Stoker Frederick Barrett saw a green tide of water come rushing in the side of Boiler Room 6. He and the second assistant engineer heard the warning bell and jumped through the electronic door just as it came slamming down.

"What have we struck?" demanded Captain Smith as he rushed onto the bridge.

"An iceberg, sir," said Murdoch. "I hard-a-starboarded and reversed the engines and I was going to hard-a-port around it, but she was too close. I could not do any more. I have closed the watertight doors."

"The watertight doors are closed? Did you ring the warning bell?"

"Yes, sir."

Smith and Murdoch moved quickly to the starboard bridge wing and looked aft. They saw the spectral shape of an iceberg blotting out the stars. The whole incident was over in ten seconds.

"Mr. Boxhall," said the captain when he returned to the bridge, "go below and inspect the forward area, then report."

Nine decks below them, the frigid Atlantic Ocean exploded into the gashed hull.

The greatest liner the world had ever seen was doomed.

Sunday, April 14, 1912

HENRY SAT ON the couch in Nichole's cabin, oblivious to the rumbling sound that moved up the ship the way a shiver moved on a thoroughbred's flank. Nichole was dead, and for a moment even the lambent gray light was extinguished. The cabin was filled with the coldness of death.

He turned on the bedside lamp and studied Nichole's face. Then he pulled back the cover. There was no sign of blood on her body. No evidence of a struggle. But he knew she had been murdered.

Tarr had suffocated her.

She looked so peaceful. Just as his father had looked when Henry had closed his eyes one gusty March morning at Cumerworth Hall, the day the first crocuses of spring bloomed under the oak trees. He had put pennies on his father's eye lids and sat by his bedside until Lord Rutherland summoned him to the study.

"You, my boy," he had said, "will be my new butler. If you're half the man your father was, you will distinguish yourself."

Now that Nichole was dead there were no more promises to be kept. Henry would tell Captain Smith that Tarr had murdered her. Tarr would be confined to his suite under guard until the ship reached New York. The ship would be met by a battery of policemen, and Tarr would be hand-cuffed and taken away in a horse-drawn paddy wagon.

Then the whole world would see Thaddeus Nugent Tarr for what he was.

Henry closed the cabin door gently behind him. There were passengers in the corridor, some in bathrobes, others with coats hastily thrown over pyjamas. Drawn from their quarters by the strange noise, they milled around telling each other what they had heard. They were curious and apprehensive.

"I say, steward." A woman in a fur coat called to Henry as he pressed his way through the throng. "Why have we stopped?"

But Henry ignored the woman. He was thinking about Nichole and how he would tell her story to Captain Smith.

The engines had indeed stopped, on orders from the captain. The *Titanic* lay dead in the water, her three active funnels blowing off accumulating steam.

Ten miles north, on the bridge of the stalled *Californian*, Third Officer Charles Groves saw a large, unidentified liner stop on the edge of the ice field. Her lights appeared to go out. Must be a passenger vessel turning off its deck lights, he thought. A discreet suggestion for the passengers to go to bed.

But the ship's lights had not been switched off: In her attempt to avoid the iceberg, the *Titanic* had veered to port. Groves first saw her at eleven-thirty. He had informed Captain Lord in the chartroom, who told him to raise the vessel by Morse lamp. There had been no reply from the *Titanic*.

Water was already spilling into the post office on the Orlop Deck. Letters were floating on the cold brine. Five postal clerks carried two hundred canvas sacks of registered mail up the iron companionway to the dry ground of the sorting office on F Deck. Water was seeping into the wardrobe trunks in the first- and second-class baggage holds. Below, Boiler Room 6 was already flooded.

In Boiler Room 5, Assistant Engineer William Harvey got the pump going, but it made little impression on the wave of green foam gushing through a two-foot hole that extended beyond the forward compartment. The lights

vent out, then came on again, and Harvey ordered that
he boilers be shut down. The stokers began the back-
breaking work of hosing down the fires and controlling the
ear-splitting rush of steam.

Taking advantage of the confusion in the corridors, a passenger dressed in a steward's jacket threaded his way
along B Deck. He carried a silver chafing dish on a small
tray. Excited passengers directed questions to him, and he
answered courteously that there was nothing to be alarmed
about. The ship would be underway once a passage through
the ice field could be found.

He stopped outside Tarr's suite and knocked on the
door.

Henry mounted the steps that would take him to the
bridge. On the forecastle deck he could see steerage passengers playing soccer with lumps of ice. There was a
slight tilt to the stairs he was climbing, which was odd, he
thought, because the water was perfectly calm and the
ship's engines had stopped.

The bridge was crowded with officers reporting for orders. Captain Smith stood in the centre of the wheelhouse.

"Mr. Boxhall, get me our exact position."

As Henry climbed the ladder to the bridge, ship's carpenter John Maxwell came up quickly behind him, then
elbowed his way through the crowd of officers.

"She's making water fast," he announced.

A mail clerk named John Jago Smith pushed behind
him. He called over the crowd of heads around the captain, "The mail hold is filling rapidly."

Henry pressed his way through. "Captain, I have to
speak to you."

"Not now, steward," an officer said. "Can't you see we
have an emergency on our hands?"

Bruce Ismay, president of the International Mercantile
Marine Company, arrived, tousled and agitated, dressed
in carpet slippers and a suit thrown hurriedly over his
pyjamas. He spoke quietly to the captain. "Do you think

the ship is seriously damaged?" Henry could read the pain in the captain's face.

"I'm afraid she is."

Fourth Officer Boxhall returned and handed a piece of paper to Captain Smith. On it was written the *Titanic*'s position: 41° 46 minutes north, 50° 14 minutes west.

An officer caught Henry by the elbow. "What are you doing on the bridge?"

"I must see the captain. There's a murderer on board."

"He can't deal with it now, man. He's got the whole ship to worry about. Can't you see what's going on?"

"But he's just killed a woman."

"Did you see it?"

"No, but—"

"We'll deal with it in good time. Now, make yourself useful below. Calm the passengers down."

Henry tried to catch the captain's attention, but the officer stepped in front of him. "That's an order, sailor."

Henry swore at the man under his breath. As he climbed down the ladder, he noticed that the angle of the steps was more pronounced than before. There was a perceptible tilt of the deck towards the bow. The *Titanic*, he realized, was sinking.

He saw a passenger holding a glass and laughing. "Waiter! Get me a piece of ice from the deck for my whisky."

Henry bent, picked up a shard of ice and handed it to the man, who dropped it into his drink.

"Look at this!" shouted the man. "Scotch and iceberg!"

Henry shook his head. How blind they were. The *Titanic* was going down. Nichole's body would be buried at the bottom of the ocean. There would be no corpse. No evidence. Just like the killing of Marsden Dewey. Nobody could bring Tarr to justice—except him.

He was the only one on board who cared that Thaddeus Nugent Tarr was a murderer.

As he walked along the deck listening to the merriment of the passengers around him, he realized that circumstances had forced him to become Tarr's judge, jury and executioner.

Would he have time for vengeance before the *Titanic* plunged to the ocean floor?

"Just come in. I've been expecting you," called Tarr in response to a knock on the stateroom door.

A steward entered, holding a silver dish.

"Who the hell are you?" demanded the banker. "I didn't order anything."

"Compliments of the captain, sir," said the steward, closing the door behind him.

"Just put it on the table." He reached in his pocket and took out a gold sovereign.

But the steward did not extend his hand to receive the coin. Instead, he lifted the lid of the salver. Under it, resting on a towel, was a Colt .32 pocket revolver. The man picked it up and pointed it at Tarr.

The banker sat back in his chair.

"So you're the one," he said. Tarr looked at the gun, then at the man's face. "But you're English," he commented, remembering the man's accent.

"I have no interest in anything you have to say, Tarr. You'll just do as I tell you."

"If it's money you're looking for I haven't got much on me. Take my wallet and get out."

"I don't want your money. I want you."

The banker let his hand slide towards his jacket pocket. "Should I know you?"

"Frankly, my identity is of no interest to you. We've never met."

"Wonderful. A man I've never met wants to shoot me. Did the Macklins send you?"

The man picked up the towel and began to wrap it around his left hand. Tarr watched him, frowning.

"What's that for?"

"It will deaden the noise."

"It's not going to be this easy, boy. I'm Thaddeus Nugent Tarr."

"Yes, you are," said the man. "And that's the reason I'm here. Go over to the promenade door and slide it open."

*   *   *

Ten minutes after the *Titanic* collided with the iceberg, the water level in the ship's forward cargo bays had risen fourteen feet above her keel. Cabin trucks were floating; a priceless copy of the *Rubaiyat* of Omar Khayyam was in a wooden packing crate. Its cover, of beaten gold, featured a bejewelled peacock, and its binding was studded with one thousand precious stones. The book was instantly ruined.

The three-hundred-foot gash along the liner's hull had exposed five forward compartments to the mercy of the sea. As water gushed in, its accumulating weight began to push the *Titanic*'s bow downwards. The situation was detected by the commutator in the wheelhouse.

"We're listing five degrees to starboard," noted Captain Smith with alarm. "Get Andrews up to the bridge immediately."

Thomas Andrews, a director of Harland and Wolff, was the man who had built the *Titanic*. During the voyage he had spent his time touring the ship, checking every detail for modifications.

That night, Andrews had been busy in his cabin sketching a new design for the first-class writing room. Its original dimensions were predicated on the notion that lady passengers needed a place to retire to after dinner while the men passed the port. But social customs had changed with the century, and women, Andrews had observed, now stayed resolutely in their dinner chairs. The writing room could be made smaller, and the extra space used more profitably.

Andrews occupied cabin A36, on the port side behind the third funnel, well away from the point of impact. Absorbed in his work, he was unaware of the accident and oblivious to the shutting down of the engines.

When Andrews arrived on the bridge, Captain Smith took him for a quick tour of inspection. They used the crew's stairwells so as not to alarm the passengers.

The mail room was a disaster. Gray-green water flecked with oil had begun to wash into the squash court. The water was already up to the foul line. When Thomas

Andrews had seen enough, the two men returned to the bridge.

"How long have we?" asked Captain Smith.

Andrews knew that the watertight bulkheads extended only as high as E Deck. With five compartments filling with water, the bow would be forced inexorably downwards. Water would flow from one boiler room to the next.

The *Titanic* could stay afloat with four of her sixteen compartments flooded—but not five.

He made a quick calculation on the back of an envelope.

"An hour and a half. Possibly two. Not much longer."

Henry pushed through the throng of passengers on the Boat Deck as he made his way to the first-class staircase. There was an air of amused tolerance about them, as if they had been aroused from sleep for a fire drill. They joked about the ice on deck and about the cold, still night.

The entire ship's company had been quietly summoned. Stewards and waiters, firemen and chefs appeared in the corridors and public areas, acting as if they were in command of the situation. To inquiring passengers they offered meaningless words of assurance and comfort.

A young boy plucked at Henry's sleeve as he passed.

"Is it true we've been torpedoed?" the child asked. He was clutching a pink metal pig with a key in its back. It was playing "Frère Jacques."

Henry shook his head. "Go and find your mother," he said, "and stay with her."

The only thought in his mind was that he must get to Tarr. There would be little enough time to confront him.

Monday, April 15, 1912

AT FIVE MINUTES past midnight, Captain Smith turned to Chief Officer Wilde and ordered the uncovering of the lifeboats.

"Mr. Murdoch, muster the passengers. Mr. Moody, assign crew members to the boats. I want all hands on deck and all officers to the bridge."

He took a scrap of paper from his pocket. It was the ship's position, which Boxhall had plotted for him. He walked quickly to the wireless room and handed it to First Operator John Phillips. Harold Bride was there, too, preparing to take over from the exhausted Phillips.

"We've struck an iceberg," the captain told them, "and I'm having an inspection made to see what it has done to us. Get ready to send out a call for assistance. But don't send it until I tell you."

Ten minutes later, Captain Smith put his head around the wireless room door and said: "Send for assistance."

"What should I send?" asked Phillips.

"The regulation international call for help."

Phillips began to flash the distress signal, CQD, followed by the *Titanic*'s call letters, MGY. For five minutes he tapped the six letters, joking with Bride as he did so. From where they sat, there appeared to be no danger at all.

The captain reappeared and asked Phillips what message he was sending.

"CQD, sir," replied the operator.

"Send SOS," said Bride. "It's a new call, and this may be your last chance to send it."

The three men laughed at Harold Bride's joke.

On G Deck where the single male steerage passengers bunked, Olaus Abelseth was awakened by the sound of water. He swung his feet to the floor and found himself ankle-deep in freezing brine. He and an Irish immigrant, Daniel Buckley, woke the other men in the room. They dressed hurriedly and headed towards the open deck. Other steerage passengers, wearing life jackets and carrying small suitcases dripping with water and parcels wrapped in brown paper, blocked the corridors. They swore in a babel of tongues as they fought their way to the staircase.

Henry squeezed his way through a group of men standing at the bottom of the staircase on B Deck.

"They say there's water up to F Deck in the mail room," he heard someone say.

"And the squash court is flooded."

"Bang goes our game tomorrow, Sidney," said another.

A large copper ashtray came bouncing down the carpeted staircase. Even the passengers knew the *Titanic* was in trouble now.

Stewards had begun knocking on cabin doors, shouting, "Everybody on deck with life belts on, at once!"

A woman wearing a long motoring coat over her night dress stepped into Henry's way. She carried a baby wrapped in a blanket. Her shoes were unbuttoned, and they flapped around her ankles.

"I say, steward. Do we have time to dress?"

"You have time for nothing, madam," he replied.

Henry moved with more urgency towards Tarr's suite. *God, don't let us sink yet*, he prayed. *Just give me a little more time. Even if I never see Kittie again. Please, God.*

He arrived at Tarr's sitting room just as an assistant purser was about to knock.

"Don't worry," Henry said to him. "I'll take care of this one."

The man turned to him and sneered. "Like hell you will, mate. He's a big tipper. He's mine."

Henry's punch caught the purser in the solar plexus. He doubled over and fell to the floor clutching his stomach. Henry stepped over him and put his ear to the door. Hearing nothing, he slipped his passkey into the lock.

As he swung the door open he felt a sudden rush of cold air. A curtain billowed across the room near Tarr's private promenade. Somewhere on the deck above, a bell was ringing.

On the promenade he saw Tarr silhouetted against the night sky. The banker leaned his elbows on the railings. Their eyes met, but Tarr did not acknowledge Henry's presence. He was listening to someone.

Henry inched forward. Through the window he could see the back of a man's head. The man was wearing a steward's jacket, and his left hand was swathed in a towel.

He saw the man raise his arm and half turn. Henry saw that the hair, flattened to the scalp, was parted in the middle.

Tarr appeared to cower. "No! Don't!" he shouted. "You can have Cumerworth Hall!"

And then Henry understood.

The man who had Thaddeus Tarr at his mercy was not a killer hired by J.P. Morgan or the Macklins. He was not a grief-crazed miner from West Virginia.

"Mr. Charles!" Henry called.

The man swivelled at the sound of his name. Tarr made a move towards him, but the man snapped the revolver into position to cover the banker.

"Who are you? Come out here."

"It's me, Henry Blexill. Your uncle's butler." He stepped onto the promenade.

"Move into the light. Beside him, where I can see you."

Henry did as he was told. "We used to box when we were children. Behind the stables. Remember?"

"You know this man?" asked Tarr.

"Yes, he's Charles Sinclair, Lord Rutherland's nephew."

"I have no quarrel with you, Blexill," said Sinclair. "Remain still. Let me do what I have to, and you won't get hurt."

"But why have his blood on your hands?"

"Because he stole my inheritance, that's why."

"What are you talking about?" demanded Tarr.

Sinclair cleared his throat. "Lord Rutherland always said he would leave Cumerworth Hall to me. And you swindled him out of it."

"Rubbish. Your uncle couldn't manage his affairs. He was speculating," shouted Tarr.

"On the basis of a forged assay report," said Henry.

Tarr turned to him, and a smile flickered across his lips. "I should never have let you go, Henry," he said.

"How do you know that?" demanded Sinclair.

"Because I found the original. There was no silver in the Los Cobres mine, and Mr. Tarr knew it."

"Business, Henry. That's all it was. Business."

Sinclair let out a groan that was half a sob.

"Did your uncle send you?" asked Henry.

"My uncle is dead."

"I'm so sorry." Henry felt tears stinging the corners of his eyes. Lord Rutherland was dead. The last link with his childhood years had gone. It was as if his own father had passed away all over again.

"He died a pauper in a miserable rooming house because of that man."

A shot rang out.

Thaddeus Tarr and Charles Sinclair stood facing each other for an instant. Henry smelled cordite. The gun dropped from Sinclair's hand and skittered across the deck.

Smoke rose from a hole in Tarr's jacket pocket. Sinclair gave a sigh and fell to his knees. Tarr caught him by the armpits and held him up.

Henry moved towards the fallen gun. As he bent to pick it up, Tarr hoisted the dying man onto the railing.

"No!" yelled Henry.

But it was too late. Tarr had pushed him over the side.

"Loyalty, Henry. That's what it's all about."

"You killed him!"

"He was going to kill me. You saw him. Now put that gun away."

"You didn't have to throw him overboard."

"This ship is sinking, isn't it?"

"Yes."

"Then it really doesn't matter a whole hell of a lot."

"It's a question of how you view human life, Mr. Tarr."

They stood six feet apart, staring at each other. They were no longer master and servant. The impending calamity had stripped away all differences between them. Their backgrounds, their attitudes, what made them laugh, what made them angry were meaningless. Henry knew they would share a common fate. And all Tarr's money could not save him from it.

Henry raised Sinclair's revolver.

"Just answer me one thing. Why did you ruin Lord Rutherland?"

"Put the gun down, Henry."

"Answer me."

Tarr breathed heavily through his nose. "He ruined himself. Pure greed."

"No. He acted on the geologist's report you made Hislop write. You encouraged him to speculate on the shares. Why? You had enough money."

"Nobody ever has enough money, Henry."

"But you didn't need Cumerworth. Why did you destroy it?"

"Because it stood for everything I despised." Tarr spat out the words. "It stood for all the power I could not have. Money can give you power, Henry, but there is something else. Morgan has it, the power that lets you sit with kings and emperors. That's what I wanted, but they never gave it to me. Lord Rutherland could have helped, but he wouldn't. I asked him to propose me for membership in his club. He smiled that superior smile and changed the subject. He was laughing at me. When I made it a condition of our deal, you know what he said to me? 'I can't in all conscience do that, Tarr.' And I could have bought and sold him a hundred times over."

"What you can't have, you destroy," said Henry. "How does it feel to have a gun pointed at you? Remember Brandon, when you ordered in your armored car?"

"That was war, Henry. They had guns, too. They blew up the mine and killed my guards. What would you have done in my place? Given them gold watches?"

"Women and children were killed. They were shot—they were burned alive in cellars trying to escape the bullets."

"The first rule is that you hang on to what's yours. People get hurt in the fight. That's life. The trouble with you bleeding hearts, you think we're civilized. Not like the animals in the jungle. But if you'd seen what I've seen, son, you'd know better. Now let's get off this ship."

"First we have to talk about Nichole, Mr. Tarr."

"What about Nichole?"

"You found her confession and you suffocated her with a pillow."

"Nichole was crazy. She was Morgan's blackmailing whore, Henry."

Tarr began moving towards Henry. "All she ever wanted was money. Just money. She didn't care about you or me. I gave her Cumerworth Hall, but it wasn't enough. She always wanted more."

"No, Mr. Tarr. I saw the blood. I know what happened in there. Stay where you are."

"I owe you now, Henry. I could make you rich. You want to be rich, don't you, Henry? Everyone wants to be rich."

"Stay there!"

"You wouldn't shoot me."

"You killed her, just as you killed Morgan's accountant."

Tarr laughed. "Believe what you want to believe. What does it matter now?"

Henry cocked the hammer of the revolver. His finger tightened on the trigger. Then he heard Cornelia's voice calling from the sitting room.

"Thaddeus?"

Her voice was slurred and tremulous. She stumbled against a table.

"Excuse me. Oh, there you are." She supported herself in the doorway with both hands.

"And Henry. Be an angel and get my wrap. These Westchester nights can be so cold."

The two men looked at each other. Henry lowered the revolver.

"Go inside, Cornelia," said Tarr. "We're coming in."

"Coming in," Cornelia repeated. "Do you hear the bells? Is it time for church already?"

At that moment there was a hammering on the sitting-room door. They could hear Hislop's voice calling, " Mrs. Tarr. I have your life jacket. Let me in."

Cornelia lost her footing and slumped into a chair. Tarr moved towards her. As he passed Henry, he said: "Let me get her and Rhonda into the boats, then we'll settle this."

Henry slid the revolver into his trouser pocket.

In the first-class smoking room, a bridge foursome in evening dress was in the middle of a rubber when an officer appeared at the door. "Men, get on your life belts," he shouted. "There's trouble ahead."

Archie Butt looked across the table at his partner, Arthur Ryerson, in disbelief. He put down his hand and rose reluctantly from the table.

As the word passed through the ship, tired passengers turned out of their bunks, rubbed the sleep from their eyes and dressed quickly. Rhonda and Georgie Skinner, dozing in each other's arms, were roused unceremoniously by a fist banging on the cabin door. They kissed each other and laughed.

"I'd better go, love," said Georgie. "Sounds like an all ands call."

In second class, Kittie and the other stewardesses advised passengers to put on their warmest clothing. Shouts of, "Everyone on deck with life belts on. At the double!" rang down the corridors as stewards flushed passengers from their cabins. Confused and complaining, the passengers poured into the hallways. The women pulled brushes through their hair, inspecting unmade-up faces in hand mirrors. Some pinched their cheeks for a little color.

The menfolk joked about the unsinkable *Titanic* and put oranges in their pockets.

In first class, maids and valets hurried to assist their employers, pulling sensible clothes from wardrobe trunks. Women in hats with fur coats over their nightdresses herded wide-eyed children before them. Passengers lined up in front of the inquiry office to claim their valuables from the purser's safe.

Each class behaved as it had during the voyage, and kept to its own deck space. Steerage passengers began to congregate on the poop deck aft. There was no panic yet, no hysteria, just a vague sense of anxiety for an adventure they could not see the end of. They stood in groups in the freezing night air waiting to be told what to do. Uncertain. Apprehensive. Newly gregarious in the face of the unknown.

A child was crying. Her father comforted her, saying: "There's nothing to worry about, dear. Not even God could sink this ship."

On the Boat Deck, crewmen wrestled with the canvas coverings on the sixteen wooden lifeboats, their fingers stiff with cold. The davits squealed as the men swung the boats over the side in preparation for lowering. Other crew members broke open the four canvas Engelhardt collapsibles stowed on deck, and prepared them for launching.

Together the twenty boats, fully loaded, could accommodate 1,178 souls. The *Titanic*'s complement, passengers and crew, numbered 2,207.

"Where the hell have you been?"

Henry was standing by his bunk, tying on his life jacket,

when Georgie Skinner came sauntering in, hands in pockets, whistling.

"Servicing one of the passengers, you might say." Georgie leered. "Gettin' a bit of revenge for you. Your old employer's daughter."

Henry's entire body clenched in anger. He went to hit Georgie, but the bulky life preserver deflected his punch.

Georgie jerked the hair out of his eyes.

"What's eating you?"

Henry sat heavily on his bunk.

"Get out of my sight."

An officer put his head around the doorway of the room. "All hands on deck," he shouted. "Make sure your life jackets are on. The passengers must see you wearing them."

Henry buried his face in his hands. He was thinking about Kittie, wondering if they would make it through the night. He wanted to see her one more time. To tell her he loved her.

He rose and walked past Georgie without a word. At the door he saw the ship's musicians, carrying their instrument cases. Some were wearing blue jackets; some wore white.

Stepping into the corridor, Henry was borne along by the crowd of passengers moving forward. At the end of Scotland Road, the passageway opened into a wide vestibule, with two staircases to port and starboard. Facing them was the Armory, where the ship's master-at-arms was busy piling small arms into a wooden box.

Tarr had sent Hislop to get Rhonda while he dressed Cornelia. She sat, dazed and withdrawn, making no effort to help her husband. Her eyes swivelled around the room trying to locate the cognac bottle.

"I knew it. I knew it," she murmured. "We should have gotten off in Ireland. Ouch! You're hurting."

"Hold still, woman," barked Tarr.

"You're too rough, Thaddeus. Nichole will do it."

"Nichole's busy."

"Daddy, what's happening?" Rhonda burst into the sitting room ahead of Hislop.

When Cornelia saw her daughter she began to cry. "My baby, my baby!" She stretched out her arms but Rhonda stood staring at her.

"They say the ship is sinking." It was more of a question than a statement. Rhonda looked from her mother to Tarr for confirmation.

"I pay a fortune for this and the goddamned ship sinks," grumbled the banker. "Here, help your mother into this contraption." He held up a life belt by one of its strings as if it were a piece of soiled laundry.

"We're all going to drown," wailed Cornelia.

"Don't just stand there," said Tarr. "Help her."

"Shall I get Miss Linley?" inquired Hislop.

"She's up on deck somewhere," said Tarr quickly. "Knowing her, she's already in a lifeboat."

At twelve forty-five, First Officer William Murdoch lowered the first lifeboat seventy feet to the glass-like water. It was Number Seven boat, the nearest to the first-class entrance. Among its occupants were actress Dorothy Gibson; French aviator Pierre Maréchal; sculptor Paul Chevre; Philadelphia banker James R. McGough; two newly-wed couples; and one of the *Titanic*'s lookouts, Archie Jewell. The other crew member was Seaman George Hogg.

The lifeboat could accommodate sixty-five people. When it touched the water it held twenty-eight.

As Number Seven boat dropped into the water, Quartermaster George Rowe lit the fuse of a distress rocket and launched it from the rail of the bridge. The stillness of the night was shattered by a thunderclap exploding eight hundred feet above the stricken liner. A shower of brilliant white sparks obliterated the stars, and for an instant gave a silver wash to the upturned faces of the passengers on the Boat Deck. Children screamed with delight, and even the lips of the adults parted in a smile. For a moment the communal apprehension was forgotten.

On board the *Californian*, ten miles away, Second Officer Herbert Stone was looking at the stationary vessel. He saw a flash of white light directly above it, and thought it was a shooting star.

He could not hear the spirited sound of ragtime emanating from the *Titanic's* first-class Lounge. William Hartley and his seven-piece orchestra had begun to play.

Henry wandered along the corridor, looking for Kittie in every cabin. The passageway on E Deck was deserted. His feet felt cold. He looked down and saw he was standing in an inch of water. Ahead of him he saw the steel-plated wall start to buckle and groan. Quickly, he headed for the staircase just as the wall swelled out, grotesquely pregnant, then burst with a sickening sound of wrenching metal. A tidal wave came roaring down the corridor, sweeping him backwards. His head hit the wall, and great balls of light exploded behind his eyes.

He splashed his face with the freezing water to clear his mind. Around him he could see the flotsam and jetsam swept up on the wake of the torrent. A man's shoe went floating by, a chamber pot, a tortoise-shell brush, a vanity case.

The force of the water carried him aft, and he fought to keep his head above water. He grabbed for door handles, but they slipped from his grasp.

Is this how I will die? he thought.

The force of the water flung him against the staircase. Waist deep in the freezing water, he clung to the banister. He pulled himself up the stairs as the water rose behind him.

Harold Bride ferried incoming messages from the wireless room to the bridge. Phillips continued to send, updating the situation with the developments supplied by Captain Smith. The *Titanic's* distress call had been picked up by several ships in the North Atlantic—the *Mount Temple*, the *Ypiranga*, the *Carpathia*, the *Frankfurt*, the *Caronia*, the *Baltic*.

The crackling buzz of the Morse tapper and the little

blue arc of electricity spelled out the extent of the disaster: "We are in collision with berg. Sinking head down."

Ships in the vicinity signalled back requests for the *Titanic*'s position. They fired up their engines and altered course to come to her assistance. The nearest ship to respond was the Cunard liner *Carpathia*, fifty-eight miles southeast of the sinking vessel.

Like ripples in a pond, news of the *Titanic*'s plight spread in an ever-widening circle. The distress signal had been picked up by a seventeen-year-old Marconi telegrapher, Charles B. Ellsworth, at Station MCE, Point Riche, Cape Race, in Newfoundland. He relayed the message to the mainland. His signal reached New York City, twelve hundred miles away, where a young student wireless operator named David Sarnoff deciphered its faint sound from atop Wanamaker's department store, a few city blocks from Tarr's mansion.

Bride went to his bunk to get his life jacket before returning to help Phillips in the wireless room. He threw a coat around his colleague's shoulders and tied his life jacket on. All the while Phillips continued to transmit without missing a beat.

Quartermaster George Rowe was setting off rockets from the bridge at five-minute intervals. As each one exploded in the black, velvety night, it lit up the ocean for miles around. The ghostly light illuminated the thirty-foot lifeboats that stood off the *Titanic*'s side, waiting.

The women, children and the few men in the boats could see the line of the *Titanic*'s bow well down in the water. Lights still blazed from every porthole and saloon window. Circles of light just below the surface of the water glowed a milky green.

They could hear the far-away sound of syncopated music. They could see figures scurrying across the Boat Deck, clambering aboard the boats.

Those on deck were no longer laughing and joking. They stood in sombre groups staring out to sea. The rockets told them just how serious the situation was. Gradually, they began to realize that the *Titanic* was going to sink.

Captain Smith, resplendent in his white uniform, moved along the Boat Deck, megaphone in hand, exhorting the women and children to take to the lifeboats.

Henry, wet and shivering, worked his way through the knots of people clustered around the lifeboats. He stared into the faces of passengers he had served and others who were strangers to him, searching for Kittie. He could hear wives pleading for their husbands to join them in the lifeboats. Some women refused to go, clinging to their menfolk, who tried to push them away.

He saw Thomas Andrews, the builder of the *Titanic*, desperately trying to drag a protesting woman towards a lifeboat.

"You must get in at once," he pleaded. "There's not a moment to lose. You cannot pick and choose your boat, madam."

Henry passed Isadore Straus and his wife, Ida. They were sitting calmly on deck chairs, holding hands, as they watched the frantic activity in front of them. For all the world it looked as if they were waiting for tea to be served.

He heard Ida say: "We've been together for forty years. Where you go, I go."

Her husband patted her hand and smiled at her.

Henry searched the line of boats, but he could not find Kittie. On the port side, the list had caused the lifeboats to swing away from the deck, making it more difficult for the crew to load passengers. Henry cut through the first-class entrance to the starboard side. At Number Three boat, forward on the officer's promenade, he saw Henry Sleeper Harper, for whom he had opened a bottle of champagne at dinner the previous night. Harper was preparing to board the lifeboat. Under his arm he carried his prize Pekinese, Sun Yat-sen. Henry had seen no other pets on deck, and for a moment he wondered if the other dogs, kennelled on F Deck, would be the first of the *Titanic*'s passengers to drown.

At Number One boat, nearest the bridge, Henry saw lookout George Symons being helped by First Officer Murdoch to clamber over the gunwales. Sir Cosmo Duff-Gordon and Lady Gordon sat erect in the middle of the lifeboat, trying not to look at the two black-faced firemen on either side of them. The boat began to be lowered. The pulleys on the davits shrieked as the boat dropped jerkily to the water. There were twelve people aboard. The crew members had difficulty unhooking the ropes because, without a swell, the sea gave no lift to the boat, so the ropes remained taut. One of the firemen was hacking at them with the blade of a small pocket knife.

Henry retraced his steps to the port side where the second-class promenade ran along the outside wall of the first-class smoking room. At Number Fourteen boat, Fifth Officer Lowe was in charge of the loading operation. The lifeboat was already half full of women and children.

Then Henry saw Kittie.

She was leaning over the railing, handing a baby to a young woman.

He ran towards her, but a crowd of men who stood watching the loading thought he was trying to jump on board to save himself.

"Women and children only," someone shouted. They grabbed him by the arms and held him back.

"I'm crew!" he protested. "I have to help."

They released him and he worked his way through the crush of weeping women who were preparing to step into the boat. Suddenly, there was a commotion on board. A fourteen-year-old boy had dived over the railing and fallen under the skirts of the women. Lowe ordered him out, but the boy cowered under the seat, sobbing. Lowe drew a revolver and pressed it against the boy's temple.

"Get out," he ordered.

Eight-year-old Marjory Collyer grabbed Lowe's arm and pleaded: "Oh, Mr. Man, don't shoot, please don't shoot the poor boy!"

Lowe smiled at her and withdrew the revolver. He turned to the teenager and said: "For God's sake, be a man. We've got women and children to save."

Sheepishly, the boy stepped out of the boat and onto the deck. He collapsed on a coil of rope and wept uncontrollably.

Kittie turned on the officer.

"Let the lad on," she said. "He's barely stopped wetting 'is bed."

"Orders are orders," replied Lowe.

Kittie bent to comfort the boy. When she saw Henry she smiled wanly and said, "I wish we'd tied the knot before we sailed."

Henry took her in his arms and kissed her.

"I love you," he said.

"Here, you two, there's work to be done," called a voice behind them.

"Stewardess Boyer," shouted Lowe. "Over here on the double. I need you."

"We'll come through, 'Enry," Kittie said. "I know we will."

"Yes."

"We'll be together in New York. We'll ride round Central Park in a 'orse and carriage like you said we would. Don't let me down."

"I promise," said Henry.

With a heavy heart he watched her step into the lifeboat. Then he retreated into the shadows to hide his tears. He hadn't cried like this since he had taken his leave of Lord Rutherland to go to America. To work for Tarr.

And then he saw Tarr coming towards him, as if his thought had conjured the man into flesh. Tarr and Hislop were supporting the distraught figure of Cornelia between them. Her feet were sliding across the deck as they guided her towards the lifeboat. Behind them, looking anxiously around her, was Rhonda.

"Make way, make way," shouted Tarr, as he cleared a path through a group of men. Officer Lowe was already standing at the back of the boat and giving orders for it to be lowered.

"Stop!" yelled Tarr. "We are first-class passengers. My wife and daughter must be on this boat, do you hear?"

Lowe surveyed his already crowded lifeboat. Then he nodded and extended his hand to help Cornelia over the railing.

At that moment a group of steerage passengers burst onto the deck. With a roar they charged at the lifeboat, beating a path with their bundled belongings.

Fearing the additional weight would send the boat crashing to the sea, Lowe took out his revolver and fired three warning shots across the side of the ship.

Monday, April 15, 1912

THE WOMEN BEGAN to scream, and Cornelia lost consciousness. She slipped through the hands that supported her and slumped onto the deck. Immediately, Hislop dropped to his knees beside her, cradling her head in his lap. He bent his head to whisper in her ear.

"We affirm that we shall heal the sick through prayer. Say it, say it. We affirm . . ."

He began to sway, his eyes closed, rocking over her. Chanting.

"Get up, man," snapped Tarr. "You're making a spectacle of yourself."

But Hislop did not get up. He placed his fingertips on Cornelia's temples and rotated them gently, his lips moving all the time. "We affirm we shall heal the sick . . ."

Tarr bent and scooped Cornelia into his arms.

"Help me, someone," he called to the people at the waiting boat.

Kittie and three other women stretched out their hands to receive the limp body Tarr held out to them as if it were a sacrifice. They pulled Cornelia onto the boat, and Kittie took her hands, rubbing them until Cornelia regained consciousness.

Henry observed the tableau. Cornelia's head lolling on Kittie's shoulder. Hislop on his knees, head bowed, tears streaming down his cheeks. Rhonda, embarrassed and perplexed, not knowing what she should do. And Tarr, breathing heavily, frowning in anger as he stared at his wife.

Cornelia lifted her head. She looked around her, dazed, unable to focus.

"Perhaps it's all for the best," she murmured, but only Kittie could hear her.

Tarr pushed Rhonda towards the railing.

"Take care of your mother," he said as he pressed a wad of bills into her hand and kissed her on the forehead.

"But what about Nichole?" asked Rhonda.

"She can look after herself. Get into the boat."

"When will you come?"

"I'll be along."

She hugged her father quickly and stepped on board. Almost immediately the boat began to drop out of sight.

"No!" shouted Hislop, scrambling to his feet. He dashed to the railing.

"Cornelia," he cried. "Wait!"

The packed lifeboat was level with A Deck when Hislop jumped. The weight of its passengers made it swing away from the ship's side. Hislop misjudged his landing, and his feet slid off the gunwales. His body was thrown back against the *Titanic's* black hull. The lifeboat swung into him and pinned him against the steel plating. Kittie and Rhonda heard him cry out. His rib cage broke with a sound like snapping twigs. For a fraction of a second Hislop was held against the hull like a pinned moth. Blood gushed from his mouth. When the boat swung away, his crushed body dropped into the sea, where it floated face down.

Several men rushed to the railing and looked at the spreadeagled figure in the water.

"Fool," said Tarr.

Hislop's requiem was a jaunty Scott Joplin tune. The orchestra had moved out of the lounge and was playing at the entrance to the gymnasium. From the galley of the first-class restaurant on B Deck rose the sound of smashing crockery. As the *Titanic* began to sink at the head, piles of Royal Crown Derby plates slid off the shelves and crashed to the floor.

Henry thought of the crystal glasses and decanters and the wines in the cellar, now at the mercy of the salt water. He looked at Tarr, and for a moment they stared at each other. Then Tarr nodded curtly and turned away. He walked towards the smoking room.

"Steward," called an officer, "follow me to A Deck."

Henry ignored him.

"I gave you an order, sailor!"

"I have other duties," Henry said as he pushed his way through the crowd of men clustered around the davits. They were staring hopelessly into the night, their eyes focussed on their shivering wives and children in the lifeboats. Immobile on a silent black ocean.

Monday, April 15, 1912

AS SUCCESSIVE COMPARTMENTS in the bowels of the *Titanic* filled with water, her bow angled into the Atlantic. With the loss of each boiler, there was less steam to drive the generators. The dynamos slowed, and power began to fade. The lights glowed orange-red. The ship's telegraph signal became fainter.

With the lowering of the lifeboats, it became apparent to those left on board that there were not enough boats to take them all off the ship. They would only be saved if another vessel arrived before the *Titanic* foundered.

Each passenger faced the inevitable spectre of death at sea in his or her own way. In the third-class dining saloon, men and women fell to their knees and began to pray, working rosary beads through their fingers. Several crewmen broke open the liquor cabinet in the bar off the Palm Court and helped themselves to bottles of gin, rum and brandy. They invited passengers to join them.

Archie Butt, Arthur Ryerson and their bridge opponents, Francis Millet and Clarence Moore, returned to the smoking room for a last hand. Benjamin Guggenheim and his valet went to their adjoining cabins on B Deck, took off their life preservers and changed into evening clothes.

"We've dressed in our best," Guggenheim told a steward, "and are prepared to go down like gentlemen." He asked the steward, if he drowned and the steward was saved, to tell his wife, Florette, he had not died a coward.

There was only one lifeboat left, an Englehardt collapsible on the port side of the bridge. Some fifteen hundred passengers and crew were left on the *Titanic*. Fully loaded, the lifeboat could hold forty-seven people.

As the boat was being fitted to its davits, Second Officer Lightoller gave instructions to crewmen to link arms and form a protective cordon around it. Only women and children would be allowed through. The crowd pushed and pressed against the human barrier, shoving wildly, cursing and shouting.

Charles Lightoller and Steward John Hardy stood on the wooden seats, helping women across the high bulwark railing and into the boat.

Twenty-five passengers were seated when Lightoller gave the order to lower away. As the frail craft jerked past A Deck, two men leaning against the railing saw that there was space in the bow. Water was already spilling over the deck up to their ankles. They decided to jump aboard. One landed upside down in the bottom of the boat; the other jackknifed over its gunwales and was dragged in. The stretched-canvas boat splashed down into the sea.

At 2:05 AM, as the collapsible pulled away from the *Titanic*, Captain Smith entered the wireless room for the last time. Chief Operator Phillips was still sending, desperately trying to raise the *Virginian*, a passenger steamer one hundred and ten miles to the north. Bride stood at his shoulder.

"Men," said the captain, "you've done your full duty. You can do no more. Abandon your cabin. Now it's every man for himself."

But Phillips persisted. His eyes were bloodshot and circled with dark rings. His exhaustion showed in the slope of his neck and shoulders. His right wrist was painfully swollen from hours of tapping.

The signal he sent was too faint for the *Viginian* to read.

"You look out for yourselves," repeated Smith. "I release you."

Tarr entered the smoking room and sat at a table. He took

a cigar from his breast pocket and bit off the end. He was about to spit into the ashtray when it slid away from him and fell to the floor. It rolled across the linoleum and hit Arthur Ryerson's chair.

Ryerson swivelled at the distraction. His eyes met Tarr's, and he quickly averted them and returned to his bridge game.

Also in the smoking room was Thomas Andrews, the *Titanic*'s designer. He sat in a leather chair by the fireplace and stared at the oil painting above the mantel. His life jacket lay on the green baize table next to him.

Tarr lit his cigar and threw the match on the floor. He patted the pocket that held his revolver.

Outside, a woman was calling, "Save me, save me."

A man's voice responded, "Good lady, save yourself. Only God can help you now."

Henry hovered in the doorway of the smoking room. He saw the bridge foursome rise. They were joking about the crazy tilt of the table. He waited for them to leave.

Then Tarr spotted him. "Come and sit down, Henry," he called, waving him over.

Henry approached the table. He stood for a moment looking down at Tarr.

"Well, here I am," said Tarr, opening his hands.

Henry took the revolver from his pocket and pointed it at Tarr.

"Is it worth it, Henry? We're both going to die anyway."

"At least I'll have the satisfaction of knowing that you died before I did."

"What's the difference? A bullet or Davy Jones's locker. Have you ever used one of those things?"

Henry looked to where Thomas Andrews had been sitting. The life jacket was still on the table, but the *Titanic*'s designer was no longer there.

It would be simple to pull the trigger. Tarr was right. It didn't matter. There would be no retribution. There was only the sea, a common fate for the innocent and guilty.

"That's why you'll always be a servant, Henry." Tarr

blew smoke contemptuously at him. "It takes guts to make a decision."

"I want you to think about Nichole for a while," said Henry.

At the bridge table, the abandoned cards slid across the table and spilled onto the floor. The lights in the room dimmed, and then brightened again. The ship seemed to heave, and her plates creaked, straining against their rivets.

"What's there to think about? She got what she deserved. She sold me out to Morgan."

"No, it wasn't Nichole. She didn't betray you. It was Hislop."

For the first time, Tarr looked like a defeated man. "Hislop?"

"Yes, the Reverend Clifford Hislop. And you know why? Because, in his own twisted way, he wanted to see justice done."

"And where did it get him?" snarled Tarr. "I'm alive and that creeping Jesus is dead." Tarr stood. "That's the difference between us, Henry. I could kill you as easy as swatting a fly. But you can't do it. I don't intend to die. I built something from nothing, and I'm not going to the bottom of the sea unless I have to."

"There's nowhere else to go, Mr. Tarr. All the lifeboats have left."

"I'm a survivor, Henry. Always have been. What good's an empire without an emperor?"

He took the cigar from his mouth and stabbed the lighted end at Henry's eyes.

Henry jerked his head back and pulled the trigger.

The shot struck Tarr above his heart. It jolted him backwards and wheeled him around. His eyes opened wide, incredulous. He went down on one knee, his hand over the hole in his overcoat.

"You son of a bitch," he murmured.

Henry placed the gun on the table and turned. He walked to the door without looking back.

Tarr felt under his coat for the wound, but there was none.

The bullet had lodged in the cork of the life preserver he wore under the coat.

The air outside the smoking room was cold and bracing. A crowd of bodies seemed to well up onto the Boat Deck, swarming like ants from below. A mass of humanity, many women and children among them, suddenly liberated from the confines of the lower decks. They were carrying bundles and running this way and that, like refugees fleeing a hostile army. They called to each other and ran to the railings, pointing towards the green signal lights shining on the lifeboats that stood off from the *Titanic*. They shouted and danced with joy, thinking ships were coming to their rescue.

Henry stood paralyzed, watching the growing frenzy of the steerage passengers as water began to wash along the Boat Deck. Above their cries of anguish, he could hear the orchestra playing the hymn, "Autumn."

The ship took a sudden lunge forward, and the bridge and officers' quarters were submerged. Around him, people were falling, sliding down the slippery deck. Above the tumult, Henry heard someone calling his name. He turned and there was Tarr.

"So you really wanted to kill me." He was breathing heavily as he drew the revolver from his pocket. "Well, now I'm going to save you the trouble of drowning."

Before Tarr could fire, Henry launched himself at the banker. The unexpected ferocity of his attack caught Tarr off guard and sent the gun spinning from his hand. All Henry's fury was concentrated in his hands. He grabbed Tarr by the throat and pressed with all his might. Encumbered by their life jackets, they circled like Sumo wrestlers.

Tarr pummelled Henry's face and body with punches, but Henry would not let go. He was not thinking of Nichole, or of Charles Sinclair, or of Marsden Dewey. He was thinking about himself, and about the anger that had simmered for so long inside him. Anger against Tarr for what he had done to Lord Rutherland and Cumerworth Hall. How Tarr had destroyed something that was fine and noble and replaced it with something that was vulgar and shallow.

The daily indignities and humiliations Tarr had inflicted upon him played out before Henry's eyes as he pressed his thumbs into Tarr's bull-like neck. At Cumerworth Hall, in the days of Lord Rutherland, Henry had enjoyed his life of service. He had been trained for it and was proud of his accomplishments. Under Tarr, his life had been servitude. In his tyrannical way, the banker had never let Henry forget who was master.

As the two men struggled, water rushed over the glass dome of the forward staircase. The intricately wrought bubble burst under its weight.

The first funnel snapped at its base. It fell crashing on the wheelhouse roof, and toppled into the water. The impact sent up a cloud of soot, which blocked out the stars. Piles of heavy wooden deck chairs broke loose and slid along the deck.

The orchestra continued to play as desperate passengers began to abandon the sinking liner. They lowered themselves down davit ropes or threw themselves from the railings, oblivious to the two men locked in combat on the promenade.

From the bowels of the ship came the sound of smashing glass and furniture. The *Titanic*'s stern began to lift ominously out of the water.

Suddenly, a wave as white as an avalanche broke across the Boat Deck, sweeping everything before it. The *Titanic* began its angled slide towards the bottom of the ocean.

The sounds of steel plates cracking and pieces of engine wrenching from their bearings rose from the belly of the ship like a symphony from hell. Showers of sparks shot up the two remaining funnels. Steam and black smoke belched into the freezing night air.

Henry and Tarr felt the stern lift under them. People screamed around them. Bodies were thrown towards the engulfing water. Still clutching each other, the two men fell, then slithered along the deck. The *Titanic* bellowed and shook in her death throes. Passengers and crew members experienced the sudden slap of freezing water, then everything went quiet.

The Atlantic closed over Henry and Tarr, breaking them apart.

Henry struggled to the surface and grabbed a railing stanchion. He looked around for the banker. The deck was at a crazy angle, and the *Titanic*'s lights suddenly went out. Then they came on again, illuminating the figure of Tarr, who was standing over him. In one hand he held a davit rope. In the other he brandished a fire axe. He raised the axe above his head and swung it at Henry. The blade rang sparks off a davit post.

Before Tarr could strike again, Henry caught him on the jaw with a left hook. Tarr went down on one knee. The *Titanic*'s lights went out for the last time.

The stern of the great ship stood two hundred feet out of the water, as terrible as the black fist of Mammon. The stress on her hull was great. Amid a series of explosions that rolled like thunder under the water, the ship broke in two, sending the aft funnel crashing down to the deck. A steel hawser snapped, recoiled and thrashed wildly. It struck Thaddeus Nugent Tarr a whip-like blow across the head, slicing his face from his skull. With a scream of agony he fell backwards into the engulfing water.

Henry felt the icy Atlantic close over him once more. The suction created by the sinking vessel pinned him against the grille of a ventilation shaft. He could not break free.

I'm going to drown, he thought.

Images flashed before his eyes. The most inconsequential details of his life shook loose from his memory as if to mock him. Rhonda handing him newly ironed bills. Kittie pinning a posy of flowers to her hat. Lord Rutherland laughing as he fished a croquet ball from the ornamental goldfish pond. Nichole with a bottle of Burgundy in her hands. A blue and gold coach moving slowly through a heat haze. Hislop's hand on his arm.

Is that all there is?

He felt strangely at peace. Death seemed to be a letting go, a final settling, a dream of sleep and warmth.

The feeling of warmth was real. It was burning his back and pushing him upwards. A gush of hot water from the boiler room rushed up the ventilation shaft and sent him spiralling to the surface. He found himself in a sea of debris, coughing and gasping for air.

The *Titanic* was nowhere to be seen.

She had sunk ninety-five miles south of the Grand Banks off Newfoundland. The only evidence of her passing was the litter—cork lining from her bulkheads, dozens of deck chairs and shuffleboard sticks, odd pieces of luggage, wooden hatches, slats from benches, a red and white barber's pole. Patches of oil glistened in the starlight, and the cries for help of those still alive in the freezing water rose like a swarm of locusts.

Fearful that water from the boilers might burst upwards and boil him alive, Henry began to swim away from the wreckage. Even in his state of shock, the cold penetrated through to his brain. His arms and legs were like lead, but he knew his only chance was to keep swimming. The knowledge that Tarr was dead was better than any life jacket. He felt a surge of exaltation, and he desperately wanted to survive. To live. To be with Kittie again.

He could hardly breathe. His lungs were burning, and he had to tread water, to rest. The green lights of the lifeboats seemed so far away. The tormented cries of the dying rang in his ears.

A dead woman, her eyes and mouth wide open, bobbed against him. Henry pushed her away and kicked furiously to distance himself from her body.

He had to get out of the water. He knew it would only be a matter of minutes before the freezing Atlantic would claim him, too. He told himself to keep moving, to keep his blood circulating. He began to sing. "Oh, God, our help in ages past, our hope for years to come, our shelter from the stormy blast and our eternal home . . ."

He could taste the salt on his lips.

"Ahoy!"

Henry stopped singing. He looked around him and saw nothing but small pieces of ice.

"Ahoy! Keep singing."

"I'm here!" shouted Henry. "Over here!"

He heard the sound of oars in the water. In the near distance he saw the outline of an Engelhardt collapsible moving towards him.

Then he heard a woman's voice, pleading, "No, not any more. We'll sink. We can't take on any more!"

But the canvas boat kept coming nearer. Henry waved his arms and sang at the top of his voice.

The boat pulled alongside him, and two pairs of arms reached for him.

"Give us yer 'and."

The green light was no longer a single point, but a blurred line. His eyes began to close. His body felt very heavy. All he wanted to do was stop moving and sleep.

"Yer 'and! Give us yer 'and!"

He tried to raise his arm, but he had no strength left. He felt himself sinking.

Then he was coughing.

His chest was tight, and he was cold. The men had their arms around him and were pulling him out of the water. The canvas boat began to tilt dangerously, and Henry heard cries of alarm.

The men dragged his exhausted body over their knees.

" 'Allo, Mr. B. I'm glad it was you."

Henry brushed the salt water out of his eyes. He looked up into the face of Georgie Skinner, who was smiling at him.

Henry began to shake uncontrollably, and his teeth chattered. Someone threw a blanket around his shoulders.

"I'm glad you made it, too, lad," he said.

He looked at the other passengers sitting huddled together for warmth. They smiled wearily at him, mostly women and children. Bruce Ismay, chairman of the White Star Line and president of the International Mercantile Marine Company, sat with his head bowed over an oar next to Chief Officer Henry Wilde, who held the tiller.

Georgie handed Henry a bottle of cognac.

"Nicked it from the bar," he whispered.

Henry took a swig. The amber liquid burned like a flame. The flavor of plums and violets mingled with oak exploded in his mouth. He was alive!

"Are you fit enough to row, steward?" called Wilde.

"I think so, sir," replied Henry.

"Then relieve one of the ladies."

Georgie moved over and made room for him to sit. Henry took an oar and, on the officer's general order, he began to pull in unison with the others.

Over the horizon to the south, blue flares were clearly visible. Everybody turned to watch them light up the sky.

"They're on their way!" shouted Wilde. "It must be the *Carpathia*."

A cheer went up from the boat. The sound carried over the water to passengers in other boats, and they, too, began cheering.

Henry looked at the sky. The black velvet night was cold, hard and diamond bright. Brighter and more beautiful than he had ever seen it. And the heavens were filled with shooting stars.

ABOUT THE AUTHOR

TONY ASPLER is known to many mystery novel readers as one of the founding members of the Crime Writers of Canada. He is the author of two short crime stories in *Fingerprints* and *Cold Blood* with a third story about to appear in *Cold Blood II*. His career as a novelist began when he co-authored three political thrillers with Gordon Pape: *Chain Reaction, The Scorpion Sanction* and *The Music Wars*. Since then he has published two novels: *Streets of Askelon* and *One of My Marionettes*. In addition to his many publications he was the first recipient of The Derrick Murdoch Award for services to Canadian crime writing.

Born in London, England, Aspler spent a good portion of his childhood in Quebec while World War II raged on back home. After graduating from McGill University in 1959, he spent six months working at the CBC in Montreal before returning to England where he worked as a writer and broadcaster for the BBC and, later, the CBC.

Wine lovers will recognize him as the popular wine columnist at the *Toronto Star*. As a wine expert, Tony has travelled the world to such exotic locations as Chile, China and Africa. As well as authoring hundreds of columns, he provided the wine suggestions for Madame Benoit's series of microwave cookbooks and is himself the author of *Tony Aspler's International Guide to Wine*, *Vintage Canada* and co-author of *The Wine Lover Dines*

With regard to the *Titanic*, Tony Aspler says, "I have always been fascinated by the *Titanic*. Her fate was like a morality play for the twentieth century. No other accident at sea, on land or in the air has captured and held the imagination of all generations since that terrible Sunday, April 14, 1912. I wanted to write a novel about what it must have been like to be a passenger on the world's most luxurious liner. Also to capture the spirit and rhythm of the age when J.P. Morgan and other robber barons became the new aristocracy. And being a mystery writer, there had to be murder involved."